PROTAGONIZED

SHANNON MYERS

Cover Design by: The Final Wrap

Teasers by: The Final Wrap

Photographer: Wander Aguiar

Cover Model: Colton Benson

Editing: My Brother's Editor

First Printing: 2019

ISBN- 978-0-9994716-7-8

 Created with Vellum

To everyone who followed their dreams, even when the world said they were too big.

ACKNOWLEDGMENTS

As always, it takes a village, y'all.

Rebecca- Thank you for once again taking my ideas and turning them into a kickass cover. You are the queen and I bow to you.

Wander- You have an eye for detail and the cover image of Colton is no exception. I am in love with it, as well as your kind and generous spirit.

The Forsaken- You guys keep me motivated when I feel like I've got nothing left. Thank you for joining me on this little journey.

Laura- Thank you for falling in love with Travis and comparing every leading man to him. It has forced me to work harder to try to top that. And I will. I'm so happy you talked me into starting a book club. Long live the introverts.

Jen & Wendi- Thank you both for your patient nudges in the right direction when I feel like I'm floundering. I know I can always count on the both of you to mention needing something new to read before giving me the side eye. I am thankful for our friendship and the support you guys give me. *You make me wanna be a better man* —er, woman.

Olivia- Thank you for believing in me when I couldn't and for staying when you could've left. Your positive energy always comes through just when I need it and I am honored to be your friend.

Ellie- Thank you for taking on this project at the last second. Your ability to find and correct my mistakes is second to none and I will have many more books for you in the future.

Shayla- Thank you for being you. I am lucky to call you my sister and my best friend. Being the older sister, I should be the wise one, but you prove me wrong time and time again. Thank you for always being in my corner. Love you, Bug.

Zach- We did it, babe. Book number nine. This past year has been rough and there were so many times I was convinced that my creative side was tapped out, but you believed in my dream for the both of us. I see you; running the house and parenting the kids while I chase these crazy dreams and I know how blessed I am. I love the life we've built, but not as much as I love you.

PROLOGUE

Detective Jake Hopkins sat in his office, bathed in the soft blue light of the computer screen in front of him. Countless times before, he'd been here, and with far less to go on.

With a furtive glance through the open door of his office, he snuck the bottle from the second drawer of his desk. He poured two fingers of whiskey into a stained police academy mug before reviewing the evidence again. Drinking whiskey inevitably led to a craving for nicotine. Knowing that it would only draw unwanted attention, he waited on the cigarette.

It had devastated the city to lose their young assistant district attorney. Worse than that, he'd lost the woman who'd kept his bed warm off and on for the past year. His might have been the greater tragedy, he thought. Jake had known she was a wildcat in bed, but never imagined that she would have been ballsy enough to go after the cartel on her own.

Hadn't he warned her against that very thing the last time they were together? However, Addison had been more concerned with the tube of lipstick she'd found in his bathroom than she was with taking his advice to heart. Jake hadn't understood her anger; she'd known what they were from the word go.

Now she was dead, and it was up to him to find her killer. At first glance, it was assumed that she'd died due to a fire in her apartment building. The autopsy showed that her lungs were clear; meaning that she'd been dead before it had even started.

It should've been a cut and dry case against the cartel, but with family members fighting over life insurance money and a shady ex-boyfriend popping up out of the woodwork, Jake was beginning to think that nothing about this would be simple. He took a long sip from the mug, letting the whiskey burn its way down into his chest.

How many cases had begun just like this? He was starting to lose count. If he was going to keep his focus, he needed to treat Addison's case exactly the same as the others. It wasn't like she was some great love of his life—she'd just been a way to pass the time.

Which reminded him—he glanced down at his watch. He'd promised Tiffany a night she wouldn't forget. His badge parted legs faster than Moses parted the Red Sea.

Jake frowned at his desk. The case would wait until morning—it wasn't like Addison was going to get any deader if he left now. She'd still be just as murdered in the morning and, in all honesty, she'd want him to kick back and unwind.

Shoot, the entire department worshiped the ground he walked on. He'd single-handedly solved more cases than any of the other detectives—combined. Jake could set fire to the entire station and instead of a reprimand, they'd just thank him for warming things up.

He deserved a night off.

With that, he downed the rest of the whiskey and grabbed his coat before heading out to clear his head. He pulled a cigarette from the pack and lit up on the walk to his truck.

What his truck lacked in luxury, it more than made up for in price. Addison had tried to talk him into a sports car, some pricy foreign shit. Jake only bought American vehicles though and the sleek black Raptor in the reserved parking space was no exception.

He was a goddamn patriot.

And, in his mind, there was nothing sexier than a jacked-up truck.

His phone vibrated from his pocket and he pulled it free with an easy grin. Jake knew it was Tiffany wondering where he was. She was getting lonely, pacing that high-rise condo by herself. He inhaled slowly, letting the nicotine hit his lungs, before telling her he was on his way.

That was the thing about Jake—he could have told her he was going to be working for a few more hours and she would have waited. And if she'd thrown a fit? Well, there were hundreds of other women who would have gladly taken her place. Everyone knew that all work and no play made Jake a real bastard to deal with.

The tires on his truck screeched against the pavement as he put the pedal to the floor on the way out of the parking lot. Yellow lights turned red, but he blew past them, flipping off any driver who had the audacity to honk.

Fuck them.

He had needs. Jesus, it had been almost three days since he'd gotten laid. That was his problem—too much pent-up aggression. Addison's case would've been much farther along if only he'd gotten his dick wet.

He pulled up in front of Tiffany's building with resolve. He'd get his head clear before reviewing the file again. Hell, he might just have the entire thing wrapped up by morning.

He whistled to himself as he took the elevator up to the

thirtieth floor, deciding that he'd make the rook buy the celebratory breakfast for him.

A week off seemed like fair compensation as well. He'd been pushing himself too hard lately. There'd still be other cases waiting on his desk whenever he graced the office with his presence again.

The first thing he noticed when stepping out into the hall was that the door to Tiffany's condo was sitting wide open. The second was the trail of candles that led out onto the balcony overlooking the city. He loosened his tie and walked out, expecting to find her in some provocative outfit. There was something caught in the railing, but the rest of the balcony was empty, save for the few candles scattered along the large stone tiles.

Jake had just leaned over to check it out when he was shoved forcefully from behind. The railing gave way, and he found that he had nothing to grab onto. His arms pinwheeled like something out of a cartoon, but the momentum from the push sent him hurtling over the edge. The last thing he noticed was the split-second flash of blonde hair retreating inside the condo. *Addison had been a blonde*, he thought, as he fell to his death.

To be continued...

ONE

A SPEAKER at a popular writer's workshop once said that the best way to write a character was to list all the things the reader would never know about him or her.

Their secrets, if you will.

Everyone had secrets; to assume that a fictional character didn't was two-dimensional and lazy.

Shallow.

What made a writer great was their willingness to go the extra mile—to investigate the characters they were bringing to life.

I wasn't a shoddy writer. I prided myself on all the research that went into each and every one of my novels. I'd also ensured ahead of time that my best friend would wipe my hard drive should something ever happen to me. There were some rabbit holes that parents should never venture down.

Here was what the world would never know about Detective Jake Hopkins:

1. He wouldn't touch beer. Whether it was a Bud Light or a hand-crafted microbrew from northern Colorado, the guy couldn't stomach the taste.

2. He told everyone that he lost his virginity when he was fifteen; in actuality, he was twenty-two. Bit of a late bloomer, that one.

3. He smoked... a lot (which was common knowledge), but tried to convince himself that every pack was his last.

4. Killing him was the best decision I ever made...

Until it wasn't.

Okay, I might've jumped the gun a bit. There had been some... strong reactions to it. Which was great because, as a writer, you really wanted to invoke powerful emotions in your readers, right?

Where was I?

Oh, right.

My newest book.

The blinking cursor taunted me. I drummed my fingers against the keys, waiting for inspiration to strike. I just needed my newest main character to start talking. It seemed like Jake had never shut up. Maybe the new detective was feeling shy in comparison.

I decided to grant her a brief reprieve before typing a few letters into the search bar on my laptop. It pre-filled the rest. Obviously, I'd been visiting this site a little more than normal.

I could stop.

This was the last time and then I'd quit—cold turkey. It wasn't an addiction or anything.

I'd been warned from the very beginning to stay away, but I didn't listen.

It started out innocently enough.

I'd stay on no more than ten minutes; just long enough to feel good. Now, it had become a seeping wound on my skin; each click of the mouse poking at the lesion over and over again just to see if it still bled. Over the last few weeks, I'd grown addicted to the pain.

The *Goodbooks* icon cheerfully greeted me from the top left corner of the webpage just as the icy fingers of dread wrapped themselves around my gut.

This was definitely the last time.

"Okay." I blew out a soft breath. "You can do this."

Detective Hopkins: One in the Chamber had an average rating of... 2.21.

Oh god.

I'd somehow lost an entire star overnight. One star just gone.

Poof.

The male cover model stared back at me, his look of perplexity matching mine perfectly.

How had I gotten this one so wrong?

"You are okay, Hayden. You are safe. You are grounded. You are balanced. You are centered." I took a deep breath to calm myself, adding, "And you are Zen," before scrolling down to read the newest reviews.

If I could give this ZERO stars, I would. I cannot believe the author had the audacity to kill off Jake after three books! Worse than that is the news that there's going to be a new Detective Hopkins novel featuring a female detective! A female! It's unheard of. I bet the author is laughing all the way to the bank at the expense of the poor readers. Well, this reader is done and I will be telling all of my friends to boycott this garbage as well. I hate when writers pull this shit.

I noted that she'd even taken the time to shelve the book as "AWFUL" and "Authors to Avoid."

Well, at least she was thorough.

I scrolled farther to find another message I was frankly getting just as sick of seeing.

Okay, you got a bad review. Deep breath. It happens to every author eventually. Keep in mind that one negative review will not impact your book's sales. In fact, studies have shown that negative reviews can actually help book sales, as they legitimize the positive reviews on your book's page.

We really, really (really!) don't think you should comment on this review, even to thank the reviewer.

Right.

All those negative reviews were just going to push my book into the upper echelons of the bestseller ether.

Any minute now.

I ignored their repeated warnings and stabbed *Accept and Continue* with a low growl.

"*Dear Eleanor,*" I began, with short angry bursts on the keys. "*I am so sorry to hear that Jake's untimely passing affected you on a personal level. It's just a friggin' book. I am not laughing all the way to the bank as writing isn't really all that lucrative of a career option. Also, my cat and I are not sorry to see you go. You sound old and crotchety.*"

I mashed the backspace button until the cursor flashed over an empty box. What was I supposed to say? *Elitist Eleanor* was only one of many angry fans.

I really thought that killing Jake off was a bold move—one that would propel me up there with the likes of Jodi Picoult and George R. R. Martin. I wasn't afraid to off my main character and carry on with the series as though nothing was amiss.

Bootsy—the cat of House McFluffsalot, First of Her Name, Queen of the Apartment and Balcony, Khaleesi of the Litter Box, Breaker of Trinkets, Mother of Dragon-sized Hairballs—chose that exact moment to jump onto my desk, minimizing the offending review and freeing me to the more important task of petting her.

"What are we gonna do? They're all jumping ship!"

Bootsy, in her infinite wisdom, flicked her tail carelessly and stretched out across my laptop.

"Well, not writing is certainly one way of dealing with the problem, but I'm not sure that it's going to help us maintain our lavish lifestyle. I mean, if I'm not writing, then the catnip and vodka are going away, Bootsy. I mean it this time."

I'd done surprisingly well as an Indie author. Not immediately, no, but the Detective Hopkins novels had been my turnaround. For whatever reason, women and men alike were crazy about the hardened detective with a penchant for whiskey and women. Problem was, I never meant to make him a likable character.

Jake Hopkins was a combination of the worst traits in men—alcoholic, workaholic, womanizer, cheater, smoker, and just an all-around dick. The man had a huge fear of commitment and probably could've solved his cases a lot faster were he not constantly distracted by every pair of breasts that came his way.

He was supposed to have been a one-off, but somehow, he took over the story and people began to demand more. I never intended to make it a series. I started countless other books but was always pulled back to his out of guilt. Given what I'd spent on cover designers and editing, I was left with no choice but to give the people what they wanted. I thought if I played by the rules for a little while, then eventually I'd be given free rein over my work.

The plan was to carry on the Detective Hopkins series with a new lead—a lead I actually enjoyed writing.

I caught a discreet eye roll from Bootsy and opened my mouth to argue when she shifted. *Goodbooks* reappeared on the screen along with another review. I pulled her limp body onto my lap and adjusted my glasses before leaning in to read it.

1 STAR! I hope someone throws the author off a thirty-story building. Would serve you right for what you did to Jake. He gave you three books and that's how you repay him? Shame on you and shame on the publisher who encouraged this.

I rested my chin against my chest and briefly debated the pros and cons of bashing my face into the keyboard by way of response. I didn't have a publisher—I didn't even know any.

Well, that wasn't exactly true.

I knew a lot of publishers.

Just not any that would publish my words.

I did, however, know of an agent.

Rachel of *The Janice Morrison Agency* had read my last *Detective Hopkins* novel and loved it—she said it had a lot of potential, but that they were looking for something a little edgier.

So, I'd gone above and beyond to deliver this time around. Maybe the fans weren't as receptive as I'd hoped, all I needed was for Rachel to see that I wasn't afraid to take risks. The *Detective Hopkins* series could go on without Detective Hopkins.

I had complete faith.

Any day now she was going to reach out to tell me that *The Janice Morrison Agency* wanted me as a client. Until that day though, I was just going to keep hustling.

It was exciting, knowing that my life was about to change for the better. I couldn't wait to announce that I, Hayden Michaels, was being traditionally published at the next family dinner. That was the next logical step after getting an agent. They'd pitch me to the big five publishing houses and then they'd battle it out.

I could see it now; my mother would weep about how she always knew I had a rare talent, while my father made a toast in my honor. My brother would choke with jealousy; finally coming to the realization that he was no longer in the spotlight.

I was debating whether it was in poor form to throw money in the air when a loud thud at the front door sent me hurtling backward in my chair. Bootsy, never one for surprises, bolted for the safety of the bedroom.

"A lot of help you are," I grumbled, before picking myself up off the floor. A quick glance through the peephole revealed my neighbor and friend since sixth grade, Aaris.

"Are you going to let me in or should I just drop these perfect margaritas all over your doorstep," she called out.

"Hey," I replied through the door. "I'm actually in the writing cave tonight."

Her smile was instantly replaced with pursed lips. "Do not give me the same lame excuses you give your family. I know you're not writing. You're stalking that damn review site, hoping someone else wanted Jake dead as much as you did. Now, let me in, bitch. It's Thursday!"

It was girl's night.

And I'd completely forgotten. I lost track of time, wrapped up in my bubble of bad reviews.

Shit. I think I was in charge of snacks.

I threw the door open and took the pitcher from her left hand while she juggled two margarita glasses in her right. "Damn, woman. You almost wasted the top shelf tequila I smuggled home from the bar the other night."

I placed the pitcher on the beige laminate countertop and gave her my best stern expression. "You stole liquor from your work? Again?"

She lifted one shoulder in a shrug and began filling the glasses. "Bryan shorted me on tips again, so I did what needed to be done."

Bryan was her tyrant of a boss and the owner of *Magenta*, 'a bar created by millennials, for millennials.' It was supposed to be sleek and sexy with its floor to ceiling windows and black leather couches.

There were television screens mounted throughout that displayed nothing but social media tweets and updates from the hot 'celebrities' of the week. To have their name up on the screen was the closest some would come to seeing their name in Hollywood lights.

The bar came complete with USB chargers on every table, for the patron who couldn't be separated from their smartphone for more than a few minutes.

Even as a millennial, I'd always found it odd. On the rare occasions that I did go out, I did it to get away from social media and the urge to spend my every waking moment online.

Plus, Bryan was a supreme douche bag. He withheld tips from the female bartenders unless they offered him something in return. Never mind that they'd been schilling beer and avoiding the groping hands of inebriated men for their entire shift; now they had to worry about their boss.

"When are you going to tell him to go screw himself and find something better?" I stopped rummaging through my small pantry, coming up with a half-eaten bag of blue corn tortilla chips. It would have to do.

Aaris perched on the edge of the barstool, somehow looking like royalty in her ratty joggers and loose fitting tank top. "As soon as this modeling thing takes off, I'm done. Until then, I'll suffer through it. My regulars make it worth it, you know?"

I found a questionable jar of salsa in the back of the fridge and placed it alongside the stale chips while nodding along. Questionable because I couldn't actually remember the last time I went grocery shopping, much less my last salsa purchase.

Tomorrow, I was going to start being a responsible adult. I'd wake up early, go for a jog, grab some groceries, learn how to cook, and then maybe I'd pay some bills.

You know, if there was enough time.

Aaris scrunched up her nose in disapproval. "Hayden, I know you're not serving this to me. Not after I went out of my way to steal good tequila for you."

I blew out an exasperated breath. "This is all I have—I've been a little busy today."

"You were on *Goodbooks* again, weren't you? Hayden, how many times do I have to tell you that focusing on the negative is a shit business plan? You're better than this."

I nodded and straightened the chip bag without making eye contact. "Look, I just need to know what they're saying. Consider it research for my newest book."

She took a sip of her drink and rolled her eyes simultaneously. "Sure. Research. And how exactly is that going to help you with your new book? You gonna bring Jake back as a zombie? I can see it now; *Detective Hopkins: Ghosted.*" She paused to laugh at her own joke. "C'mon, girl. Focus on your female detective and make all the haters eat their words."

I mulled it over, back to imagining how good it would feel to throw the phrase '*published author*' in my brother's stupid face.

On the other hand, zombies were kind of in right now. It wouldn't be unheard of to bring him back; soap operas did it all the time.

Detective Hopkins: Highway to Hell.

She sighed. "You're really considering ways to bring him back to life, aren't you? Stop. You aren't going to please everybody—you're not *Nutella*."

She was right.

I was getting far too invested in the opinions of strangers.

"Okay," I reluctantly agreed. "I'll focus on the new book and not the reviews."

This was just step one in becoming the new me.

This was the moment I'd recall when being interviewed by the *Today* show.

They'd probably have Kathie Lee interview me and I'd look her right in the eye and say, "Kath." Obviously, I'd shorten her name as we'd have become very close in the green room. Kindred spirits, perhaps. "Kath, one night over margaritas with my dear friend, I realized that life was too short to spend time obsessing over who does or doesn't like you. I took that negativity and channeled it into the mega-blockbuster book, turned movie. It's truly been a remarkable journey."

Kathie would lean in conspiratorially, she'd probably even pat my leg as she mock-whispered, "I knew from page one that this book was going to be huge."

I was plucked from my fantasy by the sound of Aaris loudly slurping her margarita.

Once she had my attention, she eyed the sad selection of snacks on the counter. "Order me a pizza while you're fantasizing about being interviewed on the *Today* show, okay?"

TWO

"IS it just me or did Jeremy Piven suddenly get hot?" Aaris asked around a mouthful of vegetarian pizza as we sat side by side on the couch.

I adjusted my glasses and looked at the commercial on the screen again before frowning at her. "Really? Him?"

I mean, I'd had quite the crush on Keanu Reeves ever since I found an old VHS of *Bram Stoker's Dracula* mixed in with my Disney movies. My father had recorded it off "the *HBO,*" and I'd assumed that it was okay for a six-year-old to watch.

It wasn't, but that didn't end my Keanu obsession. I cut pictures of him out of magazines, strategically placing them around the mirror over my dresser like he was looking down on me. Twenty-four years later and the pictures were gone, but I was still in awe of the man.

Jeremy, on the other hand? Not so much. He was definitely not in the same league as Keanu.

She continued chewing, a dreamy expression on her face. "Maybe it's the glasses. I don't know, I'd do him though. Ooh, speaking of doing, how'd the date with that guy go? What was his name? Spencer? Shawn?"

That was the thing about Aaris. She was stunning, yet always seemed to go for guys who were closer to middle age. Men who inevitably ended up being married or in the throes of a mid-life crisis.

Seriously, the girl won the genetic lottery. Her Indian father met her German mother and they fell in love, creating the three most aesthetically perfect children in the world. After moving around the world, they finally chose to settle in my city and she and I had been friends ever since.

With her long black hair and flawless skin, Aaris could've been modeling for years. Instead, she chose men who made her feel insecure and kept her working for guys like Bryan at *Magenta*.

"So close—Cole," I said with a laugh. "And it went about like everything else in my life does. Disappointingly." I glared at the half-empty margarita glass resting on the side table as I swayed slightly on the couch. I swore I wasn't going to talk about yet another failed attempt at dating, but Aaris didn't mess around when it came to alcohol.

The date with Cole had been another fail in a long line of fails. He'd seemed nice enough online but was pushy and arrogant in person. Maybe that was why it had been easy for me to write a cocky man whore like Jake Hopkins; because it was all I ever seemed to meet in real life.

Bootsy strolled past the couch, judgment evident in her stare. She'd never approved of any of my dates or even the mere mention of dates. She didn't really approve of me leaving the house period.

"Bootsy, how the hell are you?" Aaris teased, earning herself a tail flick. "She really is the cat from hell, isn't she?"

"She's not! She's a wonderful companion," I argued, my words running together thanks to the tequila.

She shook her head with a laugh. "Whatever you say. I still think she's an evil bitch." She held her index finger up. "Nay, an evil *murderous* bitch."

"Allegedly."

Aaris and Bootsy's relationship had been doomed from the start.

We'd been drinking at my apartment one night and Aaris decided to stay over—she lived across town at the time. I'd gotten up early the next morning to take a shower when I heard the screams coming from my bedroom.

According to Aaris, she'd awoken to Bootsy's paws over both of her nostrils. In her eyes, it was clear proof that my cat had tried to murder her while she was sleeping. I'd suggested that Bootsy was simply warming her paws by the warmth of her nose, but Aaris was not having it.

"Allegedly, my ass. Satan cat," she said as she stood up with a soft belch. "Pitcher's empty. Decide on a movie while I make another batch, will ya?"

I snorted, "That's easier said than done. You never like anything I pick out."

She cradled the empty pitcher in her arm like a newborn and unsteadily made her way toward the front door, calling over her shoulder, "I'm easy. Just pick something that isn't all action-y, based on a fairy tale, or with sci-fi crap. Simple."

"Simple," I mimicked as the door slammed shut behind her. I scrolled aimlessly with the remote, but came up empty-handed. Nothing was going to meet her stupid criteria.

Three sharp raps on the front door had me dropping the remote in fright. "Jesus, Mary, and Joseph, just yell. You're going to give me a heart attack." Bootsy yowled in agreement as I went over to the door.

I threw it open, ready to lay into Aaris, but was immediately stunned into silence. The man standing in front of me was most certainly not Aaris. He glanced up from the ground at the sound of the door opening and I damn near swooned. Something about him was so familiar, yet I was certain that we'd never met before.

Trust me, I would've remembered.

He towered over me; which wasn't really saying a lot as most people did when I wasn't wearing heels. His light brown hair was close-cropped on the sides, but longer on top. Every strand was combed back perfectly, except for a cowlick that poked out near the back of his head. He had a dusting of hair along his strong jawline and brilliant greenish-brown eyes that probably had the ability to hypnotize me if I stared long enough.

And he was absolutely, without a doubt, at the wrong apartment.

"Hello," he began, and a small frisson of lust moved through my veins.

I chalked my reaction up to the dry spell I'd been in as of late and nodded politely. "Hello. Can I help you?"

He lifted his hand and consulted a book I hadn't noticed him carrying before looking back at me. "I'm sorry to bother you, ma'am, but I'm looking for Hayden Michaels."

I took a hesitant step back when I realized he was holding a copy of *Detective Hopkins: One in the Chamber*. So far, hate reviews had been the only thing I'd received. I hadn't factored in the possibility of a crazed reader showing up on my doorstep to vent. It wasn't like my address was listed on the back cover or anything.

The hottie was looney.

Damn.

I forced my voice to remain calm. "I think you have the wrong apartment."

He flashed me a megawatt smile, complete with dimples. "Sorry to have bothered you, ma'am. Have a nice evening."

I closed the door and latched it before sinking down to the carpet. I'd never been more grateful that I chose not to put my picture on the back of my books.

What would he have done if I'd said I was Hayden?

Shot me?

Murdered me for offing his favorite fictional character?

Forced me up against the nearest wall and taken his frustrations out on my body in a more passionate manner?

Okay, so the last one was stretching it a bit.

The next knock at the door had me scrambling into the kitchen for a weapon. I grabbed the first thing I could find and tiptoed back to check the peephole.

"Hurry up and let me in," Aaris complained.

I quickly unlocked the door and dragged her inside, sloshing some of the margarita mix onto the linoleum floor in the entry.

She took in my weapon and carefully asked, "Everything okay, Hayden?"

I dropped the rolling pin back onto the counter and whispered, "No. Did you see a man outside?"

Her brow furrowed as she turned back toward the door. "Uh, I saw Eddie that lives two doors down. Are you sure you're okay?"

I shook my head. "No. There was a man here. He had my book and wanted to know if Hayden Michaels was here."

She nodded slowly. "And you told him what exactly?"

"I said that he was at the wrong apartment. Jesus, Aaris, why would he have my book?"

She gestured toward the kitchen. "I think the more pressing question is what you planned on doing with the rolling pin? Baking him a pie?"

I shrugged. "It was the first thing I found. I'm seriously freaking out here. Bad reviews are one thing, but showing up on my doorstep? That's psycho-level stuff, right?"

She refilled my glass and handed it to me with both hands. "Okay, sweetie. Here's what we're gonna do. You're gonna sit down on the couch and drink this, while I find something for us to watch."

It didn't escape my notice that she kept glancing toward the front door, expecting my book-wielding assailant to burst through at any moment.

I kept an eye on the rolling pin just to be safe.

———

IN MY SEVERELY hungover state the following morning, I'd almost convinced myself that the entire thing had been a joke. It was just the sort of thing my asshole of an older brother would do. Just because I hadn't invented a thing that did a thing that Oprah put on her list of favorite things, I was somehow beneath him.

I popped a coffee pod into the machine and leaned against the counter for support as it began brewing.

To make matters worse, my parents were the same. I was constantly asked at family gatherings when I planned to give up writing and get 'a real career.'

I blearily tapped out a text to him.

Nice job sending a psycho to my apartment. Don't think I'm going to forget that anytime soon.

The bright light streamed into the room through the cheap vertical blinds covering the balcony door and I winced in pain before retrieving my sunglasses from my purse. After adding half a carton of creamer to my coffee, I laid my face against the cool countertop and groaned, "Bootsy, why'd you let me drink so much last night? You know I have to write today." She wound her way around my legs, clamoring for my full attention, clearly not giving a fuck that I felt like dying.

Her meows were like ice picks to my skull, each one louder than the last. Seeing that I wasn't moving, she resorted to caterwauling. The yowls had me up and searching for her food within seconds.

I dumped a cup of dry food into her bowl with a tersely whispered, "Please, for the love of all that is good and holy, shut the hell up!"

She glared past me, toward the cabinets where I kept the canned food. "Oh, no. You are not getting that fishy smelling shit this morning."

I pushed past the nausea and sipped my cup of coffee like a frat boy chugging a pint before deciding that a second cup was a must. Once that was settled, I pulled up the manuscript for *Detective Hopkins: Angel of Death*. It was still in the very rough stages—so rough in fact that I'd only written the title so far.

I cracked my knuckles. It was time to introduce a new detective and win my readers back.

When Laura Bennett awoke out of a deep slumber, she had no idea that her life was about to change. All she knew was that, instead of Restless Leg Syndrome, she'd been cursed with a restless bladder. Luckily, Frank was on shift down at the fire station so she didn't have to worry about waking him with her frequent trips to the bathroom.

Laura went out into the living room when it became clear that she wasn't going to be able to fall asleep again anytime soon. She poured herself a brandy and walked out onto their large balcony overlooking the city. They'd bought the condo for the view—twinkling city lights reminded her of Christmas. She'd always loved the time of year when snow fell—

A knock at the front door pulled me away from Laura's condo and back into my own apartment. I sighed. I'd been on a streak there; hopefully, I'd be able to keep it up once I got rid of my visitor.

I used the peephole, but could only see the back of someone's head. Reluctantly, I opened the door a few inches, keeping the chain latched.

Oh god, it was the hottie. The psycho. Psycho Hottie.

He grinned down at me. "Me again. I was told by the front office that I could find Hayden Michaels here."

Catching a glimpse of the holster underneath his jacket did nothing for my nerves and I shook my head. "No..." I choked on the pooled saliva in my mouth, a complete giveaway that I was lying. "There's no one here by that name."

Without giving him a chance to respond, I quickly slammed the door shut and latched all three locks with shaking hands. Why would the complex give out my information? Surely, that was an invasion of privacy.

"What am I gonna do? Oh god." I briefly wondered how bad it would be if I ended up barricaded inside my apartment forever. Aaris would have to buy my groceries and take Bootsy to the vet when needed.

"Okay...everything's okay," I mumbled as I tiptoed over to my desk to grab my cell phone. I was going to call the police and let them handle this. That was all there was to it.

I'd only entered the nine when my computer alerted me to a new email and Rachel's name popped up in the alert box. My mission temporarily forgotten, I sank down onto my chair. I needed to focus on the fact that there was a gun-toting madman on the other side of my front door, but all I could think about was that *The Janice Morrison Agency* had finally recognized my talent.

"Oh my god, Bootsy. This is it. Our entire lives are about to change. No more schilling shampoo at the salon just to pay the bills." She poked her head out from underneath the couch, completely unimpressed.

Hangover forgotten, I was Zen.

Dear Hayden Michaels,

Thank you for your most recent email. I appreciate the opportunity to consider your work again for possible representation, but I'm afraid I've decided to pass. When I encouraged you to be bold in your writing, I was thinking more along the lines of a competing detective that could work as a potential love interest for Detective Hopkins. Killing him, while bold, has made any future books a little hard to market.

Please do not be discouraged as many best-sellers have been passed on numerous times prior to being successfully published. I wish you the best of luck finding an enthusiastic agent and publisher for your work.

Best,

Rachel

And now I was going to launch my laptop off the balcony.

Nope.

Still Zen.

Completely Zen.

My eyes stung from the rejection. I hadn't realized just how much hope I'd invested in securing an agent until a fat teardrop hit the keyboard, splashing out across several keys and fogging up my glasses. I was absolutely not Zen.

Thoughts of a probable killer on the other side of my door didn't even faze me anymore.

I was unmarketable.

In my infinite stupidity, I had just killed off my meal ticket. The one thing that was going to set me apart from all the other authors was lying thirty stories below his booty call's apartment. The male slut who annoyed the hell out of me had been the only thing to make me unique.

"Goddammit!" I roared.

The email continued to taunt me from the screen, so I hurriedly minimized my browser. This wasn't a rejection. It was the fuel I needed to make my next novel even better. The banging at the door began again, the sound reverberating through my skull.

"I need to speak with Hayden Michaels. It's urgent!" the man yelled from the other side.

I leaned down, resting my forehead against my knees before muttering, "This is the day from hell, Bootsy. Absolute. Hell."

"I know he's in there. Just do us both a favor and send him out!"

I paused. He thought Hayden was a man.

"He's not here," I called back. "And if you don't leave, I'm calling the police!"

"Lady, I am the police!"

Fuck.

Why did the cops want me?

I thought back over the last few days and then froze in horror.

Cole.

My failed date. I'd been convinced that my actions were warranted at the time, but under present circumstances, I was starting to think that maybe I'd been mistaken.

The gray fabric skirt along the bottom of the couch framed Bootsy's head like a little bonnet as she continued to peek out at me. The knock sounded again, and I laughed maniacally before dragging her out by her front paws and pulling her onto my lap. "Bootsy, Mommy may have messed up a little the other night. Kitty Protective Services is gonna show up and take you away."

She meowed loudly and kneaded my sweater in response.

I kissed her head and placed her back on the carpet before inching toward the door, much like I imagined a death-row inmate would walk toward the lethal injection room.

Or whatever they called it.

It wasn't like I'd ever been to prison.

Oh god. What if I ended up in prison over this?

I briefly wondered if prison jumpsuits were anything like regular jumpsuits where you had to get naked just to pee. Or were those rompers?

What was the difference between the two?

"Is this about the Cole thing?" I asked weakly as I reached the door.

"Bingo."

I set about undoing the locks while critiquing the life choices that had led me to this point. I was hungover, sans writing contract, and about to take a trip 'downtown.'

The doorknob rattled against my shaking hand. It was a shame really.

I'd hoped that the whole thing had been a ruse and he was here to ask me on a date. Or that he was a stripper posing as a cop.

Hell, at this point, I would've even settled for an angry reviewer determined to give me an earful.

The man frowned at me as he stepped inside and shut the door behind him.

That wasn't part of the plan.

He was supposed to cuff me and throw me in the back of his car. I deserved a good frisking after the morning I'd had. And, thanks to only one cup of coffee, I wasn't even sufficiently caffeinated.

"You've got a lot of balls, lady. I'll give you that, but hiding Hayden isn't helping anybody." His lips pursed as he talked, like a teenage girl, doing an obligatory duck pose selfie. It should've looked ridiculous, but I found myself mesmerized by the pout.

Women everywhere would kill to have lips like his. I could sink my teeth into a pair of lips like that. Not hard, mind you. Just playful little nips while my fingers traced the five o'clock shadow on his jaw.

I realized belatedly that he was waiting for me to stop staring and tell him where Hayden was.

I took a deep breath and pushed my X-rated thoughts aside. "Look, it was an innocent mistake, what happened with Cole. He was groping me and I—I didn't think. I just grabbed what was in front of me and then I left immediately after, I swear. I didn't know it was illegal to throw a drink in someone's face, especially if said someone's hand was working its way up the inside of your thigh. I can pay a dry cleaner bill or what—"

"Wait." He held up a hand with a frown. "You're Hayden Michaels?" His eyes moved from the crown of my head down to my socks as he rubbed absently at the back of his neck. Not content with his once-over, those same eyes came back up and rested on my lime green t-shirt. It featured a cactus in the shape of a cat.

A *catcus.*

I adored it because the cat looked like Bootsy had as a kitten. Judging by the sour expression on the cop's face, he didn't find it as appealing. The temperature in the room seemed to go up several hundred degrees as he observed me.

I nodded at his question, this time with reservation.

He was about to go looney on me. I just knew it. Even his posture screamed that he was holding himself back. The cuffs were going to come out and then I was definitely getting hauled to the clink.

His eyes narrowed as he studied my face. "Well, I'll be damned. You look nothing like I expected. I could've sworn you were a man."

I gave him what I hoped was a condescending smile, but in all actuality, probably missed the mark. "I'm very much a woman," I answered. "Who the hell are you?"

The man's eyes glinted briefly with a flash of anger, but it was gone before I could really question it. "I'm Detective Jake Hopkins and I've got a bone to pick with you."

THREE

OH GOD.

I rocked back and forth on the carpet.

It had happened. It was bound to sooner or later. I'd spent too much time lost in my own head and now I was hallucinating my characters. I eyed 'Jake' again. I'd at least give myself this—he looked even better than I'd written him.

"So, you're not arresting me for what I did to Cole?" I asked, my voice laced with hysteria. *Could he even arrest me?* I was unfamiliar with fictional cops and their jurisdictions.

Those lips pursed again, and he shook his head. "Uh, no. It sounds like he got just what he deserved. I'm actually here because I want you to bring me back. Fix the ending to *One in the Chamber* and I'll be out of your way."

I nodded slowly. "Oookay. That's it? Great."

With that, I quietly got up and went into my bedroom, taking the time to close and lock the door behind me.

"Okay, I am Zen. I am not crazy. That's me, cool as a cucumber."

The door rattled as my hallucination hit it. "Hayden, we need to talk. Open up."

Maybe it was that tequila that Aaris bought. That had to be it. I'd heard of this sort of thing happening at a few Mexican resorts. They'd serve tainted liquor and people were either dying or waking up with no memories.

I'd bet anything that Aaris was having a hallucination of her own. Probably with Jeremy Piven.

I shuddered at the thought.

I took a deep breath and looked at the bedroom door. I just needed to write and get the crazy out.

A gallon or two of water probably wouldn't hurt either.

I threw open the door to Hallucination Jake just as he was about to knock again.

"You're not real," I muttered as I strolled with resolve toward my computer. The small lines that appeared on his forehead obviously wanted to disagree with my assessment, but I continued on my mission.

Where was I?

Oh, right. I sat down and began.

Laura loved to sit, curled up by the fireplace, watching the city lights twinkle down below.

"Did she now?" a soft voice said in my ear.

I jumped, and the movement sent Bootsy scurrying out from under the couch and for the bedroom. "Thanks for your assistance," I grumbled after her before picking up the laptop and moving to the couch where he couldn't see what I was typing.

Maybe I just needed to write about Jake in order to make him disappear. That was all this was—my muse demanded closure for his storyline.

If her bladder hadn't given her grief, she might've missed the detective as he fell past her window, a look of absolute terror etched onto his face.

"I wouldn't say it was absolute terror," the figment of my imagination called out from the kitchen and I froze.

Oh my god. He knew what I was writing. What if he wasn't an illusion? Maybe he was a hacker. Yes, that was exactly what he was. He probably thought that he'd show up here and blackmail me into changing the ending.

The question was, how was he hacking me from the kitchen?

I grabbed a notebook from my desk and scrawled out:

Laura watched in horror as he fell to the street below. The brandy slipped from her hands and shattered against the stone pavers on the balcony.

"Why is she drinking a brandy? Have we gone back in time? Does anyone under the age of forty drink brandy?" He leaned across the bar and asked with a laugh.

I dropped my pen with a squeak. He was ten feet away. This was impossible.

So, he wasn't a hacker. Definitely a make-believe character. Great —and here I'd been hoping that I hadn't gone off my rocker.

Ooh, off my rocker. I feel like that's something Laura would say.

I wrote it down and Jake let out another loud chuckle. "Now I know she's eighty."

"Oh my god, I'm insane. I'm insane!"

Jake moved to the chair across from me, pouty lips on full display.

"I would have to agree with you. Who else cuts a man down in his prime?"

His voice was deep and measured, with every word sending a tremor through my body. It was a good detective voice. I'd confess to anything if I was locked inside an interrogation room with him.

If sin could talk, it would absolutely sound like him.

I needed a solution to this problem, but Jesus, I couldn't think with him so close to me. I stepped around him and walked out onto the balcony, taking deep breaths in an attempt to clear my head.

Clearly not taking the hint, Jake followed me out. "Look, I know this is a lot to take in," he began.

"A lot to take in? No. Having fictional characters show up on my doorstep is an everyday occurrence around here."

He tested the railing in several places, tentatively resting his arm against it before pointing toward my face. "Tell me, do you typically wear sunglasses around your apartment?"

I reached up and touched them. In the chaos, I'd forgotten that I had them on. "Well, Jake, when I'm hungover as fuck I do."

Confident in the security of the railing, he brought his other arm up to rest, while staring across the complex. "I know you're having trouble coming to terms with this, but I don't have a lot of time. Addison's killer is still on the loose and slipping farther away the more time I waste dicking around with you. Now, I didn't want to have to bring Rachel into this, but you're a loose cannon. And unless you set things right, you can kiss any agent goodbye."

The blood drained from my face. How would he have known about that? How would a fictional character have insight into what was going on with a potential agent?

He wasn't fictional.

This was like that movie... what was it called?

Snatch...

Splat...

SPLIT!

I obviously had Dissociative Identity Disorder and he was just one of my personalities. A personality who had obviously waited until I was asleep to sabotage everything.

Son of a bitch.

If I punched him, would it be like punching myself?

I slowly backed away from him and into my apartment. He turned just as I flipped the lock on the sliding glass door.

"Hayden," he warned. "Open the door. Now!"

I shook my head and he slammed an open palm against the glass, rattling it enough to send a little black and white fur ball into the living room to investigate.

I gave her a sad smile. "Bootsy, honey, Mommy's personality is just a little angry right now. He'll calm down after a few hours on the patio." She probably knew all about him. Poor thing had always been skittish, and I'd just chalked it up to her being a weird cat. But, it was me the whole time. I'd traumatized her with my other personalities. She probably would've been better off with Kitty Protective Services. At least with them, she'd know what to expect.

I made a note to myself to research Dissociative Identity Disorder later. There was so much I was going to need to learn. Maybe I could even email Rachel and apologize for my alternate personality.

Well, obviously I wouldn't word it that way.

I walked over to the door and Jake brought his hands down to rest on his hips. I had an idea. It was a little crazy, but the entire situation was far from normal. I wasn't exactly familiar with the entire ritual, but I had the gist of it down.

"I recognize that you are the part of my personality that has trouble letting go and moving forward," I began. "I recognize that and I release you from me. By doing so, I also release myself from you."

His eyes narrowed and I waved my hand mystically in front of my face. I wasn't sure if the gesture was helpful or not, but it seemed necessary in ridding myself of Jake. Any moment now. It was going to work.

Those same eyes turned positively murderous when I brought the palms of my hands together in a praying motion and extended them toward the glass. "Namaste. Farewell."

He brought his fist up to the glass with a thud. "Oh, no you don't," he growled. "Don't fucking namaste your way out of this! You killed me! I want to come back. End of story."

Jake continued spewing obscenities at me from the other side of the glass and I waved back cheerfully before retrieving my laptop from the couch.

Maybe it took a few minutes to kick in.

Now, how to figure out what was sent to Rachel. I was skimming my sent folder when my cell rang. "How did you get this number?" I answered tersely, by way of greeting.

Aaris gave a weak laugh before grumbling, "Girl, check the caller ID. Listen, I'm glued to the view across my balcony just as much as the next single red-blooded female in this complex, but do you think you could tell your hottie to keep it down? Some of us are still trying to recover from last night."

I gasped. "You can see him?"

"Sweetie, see him, hear him. If I could make it more than three feet from the toilet, I'd attempt to taste him. Jesus, what was wrong with that tequila? I mean, we only had two pitchers." She belched into the phone and paused. "Sorry, false alarm. Seriously, though. Why have I never seen this sexy as fuck man before? And why, in God's name, are you keeping him locked away on your balcony? Put him back in your bed where he belongs."

He wasn't a hallucination or some hidden aspect of my personality. He also wasn't a hacker. He was a man who was insisting that he was Jake Hopkins. Not only that, but he knew what I was writing.

It didn't make a bit of sense, but he was real.

"Um, Aaris? He says he's Detective Jake Hopkins."

I was expecting her to tell me to lock myself in the bathroom and call the cops when I heard a soft moan. "Jesus, this could be the remnants of the tequila talking, but he could say he was Donald Trump and I'd find a way to roll with it for the night."

I cringed at the image her words conjured up.

"Okay, I'm going to have to call you back."

"Mmm hmmm... I see how it is. You're gonna take my advice and get rid of your coochy cobwebs. Good for you, sweetie. Just give me sixty more seconds with his backside please," she begged.

I ended the call and stared blankly at the balcony door. Jake met my gaze and gave me the middle finger before insisting again that I let him in.

Maybe he was just a crazy reader—like whatshername in *Misery*. He probably just wanted to bash my ankles in and tie me to a bed.

The last part dredged up some conflicting thoughts and I had to physically shake my head to clear them away.

"Focus, Hayden," I chided.

I was just going to let him know that I'd been on the phone with the police. The actual police.

Yes, that was a good plan. He'd shimmy down off the balcony and be on his merry way back to Crazytown. Then, I'd be free to delve back into Laura's story.

"I've called the cops," I yelled toward the glass door as I retrieved my laptop from the couch, returning it to the desk in the corner. "They'll be here any minute."

Great. In addition to a tequila-induced headache, my caffeine had gone ice-cold on me.

I carried the coffee mug over to the microwave and nuked it for thirty seconds, feeling better than I had all morning. So, maybe I'd had a delusional man bust into my apartment, trying to convince me that he was a fictional character.

Surely, Hemingway had dealt with his fair share of crazies.

At the loud series of beeps, I retrieved the cup and added another healthy pour of creamer. Bootsy smiled up at me from a refrigerator magnet with the words, "Mama's Little Khaleesi" dancing above her head.

It was my favorite and one of the rare pictures I had of her where she appeared to be happy.

Before I'd even slipped my fingers around the now steaming mug, a hand clapped down hard over my mouth. Instinctively, I bit down and threw my head back, connecting with something solid.

"Holy shid! You bid me and bucked up by node!" Jake shouted, managing to latch onto my bicep just as I made a run for the door.

I would've laughed at his poor attempts to speak through the blood running down the back of his throat, you know, had I not been running for my life.

Instead of breaking free, our feet tangled together and we went down in a jumbled heap on the linoleum floor of the kitchen. I let out a hoarse scream, the sound piercing my skull in thousands of places. His hard body moved, effectively keeping me pinned against the black and white squares. He was probably bleeding all over me.

"Let me go! I've called the cops—ow!" I let out another shriek, hoping that a neighbor would hear it and come to my rescue. Said shriek died in my throat at the feel of a cold barrel against my temple.

"Led's try thid again." I let out a startled squeak from the bite of a metal handcuff tightening around my wrist but fought the urge to shout again. I had no idea how itchy his trigger finger was and now was not the time to find out.

He rocked back on his heels and yanked me to my feet. I struggled in his grasp as he dragged me back into the living room before forcing me onto my desk chair where he promptly snapped the other cuff around the metal armrest with an ominous click.

I looked up at him in fear. I was alone inside my apartment with a nutcase. A nutcase with a gun and a sturdy set of handcuffs. He could do anything, and I'd be powerless to stop him.

I swallowed the bile that rose up in my throat and forced myself to appear unfazed by this most recent development.

Jake retrieved a roll of paper towels and mopped up the blood on his face. And then the blood on the linoleum.

My captor was goddamn *Mr. Clean.*

He tore another towel off the roll and rolled it up before inserting it up under his top lip. It gave him the appearance of a boxer who'd endured a very rough fight. The fullness of his lips was magnified by the positioning, giving him an almost comical appearance.

The fact that there was still a gun in his hands had me rethinking the flurry of jokes that popped into my head. We sat in silence until the bleeding slowed, then stopped.

Jake removed the towel and coughed to clear his throat. "You didn't call the cops. And you're not going to. See, the thing is, you locked a detective out on your balcony. I don't think that'd go over real well with them. Lucky for you, I picked the lock."

"You're not even a real cop," I huffed.

"You wanna play good cop, bad cop? Well, guess what, Sweetheart? Good cop is fucking done for the day and now you've got me. Here's how this is going to work. Your pretty little ass is gonna sit in this chair until my book is where I want it—"

I jutted my chin up at him in defiance even though my heart was pounding like it did when I attempted exercise-type things. "And if I refuse?"

He holstered his gun and ran a hand over the scruff on his face with a harsh laugh. "If you refuse? Christ, is ruining people's lives something you do for sport? If you refuse, then what happened with Rachel is just the beginning. I will drag your name so far into the mud that there won't be a chance in hell of you getting it clean again. You'll have to kiss your dream goodbye because no one wants to read books written by a plagiarizer."

Spittle from his mouth landed on my cheek and I brought my free hand up to brush it away. "I am not a plagiarizer, you—you dick. I put everything into those books!"

He grinned, both dimples on full display. "Everything, huh? You can't even write a decent sex scene. I wouldn't say you put 'everything' into it."

I strained against the cuffs. "Did you just use air quotes?"

He stepped around the chair, forcing me to turn to keep him in my sights. "Face it, Hayden, your writing is tame. Safe. No publisher wants that. You just don't have what it takes—"

"Motherfucker!" I roared. "I had enough to throw you off a building, didn't I?"

He spun my chair and sat down in the armchair across from me. "And how's that working out for you? Readers just going crazy for your next release?"

Bootsy's yowl stopped me from unleashing another stream of obscenities at Jake. She wound her way through his legs, paying absolutely no attention to the fact that I was handcuffed to a chair. Her howls grew in frequency and intensity, yet Jake stood completely still.

"She's feeling stressed out. She needs to be petted and told she's pretty."

He rolled his eyes. "You're joking, right? She's a damn cat, what does she have to be stressed about?"

I paused as the magnitude of my situation hit me full on. I was arguing with a character I imagined in my head and he was exactly like I'd written him.

A complete jackass. It made me remember why that thirty-story fall had been so exhilarating to write.

I inhaled and tried to center myself. "She's been exposed to a lot of crass language—"

"Most of which came from you," Jake threw in.

I cleared my throat. "As I was saying, Bootsy has been through a lot today and I think she needs some calm-down time."

He crossed his arms, causing his shirt to strain around his very muscular arms. His biceps had little baby biceps. What I wouldn't give to squeeze—*no, I was in control of my emotions.*

I was not going to fall victim to his charms.

"So, you're telling me that your cat, Bootsy, needs to have a time-out? Bootsy. That's literally the cat's name." He said the last part as a statement, as if calling a cat, Bootsy, was unheard of.

I nodded. "Yes, Bootsy. The cat of House McFluffsalot, First of Her Name, Queen of the Apartment and Balcony, Khaleesi of the Litter Box, Breaker of Trinkets, Mother of Dragon-sized Hairballs.

She gets stressed out from time to time so I let her watch bird videos on my iPad, just until she's found her Zen again."

Jake let out a low whistle. "Jesus Christ, lady. You're a fucking lunatic."

And that was when I knew for sure that Jake and I were not going to be close friends. In fact, I had illusions of shoving him off of my own balcony. You know, just to see if it stuck the second time around.

My nose whistled at the force of my inhale. "You know, for a cop, you're pretty stupid. Do you really think that insulting me is going to make me more likely to help you?"

His jaw ticked in anger as he leaned in, resting his forearms on my knees. The heat from his body seemed to move straight toward my core, proving yet again that I was experiencing quite the sexual drought. "I know it might not mean much to you, but I had a life before you started meddling. I had plans."

But, he hadn't.

If he was who he claimed to be, then he had nothing going for him, other than being the department's golden boy. Well, that and the fact that his bedpost had been whittled down to a toothpick thanks to all the notches in it.

I snorted at my own joke.

"You really are unhinged. Positively mental," Jake noted dryly.

"So, if I don't help you, then my writing career is over. What happens if I do help you? Do you just go away and everything goes back to the way it was before?"

He nodded. "I'll go back, and it'll be like I was never here. Look at me, Hayden. I'm thirty-four. I'm in the prime of my life here. I'm not ready for the retirement home."

"Retirement home?"

"Yeah," he remarked pensively. "That's what happens to characters when they're 'killed off.' They end up in *Sunset*; completely off the pages and away from the action. Usually, it's your run-of-the-mill villains, but occasionally you get some older characters. If George has been at it, you get an influx of protagonists and some bad *'Winter is coming'* jokes. That's not really the point. I'm not cut out for a life like that. I can't sit around playing bridge and eating tapioca pudding like I haven't got a care in the world."

I sat, openmouthed. I'd never considered what happened to characters once they were written out of a story. In all honesty, I'd never considered them as anything more than a figment of one's imagination.

Jake sighed. "You've never killed a character before, have you?"

My phone buzzed just as I shook my head and I instinctively reached for it. Jake was faster. "Who's Reid?"

"My brother."

Of course it would take him this long to get back to me. He had a 'real job.' Maybe if he'd been better at replying to my texts, I wouldn't be in my current situation.

"Well, you can rest assured knowing that he 'had nothing to do with a psycho showing up on your doorstep' and 'maybe you should consider the possibility that your own actions have gotten you into yet another mess.' Sounds like a great guy."

"Says the man who held a gun to my head and handcuffed me to a chair," I quipped.

"Oh, I wasn't being sarcastic. I commend any man who's managed to put up with you for longer than an hour or two and offer my sincerest sympathies."

My head was pounding from the residual effects of tequila and adrenaline, leaving me in no mood to deal with any more shit. "Jake, with all due respect, I'm not going to change the ending to your story, and I suggest that if you want a different version, then you write it yourself."

I was rewarded with the sight of his jaw clenching before he jumped up and began pacing my living room.

He spat out through clenched teeth, "I can't change the ending myself, Hayden. If a writer kills a character, then only that fucking writer can fix it."

I matched his pouty-lipped expression with one of my own.

"Well then, Detective, sounds like you're out of luck because this fucking writer is working on a cozy mystery."

His fury gave way to confusion as he scratched the back of his head. "What the hell is a cozy mystery?"

I gestured with my free hand. "Cozy mystery—Cozies. Everyone knows what those are." At his blank expression, I elaborated. "They're crime novels where the main character is usually both a woman and amateur detective. She runs a bakery or works as a reporter; something that helps her interact with the people of the town she lives in. There's very mild profanity and no sex scenes. Nice and tidy."

His lips moved back into their trademark pout. "Well, I have to say that the fade to black scenes are going to be right up your alley; although I'm not sure about the cursing, as you have the filthiest mouth out of any woman I've met. And I've met some filthy ones."

He said the last bit with a wink, and I rolled my eyes. I was well aware of his exploits. I'd written them, after all. "I'm quite familiar with your extracurricular activities—"

"I highly doubt you have any insight into what went on 'behind closed doors,'" he interrupted. "You never wrote it. I'll have you know that the women I spent time with were not only beautiful, but intelligent and cultured. We had amazing dinners and watched foreign films; hell, sometimes we even talked about the future and where we saw ourselves."

Everything he'd just described was exactly what I'd been combing the city looking for. The deep timbre of his voice intoxicated me; making it almost impossible to have a coherent thought.

"Really?" I asked, my voice much breathier than it was only moments before.

His lips turned up into a wicked grin. "No. We fucked. Like normal people."

The spell he had me under broke and I dropped my shoulders in disappointment. Not only were there no good men left in the world, there were apparently none left in books either.

"Good to know. Now, if you'll excuse me, I have a novel to write. I just need you to uncuff me and see your way out."

Jake nodded and came back over to where I was sitting. I dutifully raised my arm as far as the cuffs would allow, waiting for him to free me.

Instead, he sat back down in the armchair and picked up one of my magazines. "Go right ahead. I'll just sit here and offer helpful input as needed."

I rattled the cuffs loudly against the metal on the arm of the chair. "Trust me, your input will not be needed."

He looked up from over the top of the magazine. "Oh, I think it will. And, since I have nothing else going on, I can give this my complete, undivided attention."

I was going to murder him... again. Just as soon as I figured out how to pick the lock and free myself.

FOUR

A CLOSE FRIEND or loved one might drop out of sight today. You may panic when he or she doesn't return your phone calls. Don't jump to conclusions, dear Libra. They're preoccupied with matters that, for the moment, appear important and will contact you in time. When you do finally connect, you could hear some interesting news. Relax, go about your business, and look forward to the call.

"Do you have any food around here?"

I jumped at Jake's voice and quickly switched my laptop screen back to the book I'd been avoiding writing for the last two hours. I claimed I was doing research any time he peeked over my shoulder.

If he suspected that it was bullshit, he was keeping it to himself for the time being. I'd also secretly been emailing Aaris, but unsurprisingly, had gotten no response. Knowing her, she was still curled up in bed, sleeping off her hangover before her shift at the bar later tonight. My horoscope only confirmed that suspicion. I hoped that her 'interesting news' would involve ways to make Jake disappear.

Permanently.

For now, I was left to fend for myself with my captor.

"I was supposed to grocery shop today. Instead, I ended up being kidnapped and held hostage by a fictional detective."

He nodded along as I spoke before adding, "Yeah, I didn't need your life story. A simple 'no' would've worked." He sighed and looked around the tiny kitchen, but food didn't magically appear. "I'll run out and pick something up."

My stomach began to grumble, effectively destroying any chance of me pretending I wasn't hungry. The queasy fog brought on by the tequila had dissipated sometime over the afternoon, leaving me ravenous.

It took my brain a second to latch onto his words. He was leaving to go get food. I was going to stay behind in my apartment.

Alone.

This was my chance to escape; or at the very least, alert Aaris to the fact that I was being held against my will. Not that I was convinced she was going to offer much help. She'd probably volunteer herself as tribute.

If I played it cool, there was a small chance I'd be out of this mess in no time. I went back to staring at the computer screen, clicking the mouse at random.

Completely casual.

Not at all suspicious.

"Are you hungry?" Jake leaned down into my line of vision and I shrugged.

"Maybe."

"Maybe. So, I'm gonna take that as a no. Looks like I just need to grab enough for me."

"Fine," I muttered under my breath.

"I'm sorry, did you say something, Hayden?"

"I said." I stretched my arm, testing the cuff around my wrist, much like a dog would a leash. A couple more inches and I would've been close enough to wrap my hand around his throat. I let out a disappointed sigh. "Yes, I'm hungry."

I'd already pointed out the flaw in his plan when I demonstrated my inability to type with both hands. He'd simply suggested that I just type with the one I had.

In response, I'd given him a choice finger from said hand.

Fictional Jake would've understood, as nothing was more important than one's career. Actual flesh and blood Jake was going to be taking another swan dive off of a high rise if he kept it up.

"Okay then," Jake continued, seemingly ignoring my attempts to strangle him by using the Force. "You sit here and fix the book while I go grab us some grub."

I kept my eyes fixed on the screen. I had a feeling if I looked at him, I'd give away my plan to escape. "Whatever you say, Captain. I'll just be here, not writing this book."

His lips brushed against the shell of my ear and a small tremor worked its way through my body as he whispered, "It's Detective, beautiful. Surely you didn't forget that already?"

Oh, he was good.

I pressed my free arm against my suddenly interested nipples and squeaked out, "Of course not."

He pushed off of the chair and I fought the urge to beg him to come back.

"Dry spell," I muttered.

Jake paused as he reached the door. "Did you say something?"

Kiss me.

"No?" A bubble of laughter rose in my chest that I tried to disguise as a cough.

His brows dipped down. "You're sure you'll be okay if I run out? You're not going to try anything stupid?"

I shook my head, knowing my tongue was a traitorous hussy. My mind was filled, not with thoughts of escaping, but of all the things I could do to the detective's body.

Not murder-y type things either.

One minute he had me straining at the cuffs like a possessed person in my attempts to end his life and the next, I was—*well, I was in big trouble.*

That was all there was to it.

"Okay. I'll be right back."

The door closed behind him and I let out a rough exhale. *Oh my god. What did that man just do to me?*

I heard the heavy tread of his boots on the stairs outside as I regained my bearings and remembered my mission. I had to get out of these cuffs and find help. I pulled the bobby pin from my hair and began jamming it into the lock at random. I'd seen this done on television, but hadn't ever attempted it myself.

"Maybe I'm supposed to use the end with the prongs." I spun it around and stabbed it several more times before sighing again. "Jesus, Hayden. You're sitting in front of the GD computer. Google it."

Bootsy wandered out into the living room and observed my efforts in silence.

"In a few clicks of the mouse, Mommy will be free and we'll get the hell out of here. Okay, here we go. Remove the plastic tip. Got it. Bend into a ninety-degree angle. Okay. Insert into the upper portion of the lock halfway. Be sure not to enter it fully or it will not bend into the proper shape."

I worked to follow the instructions. "Does this look like an 's' shape, Bootsy?"

I held up the now jagged bobby pin, but she was fixated on the front door. She let out a soft meow before resting her front paws against it.

I frowned and went back to the lock. A few more bends and I'd be free.

Three bobby pins and a million curse words later, I rattled the cuffs in anger. It was hopeless. Even with clear-cut instructions and pictures, I was still chained to my damn desk chair while my cat pined away for my captor.

I rolled over to the door and bent to scoop her up, but she skittered away at the last second.

"What. Are. You. Doing? You don't even know him!" I hissed.

Bootsy bolted under a barstool and watched me slowly roll across the carpet. Realization hit and I jumped out of the chair before scrambling toward her. "Climb in the chair, baby. We're gonna have to take it with us."

Instead of cooperating, she bolted out from under the stool and took off for the bedroom. If I knew her, she was sitting happily underneath the bed, right in the spot she knew I could never reach.

Especially not while handcuffed to a chair.

Okay, I'd come back for her after I got help.

I rolled the chair out onto the landing and eyed the concrete stairs with loathing. The four flights were a pain in the ass, even on my best day. To conquer them with a chair was going to require my entire focus.

After running several scenarios through my head, all of which ended with me lying bloody and broken on the floor below, I decided to walk down backward. I took the first tentative step before pulling the chair down after me.

I winced as it landed on the stair with a loud thud. This wasn't going to be quite the covert operation I had hoped it'd be. I slowly made my way down, the wheels making a bone-jarring thud with each step. I paused to take a breath on the landing. There were still three more flights to go and, despite the cool fall temperature, sweat was forming around my hairline. Once I reached the bottom, I was going to have to cross the courtyard and then up another four flights to get to Aaris.

I might as well have been scaling Everest. "See, this is what happens when you open the door to a complete stranger; even one who claims to be a cop," I ranted to myself as I dragged the chair down the next flight.

Four flights and one soliloquy later, I reached the ground floor.

"Going somewhere?" Jake asked with a wry smile as he materialized from around the corner. I jumped back with a choked scream.

"I—how did you—I—"

He raised his eyebrows as I tried and failed to complete a sentence.

"I just—you were—food," I sputtered and was rewarded with his amused pout.

"Damn, you just have a way with words. It's no wonder you're a writer. If I interpreted correctly, you're curious to know why I'm here. Well..." He leaned against the brick exterior. "Let's just say that I had a feeling you'd make a break for it the second I turned my back."

"So, you've been sitting down here for the past forty-five minutes doing nothing?"

As if it had been summoned, a vehicle pulled up and parked. It even had an *Uber* decal on the windshield. Jake reached into the back pocket of his jeans for his wallet before answering. "I wouldn't say I've been doing nothing. Why don't you go back upstairs and we'll eat."

"But, you could've stayed in the apartment the entire time. We might've avoided this entire situation," I stalled, gesturing toward the chair chained to my wrist.

"I needed some air. By the way, that was one hell of a speech you made on your way downstairs." With that, he turned away and greeted the delivery driver.

I'd been dismissed.

He hadn't even seemed all that surprised that I'd been planning to make a break for it. Hell, he wasn't concerned that I might run now.

I stared longingly across the small courtyard separating me from Aaris. It might as well have been hundreds of miles. My shirt was soaked with the sweat running down my back and my calves ached from carrying an extra fifty pounds down the stairs.

I rolled the chair back over to the stairs, feeling much like the mice in *Cinderella* probably had as they'd rushed to get the key up to the attic. Aaris and I had talked about getting an apartment with a doorman and an elevator. Once we realized that we were in the wrong tax bracket, we'd ended up here.

And this was nice.

But, right now? I would've killed for that elevator.

I paused on the second step. *Why was I retreating to my apartment?* Jake hadn't demanded it or threatened me with the gun again. I wasn't some meek little hostage—granted, I'd never been held hostage before—but I imagined that I'd never let someone with a gun order me around.

Common sense demanded that I absolutely should let the someone with a gun order me around, but according to my parents, I'd never had much of that either.

I watched Jake approach the delivery driver and once it seemed that they were deep in conversation, I bolted through the breezeway.

If I took a left, I could cut between two of the buildings and make my way back to Aaris' apartment. I decided that it was a brilliant plan just as the rubber on my flip-flop buckled beneath my foot, sending me sprawling face down onto the concrete. The sudden change in direction sent the chair crashing down on top of my prone body.

A weak mewling sound escaped my lips as I lay prostrate on the pavement.

"Damn you, flip-flop. Damn you straight to hell," I groaned. Defeat washed over me at the heavy footsteps coming up behind me. The deep laugh that joined them just added insult to injury. He hadn't even run after me. It was like he'd known that I wasn't going to get very far.

"Okay, *Speed Racer*. Let's get you up."

I went limp, forcing Jake to work to get me off the ground.

"Leave me here to die in peace," I mumbled, earning yet another chuckle from him as he brought me back to my feet.

"If you think that's bad, you should try falling thirty stories," he observed as he pulled the chair up. The retort on my tongue died as the most amazing scents rose from the paper bags on the ground.

"Oh my god, did you get burgers?" My mouth began watering and all plans to escape faded away in the face of greasy goodness.

Jake checked me over before answering, "Well, that depends. Are you going to be compliant?"

I nodded, and he unlocked the cuff around the chair. My relief was short-lived as he snapped it around his own wrist. I was now cuffed to him. A six-foot-six wall of muscle. The proximity made my brain go haywire.

"What are you doing?" Thanks to our height difference, my arm was bent near my head like a bird's wing.

He bent to retrieve the bags of food. "Making my life easier." He dropped the bags into the chair and began rolling it back toward the stairs, pulling me reluctantly along with him.

"So, you're not going to make me drag the chair back up by myself?"

With narrowed eyes and pursed lips—I was beginning to suspect that it wasn't a pout and more just how his mouth was—he bit out, "Look, I know you think I'm a prick, but I'm not making you pull the damn chair up four flights of stairs... even if you did throw me off a building."

I yanked my arm back, forcing Jake to stop. "You're just going to keep bringing this up, aren't you? Well, I'll have—"

"Jesus, Hayden. Do you ever stop? I just offered to carry the damn chair and you're picking a fight."

"You should carry the chair. It weighs like fifty pounds. I could've gotten hurt and then where would you be?"

He lifted the chair with one hand and smirked. "Fifty pounds? This thing can't weigh more than fifteen, tops."

"Fifteen? You're obviously impaired. It's a beast and I'm lucky to have made it down the stairs in one piece."

Jake simply raised his eyebrows and continued to move effortlessly up the stairs while I panted and did my best to keep up. The smell of fried goodness was the only thing that kept me from lying down on the stairs and accepting my imminent death.

"Did you pay for the food?"

I wasn't sure what possessed me to entertain the fantasy I'd been presented with, but if he was fictional, then it wouldn't make sense for him to have actual money.

He paused as we reached the fourth floor. I noticed that he hadn't even broken a sweat and was breathing normally while I wheezed like an old man who'd smoked a pack a day for the last fifty years.

And he was the smoker!

"I have money. Law enforcement isn't a volunteer position although it sure as hell feels like it in the early days." With that, he began rolling the chair toward my front door.

I nodded dumbly before being pulled along. It still didn't make sense. Was his money good here too?

It was at that moment that my neighbor, Eddie, poked his head out of his apartment. I wrinkled my nose at the strong chemical smell emanating from behind him.

"You okay, Hayden?" he asked as he took in the handcuffs and chair before his bloodshot eyes came to rest on Jake.

Okay, so Eddie could see him too.

That meant it officially wasn't tainted tequila.

Not that I necessarily trusted Eddie's judgment; I'd witnessed my neighbor conversing with a trashcan on more than one occasion. I blamed his bizarre behavior on the strange stench that seemed to linger around his apartment.

Jake stiffened next to me and I knew that he must've put two and two together a lot faster than I had. If this were a *Detective Hopkins* novel, then Jake would be pulling his badge and laying on the charm.

"She's good. Aren't you, sweetheart?"

I nodded again on autopilot. He was going to reference something sexual and pull his badge in three, two, one...

"She's into some kinky shit and I'm just happy to oblige, you know? Listen, speaking of illicit activities, what do you have going on in your apartment?" He gestured with his free hand and I realized that the sly bastard had done it. He'd pulled his badge.

Eddie's face paled instantly, and he retreated into his apartment without another word. The door clicked shut softly behind him, followed by the scrape of the chain as it was latched.

What the hell had just happened?

Jake had managed to scare the shit out of Eddie, while ensuring that he didn't try something stupid, like helping me escape. And he'd done it in perfect character.

I was both in awe and enraged at him.

My mouth hung open while my eyebrows had permanently become part of my hairline. "Why would you do that? He's my neighbor..." I dropped my voice to a harsh whisper, "Now, he thinks I'm into kinky fuckery."

He nonchalantly pushed the chair to my apartment door and let himself in. "You're really worried about the crackhead's opinion of you?" He said it slowly, his tongue poking into his cheek.

I sighed. "I know what you're thinking, but Eddie isn't a crackhead. He's a mechanic, so he always ends up covered in grease and chemicals by the end of the day."

Even as I said it, I knew it was complete shit. It was the same thing I'd told my parents the first and only time they'd visited me. Somehow, it was better to imagine Eddie as an average blue-collar man rather than admit that I lived just a few feet from a crack-house —er, apartment.

The latter didn't leave me with warm fuzzies.

Jake used his leg to kick the door shut behind us before placing the bags of food on the small table set off to the side of my kitchen.

"Okay, lady. Your neighbor is a mechanic and I'm the Pope. Can we eat now and fight later?"

No, we couldn't fight later. I was a here and now kind of girl. I wasn't going to just let Jake win without a—*oh my god, were those egg rolls?*

My mouth began watering again as he pulled burgers and salads from the bag. Either he had quite the appetite, or we were expecting company.

He looked up at me. "I didn't know what you liked, so I got a little of everything."

Things the world would never know about me:

1. For other women, it was fancy jewelry or handbags, but it had

been a long-running fantasy of mine to have a man shower me with food like something out of *Pretty Woman*—you know, *"I didn't know what you liked, so I took the liberty of ordering everything on the menu."*

My heart flip-flopped in my chest. It was the kindest thing anyone had ever done for me. If only he were someone I actually liked.

He turned the bag upside down and a flurry of cocktail napkins rained down onto the table top. Somehow, without knowing a thing about me, Jake had gone and gotten food from my favorite restaurant, *5280 Taproom.*

Not that I was going to let a detail like that sway my opinion of him. He was still a complete bastard, and I was still very much hand-cuffed to his side. That was how he'd managed to be so successful; he started off really sweet and then BAM—interrogation out of nowhere.

I wasn't going to let my guard down just because a fictional detective had gotten me dinner. I was being held against my will and —*buffalo wings?*

Goddammit, he was backing me into a corner here. Those wings were my kryptonite. I would've offered to carry drugs in my hoo-ha for Eddie if it involved 5280's famous wings.

No.

I would've offered to wipe the slate with the last *Detective Hopkins* novel if it meant more wings. He was bringing out the big guns early.

I was in huge trouble here.

He had to go. Right after I finished eating, he was gone.

Mmm hmm...

FIVE

I SWEAR I TRIED.

I was going to boycott eating as a way of regaining control of the situation. I really was.

"You gonna make it over there?"

I stripped the rest of the meat from the buffalo wing with my teeth before moaning orgasmically around it. "Ohmygod, sooooooo good."

Jake's expression was pinched. "Yeah, you have a little something just there... and there... pretty much all over your face." He gestured with the hand that was still cuffed to mine, forcing my hand toward my face with each move.

Instead of searching for the nearest napkin, I rested my forehead against the tabletop and soundlessly shook with laughter.

I'd been on hundreds of dates in my quest to find 'the one,' and I typically spent most of it obsessing over the menu. I passed over my favorite dishes in favor of something that wouldn't make a mess. I also never ate enough to fill me up.

I had just done both with the most attractive man I'd ever met and had no regrets. It was exhilarating. Granted, we weren't on a date, so it didn't really count.

But, damn did it feel nice to just not care.

Jake seemed to be ignoring my mini break with reality. I turned my head and found him watching me curiously. "You doing okay, Hayden?"

The urge to giggle faded and I nodded, suddenly serious again. The moment was gone, and I was left with a sauce-covered face and a longing for a bubble bath to collect my thoughts.

I grabbed a cocktail napkin and dabbed at my face. "I think I'd like to take a shower."

He continued staring at my face. "That's probably a good idea." My stomach protested against the tightness of my denim jeans as Jake pulled me toward the bathroom like a convict.

"Um, Jake? I'm not comfortable showering with you in the room."

He didn't respond as he yanked the shower curtain back, and it took me a minute before I realized that he was searching my bathroom for contraband. Just like a real cop. I wasn't sure why he bothered. Even if I found a weapon, the bathroom was windowless. I had nowhere to go.

After checking behind the toilet tank, he crouched down and began going through the small cabinet beneath the bathroom sink, forcing me up against his body with every movement of his arm.

I held my breath as he knocked a box of tampons aside, thanking the gods above he didn't rifle through it in his quest to find something illegal.

"Jake?"

I was bent in half, with my face pressed up against his shoulder as he meticulously went through everything I owned. I made the mistake of inhaling. He didn't smell like cigarettes, which was what I'd been expecting. It was something else...

Campfire.

Like the ones I sat around, roasting marshmallows, when we went to the lake house in the summer. But, it wasn't just campfire.

There were definite hints of spice too. He was smoky spice and woodsy cologne all rolled into one.

Like a campfire made of spicy cologne. And marshmallows.

No.

I was not going to think about that.

He came up empty-handed, and I had to fight the victorious smile threatening to take over my face at the metallic click of the handcuff being removed. I stretched like I'd been imprisoned for years and not just the better part of a day. One of Jake's massive hands closed around my left wrist. My pulse picked up as his thumb traced the red line of irritation left by the metal.

I felt like a robot that had been thrown into a swimming pool; his touch had my entire body short-circuiting. I could do nothing but watch as his fingers delicately stroked the inside of my wrist. The bastard had rendered me speechless.

His hand dwarfed mine, making me feel much smaller than I already was.

Big hands meant a big—

"It's clear." Jake released my hand, and I gazed up at him stupidly, pushing the dirty thoughts I'd been having back into the recesses of my mind.

Clear?

"Your, uh, bathroom—all clear. I'll just be,. He clicked his tongue against his teeth and pointed toward my bedroom.

I closed and locked the door before leaning over the sink with a gasp. *What the hell had just happened?*

I caught my reflection in the mirror and winced. Several strands of hair had freed themselves from my bun during my escape attempt and were now defying gravity above my head, giving me the appearance of someone who'd had a balloon rubbed on their hair. I also still had orange wing sauce around my mouth and, inexplicably, on the bridge of my nose. Yesterday's mascara had transferred onto my eyelids and the skin beneath my eyes.

I looked like an electrified raccoon.

With a sigh, I added a healthy amount of bubble bath to the tub and began filling it before scrubbing my face until it was spotless. Suddenly overcome by the events of the day, I sank down to my knees on the cold tile and retrieved the box of tampons that had surreptitiously escaped Jake's notice. So, I had a few secrets of my own. Everyone did.

• Confession: I was a stoner. Well, sort of stoner. I hated smoking but loved edibles. Luckily, I lived in a state where marijuana was legal. Unluckily, I had two of the most conservative parents known to man and had been forced to resort to hiding it just in case they ever dropped by, unannounced.

I dumped the tampons into my lap before retrieving the small cylindrical container from the bottom. I popped the citrus gummy into my mouth and eased into the bubble-filled tub with a contented sigh.

I hadn't ever understood my family's opposition to weed. My mother had had a prescription for Xanax for years, one she refilled like clockwork. I'd simply chosen a more natural approach to treating my anxiety.

Not that I'd ever admit to it. Aaris was the only one who knew, and she'd been sworn to secrecy years ago. I simply nodded and smiled as they lectured me on the dangers of drugs and the importance of always being alert—because dealers were waiting on every street corner, just itching to shove weed down unsuspecting people's throats.

I snickered at the thought and leaned back, massaging my sore wrist. The water lapped at my raw skin as I moved my thumb back and forth over the affected area, completely lost in thoughts of Jake.

Twelve hours ago, he was just a figment of my imagination and now, he was here, in the flesh. In my mind, he'd always been this abstract object. It was a bit like standing next to a painting. Up close, things were blurred. I'd known his personality and mannerisms, but his physical appearance had always remained elusive. He was like something from a dream with features that were never clear. Now that he was in my apartment, it was like taking a step back and seeing the entire painting for the first time.

And it was a fucking magnificent thing to behold.

I closed my eyes and let the weed spirit my worries away. I knew I needed to come up with a rational answer as to how Jake was here, but I was distracted by muscles and sheer masculinity. Being pinned against the kitchen floor was the most action I'd gotten in quite some time. I clenched my thighs together as I pictured Jake above me. The hand that was aching only moments before, drifted down my body to relieve another sort of ache altogether.

My hand froze as the small part of my brain that was still very much rooted in reality chose that moment to helpfully remind me of the gun against my head and the fact that the douche bag had cost me a publishing deal.

I sat up with a low groan, sloshing water and bubbles over the side of the tub. "This is just a dry spell," I whispered. "You are not attracted to your kidnapper. That would be crazy and irrational. You are not crazy and irrational."

However, I was talking to myself, so perhaps, the jury was still out on that one.

I waited until the skin on my fingers shriveled up like prunes before reluctantly pulling the drain. Instead of spending my free time coming up with a plan of action, I'd fantasized about my captor.

And I still didn't know what I was going to do.

I wasn't willing to change the ending to *One in the Chamber* even if it would mean my freedom. I'd committed to that ending and, for lack of a better term, had pulled the trigger. It was too late.

I snagged a gray cotton cami and black lounge pants from the hook on the back of the door and then took my time pulling my damp hair back up into a bun.

At least I wasn't going to have to face him naked.

I inhaled deeply and took one last look in the mirror. My face couldn't hide my emotions. I was scared shitless to face him without a solid idea of what I was going to do.

"You are calm. You are safe. You are Zen," I whispered before unlocking the bathroom door.

I almost stumbled over Jake as I opened the door. He was leaning against the door frame with Bootsy curled up asleep in his lap. His massive arms were cradled around her body protectively.

Jealousy sucker punched me in the gut while lust dealt the death blow to my ovaries.

He gently placed Bootsy on the carpet before standing and stretching. She gave him an irritated look before curling into the fetal position and resuming her nap.

His position put me right at eye level with his stomach. His t-shirt rode up and my eyes were drawn to the covering of light blond hair that trailed down his abdomen before disappearing into his jeans.

My heart beat out a steady message—*touch... touch... touch.* My brain sent one of its own—*dry spell... dry spell... dry spell.*

I forced my eyes up, hovering much longer than necessary on his broad chest.

Touch.

Then, they moved up to his strong jawline dotted with stubble. He watched me with pursed lips, and I had a feeling he was not fighting the same emotional tug-of-war I was.

His eyes were heavy-lidded, with each slow blink giving me the impression I'd woken him unexpectedly. He had a nose that slightly turned up at the tip. I'd long associated snub-noses with condescending bitches, thanks to some unfortunate run-ins in high school, but Jake made it work to his advantage. Eyes that I'd often described as a dull flat brown were more of a deep amber, flecked with gold and green. Like an olive.

How had I missed so much?

The corner of his mouth turned up ever so slightly as he reached out for my hand. "Is your wrist okay?"

Touch...

I stared at my wrist dumbly before returning my gaze up to his face. His thumb traced around the red groove left by the handcuffs as he waited for an answer.

Say something...

I nodded slowly, absolutely certain I would sound like a porn star in heat if I used my voice.

He moved and began walking me back toward the bed and my brain, which had protested almost everything, remained silent.

"You sure?" he murmured.

I nodded again. In fact, I wasn't sure that I'd ever stopped nodding. I was like one of those bobble-head dogs that sat on the dashboard, constantly in motion. His legs brushed up against mine, sending me scurrying up onto the mattress.

Click, click. One cuff bit into my wrist at the same moment the other closed around my wrought-iron headboard.

"Good." He leaned in and whispered against my ear before slipping out of the bedroom with Bootsy right on his heels.

Dry spell...

SIX

I WAS APPROACHING hour thirty-three of my imprisonment.

Number of text messages received: 0

Number of voicemails received: 0

Number of violent thoughts: twelveteen million.

The past day and a half had been nothing short of a nightmare. Jake had refused to listen to reason and kept me chained to the bed all night. And by reason, I mean me, screaming about all the ways in which he could fuck himself.

And I don't mean chained to the bed in a sexy, bodice-rippery sort of way, but more in a *'it puts the lotion on its skin'* way.

He escorted me to the bathroom when I needed to go and waited outside the door like my warden. Had there been a window, I was certain he would've made me pee in front of him. I might've been touched by his kindness in allowing me to go the bathroom at all; you know, had he not immediately chained me to my desk chair and insisted I write afterward.

Sick bastard.

"'This series had me glued to my chair—keyword, had. Detective Hopkins always ended up in the middle of chaos, which made for a quick fun read, if you put zero effort into reality. Addison was a little too dumb and naïve. And the author never explained how Jake would automatically suspect the cartel for her death. No police procedure was followed. I'm out. The next book sounds good, but without Jake, what's the point?'" Jake read from the couch.

I took a deep breath to center myself and returned to my novel. So far, I'd managed to read four *Ranker* articles and discovered that people experienced some strange shit out in the forest, reinforcing my decision to never visit any heavily wooded areas. Jake, on the other hand, had discovered *Goodbooks*.

"Jake," I said, much louder than was necessary while punching at the keys on my laptop. "Who was very much still dead, lay at the bottom of the building in pieces. The detectives were going to have a hell of a time piecing him back together!"

Jake lay across the couch with his cell phone in his hands, giving no indication that hearing me narrate his death was upsetting him. Bootsy, the two-timing pussy, was curled up at his feet.

When I paused, he lowered it and peered at me. "You used *pieces* and *piecing* in the same paragraph." He retrieved the newspaper from the coffee table and began reading.

"And?"

With a sigh, he brought it down again. "And, it's lazy storytelling. You have a thesaurus literally within inches of you, yet you're going to stick with variations of the word 'pieces.' You would never consider that there might be words like portions, bits, segments, or parts that could be used. It says a lot about how you value your craft. Really. Keep up the good work."

The paper went back up, and I resisted the urge to launch my coffee cup at it. Mainly because it was still three-quarters of the way full and I knew I was going to need all the caffeine I could get to survive the rest of the day with Jake. The warden had allowed me one cup; I doubted I'd get another if I tossed it at him.

I turned back to my computer with a sigh, taking care to rattle the chain around my ankle as loudly as I could manage. Jake quickly learned that handcuffing my arm very much prevented me from reaching my laptop. So, instead of heeding my advice to just remove the cuffs completely, he chained my legs to the metal spider legs of the chair base.

In spite of the hour, Laura could see that there was a crowd quickly gathering on the street below. She slipped on a pair of snow boots and took the elevator down to join them.

The police had arrived by the time she made it outside and fat flakes of snow were just beginning to drift down lazily from the sky. Unfortunately, they hadn't quite managed to cover the poor man... or what remained of him. There appeared to be body parts scattered across a one block radius, leaving his identity a complete mystery.

"That's better. It leaves the book open to me coming back," Jake noted from the couch.

My eyes rolled back so far that I managed to catch a glimpse of my brain.

"But," Jake cut in. "And I mean this with all due respect, if the victim is scattered on the street, how would she know whether it was male or female?"

I ground my molars together, a habit my dental hygienist was constantly urging me to quit, and tapped at the keys. Ignoring his input and continuing was in my best interest.

It was also in his best interest.

She huddled next to a younger couple that lived in the condo next door. She'd never spoken with them personally but had seen them on the elevator and in her small café on the ground floor of the building. They still had the spark of new love radiating about them...

"And, it sucks again," he groaned from the couch. "Get to the good part."

"I already did," I answered sweetly, turning to him. "When you took the express elevator down from Tiffany's condo."

It filled me with endless pleasure to see the edges of the newspaper crumple beneath his tightly clenched fists. Satisfied that I'd shut him up for a while, I turned back to my laptop.

Laura had never seen a dead body up close. She'd always imagined that if she did, it would evoke a visceral reaction in her. And it had. It wasn't one of outrage and worry that she could be next; although both weighed on her mind. No, as she watched the police secure their crime scene, she'd focused on the crowd gathered around her.

Any one of them could've been the killer.

The thought consumed her until she was searching faces for signs of guilt. Was the young couple next to her clinging to each other due to the frigid temperatures or out of culpability? What about the young woman being questioned by the police? After all, it was her apartment he'd been in.

"Is this what a cozy mystery is? Some nobody, searching crime scenes for perps because she received a criminal justice degree from the 'internets?' The police wouldn't release which apartment the victim was in, so again, how would this 'sleuth' be privy to it? Jesus, Hayden. With me, you half-assed it, but at least you were trying. Just admit it—you're phoning it in."

Damn. And here I'd thought that my last comment would keep him sulking for at least half an hour.

Phoning it in?

This dickhead didn't know me.

I brushed off my irritation and pulled up my horoscope, needing the distraction. Today had been an absolute wash, but tomorrow had to be better. I'd reached rock bottom, it could only go up from here.

A message or phone call from someone dear who lives far away could arrive today. You've been thinking about this person for a while, Libra, so don't be surprised if you hear from him or her. You're especially attuned to the thoughts and feelings of others right now. In fact, you may feel especially inspired to work on projects of your own, as ideas are likely to fill your head. Have fun!

Oh, I had ideas filling my head, alright. Unfortunately, none of them were going to help me finish this novel on time. And, unless there was some great distance between mine and Aaris's balconies, I didn't know anyone who lived far away. What a load of generic garbage.

I needed a horoscope that actually fit my situation, like:

You're being held captive in your apartment, dear Libra. Not to fear, a close friend will make her appearance known and free you. Grab your trusty smudge stick and send this fictional demon back to hell.

I smiled. That one was much better.

"Here's a good one—" I glanced over to see that Jake was once again glued to his phone. "My cell service was shit back home. It's nice to not have to wait for websites to load. Where was I? Oh, here it is—'I was a huge fan of Hayden's, but I'm afraid I've lost my faith in him as a writer. I can no longer trust him to deliver a solid book. His romantic suspense series, Blood Letters, had me pulled into the story from page one. Since then, his books have become nothing more than meandering drivel. There's no cohesive plot—and what is the purpose of mentioning Jake's wandering eye every other page? We know, the guy gets around. He's a damn good writer, that's a fact, but it's like he's writing for someone else in this series. Certainly not the readers who have been with him since book one.'"

I pinched the bridge of my nose and focused on my breathing. I was balanced. I was centered. Inside, I was... well, I was seething.

"'One in the Chamber wants to be deep, but comes across as trite and shallow. Ending this book with a cliffhanger would've been acceptable, you know, had there been any redeeming qualities in the main characters. With the earlier work, I was convinced that Hayden was the next Nicholas Sparks. Now, I'm convinced that Hayden is a frat boy who probably wouldn't know a balanced character if it was doing a keg stand right in front of him.' That's good constructive criticism," Jake paused to note.

I buried my face in my hands with a groan.

"No, really. You're getting caught up in the stereotype. You've kept your characters two-dimensional. This is something I can help you with in the book. With a little insight, I think we can turn this whole thing around." He continued reading the review aloud, eviscerating my career with every word.

Apparently, I'd been putting too much of the frat boy lifestyle into my books. Because, obviously, I was a man. What woman could ever be named Hayden?

• Confession: When I was nine, I wrote a book. Nothing fancy, but god, was I proud of it. I'd even taken the time to draw my own illustrations on each page with colored pencils. When I asked my parents for one of my school pictures to tape to the back, my father informed me that it was better if people not know I was a girl. He said they'd be more likely to take me seriously if they thought I was a man. It was why he'd chosen the name Hayden. As sexist as it was, it stuck with me and I'd never felt comfortable using a photo since.

I knew Jake was expecting a snarky response, but I was still reeling from the review. The reader had been 'bored as hell' for the first half of the book, but finally became invested by the second half—until I threw Jake off a balcony.

I stared blankly at the word document in front of me, my muse beaten to the point of silence. The cursor flashed, taunting me. Each flicker was like a beacon, alerting the world to my failure.

Blink.

Failure.

Blink.

Failure.

My throat began to tighten, eyes stinging with unshed tears. Jake must've sensed something was off because he stopped reading. I felt his eyes on the back of my head and my skin flamed with disappointment? Anger? I didn't know.

I blinked rapidly, my teeth sinking into my lower lip, gnawing away at the last remnants of lip balm. I'd sworn I was going to break the habit but, like so many other things in my life, hadn't succeeded.

Blink.

Failure.

"Hayden." Jake's voice was soft. A loud knock at the front door silenced whatever he'd planned to say next. He was up off the couch with his gun drawn before Bootsy even had a chance to react.

He'd lost his boots at some point and was now padding across the carpet in his socks. Inexplicably, that irritated me more than him commandeering my couch and my cat. Socks indicated familiarity and a sense of being at home.

This wasn't his home, and I certainly didn't want him getting comfortable.

"Does anyone know I'm here?"

I shook my head. "Wait, yes. Aaris does. That is, if she remembers anything post-hangover."

He checked the peephole. "What does she look like?"

"Gorgeous. Tall. Looks like she fell out of a fashion magazine?"

"Would she have gone for backup?"

The sheer absurdity of it all had me mashing my lips together to keep the laughter inside. "Backup? Jake, this is the real world. Just let her in; if you don't, she'll definitely get the police involved. The real police," I amended.

He nodded and holstered his gun before unlocking the door. "Aaris?"

She strolled past him and into my apartment with a frown. "I'm going to quit! I can't work like this anymore. I was supposed to have the early shift last night, but then Kara called in, so I had to stay and close. You know how hungover I was, so I'm sure you can imagine how well that went. I paid out the bartenders and then Bryan called me into his office. Accused me of drinking on the job and—holy shit, sweetie, are you handcuffed to the chair?"

I nodded. "Oh, well, yeah. But, what happened with Bryan?"

Jake leaned against the front door with a bemused expression on his face.

"Who the hell are you?" she asked, clearly noticing him for the first time. Perhaps, he should've had his ass greet her at the door. She'd seemed quite familiar with that yesterday.

"It's Detective Jake Hopkins. You know, from my books."

Her mouth fell open and her eyes darted from him to me and back over again, like a tennis ball at Wimbledon.

"Jake from the books, why do you have my best friend handcuffed to a chair?"

He dragged his thumb along the side of his mouth. "We, uh, had a difference of opinion on how to write the next book."

"So, you handcuffed her?" I winced as her voice went up several octaves.

At some point during the commotion, Bootsy had joined Jake near the door and they both eyed Aaris warily.

Jake crossed his arms over his chest defensively. "She threw me off a thirty-story building! Don't let the sad expression fool you; your best friend is a sociopath."

She made a sound that could only be described as something between a groan and a scream before pulling her cell phone from her purse. "Oh my god, you really think you're a fictional character? Hayden, honey, I'm calling the police."

Jake put a hand on his holster. "Don't do this, Aaris. I will be forced to restrain you if you don't put down the phone. Hayden, tell her."

He looked to me and I shrugged helplessly. I was the victim here; he'd do well to remember that. "What am I supposed to tell her exactly? I'm just the resident sociopath, remember?"

His brows knitted together. "Goddammit. Tell her that I'm Jake."

"This man says he's Jake."

He rolled his eyes and gave me a thumbs up. "Thanks for that, Hayden. Super helpful."

Aaris's breathing had turned ragged, and she gripped the wall behind her for support. "P-prove it."

"Excuse me?"

"You heard me. If you're Jake, then prove it. There's got to be something that proves you're him—something that's not in the books. Hayden can verify."

Oh, she was going to eat him alive.

I wasn't sure why I hadn't thought of making him provide proof. Probably because he had me handcuffed before it could come up in conversation.

She stared meaningfully at me and, unsure of what she was trying to communicate, I returned it. That earned me another eye roll and an exasperated sigh. "I need a suggestion. What is something that only you would know?"

I wracked my brain. "Uh, his mother's maiden name?"

"Olson," Jake replied. "Next?"

Aaris looked to me for confirmation and I nodded.

Lucky guess.

"Okay, where did you go to high school? Is that something you know, Hayden?"

I nodded. I'd created an elaborate back story when it came to Jake but had kept the details to myself. It hadn't seemed important enough to add into the novels.

He paused and looked up at the ceiling, and I knew we'd busted him. He wasn't Jake—he really was just some crazed reader.

"Well, Aaris," Jake announced like he was hosting a game show. "That would be the completely fictional Sierra Pines. Home of the fighting Bobcats." He didn't smile, but the corner of his mouth turned up ever so slightly at my facial expression.

I looked like a fish out of water, gasping and spluttering in shock. "How?"

His lip twitched. "Ask me another. This is fun."

"Tattoos?" Aaris blurted and I nodded vigorously.

"Yes, tattoos!"

I visualized my make-believe detective, suddenly convinced that the other two answers had been mere flukes. Jake had some very distinct pieces.

He sighed. "Should we start with the family tattoo? Where the f is actually the branches of a tree? Or, were you referring to the bridge? Because sometimes, you have to see—"

"Where you came from to know where you're going," I finished with a whisper. "You're really him."

Satisfied with the interrogation, Aaris crossed the room to him. "I'm going to need to see them." His eyes narrowed and she added, "For verification purposes."

Jake turned away from me and unbuttoned his shirt, while I strained against the chair, hoping to get a better look.

"There. Are we all good now?"

Aaris's eyes widened and she nodded dazedly, never once taking her eyes off of his chest. The cuff around my ankle rattled against the chair, but he kept his back to me.

"Hayden," Aaris murmured. "I want one of my own."

Her hands snaked around his biceps, kneading at him like Bootsy did when she craved attention. "Is everything real?"

I infused as much boredom as I could into my voice. "I wouldn't know. I really thought I was the only one on this crazy train."

"Tickets for two, please," she purred. "Jesus, it's like he was carved out of stone."

Jake dropped his hands and began refastening the buttons on his shirt. "Yeah, uh, I can hear you."

"Sweetie, I don't care." She continued squeezing him. "I told Hayden not to kill you off, but she wouldn't listen. She just got so caught up in getting this publisher's attention—"

"Aaris!" I shrieked.

She stood on tiptoe and peered at me over his shoulder. "What? I did tell you."

Jake's eyes flashed with amusement as he turned back to me. "I like her."

There was nothing sexual in the way he said it either. It was just further proof that he had to be fictional. There wasn't a man alive that was oblivious to her beauty.

She kept his arm pinned in her hands, even as he tried to sidestep her grasp. "Holy hell, you're like a superhero. Tell me, do you have a brother?"

No.

Another thing the world would never know about Jake? His parents were killed instantly when a robbery suspect ran a red light and t-boned their car following a high-speed chase with the police. He had no other family members and spent a year in foster care until he turned eighteen.

"I actually have a sister."

I froze. "No, you don't. You were an only child and with the tragic loss of your parents as a teen, you decided to go into law enforcement to prevent another child from experiencing the same tragedy. I know everything about you!"

My voice got a little shrill toward the end and it sounded like I was reading from a script, but I lived and breathed Detective Jake Hopkins.

He smirked. "You think you know—"

I began ticking things off on my fingers. "No, I do! Your mother loved, uh, crafty stuff. She was into cross-stitching and whatever. And, and your dad—he was a former Marine, so he was strict with you, but you never once doubted that he cared. The loss of them made you who you are. You didn't have anyone else to turn to, so you became your own hero of sorts." I wracked my brain, trying to drum up more evidence.

Aaris's eyebrows shot up. "I never read any of that—"

"It's because she never put it in the books. She made vague references to my family, but never clarified whether they died or were on an extended vacation." The slight quirk of his lips incinerated me. "My mother still enjoys cross-stitching and whatever, in case you were wondering, but, go on. Continue with your list."

"She looks like she's about to combust, doesn't she?" Aaris noted dryly.

How was it possible that I knew so much, yet so little?

SEVEN

"DO you want the last egg roll?" Jake asked around a mouthful of food.

It appeared like the universe was going to be doing everything in its power to keep my libido in check. It didn't matter if he had half a burger in his mouth or not, if Jake had something to say, he was just going to say it. Flying bits of cow, be damned.

And, the smacking...

I grimaced and shook my head. "I'm suddenly not hungry."

"Why?" A masticated piece of what appeared to be hamburger bun landed next to my laptop. I stared at the soggy piece of bread and felt the bile in the back of my throat.

Knowing if I looked at it much longer, I'd run the risk of hurling onto my laptop, I reluctantly brought my eyes up to meet his. "I'm..." Deep breath. Swallow. "I'm just not hungry." I looked back down at my laptop, dismissing him.

Aaris had left us alone again to go back to the job she'd sworn she was quitting. By now, I knew that her threats were hollow, but listened to her vent all the same.

Jake allowed her to leave only after she promised that she wasn't going to tell anyone that he was here. She nodded along and repeated the words, but her gaze never left his arms. She'd stumbled out of my apartment like a drunk.

He'd officially rendered my best friend useless. She wasn't going to tell anyone that he was here. So, once again, I was back to square one. I was going to be Jake's prisoner until I changed the story.

Unfortunately, no matter how much I tried to center myself, my mind had taken those negative reviews and put them up on the big screen.

"Hayden could be a good writer if he had any inkling how to plot or tell a story. In my honest opinion, he's highly overrated as a writer."

Six books.

I'd written six books, but it was hard to find the accomplishment in any of it as I stared at the mostly blank word document in front of me.

What if I didn't have it anymore?

That scared me even more than the bad press. What if it was a fluke? I'd known after the *Blood Letters* trilogy that I wanted to write about a detective. *Blood Letters* had flirted with the thriller genre while still remaining heavily ensconced in the romance territory. Each book featured a main character searching for love after tragedy. There was enough suspense to keep the reader hooked while allowing the main characters to find their soul mates. *Detective Hopkins* abandoned any pretense of romance and happily ever afters before plunging headfirst into the waters of crime fiction.

I'd spent many a summer afternoon in the small pool house behind my great grandmother's house, lost in a world of earnest detectives and corrupt mob bosses. The apartment had belonged to a great uncle that had moved on to bigger and better things, leaving his family and hard-boiled fiction behind to gather dust.

The wall that faced the pool was entirely made of glass and was therefore subject to the afternoon rays that bounced off the water. It had also been built without air conditioning, leaving me to often wonder if that was the catalyst in my great uncle taking off. I'd prop myself up against the wooden frame of the old waterbed, amid the mildewed cardboard boxes, to read for hours.

The men wore suits and smoked like freight trains, while the women were mysterious and seductive femme fatales, leading the hardened detectives into dangerous situations. And I loved everything about them, especially the fact that there never seemed to be a happy ending. It was such a contrast from the fairy tales I'd cut my teeth on.

So, after *Blood Letters*, I branched out into noir fiction, creating a detective who was more villain than hero. The night before *Detective Hopkins: Body of Proof* released, I couldn't sleep. I'd become convinced that my readers were going to hate it because it wasn't romance and anything remotely romantic was done off-page. I finally convinced myself that it was just one book. If they hated it, I'd simply go back to romance.

They went crazy for him.

My inbox was flooded with readers asking when the next book was coming out... what his next case would be... some even wrote me to offer themselves up as the inspiration for his next love interest. Even my brother's girlfriend, Emily, had loved it and asked for more.

It should've been good news. I'd gotten to write in the genre I'd loved as a young girl, but it felt like something was missing. It took me three books, but I finally figured out what that something was.

The men were the heroes, and the women were nothing more than pretty distractions. Growing up, I'd never read one story where the woman saved the day. They were one-dimensional figures whose superpower was rocking a pair of stilettos.

So, I killed Jake off, thinking that my female readers would support my decision to revamp the series with a female lead.

Girl power and all that.

Now I was without an agent and facing the wrath of a very angry detective.

"You need coffee?"

I jumped at the sound of his voice and was surprised to see that all traces of Jake's hamburger were gone. He sat on the edge of my desk, watching me curiously.

"What?" I asked, fighting to pull myself from the realm of bad book reviews and antihero detectives.

"You zoned out on me. I asked if you needed coffee. We've got a long night of writing ahead."

My upper and lower molars connected at the use of the word 'we.' As if he was going to be sitting down to write anything. I knew what he'd be doing; sitting on the couch, offering unsolicited advice.

I nodded. It was going to be the longest night of my life. It almost made me miss being handcuffed to my bed.

Almost.

The coffee maker grumbled to life, struggling just like I was to do its job. I highlighted a word and deleted it before promptly rewriting it again. The last two hours had been some variation of this exact thing. At this rate, *Angel of Death* would be complete in five to six years.

The coffee maker gave its final phlegm-laden groans, filling the air with scents of caffeinated goodness. Maybe a strong cup of coffee would jolt me out of this fog.

"Do you want cream?" Jake called from the kitchen before lowering his voice. "Or does Satan drink it black?"

"I heard that and if you think that I'm going—"

A deafening boom filled the room and the balcony door splintered into a series of cracks before my chair was flung backward onto the carpet.

Jake had me and the desk chair pinned beneath his body, like a massive riot shield, while my addled brain tried to determine what the hell had just happened.

It took a full minute for the tail end of our conversation and the images of my door imploding to align. My heart pounded in terror and I began hitting Jake.

"You broke my door!" I croaked, as I was pushed farther into the chair. My hands connected with his shoulders repeatedly, but he kept me pinned down.

"Goddammit, Hayden, stop fighting me!" He shifted in an attempt to block the next blow and I suddenly felt the presence of a new weapon altogether.

A very large weapon.

I halfheartedly swatted at his arms as every one of my biological instincts urged me to arch my hips and find that weapon a good home.

"Is that a gun in your pants or do desk chairs get you going?" I panted, partly from his weight on me and partly from the fact that my libido had taken the reins.

He pushed himself up onto his hands and glared at me. "We're under attack and you think now's a good time for sex jokes? Is this something you experience often?"

I tried to think of the last time I'd been pinned to the carpet by a man and came up blank. I was certain that if I'd ever experienced this, I'd remember it. It'd be one of those memories I'd hold on to even as I wasted away in the nursing home. I would entertain all of my nurses with tales of my conquests. They'd call me the sexy granny... no, maybe the sexy maven. Maven seemed distinguished.

"Not this, Hayden," he ground out through clenched teeth. "The door. Someone shattered your door."

"You. You shattered my door," I helpfully pointed out.

His gold eyes glinted with barely constrained rage. "Sweetheart, I'm going to assume you hit your head on the way down because I was in the kitchen. That loud bang? That came from the balcony. The balcony is on the opposite side of the apartment from the kitchen. Do you understand?"

A fresh wave of anger swept over me at his slow, measured tone and I thrust my fist up into his jaw. His nose wasn't going to be the only thing that was bruised. The force of the blow sent pain radiating from my knuckles down to my elbow. "Don't talk to me like a damn child!"

He blinked slowly and then rolled off of me. "Stay here, Rocky."

I ignored his little dig and began checking my hand. If Jake's body was made of stone, then his face was made of granite. I opened and closed my hand, trying to alleviate the stinging. He hadn't even reacted like someone who just almost got knocked out. Just further proof that he was not human.

I lifted my head off the carpet in an attempt to see what he was packing in those jeans. Instead, I was treated to the sight of his ass as he crept toward the balcony door. I wanted to point out that a crouch for him was the equivalent of most people standing up normally, so he wasn't quite as inconspicuous as he imagined. I decided against it when he turned and I saw the intense look on his face.

He reached the opposite wall and contorted the upper half of his body to check the balcony. "I think they're gone," he whispered.

I rolled my eyes and whispered back, "Are they? That's a shock. I thought they'd want to stick around for coffee."

Jake dropped his hand from the handle of his gun and pinned me with a hard stare. "Your life is in danger—"

"Your life is in danger," I retorted, like the mature twenty-seven-year-old I was.

He sighed and began the tedious task of sliding the balcony door open while keeping the glass intact. "It's a damn good thing you have double pane glass or the projectile would've come into the apartment."

Knowing my luck, 'the projectile' was probably a Canadian goose who'd mistaken my sliding glass door for a beach in Mexico. A pigeon had committed suicide in a similar fashion last fall. Bootsy had proudly brought me the corpse.

I cracked my neck and tried wiggling my toes to regain feeling in my feet while Jake prowled around the balcony with his gun drawn. It didn't escape my notice that he tested the railing three separate times before leaning over to check below.

I would've told him that he'd been reading too many crime novels had he, you know, not been the main character in one. He was just doing what I'd written him to do. And it was only human nature to be wary of balconies after falling thirty stories; he was just reacting the way anyone else would in his situation.

Speaking of behavior though, I had yet to see him light up a cigarette. It was completely out of character. Between that and coffee —*oh, my coffee!*

I arched my back and tried using my legs to flip the chair onto its side. If I worked hard enough, I could crawl to the kitchen and retrieve my mug. Jake could search the balcony for clues until morning as long as I got my caffeine.

With one great heave, I threw my body weight to the right and tipped the chair. When I saw it, I let out an involuntary squeak of shock.

My *Write Like A Motherfucker* mug lay on the kitchen floor in a pool of coffee, but the handle was completely detached. That bastard destroyed my favorite cup and was now wasting precious time searching for a dead bird instead of dealing with the more pressing tragedy.

My lips began to quiver, and I mashed them together in a futile attempt to stop the tears that were inevitably coming.

He was as big as a damn redwood, what did I think was going to happen when he forced himself into my tiny kitchen?

"You are safe. You are grounded. You are balanced. You are... uncaffeinated." A soft sob broke free, but I tried passing it off as a sneeze.

Jake spun around on the balcony. "Hayden?"

I shook my head. "I'm f-fine." Another one slipped out and before I knew it, I was having a full-blown meltdown on the linoleum.

The cuffs fell away from my ankles with a soft click. Jake lifted me out of the chair and, instead of giving him a piece of my mind over the mug, I just wrapped my arms around his neck, buried my face in his shirt, and inhaled deeply.

Because I was so traumatized.

I wanted to get tangled up with him.

That was obviously just a side effect from the sudden altitude change.

"Hayden?"

"Hmmm?" I answered, sleepily, face and hands still very much attached to his shirt. At some point, I'd stopped crying and sent my olfactory system into overload trying to identify all the various scents that made up Jake.

"You-uh, you have to let go now." His voice was lower, not like he was whispering again, but the tone was different. Deeper.

His fingers lightly moved up and down my spine and I reluctantly pulled myself away to meet his laser stare. We were on the couch; well, Jake was on the couch. I was sitting curled up in his lap.

I was no better than Bootsy.

Before long I'd be rubbing my body against his legs and—*Jesus, what was wrong with me?*

I scrambled back onto the next cushion and perched near the side arm of the couch. A change of topic was in order. "You broke my favorite mug," I stated flatly.

"Your life is in danger," he answered in kind.

We stared each other down, neither of us willing to break first in order to hear the other person out. Bootsy poked her head out from beneath the couch and watched the standoff for a few minutes before disappearing again.

"Hayden," he prodded.

"Jake."

He scratched an invisible itch on his temple with a wince and sighed heavily. "Aren't you the least bit curious to know what I found?"

I crossed my arms over my chest defiantly. "Aren't you the least bit sorry that you broke my favorite mug? What am I supposed to drink out of now? A generic one?"

"Hayden," he tried again, but I turned toward the wall, choosing to give the clumpy textured patches the attention they'd been missing. "Hayden, damn it, look at me. You're in danger—"

"From what? The Canadian Goose Mafia?" I snorted at my own joke but quickly realized that I was the only one laughing. Jake pursed his lips, clearly waiting for me to get ahold of myself. "C'mon, Jake. It was a bird. A poor, misguided bird who made bad life decisions that led to my balcony. He was probably strung out on some bad seed..."

My voice trailed off as Jake held his phone up to my face. I squinted and pushed my glasses back up onto the bridge of my nose, trying to see whatever it was he'd seen when he took the picture. The blood drained from my face when I spotted it sitting near the broken glass.

"That looks like a brick." I was back to whispering, in case the alleged brick sniper was perched on a nearby balcony, listening in, just waiting for the most dramatic moment to lob another 'projectile' at my head.

He stood up and went back out onto the balcony, returning with said brick in his hand. I backed myself up onto the arm of the couch back arched like Bootsy's when she was startled. He moved his hand up and down. He was either trying to determine its weight or looking for a place to shove it.

"I've got a proposal—my life, in exchange for yours. You get me back into my story and I'll find out—"

"Whoa, whoa, whoa." I held up my hand. "Wait a second. I'm supposed to just agree to this negotiation? For all we know, it was just some drunk kids. My life isn't in danger. I've got some angry readers, but that's to be expected after the last book."

Jake shook his head and rapidly lifted and lowered the brick. He was definitely deciding where to hit me with it. "Someone's sending you a message."

He turned it over and the laugh died on my lips as the cover model for *One in the Chamber* looked down at me from his brick prison cell.

I DUMPED another dustpan of glass shards into the trashcan. "Do you think we got it all?"

Jake peered down through the wooden slats of the balcony and smirked. "Well, if we don't count what went onto your neighbor's patio, then yeah, we're golden. Are you sure you don't want to sit down and let me finish? You've had a pretty traumatic night."

I shrugged. "I'm okay."

Not only had someone thrown a brick at my apartment, apparently they'd decided to discard their copy of *One in the Chamber* in the same manner too.

It was like something out of one of those cheesy made for TV movies. The overdone brick through a window trope. The truth was, I didn't know what to make of any of it. I couldn't imagine anyone hating the book enough to try to commit a murder.

Jake hadn't given up as easily and had been peppering me with questions about anyone who might wish me harm. With the exception of Cole, the date from hell, I couldn't think of anyone.

On top of that, if I wanted to avoid situations like the one I presently found myself in, I was going to have to come up with a way to resurrect a detective after his swan dive off the high rise.

When he wasn't interrogating me about the whereabouts of my enemies, he'd insisted that I sit down and rest. At the computer.

As if I could just magically summon up the words and get him back into the book by sunrise. It was unfathomable. Not only that, but Laura had hightailed it out of my head right about the time my balcony door had a brick thrown at it.

So, now I had no one to solve Jake's case and, without someone to solve his case, there was no realistic way to bring him back into the story.

I put the dustpan back under the sink and moved on autopilot to the couch. I just needed one good idea. Something to break through the block...

"Hayden?"

I jerked awake. "I wasn't asleep!"

Jake pursed his lips and nodded condescendingly. "Of course you weren't. It's completely normal to rest your head on your chest and snore for an hour when you're brainstorming your next bestseller. I solve most of my cases in the exact same way. I can't wait to hear what you came up with."

I groaned, wishing I'd taken the opportunity to snag an edible once the handcuffs were off. I found my tolerance to him got higher at roughly the same pace I did. "I'm tired, Jake. And, in case you've forgotten, I haven't agreed to the terms of your deal. I have a storyline in place that doesn't involve you miraculously reappearing."

"Fair enough." He reached for my hand. "Let's get you to bed then. You get a good night's sleep and we'll talk in the morning."

I reluctantly took it and let him lead me toward the bedroom, too exhausted to put up a fight. He waited outside the door as I changed into my pajamas and washed my face before leading me over to the bed like a parent. I lifted my wrist dutifully.

"What are you doing?"

"Waiting for you to handcuff me to the bed," I answered with a yawn.

He grinned. "If I had a dollar for every time I heard that."

I frowned. "You would. Look, are you handcuffing me or not? I just want to sleep until my life makes sense again."

Jake moved to the small window next to my nightstand and lifted a wooden slat. "I don't want to keep you prisoner," he said absently, as he searched the parking lot down below. "I thought my offer was beneficial for both of us. I've never had a case I couldn't solve, you know it's true."

He'd never had a *fictional* case he couldn't solve. This was the real world though and villains here rarely followed a script.

Bootsy jumped up onto the bed, having been M.I.A. for the better part of the evening.

Jake turned back to the bed and began waving his index finger at her. She flicked her tail and looked up at the ceiling.

I cracked my neck and settled against the pillows. "Jake, what the hell are you doing?"

He kept his focus on Bootsy as he answered. "I'm playing with her. Does she do any tricks?"

I definitely should've had the edible. "Tricks? Dogs do tricks, Jake. Cats are companions."

"Look at her tail though. That means she's happy."

I lifted my head to look at her. "No, she's actually pissed. I'd stop before she decides to shred your finger with her teeth."

He gave it up and sank down onto the carpet. "I was thinking that maybe I should stay in here tonight. Just in case they try something else."

My eyes popped open. "No. Absolutely not. I am not getting pubic lice or whatever the hell else you carry. You can stay on the couch or at the *Super 6* down the road, but not in here. Nope."

I closed my eyes and refused to look at him again. It was a dick move, but I couldn't tell him the truth. What was I supposed to say? *'Hey, sure, stay in here with me and I'll try not to dry hump your leg?'*

The dry spell, coupled with his appearance, was wreaking havoc on my lady organs.

"Goodnight, Hayden."

I slowed my breathing down and pretended to be asleep. I was afraid if I opened my mouth to tell him goodnight, then everything else would come falling out with it.

I had to agree to his terms and get him back into his book even if it meant career suicide. If he stayed here, then my heart wouldn't stand a chance. I fell into a restless sleep, riddled with guilt and confusion.

Who wanted me dead?

EIGHT

"YEAH, put it there. I want to see everything."

I sat up in bed with a jolt at the unfamiliar, and downright porno-graphic sounding, conversation taking place outside my bedroom. A quick glance at the clock confirmed that it was just a little after eight, yet my apartment had suddenly become a hub of activity.

I relieved my bladder and put on a robe before venturing out into the hall to investigate. A couple of guys were up on ladders, drilling into the ceiling, while several others were grouped together outside the open front door. I didn't recognize a single face.

"Jake?" I called out hesitantly.

He stepped inside from the balcony, cup of coffee in hand and looking like a million bucks. "Good morning."

Nothing about his stern expression or clipped voice indicated that it was indeed a good morning. I'd definitely overstepped the line between trying to keep my panties on and downright obliterating the man's character.

"Hey," I tried. "I'm sorry about last night—"

He stepped around me. "No need to apologize. I get it; we're not friends." He was right, but the words still stung. "I've got the guys installing security, so we'll have eyes on this place at all times. I also talked to the complex and they'll have someone out for the door in a few hours. I told them I wanted the glass reinforced."

He paused, clearly wanting to say more. "I think you've been briefed on everything, Ms. Michaels. Have a nice day."

Ms. Michaels?

Oh, he was definitely pissed.

I stood in half-alert shock when he turned away and stepped back out onto the balcony.

"I'll do it."

Jake looked back at me before taking a sip from his coffee mug, his eyes never once leaving mine. I was being investigated without words. "That's great, Hayden," he finally noted in a voice heavily laced with sarcasm. "You're a real humanitarian."

"Hey!" I protested. "This is what you wanted."

Wasn't it?

"Look, lady. If you're expecting me to fall at your feet in gratitude, then you're going to be sorely disappointed. You hold up your end of the bargain and I'll hold up mine." This time he didn't wait for a response before striking up a conversation with the two men working on the balcony.

Bootsy appeared out of nowhere and began winding herself through my legs, apparently having realized over the last few hours that, while Jake was great, he didn't know where the food was kept.

She met my bewildered gaze with a look that seemed to suggest she'd decided to hold me personally responsible for the entire debacle.

"Yeah, well, that makes two of us," I said, more to myself as she continued to glare at me. Knowing I wasn't going to win the argument, I went for my secret weapon; a tin of the most noxious smelling cat food known to man.

Bootsy tried to play it cool, but not before I saw a look of complete adoration in her eyes.

"Look who's reclaimed her pussy," I noted victoriously.

"What the hell did you just say?" I jumped in fright as a man swung down off the ladder in the dining room.

"I—" I froze.

I could've sworn they'd all migrated over to the front door. My cheeks burned with embarrassment and I instinctively turned toward the balcony, hoping for an assist.

Jake, however, had his back to me and was obviously still pretending that I didn't exist.

"Look, miss, I'm half deaf, so you're going to have to speak up." He leaned in over the counter.

I took a half-step back, my eyes darting around the kitchen like ping-pong balls. "I—"

Think, dammit.

"I said, 'Oh, this tuna looks juicy.'" I tapped a finger against the tin of cat food for good measure and added, "Yummy."

He looked at the can and then back up at me skeptically. Completely going for broke, I began patting my stomach and nodding like a loon.

"Sweetheart, that's salmon," he gruffly stated. "And cat food."

I kept nodding, even as he went back to work, mumbling something about the pretty ones always being bat shit crazy.

Once he was out of earshot, I turned on Bootsy, hissing, "You made me look like an idiot!"

"Oh, I don't think you needed the cat for that." Jake leaned against the fridge.

"How much of that did you witness?"

He smirked. "I caught you pantomiming the deliciousness of the cat food. Is that something you do to convince the cat or yourself?"

I placed my forehead against the countertop with a groan.

"I'm actually not here about that though. I'm here on business."

I looked up with a frown. "Why are you talking like you just arrived? You've been here for two days. Stop acting like you're running an actual investigation."

"Ms. Michaels, I'm afraid I'm going to need to question you. We need to know your habits, see if we can establish your whereabouts over the last week or two. It might help us come up with a motive for who would want to hurt you." His tone remained even, a testament to how many times he'd made this exact speech.

What the actual fuck?

And, who was 'we?'

"Wow. I guess we're moving right past pleasantries this morning, aren't we? And I haven't even had coffee yet."

Bootsy began yowling and pawing at the belt of my robe. I took the can opener and turned it forcefully around the can before dumping the toxic fish parts onto a paper plate.

Jake's self-righteous smirk faded almost instantly. His skin had even taken on a greenish tint. "Oh my god, what the hell is that?"

"Breakfast," I said with a grin. "You know, for people who are here on official police business. Eat up, Detective."

He grabbed my bicep and lowered his voice. "What do you want, Hayden? I'm too friendly last night, but this morning it's too formal. I'm just trying to do my job so that I can get home. Is that too much to ask?"

"Oh, it's Hayden again? Make up your damn mind, Detective Hopkins. You're giving me a headache."

"Fuck me," he muttered.

God, I would.

And that fact irritated me to no end.

I took a moment to ogle him as he rolled his eyes. Today, he was wearing a heather blue t-shirt with a small white flag screen-printed on the sleeve.

He was my enemy. I needed to remember that.

"How about this? You call me Jake, I call you Hayden, and then you tell me what it is you do all day?"

I crossed my arms over my chest. "What are you implying? That I don't write all day? You think I'm lazy? Is that it, Jake?"

He dropped a fist onto the counter. "Jesus Christ, lady. I'm getting nowhere with you. Just go get dressed."

"She's a handful, isn't she, boss?" A worker materialized from the hallway. He winked at me and my brow furrowed. I couldn't place him, but maybe he'd done work on my apartment before.

I turned my attention back to Jake. "I don't know if I want to go anywhere with you."

The other man chuckled. "That's right, lady. You reclaimed that pussy. He better recognize."

Oh, shit.

Someone had heard me after all.

Jake frowned. "She what?"

"I'll be ready in five," I blurted before all but running from the kitchen. The worker's laugh followed me down the hall and into the bedroom.

"OKAY, now when we get there, act normal. Order whatever you usually get. Sit where you normally do. That kind of thing. Don't get too focused on looking for a suspect. That's my job." Jake hit his turn signal and switched lanes. I was riding shotgun in the shiny black Raptor I'd written for him and, any moment now, I was going to wake up back in bed, having dreamt this entire thing. I rubbed my damp palms against my jeans and focused on my breathing.

After getting dressed in record time, Jake had wanted to know my schedule for a typical day. When I mentioned that I wrote at a local coffee shop a couple of times a week, his eyes lit up. I was relieved that I'd left out the fact that I worked at a salon in the afternoons and evenings because there was not a chance in hell of me letting him tag along there.

We pulled into the parking lot and Jake turned to me. He studied me for a second, giving a slight head shake at my *you've got to be kitten me right meow*, t-shirt. "This is the place?" He looked through the windshield at the *Cold Brews Co.* sign and then back at me. "It looks like a bar."

"No, their specialty is cold brew coffees—look, is this a good idea?"

Translation: Is this safe?

He nodded. "I'm not going to let anything happen to you."

The thought that someone, besides Bootsy and Aaris, wanted to keep me safe did weird things to my heart, even if it was coming from Jake. I fought the urge to pump my fist in the air while laughing like a lunatic.

"After all, you're my meal ticket. If you get dead, I can't get back home," he finished with a pouty smirk.

Oh good, the limbic rage was back. I'd been worried it was gone forever once the handcuffs were off.

"Why do you do that with your mouth?" I snapped, as I unbuckled and climbed down to the pavement.

"Do what?" He pursed his lips again.

"That! You're doing it again."

At his blank expression, I forced my own lips into a duck pose as he held the coffee shop door open for me. "Like this."

"Why are you doing that to your face? Stop. People are staring." He hissed, glancing around.

"You look like that all the time."

"Good Morning, Hayden," my favorite barista, Damien, called over the espresso machine as the door jingled above our heads, announcing our arrival. "The usual?"

I immediately softened my expression, trying to channel the joy and tranquility that tried to flee when Jake entered a room. "Yeah, that'll be perfect. Thanks, Damien. How'd Paul do on his test?"

He poured steamed milk into a paper cup for a to-go order with a dramatic eye roll. "Nailed it. Like he does everything else. I just have to talk him off the ledge every time though. How'd I end up the motivator in this relationship? I swear."

"Because you're a positive person and deserving of all the good things life has to offer," I reminded him as I selected a bottled water from the refrigerated case

"I just come here a couple of times a week, but know everyone's life story," Jake quietly taunted at my back, his body inches from mine. A shudder worked its way down to my toes as the scent of campfire and pine flooded my nostrils.

Were there notes of citrus layered in there? No, I was definitely detecting hints of clean laundry that had been dried on a clothesline mixed with something.

Gah, what was it?

I wanted to lean back and rest my head against his chest while looking up at him adoringly. Just like I'd witnessed the younger couples that frequented this place do on more than one occasion. But this time, it'd be me experiencing something other than abject disappointment.

Me and my very own tree.

And I'd climb that redwood every day.

Just doing my part to save the earth, kids.

I was struck with the image of massive hands on my hips, pinning me in place. I'd just bet that his fingers would curl in possessively, marking me as his to anyone who dared to look. The cold air blasted around bottles of juice and water, yet inside, I was sweltering.

His proximity was messing with my brain waves. I straightened with a shaky exhale and carried my water over to the register, doing my best to ignore my flushed cheeks and the giant I came in with.

Damien added a heart to the foam and handed me my caffè mocha before noticing Jake. "Hey, you brought a friend," he exclaimed in his typical sing-song.

I shook my head. "We just came in at the same time. I don't know this man."

I wasn't just imagining all the ways I'd like him to defile me in front of the poor beverage case, either, in case you were wondering.

"Are you sure you don't want to get to know him?" he stage-whispered, raising his eyebrows up and down suggestively as he snagged me a cinnamon roll from the case.

"Oh, no. I've got quite enough excitement in my life."

Damien gave Jake another once over. "If you say so. I personally think when excitement comes packaged like that, you thank the universe and don't ask questions. But, that's just me. How's Bootsy doing? Is she still loving her holistic food?"

"Yes. It has made such a difference with her..."

Shit, what was it supposed to do?

"Poops?" I offered hesitantly just as Damien suggested, "Her coat?"

He frowned. "It shouldn't have changed her bowel habits. My girls didn't seem to be any different. Maybe check with the company—"

I waved my hand. "Oh, no I meant that she was much more 'regular,' if you know what I mean. Poor thing, uh, couldn't get the job done before. This food has really taken in her interconnectedness with her, um, environment. She's living her best holistic life now."

I made the mistake of looking over at Jake. He stood at the counter with wide eyes and a *what the fuck are you talking about* expression on his face.

• Confession: I never actually bought the cat food that Damien recommended. I went to the pet store with every intention of purchasing the *all-natural, chock full of vitamins and omegas, and completely grain-free* canned cat food until I saw the price. At six bucks a tin, I decided that I would just let Bootsy continue her unwholesome lifestyle. Unfortunately, Damien asked about it the very next time I was in, and instead of coming clean, I told a little white lie. He'd just made it seem like letting your fur baby eat anything else was bad pet parenting. And, it wasn't like he would ever know. He wasn't going to show up to my apartment, demanding to see the contents of Bootsy's litter box.

Damien nodded. "Well, let me know if you need anything else for her. Oh, have you noticed how much more connected she is spiritually to you now? I swear, I recommend it to everyone."

I avoided Jake's penetrating stare as I paid before patting the front pocket of my backpack. "Definitely. So... Zen. Well, I better get to it."

"Same. I'll come by and check on you in a bit."

I stuck the bottle of water in the side pocket of my bag, juggling the cinnamon roll and mocha as I made my way to the wooden table near the back. It was the only table with an outlet that was out of direct sunlight.

Next to it was an old wooden hutch that held cream and sugar. I found that it was the best seat in the house for eavesdropping, which was a win-win for an author in need of a story.

I loved everything about coming here. From the exposed brick walls and ceiling beams to the vintage signs and old produce case turned bookshelf, it was the perfect place to let my creativity flow.

Jake solved his first case here. Incidentally, he also fell off a balcony at this very table. It held a special place in my heart.

"I'm going to sit on the other side of the room," Jake said in a low voice. Instinctively, I turned to where his voice came from just in time to see him add sugar to his coffee.

"No, don't turn around. You and I aren't having a conversation."

He was going to add precisely two and a half raw sugars, keeping the other half in his pocket for his next caffeine fix. When I heard the distinct sound of paper being folded, a victorious smirk spread across my face. God, I loved being right.

"Why are you smiling?" He kept his back to me, so it appeared as if he was having a conversation with the various creamers.

"I'm not." My grin widened.

He sighed. "You are. I can see your reflection in the carafe. What about this investigation is funny to you? See, someone shoots up my door, I'm not laughing. Then again, I'm not trying to have a spiritual intervention with my cat."

My smile faded, and I turned all of my attention into retrieving my laptop from the backpack at my feet. "You're just so—" What was he? "Predictable. Everything you do is exactly the way I wrote it.

Sometimes, I'm even convinced that I know what you're going to do next before you do."

I saw him reach for a stirrer in the reflection of my laptop screen. Judging by how vigorously he was using it, I'd gotten under his skin.

"You're probably right," he finally conceded. "You are, after all, operating on an entirely different plane than the rest of the world. I'll be across the room; try to act normal."

I bit the inside of my cheek. "And how am I supposed to do that when you're watching me from across the room?"

"Just write the book, Hayden. Don't worry about who's coming or going. Let me handle that. Tap your finger twice against the table if you understand."

I did, feeling like a secret agent in a summer blockbuster.

With villains at every turn, there was only one woman capable of saving the world. All she needed was her trusty laptop and some caffeine—

"Hayden, I just needed you to tap twice. You can stop now." He snagged a newspaper off an empty table and tucked it under his arm before moving toward a table near the front. From there, he'd be able to see everyone coming and going.

I took a bite of my cinnamon roll and cracked my knuckles before pulling up my manuscript.

Alright, Laura. Let's solve a mystery...

Laura stood, shoulder to shoulder, with some of the city's most upstanding citizens. It was unfathomable to think that any one of them could've been responsible for the body lying in the street, but her instincts told her that was exactly the case.

My mind went blank, and I began distractedly counting each pulse of the cursor. I was simply rehashing what I'd already covered.

In all honesty, I had no idea what to do with Laura. Jake had pointed out her implied elderliness more than once and now I couldn't help but picture her as some blue-haired granny with a cane.

How was she supposed to solve a murder?

Plus, by mentioning her husband early on, I'd destroyed any chance of adding a love interest for friction. It was shit.

I tried again.

Laura stepped away from the crowd and searched for... a way out of this story. She'd gotten roped into playing the main character after the author killed off the other one. Laura didn't want to be next.

Laura was fucking everything up.

Jake caught my eye and frowned from over the newspaper. Obviously, he was enjoying the drivel I was spewing out about as much as I was.

I took a long drink of coffee, but the caffeine only confirmed what I already knew. I needed a new main character. Someone who was younger. Female. Maybe she'd been exposed to law enforcement by a former boyfriend or family member. Just enough that she'd know her way around a crime scene—*oh my god.*

My legs caught the edge of the table as I quickly stood up, rattling the plate containing my half-eaten cinnamon roll. I just needed to act discreetly.

Jake had the paper up again, reading, so I couldn't signal for Plan A, which was for him to meet me in the bathroom. I was going to have to go with Plan B. I walked over behind his table and looked out the large glass garage door that they opened during the summer months.

Realizing I still hadn't grabbed his attention, I stretched my arms overhead and yawned loudly.

"Hayden, what the hell are you doing?" he asked, without lowering the paper.

"I have a question," I said, much louder than anticipated. I tried again, this time lowering my voice. "I have a question. About the book."

When he remained quiet, I continued. "I think you're right about Laura—oh man, what a beautiful day it is! Sorry, I thought that person was coming over here. We gotta stay discreet, right? So, I'm starting to think that maybe she's not the right character. I was wondering if maybe—"

Jake dropped the newspaper and pushed his chair back away from the table, the legs scraping loudly against the concrete floor.

Good. We were going to discuss this like real people and not spies. Although I really felt like I was starting to get the hang of it.

"Our cover's completely blown. I'll be out in the truck." I followed his gaze over to the counter where Damien was waving slyly at me.

I returned it and turned back in time to see Jake disappear through the front door.

Shit.

"Decided you were in the mood for some excitement, after all?" Damien carried a damp cloth in his hand, but he wasn't here to wipe down the table. He was here for the dirt.

"Um, well, I tried. Got shot down. Better luck next time, I guess." I kept sneaking furtive glances toward the parking lot, hoping to catch a glimpse of my surly detective.

Well, not mine, mine.

"He's kind of a pretty boy, isn't he?" Damien asked.

I nodded. "Yep. It wouldn't have worked out. Bootsy's the most high maintenance thing in my life. I don't have room for another. Would you mind boxing up my cinnamon roll and getting me a to-go cup? I'm just not feeling my muse this morning."

"Sure thing."

It was supposed to be part of the cover, but I realized that there was no scenario where Jake suddenly developed feelings for me. He'd said just as much before we came in.

Damien brought me my food items as I packed up the laptop, consoling me with promises of what he'd do to Jake's drink if he ever bothered showing up again. By the time I made it outside, the air had turned cooler and clouds darkened the sky. I walked around to the back parking lot.

"I think they saw us come in together," Jake said, by way of greeting, as I struggled to climb up into the truck with full hands

"Oh, hey. Hello. I'm doing great, thanks for asking, Jake."

He leaned across the seat and took both the coffee and the cinnamon roll from my hands before helping me up. "Hi, Hayden. This will come as a bit of a shock to you, but you stick out like a sore thumb."

I snapped the seat belt into the buckle. "I do not! I was inconspicuous."

He put the truck in reverse just as the first drops of rain began to fall on the windshield. "You were about as inconspicuous as a beer vendor at an AA meeting. And what the fuck was that cat food conversation?"

"You told me to be myself!" I bit out.

"Yeah," he agreed before merging into traffic. "That was a mistake."

"You coming back to life was a mistake," I muttered to the passenger side window.

He prodded. "C'mon, Hayden. Surely you know that this operation failed miserably?"

Why couldn't he have been hideous? At least then the exterior would've matched the interior.

"Any good stalker worth their salt is gonna stake out the parking lot. So, probably. Maybe. Alright, fine. Yes. There's a very good chance that if someone was watching, they probably saw us together. It's mostly my fault."

"Mostly?" Jake asked, with a quirked brow.

"Yeah, I wasn't thinking this morning and I put on my oil spray."

He stopped at a red light and turned toward me. "You put on oil spray." His speech was slow and measured like I'd suddenly stopped speaking English. "What does that mean exactly?"

"Oh, I'm an empath, so if I don't use my spray every morning, I am drained by lunch. You know, it gets way too people-y out there."

Instead of agreeing, Jake signaled and pulled into a gas station. "Hayden, I didn't understand two words of what you just said. What the fuck is an empath and how does oil spray factor into this investigation?"

Seriously? What planet was he living on that he didn't know about oils and empaths?

"My spray repels negative energy, so it's a protective measure. It blocks any energy attacks and keeps me running on a full tank. It's vital when I'm in writing mode."

His eyebrows lifted. "So, let me get this straight; the spray kept the stalker away?"

"Not exactly," I admitted with a sigh. "I have my crystals too. I swear, I didn't even think about it being a problem. It's just a habit to keep them in my purse. I mean, it's not like I typically go out in search of negativity."

He shook his head. "So, the crystals and sprays keep you safe from the bad people?"

Finally.

"Yes," I nodded happily. "And, with the work that you do, you could really benefit from it. I'd start small. Maybe keep some black tourmaline in your truck and house. Oh, amethyst would be a good one for you; they work as both a protector and a stress reliever. It'd definitely make things more bearable for you at work. Hematite's another—"

"Sweetheart, there's not enough oils and crystals in the world to make some people bearable. Do you catch what I'm saying?"

I opened my mouth to respond, but only managed a growl. The

back of my eyelids burned, and I knew that if I tried to talk, it'd just come out as a sob. That, in turn, would just freak Jake out completely.

I hated that about myself. Other people got mad and spoke their minds. Me? I cried and babbled incoherently.

Aaris once informed me that I got 'wet angry.' According to her, the majority of my emotions, including anger, were expressed through tears. Aaris? She was in a separate category known as 'dry angry.' She expressed her anger like anger—it both amazed and scared the hell out of me.

We drove in silence for about ten minutes before he asked, "What are you thinking?"

I turned away from watching the raindrops race each other across the window to answer. "I was just thinking that thirty stories wasn't high enough."

NINE

"DO YOU THINK YOU'RE SAFE?" Aaris asked as she looked across the complex from my balcony.

The calls and texts to me had begun shortly after she woke up to see an entire crew of men in my apartment. In hindsight, I probably should've given her a head's up, but I could barely wrap my own mind around it. She'd offered to come over and spend the afternoon with me, effectively saving me from Jake.

"I don't know." I shifted the laptop on my legs and pulled the blanket up higher. It had rained on and off most of the day, leaving a damp chill in the air. It wasn't really balcony weather anymore, but Jake's presence seemed to fill the entire apartment, forcing me to make the best of it outside. It also helped that I'd been high since we got back from the coffeehouse.

Aaris pulled her own blanket up under her chin, tucking her arms inside. "What if it's him?"

"What do you mean?"

She glanced back through the brand new sliding glass door before lowering her voice. "I just think it's coincidental that you've never had anything like this happen before, but he shows up and suddenly you've got a deranged stalker?"

It was suspicious timing, but hadn't Jake been just as thrown as I was when it happened?

"I don't understand the benefit of destroying my door, only to have to buy another. On top of that, the security system he put in can't be cheap." I looked up at the solid green light on the camera mounted in the corner.

She leaned across her chair. "Hayden, he got you to agree to bring him back into the story. It's what he came here for, right? He makes a demand, you refuse, and then your door has a brick thrown through it. I don't know; it just seems like he's the only one benefitting from this."

I closed my laptop, deciding to give up any pretense of writing. "He did offer to keep me safe in exchange for his life," I reminded her.

"Safe from who exactly? Him?" she hissed. "Look, I'm not trying to tell you what to do, but just promise me that you'll be careful. If you need to stay at my place, you can."

I shook my head. "I'll be fine. Don't you need to get to work?"

Aaris burrowed deeper into the blanket with a soft groan. "Yes, but I'm stalling for as long as possible. Have you thought about reaching out to the police?"

I laughed softly. "And tell them what exactly? That a fictional detective is holding me hostage until I rewrite my story? Promise me you'll come visit me in my newly padded room at the psych ward."

"I'm serious. I don't trust this guy. His motives are questionable and you gotta go where the money leads."

I leaned forward with a frown. "What does that mean exactly? Go where the money leads?"

She shrugged. "I don't know. It just seemed like something that a detective would say. I guess you need to look at who benefits the most from this 'attack.' Spoiler alert—it's him."

That was it.

The key to solving Jake's murder lay in my ability to determine who would benefit the most from his demise. It seemed simple enough, but a man like Jake had plenty of enemies.

Aaris patted my leg through the blanket. "Just think about what I've said. And you better call me if anything else happens. I don't want to drop dead of a heart attack, thinking someone killed you; or worse—that you'd been evicted."

My lips inched up into a slight smile. "Yes, that would be much worse."

She stood up and stretched. "It would be. I'd have to drive to visit you for girl's night and then I'd have to stay the night because you know I'd be too drunk to drive myself. At least if you were dead, I could just move your ashes into my apartment and then we'd always be together. Just a little pour of top-shelf liquor in your urn and it'd be like old times."

I moved my laptop to the small stone table beside my chair and wrapped her up in a hug. "I love you, you psychopath. I'll try to not get evicted while you're at work."

"Love you too. I'll text you tomorrow when I'm up." She gave me a worried look, prettily packaged in a close-mouthed smile.

"I work tomorrow, but I'll text you when I'm off."

She slid the door open and walked right past Jake and Bootsy as if they were invisible. I envied her dry angry skills before returning to my now cold chair.

I couldn't stay outside forever. Eventually, I was going to have to go inside. I'd been ignoring him since we'd gotten back to my apartment and, somewhere over the span of a few hours, it had become a game.

Neither one of us was willing to crack first though. Jake had slipped once but covered it by finishing his thought to Bootsy.

As if she gave a damn whether he ordered dinner or not.

I was feeling strong though. I had a book to write, so I could technically go weeks without needing to interact with the world around me. I'd done it before.

Aaris had once found me at my computer in food-stained clothing and unwashed hair, mumbling about the mob being after Jake.

I slipped another gummy from my pocket and popped it into my mouth. Maybe that had been the problem. I'd been trying to write sober. Any minute now, Laura was going to re-emerge from her hiding spot and start giving me the story.

I browsed my social media while I waited for inspiration and my high to kick in. I scrolled past the posts from people I knew in high school, bragging about the intelligent or funny thing their kid had done.

Big deal.

Bootsy did funny and intelligent things all the time. It didn't mean I needed to post about it though.

Several posts referred to some vague incident that no one but the poster would know anything about and I rolled my eyes as I scrolled past them. Almost every other post was related to book releases, and I felt the smallest twinge of envy.

It came so easy for them. A new release every month that soared to the top of the charts while I struggled to even get my words onto the computer.

Speaking of people who never seemed to have to try, there was a new post from the *King of Fuckersville* himself, my brother, Reid. If that wasn't an indication that it wasn't my night, then I didn't know what was.

Apparently, he was spending the long weekend in Chicago with his perfect girlfriend Emily, judging by the obnoxious ChiTown and Windy City hashtags. I exited the page and stared at the blank screen in frustration.

When was it my turn?

The door opened and Jake stepped out and I resisted the urge to look up at the stars and shake my fist. *Thanks, universe. A simple never would've done the job just fine.*

"I brought you some water."

And I was the winner of the quiet game. I took it from his hand, placing it next to the chair without a word. He may have forfeited, but I was still very committed to not speaking to him. Instead of taking the hint, he sat down in the other chair and stared at me.

"What?" I finally asked without looking up from my screen.

"It's cold out here. Wouldn't you rather be inside?"

"You were inside, so, no." I met his gaze. "Just admit that you came out here to smoke."

He smirked. "I don't smoke. That shit'll kill you."

"But, but," I spluttered. "I wrote you as a smoker."

"And I'm a good actor. I only inhaled when you specifically wrote it. Otherwise, fake it 'til you make it, right?"

I frowned. It wasn't right. Everything else I'd written had proven to be true; how could he not be a chain smoker? He'd picked up the habit after spending time with one of the veteran detectives. A detective who had a pack a day habit.

"What about Sergeant Strauss? He was your mentor until that street gang in *False Evidence* took him out. One wrong turn and he was gone forever. You were promoted to take his place and you smoke because it reminds you of him—"

His lips looked like they were caught in a tug of war between a smirk and a pout when he interrupted. "Well, he's still around and I see him from time to time. Oh, and he's not a smoker either. Are you okay, Hayden? You look like I just told you Santa's not real."

"I thought you had to be just like I wrote you," I responded weakly.

He kicked his feet up on the balcony railing, obviously confident that it wasn't going to give way, dragging him over the edge to his second death.

"Think of it like this; you watch movies, right?" I nodded and he continued. "Okay, so you see a movie where your favorite actor has an American accent, but you know he's British. It's just an act."

I thought about it. "But, that doesn't explain the sugar thing! You used two and a half packets exactly. And then the thing with my neighbor; you did exactly what I thought you would!"

He moved his hand down, urging me to lower my voice. "I'm sitting in the same zip code as you, there's really no need to yell."

I covered my mouth. I hadn't realized I wasn't speaking normally. Just like I was starting to lose track of how long we'd been having this conversation. It felt like years.

"To address your concerns, some of what you're seeing is my mannerisms. There's a difference. So, yes, you might see me do some things, but it doesn't mean you know me."

Well, that was a slap in the face. I gave life to this asshole, but you'd think he'd just done it himself. Ungrateful prick. If this was what parenting was like, then I had no plans to ever sign up.

I crossed my arms over my chest and gave a condescending smile. "Well, thank you so much for enlightening me, Detective. It's been a real pl—"

"Are you high, Hayden?" Jake leaned closer to me, studying my face intently.

Instead of boldly telling him to fuck off, I found the neighboring building interesting.

"Hayden," he warned before standing up.

"No." My voice cracked, suddenly becoming high-pitched.

Jake moved into my line of vision, guiding my eyes back toward his with his hand on my jaw. "Look at me." I did and he sighed. "Your eyes are bloodshot. Did Aaris bring you drugs?"

I refused to answer, instead watching him warily, like an animal caught in a trap.

His fingers moved down to my wrist and I jerked my hand back.

"Calm down. I'm not getting the cuffs. I just wanna check your pulse." He reached for me again and I reluctantly let him take it. "It's fast. You wanna tell me what you took? You don't smell like it so I know you weren't smoking."

He smelled me?

I briefly wondered if my scent had affected him on an

emotional level. Maybe he was fighting his own biological reactions and the urge to screw my brains out against the new door. Perhaps if I said nothing and just continued to blink at him, he'd act on those urges.

His eyes narrowed and he knelt down in front of me. "Hayden?"

Blink.

Blink.

This one was hitting me harder than the others had. I felt all floaty. It wasn't a bad feeling; just different.

I really should've eaten dinner.

"Why'd you come out here? Haven't you done enough today?" I was mad, but my words sounded sleepy.

Jake rocked back on his heels. "I brought you water, remember?"

"But, that's not why you came out." I realized I was shaking my head too much and worked to stop it.

"You're right," he admitted. "I came out because you don't have any holistic cat food. I checked."

A giggle burst from my lips. "Why, were you hungry? Did you need an all-natural snack?"

His lip curled up in disgust. "What? No, I just meant that I've looked all over your apartment and you don't have one thing with the word holistic in it. You're full of shit."

"Wow. Hey everyone, Detective Hopkins here can't figure out who wants me dead, but at least he knows what my cat's eating!"

Jake clapped a hand over my mouth. "Jesus, Hayden. Lower your voice. Why'd you lie to that guy?"

I stared pointedly at him until he lowered his hand. "That guy? You mean, Damien? Why do you care?"

"I don't." This time he looked anywhere but at me.

He so did.

"You do. Why?" It was just cat food, surely he wasn't going to shame me for choosing not to spend more on the cat than I did myself.

His eyes met mine and even with him kneeling in front of me, we were roughly the same height. The amber in his eyes appeared softer, muted by the dim light streaming out from the living room.

"You lied to Damien. Who's to say you're not lying to me?"

And there it was. His biggest fear was that I'd screw him over. It didn't speak highly of my character.

I took my glasses off and put them on the table before massaging my eyelids. "Look, Jake. I didn't buy the food, okay? It was crazy expensive. I didn't want to have to find a new coffee shop, so I told a little white lie."

He pursed his lips and nodded. "Lying was easier than just telling him that?"

I sighed. "He's like really into giving his cats the best of everything and thinks that anyone who doesn't isn't fit to own one. It was either lie or endure shaming every time I needed to get out of the house to write. And I really like that coffee shop the best."

Jake stood up to stretch his legs before moving back into his chair. "Do you really think his cats are more connected to him spiritually?"

I snorted and shook my head. "I have no idea. Maybe?"

"Well, I guess you'll never know," he said with a grin.

"It's definitely my loss." Another giggle slipped out and I paused to consider whether it was from him or the gummy.

Probably the gummy.

"How's uh, how's it going with Laura?" he asked, suddenly looking intent again.

I groaned and leaned back until my head rested against the composite siding of the building. "Terrible. You were right. It's all shit."

"I never said it was shit," he finally admitted, startling me out of my oblivion. "I did think she was coming across much older than you intended though. Maybe you just tweak—"

"No." I sat up again. "No. I need someone younger. You said you had a sister."

"You want to use Jessa?"

His tone implied that it was a crazy idea, but the weed had

dissolved the filter between my brain and my mouth. "But, she's younger, right? And she has the same last name! I wouldn't have to change the title. And she's younger!"

He nodded with a smirk. "Yeah, you said that one already. What if you just tweaked Laura's character? Then you don't have to scrap what you've already written."

"Really? You think I'm worried about losing all of eight-hundred words? It's shit. I know it and you know it. But, you know Jessa and you could help me get into her head. How cool would it be if your sister is the one who solves your case and brings you back? And then you guys could team up and Rachel would see that I found you a female counterpart and she would change her mind and I would get—"

He held up a hand. "Whoa, slow down. I think you're getting a little ahead of yourself."

I sighed again. "It's a bad plan, I know. I just worry that you were it—like what if I can't write another character?"

We both slipped into silence, allowing the low din of the traffic below us fill the void.

"You'd like Jessa. She's twenty-six. Terminally single. Oh, and she always speaks her mind. She'd definitely give the detectives hell."

I turned to him in surprise. "You're going to let me use her? Did we just agree on something?"

He nodded. "I think we did. Now, let's get you back inside. The weed may have dulled your senses, but it's fucking freezing out here."

"I'm not high, Jake," I argued as I unfurled myself from the chair. My head swam with dizziness, just like the time I rode the teacups at the carnival, but I refused to let him know that.

I made it three steps before the ground began to shift unevenly beneath my feet. I stumbled and managed to right myself just before falling again.

Jake caught me by the waist and guided me through the door. "Alright, Cheech. Let's go."

"But," I protested. "But, my parents don't know." I waved at Bootsy as she peered out at me from under the kitchen table.

Sweet little thing. I just loved her to pieces.

"Don't worry," Jake said with a laugh. "It'll be our little secret." He kept his arm around my waist as he led me to my bed.

We'd had our first agreement and he was going to keep my secret. We may not have been friends, but at least we were no longer enemies.

TEN

"SHIT," I exclaimed, stubbing my toe on the edge of my dresser. "Shit, shit, shit."

I'd overslept and was now either going to work with bedhead or sans caffeine. As I passed the bathroom mirror, I decided it was going to have to be the morning coffee. And I worked the long shift today.

I bent over and hit my head with several shots of dry shampoo, praying it was enough to take me from homeless drug addict to radiant rainforest goddess, like the commercial had implied.

I stood up to see several white patches of dry shampoo, but mostly it looked just as it had before. I ran my fingers through it hurriedly, hoping to distribute the powdered residue across my scalp.

"Shit," I cursed again. Messy bun it was. I bent down again, gathering my thick hair into an elastic holder. Once I was satisfied that it would pass for work, I headed for my closet.

"Hayden?" There was a hesitant knock at the bedroom door.

"Um, not right now, Jake," I panted as I worked to get the tight denim of my skinny jeans up over my hips.

The door burst open and my hands moved up and down simultaneously, trying and failing to cover all my exposed parts.

His own hand went up over his eyes. "Sorry. God, am I sorry. I thought you were getting high again. Next time, tell me you're changing."

I dropped my hands to hips. "Excuse me? How about next time don't barge into someone's bedroom! Now, if you'll excuse me, I'm running late." I finished shimmying into my jeans and walked into my closet for a shirt.

He followed me in, somehow keeping his eyes averted. "Late for what?" he asked the ceiling.

"Jake, I'm down here."

He looked at my head before his gaze roved downward. "You're late for—is that a cat tattooed on your hip?"

I snagged a t-shirt off the hanger. Today's choice was three cats in space suits—*catstronauts*. I glanced down at my hip as I slipped it on. "Yeah, so?"

Jake let out a low chuckle. "You have a cat tattooed on your body. As if the shirts weren't enough."

I shrugged. "I don't see what the big deal is. You have cattoos."

He stayed on my heels as I moved around the bedroom, picking up various clothing and pillows in an attempt to find my shoes.

"You called them *cattoos*."

I looked up at him. "No, I didn't. I said tattoos, obviously."

He shook his head with a smirk. "No, you didn't. That's what you call it, isn't it? Your cattoo?"

"Jake, I'm really in a hurry." My cheeks flamed, and I bent down to see that my shoes were under the bed. Right where I'd left them. I quickly slipped them on and ran into the kitchen to dump some dry food into Bootsy's dish.

She popped out of her hiding spot only to scowl when she realized I wasn't giving her the good stuff.

"I'm sorry, baby. Mommy's running so late."

She dismissed me with a flick of her tail and returned to her hiding spot under the couch.

Jake caught my arm before I made it to the front door. "Last time, why are you running out of here?"

"I have to go to work."

Lines appeared on his forehead. "You work from home, don't you?"

My arm heated under his grip and I swallowed thickly, unsure of what to tell him. "Um, well, I also work at a salon too."

His eyebrows went up, and he nodded slightly. "It sounds like killing me off has worked out really well for you. Let me just grab my jacket."

"Oh, no," I protested. "That's really not necessary. You'll be bored out of your head."

"I'm going with you. It's not safe for you to be out on your own right now," he called from the bedroom.

Somehow, in spite of the morning traffic, Jake got me to the salon with two minutes to spare. I tried to get a rundown of our script, but he just waved me inside and told me he'd handle it.

I slipped in the back door and made it up to the front without being seen. The next half hour was spent arranging the designer shampoos and conditioners and dusting along the shelves.

The owner, Shelley, had every wall painted dark red and adorned with mirrors. The ceiling was black, casting the entire salon in darkness, save for the iron sconces along the walls.

I'd decided not long after starting, that she'd been aiming for red room and landed somewhere in the vicinity of fourteenth-century dungeon. Which was definitely what you wanted when you were coloring hair.

Not only that, but the salon stayed open until two in the morning. If it was a good day, then the drunk college girls stayed at the bars. If it was a typical day, then they were staggering in with their girlfriends, demanding some extravagant service. Because nothing said good idea quite like a fifth of Jack and a pixie cut. These same girls would also throw the unholiest of fits if I couldn't get them exactly what they demanded.

Unfortunately, it was the only business that paid what I needed and worked with my writing schedule. So, I learned to fake a smile and give them what they wanted.

"Morning, Hayden," Kamdyn called out as she unlocked her room.

She normally hung out at the front until her first client arrived. I frowned and followed her into her booth. "Hey, are you okay?"

She put her purse on the counter and turned around to face me. Her eyes were rimmed in red and it was obvious she'd been up crying most of the night.

"You were right. He dumped me." Her voice squeaked as she fought off another round of tears. "By text."

Kamdyn had been dating a guy for the last few months that was a perpetual man-child. She put all the effort into the relationship while he reaped the benefits. If she ever pushed for him to take the initiative, he'd guilt her with how many hours he'd put in at work or how much he had to get done around his place.

He'd shown up at the salon once, not to surprise Kamdyn, but to borrow some cash from her until he got paid. I'd gotten such a bad vibe from him that I'd encouraged her to drop him.

Like most rational people, she hadn't taken my bad feeling as fact and continued dating him.

She pulled up the text and handed her phone off to me.

I'm sorry. I just can't do this. Just leave my stuff on your porch.

"Just leave my stuff on your porch?" I repeated loudly. "Oh, please tell me you didn't."

She winced and nodded. "I thought it'd be easier for him to go with me at work—"

"No, Kamdyn. You burn his shit or toss it off an overpass, but you don't just lie down and hand it over."

I couldn't fathom how she'd ended up in her current situation.

She was tall and carried herself like an Amazonian princess, with long blonde hair and icy blue eyes. She had a great sense of humor and curves for days. I knew for a fact that, despite what most women thought, men (including my prick of a brother) loved a girl with meat on her bones.

She was the perfect package yet, like Aaris, she was constantly attracting losers.

Her lip started quivering again. "I—I just thought—"

I pulled her into a rough hug, feeling very much like the tiny hobbit that tall girls carried around in their pockets until something went wrong.

"You are safe. You are balanced. You are grounded. No, look at me." She blinked through the tears. "You are worthy of all the good in the world. Listen, I gotta get back up front and unlock, but just remember that, okay?"

She nodded and dabbed at her eyes. "Thanks, Hayden. You always know just what to say."

I left her with a box of tissues and jogged back up toward the counter, running smack dab into a warm body. "Oof," I exhaled.

Large arms came up and pinned my biceps. "Hey, slow down, darling."

I scrambled back at the sound of the voice. It was one of our regulars—*regular sleazeball*. Both he and his wife came in once a month, but never together. She had a look of displeasure permanently engraved onto her face but was generally polite and quiet. He, on the other hand, was a schmoozer. He'd flatter the girls with compliments before trying to grope their asses.

You know, a real gentleman.

I usually made a point of taking my lunch break when he came in so that I never had to interact with him. The stories I'd heard were bad enough. Worse, he was in politics. Shelley and her pinched face were against anything that might result in bad press for the salon. So, she ignored the complaints and catered to the bastard every time he came in.

I deftly sidestepped his arms and backed up toward the front doors. "I'm so sorry, Rob. I was in a hurry to get the doors unlocked and didn't see you." My words sank in and I slowly asked, "How did you get in?"

He gave me his megawatt smile and laughed. "I came in through the back door. I was told you girls wouldn't mind."

Gross.

Somehow, I kept the smile plastered to my face as I walked backward. He spotted Kamdyn and marched into her booth for a forced hug while I fled for the safety of the front doors.

Jake was waiting near one of the cement columns with two cups of coffee. He frowned when he saw my face. "What happened?"

I laughed nervously. "What do you mean? Nothing happened. I was just unlocking the doors. See, all unlocked. Everything's fine."

He quirked a brow but handed me a paper cup. "Half and half with a splash of coffee."

I took it and pointed at his. "Coffee. Black. With two and a half raw sugars."

The corner of his mouth turned up as he sat down on the grey microfiber couch. "Maybe," he hedged.

THE MORNING PASSED IN A BLUR, with Jake blending in seamlessly with the clients. He sat with a magazine and sipped his coffee, watching the traffic come and go.

I buzzed all available stylists when a walk-in showed up just after noon, demanding a color and cut. Kamdyn popped up behind the desk seconds later.

"Spill it. What's her energy like?"

I clutched my chest to calm my racing heart. "Well, mine is a little startled. Thank you for asking. Hers is—uh, she's okay. A little frantic."

"Mmm...put her with Tori. You know she loves the drastic ones."

I began entering her information into our system before assigning her to Tori. She loved college girls and their daddies' credit cards.

"What's going on?" Jake approached the desk.

Kamdyn's face lit up, and she thrust a hand toward him. "Hi, I'm Kamdyn. I don't believe we've met."

He took her hand. "Jake."

"Are you here for an appointment?" she fished. It appeared that after three hours, she had fully grieved the loss of her relationship.

"I came by to see Hayden, but I could use a trim. What do you think?" He lowered his head and Kamdyn's hands went right for his hair.

It left me with a sudden urge to stake my claim.

Oh, I made that. It's mine.

Please don't touch it. It's very expensive.

I shook my head to clear my thoughts and turned back to the computer, craning my head ever so slightly to give them the side eye.

"You've got great hair, does anyone ever tell you that?"

Only every woman he meets.

"Only every woman I've ever met," he answered with a smirk.

"I bet," Kamdyn murmured as she continued to run her fingers through it. "So, are you Hayden's brother... or cousin?"

Translation: Can I hook up with you to get over my broken heart?

"What would you say we are, Hayden?"

I gave up any pretense of typing and turned my chair toward them. "Um..." *Bastard.* He'd assured me that he had a cover. "Don't you want to tell her?"

The pouty smirk was back. "Nah, I thought you would."

When I grinned, his smirk faded slightly. "I absolutely would. I just didn't know if it was okay to admit it to a stranger. I'm his AA sponsor."

Kamdyn brought her hands back down to her sides slowly. Jake looked both amused and frustrated.

"It's true," I continued, like either one of them cared. "It's my lot in life to make sure this big lug doesn't hit the bottle again. And Jake, we talked about this; no dating your first year sober."

He mouthed something that looked suspiciously like, *who said anything about dating?* When that failed to hit the mark, his eyebrows lowered and he bit out, "Why don't you tell Kamdyn how you came to be my sponsor."

"Yeah," she added with narrowed eyes. "Don't you have to be in AA yourself to become a sponsor?"

I nodded wisely. "Yes. I got into the liquor cabinet when I was sixteen and just." I pantomimed drinking. "Hit the sauce. My parents found out and sent me to AA."

Jake scratched at his jaw, clearly fighting to keep a straight face, while Kamdyn stood with her head cocked to the side.

"You're telling me that your parents put you in *Alcoholics Anonymous* after you drank one time at sixteen?" she asked.

"Yes. They saw a problem and corrected it. Who knows where I would've ended up had they not intervened." I was floundering and, judging by Jake's closed eyes and shaking head, he knew it.

"It's true," he admitted, much to my surprise. "I'm Jake and I'm an alcoholic. I owe a debt of gratitude to Hayden. The speeches she made during AA were so inspiring—the time she relapsed and woke up naked on a seesaw at a playground or when—"

"We don't need to bore her with all that, Jake," I cut in. "Let's leave some of it anonymous."

Kamdyn frowned. "I don't understand how you became a sponsor though. Is that something you just volunteer for?"

I shook my head. "No, you've got to start at the bottom and work up to sponsorship. There are twelve levels total—"

Jake grinned again. "Why don't you tell her the levels?"

"That's a great idea," I forced through clenched teeth. "Um, well, you have the sweeper level. And then the coffee level. Which is, of course, followed by the donut level."

Tori walked up, effectively saving me from having to BS my way through any more levels.

"What do we have?" she asked while surveying the front.

"Cut and color. Head's up, she's a little off."

She leaned in. "What do you think?"

I watched the girl flip through a magazine, legs bouncing in anticipation. Her jet black hair hung almost to the seat.

"I think she's going to want to go blonde; either that, or she's going to want an off-the-wall color, which will still involve a lot of bleach."

Tori nodded. "Thanks, babe. You're the best."

"What was that?" Jake asked.

"Oh," Kamdyn replied. "Hayden's like a psychic when it comes to people. She picks up on their energy."

One brow lifted. "Really? That seems like a fun trick. What's my energy like?"

I shook my head and turned back to the computer, marking Tori as 'unavailable' for the next three hours. "I'm not-"

"Oh, come on! Read his energy. It'll be fun!"

I knew Jake's energy; I'd picked up on it the moment I let him into my apartment.

He rested his forearms on the counter with a smirk. "C'mon, tell me."

I frowned at the fact that my heart beat a little faster when he leaned in closer and whispered, "You scared?"

Kamdyn fanned herself from behind Jake and mouthed, *he's so hot.*

I froze with my fingers still hovering over the keyboard. "You're—"

What was I going to say?

You make me feel things I haven't felt in a long time?

I don't know whether I want to murder or make out with you?

I settled for, "You're... overwhelming."

His lips pursed, and he nodded to himself. "Overwhelming..."

I looked back down at my keyboard as my cheeks burned with

embarrassment. I hadn't planned on admitting it. At least not out loud.

Without another word, he pushed off the counter and went back to his chair by the door. Kamdyn looked at me in confusion before hissing, "Overwhelming? What does that even mean?"

I shrugged. "He's just—"

"A Greek god? The finest man to ever grace the doors of this salon? My next mistake?" She leaned on the granite counter, eyes glued to the back of Jake's head.

"Kam, you don't want a guy like that. It would actually be worse than being dumped by text. Just..." I paused. "Just know your worth... and then add tax."

She turned away from her Greek god and squinted at me. "I don't know what's going on between the two of you, but I'm going to find out."

"Oh, good," I said, rolling my eyes. "Will you let me know when you do?"

"C'mon, Jake," she called. "Let's get you that haircut." She led him into her booth before pointing her index and middle finger at her eyes and then back at me.

"Thanks for all of your great advice, Hayden," I muttered under my breath. "I'm just going to disregard every bit of it."

I wanted to hiss at her, like Bootsy did when I took the tablet away from her while she was watching bird videos.

"How was your break?"

I jumped and spun around to face my boss. "Shelley, hi! I —well, I—"

"Listen, I was on a cruise and we were in Grand Turk- you know, Turks and Caicos? Well, it didn't even feel like fall. So sunny and warm. And humid. God, my hair looked like a frizzy nightmare for the majority of the trip."

She continued gesturing with her hands, describing her trip and all of the ways she'd been disappointed. Any time she traveled, she shut the salon down, so that her stylists could travel too. She seemed to live in a world where everyone had a disposable income and wasn't depending on their next paycheck to make rent.

I nodded and smiled as she rambled on about pristine beaches and drinks with umbrellas in them, but I'd completely zoned out of the conversation. I blocked the sound of Shelley's voice, straining to hear what was being said in booth number seven.

Kamdyn wasn't thinking clearly; obviously. She'd just been dumped. Maybe she felt she needed to flirt with a man to feel better about herself.

I gnawed at my lip, ridding it of the lip gloss I'd painstakingly applied in the bathroom an hour ago. My stomach was in knots and Shelley had yet to pause to take a breath.

There was a soft thump and then a giggle and I was convinced that if I'd had anything other than coffee in me, it'd be making a reappearance right about now.

What if they were screwing each other's brains out under one of the hair dryers? I could picture it, the two of them just going at it like majestic giraffes, with no regard to the feelings of the fun-sized receptionist at the front.

"Hayden?" Shelley waved a hand in front of my face. "Did you just hiss at me?"

Damn it.

I shook my head. "No, I coughed. My throat was dry." I tried to recreate it but only succeeded in sounding like I had emphysema.

"Do you need a lozenge?" Shelley offered. "They're good for lubricating your throat."

"You need throat lubricant, Hayden?"

I spun around, expecting messy hair and a guilty smile, but Jake looked the same. His hair was shorter on the sides, but his face had no traces of the cotton candy pink lipstick Kamdyn was sporting. I breathed a soft sigh of relief that it had just been a haircut.

"I'm good, thank you," I replied, jutting my chin up.

My boss extended a hand across the counter. "Hello, I'm Shelley. And you are?"

"My parole officer," I interjected as Jake reached for her hand.

Shelley's phone buzzed, and she stared at it distractedly. "So nice to meet you," she replied, without once looking up. "I'll just be in my office, Hayden."

Jake moved around the counter until he was facing me. "Miss me?"

"Not really. I see that Kamdyn got you taken care of."

He smirked. "Oh, she sure did."

He didn't elaborate, in an attempt to bait me into asking. Instead, I smiled primly and focused on the computer screen, clicking on various appointments at random.

Oh, she sure did.

What did that even mean?

I kept my chin high when Kamdyn walked up to get her next client, even as I searched her face for clues. She looked the same; lipstick still in place, no beard burn or strange white stuff dangling from her ear... the evidence reaffirmed that nothing happened.

Kamdyn sent her client down to her booth before making her way over to us. I relaxed my shoulders when neither of them fell into a passionate embrace, cursing my overactive imagination.

She handed him a piece of paper that looked suspiciously like a page from her planner. "Hey, you left this behind," she teased. My heart did a swan dive out of my chest onto the stained concrete floor beneath my chair.

Jake didn't return her smile. In fact, he suddenly looked uncomfortable. He took the paper from her hand and shoved it into the pocket of his jeans. "Thanks."

"Call me later, okay?"

He nodded but kept his eyes on me.

A flush crept across my cheeks and I forced out a hollow laugh. "Well, that didn't take long."

I grabbed my bottled water and took a swig, feeling off-kilter.

"Are you jealous?" He leaned in with a slow smile.

I released my clenched jaw with a direct, "No, I expected it from you."

He pursed his lips. "You're not mad?"

I took another drink in an effort to stall before admitting, "I just met you two days ago. Not only that, but you pulled a gun on me. So, no, I'm not mad. I'm disappointed because Kamdyn is someone I work with and she's going through a rough patch—"

Jake held both hands in front of him. "Whoa. Nothing's happened, okay?"

"It's just... what happens when you go back? She's not some random girl you met in a bar. She's going to have a lot of questions that I can't answer without ending up in the mental ward," I softly explained, tracing the patterns in the granite with my finger.

I didn't ask what was going to happen to me when he left because I was afraid I wouldn't like the answer.

ELEVEN

Jessa Hopkins was not having a good day. Her flatiron had kicked the bucket that morning, leaving her with hair that was only half straight. The other half was a Medusa-level mass of unruly waves.

It was a good metaphor for her life, really. Just when one aspect seemed under control, another exploded in a fiery fashion.

She'd arrived at her day job ten minutes late and officially out of good excuses. Instead of another reprieve, she'd been given a small cardboard box to hold two year's worth of trinkets and mementos before being sent down in an elevator with security.

And, as if her day couldn't get any worse, it appeared she'd been stood up. Again. She tapped a manicured nail against her wineglass, wondering how many of her vices she was going to have to give up now that she was unemployed.

Booze or beauty?

Had she not been sitting alone at a table meant for two,

she might've found humor in the fact that, because of her side job, she only ever attracted married men.

That had been the point after all.

Still, she never imagined that her nights would be spent in seedy bars or up on fire escapes, trying to capture infidelity on film.

Wasn't PI work supposed to be more exciting?

No one ever came to her with a missing kid or spouse; hell, she would've even settled for a missing dog.

No.

Everybody wanted to catch their partner cheating. Sometimes, they wanted to use her as bait, while other times, it was strictly behind the lens work.

Her older brother, Jake, had warned her it would be like this. He'd even insisted she get a nice desk job somewhere; said she was too naïve to be running her own agency.

At the time, she'd chalked it up to a jealous cop, afraid his baby sis was going to steal his business.

"More wine while you wait?" the waiter asked, with the slightest hint of irritation. Jessa shook her head.

She didn't know why they bothered with pretenses; they both knew that her date wasn't coming. And without a date, his chances of a great tip dwindled with each passing minute.

So, he'd hovered; refilling her water glass and doing his damnedest to get her drunk. It wasn't going to work though; she had a case waiting. Some entrepreneurial type who spent time overseas had become convinced that his fiancée was sleeping around on him.

She was.

They always were.

From what she'd seen online, the fiancée had found one thing desirable—his wallet.

It was better this way. She'd make a quick buck, and he'd get out without alimony and litigation. A broken heart would heal. A broken bank account was another story altogether though.

She asked for the check and observed the other couples. Over the years, it had become something of a game. She could pick out the mistresses from the wives as if they had signs flashing above their heads.

As she slipped on her jacket and walked out, she gave a brief glance back before shaking her head. Sooner or later, she'd see every one of them in her apartment office.

She needed business cards. Something she could casually drop at tables when she was out being stood up for the third time in a week.

When Jessa reached her car, she studied her reflection, trying to see the girl she once was underneath layers of makeup.

She pulled up outside the high-rise, double checking the address in her GPS before looking up. All the way to the thirtieth floor up. Her client had been specific about which direction the balcony faced and how to best access it. He'd also been very adamant that she arrive before ten.

Hell, he'd given her so much that she wondered why he hadn't just handled it himself. She wasn't in a position to turn down the cash though.

Several swigs from the flask of whiskey in her jacket pocket and a few hundred curse words later, Jessa began scaling the rickety fire escape of the neighboring building, all while keeping the elusive thirtieth floor in her sights. Based on the architecture, she guessed the building to be a century-old, at least.

Fire escapes were the same on any building in the city. It was like climbing an old ladder that had been screwed into the brick facade. Each step could be her last.

She kept her footsteps light as she crept past a well-lit window. Inside, a couple of kids were spaced out in front of the television, both oblivious to her presence just a few feet away.

Jessa paused around the twentieth floor to catch her breath and collect her thoughts. She didn't know it yet, but what she was experiencing now was the calm before the storm.

She pulled the camera from her shoulder bag, aiming it at the opposite building and adjusting the focus as needed. Best-case scenario, the fiancée decided to screw the guy on the balcony. Worst case, they had the blinds closed, forcing her back down the fire escape and to her back-up plan.

She'd delivered food and flowers before to gain access to a building, but the photos were always better when the target was unaware. Showing up at the door left room for excuses and excuses meant she didn't get paid.

A flash of black passed in front of her lens and she trailed it through the viewfinder. It looked like a piece of fencing. She corrected the focus as something larger swooped into view. Either she was looking at a very large bird or—*oh, Jesus. It was a person.*

A strangled sob escaped her throat, and she mashed the shutter release repeatedly, capturing every second of the person's descent. It was a man; of that much she was certain.

He hit the ground, and she winced before falling back against the rough bricks with a soft cry. She'd just witnessed a man die. Not only that, but she'd captured it on her camera.

What had possessed her to do that?

She'd never be able to pinpoint what made her look up; maybe just a crazy hunch, but there was someone standing on a balcony with a piece of missing railing.

She fumbled in her bag for the telescopic lens while keeping the individual in her sights. A quick count up from the bottom confirmed that she was looking at the balcony on the thirtieth floor.

Jessa quickly attached the lens and discovered that there were two people on the balcony. Two women. And neither seemed particularly disturbed by the fact that someone had just fallen to his death.

She moved up the next flight of stairs, snapping photos until they disappeared back inside.

Call the cops.

She dialed the number with shaking hands and gave them the details. Later, she'd realize that she never mentioned the photographs to the emergency operator or specifically what she'd witnessed.

It wasn't as if she could know, but that decision saved her life.

"WHAT DO YOU THINK?" I asked hesitantly.

It wasn't much of a story yet, but I'd spent the last week taking notes from Jake on everything there was to know about Jessa Hopkins. And I found that, unlike Laura, Jessa had a lot to say.

Aaris's eyes rapidly moved left to right as she scanned the screen. "Hayden, this is good. This is damn good. So, who did it?"

I frowned. "What do you mean?"

She pointed at the computer. "The push heard round the city. Who shoved him off? And who were the two women?"

I shrugged. "I don't know, Aaris. I just got into the story. I'm still trying to figure things out myself."

She took a drink of her grapefruit and vodka—yet another bottle she'd managed to smuggle home from the bar. This time in her bra. I didn't get into the logistics. I wasn't sure I wanted to know.

"Hayden, listen to me," she hiccuped. "I need to know who killed Detective Douche and I also need to know who the fuck that is." She pointed at a large figure on the other side of the balcony door.

I let out a cry of surprise before scrambling away from my desk and into the kitchen for the rolling pin.

"Jake!" Aaris called out. "Jake come in here... someone's at the door, Jake!"

"Aaris," I hissed as I crouched down near the cabinets. "Jake isn't here!"

That was right. The detective who'd sworn to keep me safe had abandoned me in favor of dinner with Kamdyn. Which was fine because I was completely capable of taking care of myself.

Like now.

Aaris had begun spinning circles in my desk chair, unbothered by the fact that there was someone actively trying to get into the apartment.

"I've called the police," I announced to the door.

"Ooh," Aaris exclaimed. "Tell them to send the hot ones!"

I sighed and shook my head.

"Hayden," a male voice said. "It's me, Max."

"Hayden! It's Max!" Aaris collapsed in a fit of giggles against the desk.

"Yep, heard that. Thank you very much, Aaris." I dropped the rolling pin onto the counter with a thud.

Jake had introduced me to Max a few days ago. Apparently, he'd served in the Army and had been traveling around the world ever since. Jake trusted him with his life. It was enough for me. The rest was just details.

I lifted the security bar and slid the door open.

"He didn't tell you I was here, did he?" he asked with an easy smile.

I shook my head and rolled my eyes dramatically. "Not one word."

Why would he have told me that Max was on bodyguard duty when he was preoccupied with thoughts of getting his dick wet?

"You good?" Max asked with a furrowed brow. "You just growled."

I paste a smile onto my face. "Growl? Me? That's ridiculous. I was clearing my throat."

"Are you real?" Aaris had abandoned her post at my desk and was walking in a slow, unsteady circle around Max.

"Aaris, you can't ask people if they're real." I turned to Max. "You are real though, aren't you?"

He glanced around the apartment, looking for answers. When his eyes landed on the vodka bottle, his eyebrows moved up. "Ah, how much have you ladies had?"

Aaris chose that moment to trip over her own foot. She fell into Max, her hands pawing at his chest in an attempt to break her fall. His hands clutched her waist, pulling her body up and into his. I was mesmerized. It was perfectly synchronized, like one of those elaborate dips you'd see on a televised dance competition.

Max was built like Jake and had the hardened look of someone who had killed before, but there seemed to be a softness underneath the rough exterior. Unlike Jake, he also seemed capable of letting his guard down, even if it was brief.

I guessed him to be in his mid-thirties, with light brown hair that was slightly thicker than Jake's and a full beard that would make a lumberjack jealous.

The day I met him, he'd immediately taken to Bootsy and had even produced a treat from his pocket for her.

What kind of man carried treats in his pocket?

A great one, in my opinion. In fact, Max was just the type of guy I needed in my life. He was kind, thoughtful, and sexy as hell. He also hadn't handcuffed me to anything, which was a definite plus.

Unless of course...

"So, how long have you been sitting out in the cold?" I asked, instinctively wrapping my arms around myself.

He glanced at the digital clock on the stove. "Almost three hours —so, not too long."

Aaris had begun petting the front of Max's shirt vigorously, like an animal in need of calming. Instead of moving away from her, he appeared to welcome the contact.

And I kissed my chances of seducing him goodbye.

He reminded me of the feral cats that used to come up on the patio at my parent's house when I still lived at home. At first glance, they were made up of nothing more than aggression and wariness. I knew that if I turned my back on them, I ran the risk of losing whatever food I had on me or ending up with claws embedded in my skin.

As they got more comfortable though, I'd see something that had been previously overlooked. Trust. And once they trusted me, the guard came down, revealing a need to be touched and fussed over.

"How's the book coming, Hayden?"

I reclaimed my desk chair and pulled the manuscript up with a nod. "I think it's finally coming together. It just took several rewrites and then scrapping the entire thing in favor of a new main character."

Max walked Aaris over to the couch. "Why don't you sit right here?"

She flashed him a blinding grin and patted her thighs through her jeans. "Why don't you sit right here?"

His eyes went wide, and he looked to me for help. He was probably married... or engaged. There had to be something wrong with him; for one thing, he was about ten to fifteen years younger than the men she normally found attractive.

I just shrugged and turned back to my desk with a muttered, "Not my circus... not my monkeys."

I resisted the urge to pull up *Goodbooks* and instead clicked the mail icon. I hadn't checked in three days and suddenly had this irrational fear that Rachel had written to say that she'd confused me with another Hayden Michaels and I'd missed it.

She'd probably admit that she felt like such a fool when she made the connection. Maybe I'd make her wait a few days for a response, just to make a point.

Or was it better to be gracious and accept right away?

I had to do something. My mind kept drifting back to thoughts of Jake and Kamdyn. I wondered if they had anything in common or if dinner had been a mere formality before jumping into bed together.

The thought of their sweaty bodies coming together made me feel sick because who wanted to see two Vikings bumping uglies?

It had nothing at all to do with jealousy.

There was nothing to be jealous over. Jake wasn't my boyfriend. He was just some fictional character who showed up and held me hostage before offering to protect me.

Yep. Nothing weird there.

A cursory glance of my inbox proved that, once again, I'd let my imagination take over. There were no emails, begging for a second chance.

There was one from my mother though. And I was going to absolutely avoid reading that one for as long as possible.

Wait a second...

I found an unfamiliar name nestled in between a credit card offer and a coupon from the *Bath & More* store.

Maybe it was another agent...

Ordered One in the Chamber for a light weekend read.

Little did I know where it would lead.

You have one final shot to bring Jake back from death.

Don't heed this warning and you'll take your last breath.

The great jewel must return from whence it came before the next full moon.

If you refuse, you'll be dead soon.

What happened to your door was just the start.

Believe me when I say that taking you down is an art.

Maybe not...

I choked back a nervous laugh and reread it. I wasn't sure I would've chosen to rhyme the entire thing if I wanted to be taken seriously, but the threat was unmistakable. The sender knew about the door.

"Max?"

He must've heard the fear in my voice because he was over to my chair within seconds. "What happened?"

I pointed at the screen. "I don't know if it's real or a joke..." My voice trailed off weakly. I was suddenly without words. I'd almost convinced myself that the brick through the glass had been random; completely unrelated to me or my books. This remedied all uncertainty.

Aaris lay with her head resting against the back of the couch, breathing softly. I wasn't sure if she was asleep, awake, or some weird area in between. Regardless, she didn't join us.

"Do you think we should call Jake?" I tried to inject as much strength as I could into my voice, but it still came out sounding small.

Max bit the corner of his lower lip and leaned in to study the email. "I don't think so," he answered distractedly. "He's in an interrogation at the moment. So, let's try to get a trace on the IP address."

I narrowed my eyes. "Interrogation? Is that what he told you? He's on a date, Max! A date! He knew you wouldn't babysit me if he told you what he was really doing. Son-of-a-prick!" I slapped my hand against the side of my desk.

"Marco!" Aaris bolted up on the couch with wide eyes.

Max clicked the mouse, opening several smaller screens. He never once broke eye contact with the information in front of him as he calmly replied, "Polo."

I sighed. I was going to need an entire pot of coffee.

"Jessa?" He whispered, "Why are you calling?"

Because she'd just watched a man die?

Because she couldn't get in touch with her brother?

She didn't know why her lover had become her last resort as she sat shaking in bed. She couldn't sleep, no matter how hard she tried. Every time she forced her eyes closed, she saw his body falling and heard the sound of him hitting the pavement.

Jessa had been up too high to hear it as it happened, yet

her mind had helpfully supplied a soundtrack, forcing her to relive it over and over again.

"I," she tried. She couldn't tell him without exposing what she did for a living and where she'd been.

"Are you imagining me there with you?"

She exhaled slowly, knowing by his tone that he'd left his wife sleeping and slipped into another room. His voice would grow bolder and he'd talk about the things they would do when they were together again.

"Chad," she tried again. She had to tell someone what she'd seen; someone who could just hold her until the shock wore off.

Her phone buzzed against her ear and she pulled it back to see a text from a blocked number.

Don't tell anyone what you saw tonight. It's not safe. Meet me at 5 AM... same spot.

Fear wrapped around her chest like a vice, squeezing her lungs until each breath became an effort.

Chad softly called out her name several times, but she remained silent, the words taunting her from the back-lit screen. It was why she'd called Jake in the first place—he dealt with death every day. He would've known what she was going through.

He also would've known how the hell to deal with this, she thought wryly.

"Chad, I—I have to go."

He let out a soft curse. "Is this because of tonight? I would've come, baby. She was just busting my balls about not spending enough time with the kids. Let's get away for the weekend. Just you and me. I'll tell her that I have to work."

There it was.

The elusive target she'd been hunting for eight months, handed to her on a silver platter. And now that it was out there, she felt nothing.

Jessa had gone up that fire escape a disgruntled PI focused on getting the shots and getting paid. She'd done it so she could go home and mope about the fact that her boyfriend was always going to choose his family over her.

Now, she was a witness to a murder and possibly in danger. She hadn't been afraid in a long time; and she no longer wanted the man on the other end of the line.

It didn't matter how old she was, she still needed her brother to tell her that everything was going to be okay.

I CHECKED the clock and leaned back in my chair with a sigh. It was almost one and Jake still wasn't home—well, not home, but back to my apartment.

Max sat on the couch, watching a football game on mute, while Aaris lay with her head against his shoulder, sleeping off her drunkenness.

It didn't matter how many times I asked, he refused to tell me what his search turned up. I decided then that he wasn't as great as I'd previously thought. When he turned my laptop back over to me, I'd immediately pulled up the history, which had been cleared out, leaving me with zero answers into who wanted me dead.

He'd been texting someone on and off since then, but would just shake his head when I looked over at him. He caught me staring again and motioned to Aaris. "Is she always like this?"

I cocked my head to the side, trying to decipher his meaning. If he was referring to her being a magnet for emotionally, and sometimes completely, unavailable men, then yes.

"Do you mean the drinking?" I ventured.

He nodded, doing his best not to wake the drooling mass at his side.

"Um, just lately. Her job is... difficult. Plus, it's like a proven fact that the alcohol she steals from the bar is tainted. You know, like what they talk about happening at resorts?"

He pressed his lips together and nodded. "So, we're just going to gloss over the fact that you drank the same vodka that she did and you're fine?"

Shit.

He had a point.

"Well, that's because she has antibodies—"

"Are you always this full of shit when you don't know the answer to something?" he asked with a grin.

I returned his with one of my own. "No... maybe."

God, maybe I'd been wrong about him. He really was great even if he was keeping things from me.

The captivity was getting to me. I was experiencing that thing that hostages got—*Munchausen Syndrome by Proxy.* I was developing feelings for my captors. At least it wasn't because I had horrible character judgment.

We both froze as the knob on the front door began to turn. Max shifted Aaris toward the opposite end of the couch and moved silently toward the door. The way he kept a hand on his hip holster reminded me of Jake and I got angry all over again.

Who went on a date when they were supposed to be protecting someone? Kevin Costner never would've done that to Whitney Houston.

Max checked the peephole and smirked. "Well, well. It looks like somebody forgot to snag a key before he took off on a date."

I chewed at the corner of my lower lip and leaned forward in my chair. "Don't let him in."

Max shook his head with a smile and unlocked the door.

"You needed me?" he practically sang as he entered.

The glee I'd felt only moments ago was gone, replaced with the overwhelming urge to roll my eyes until they stuck that way. "Oh, no. We're fine, Jake. Thanks for showing up though."

He shook hands with Max before pinning me with his sleepy glare. "Hayden, so happy to see that you waited up for me."

I crossed my arms over my chest, tapping my index and middle fingers against my bicep. "I was working late," I bit out. "Where the hell have you been?"

Max clapped Jake's shoulder. "We'll talk more tomorrow. I'm going to get this one back to her apartment."

"Wait," I protested. "You don't have to leave. Jake can leave. You and Aaris can stay."

Jake followed him to the couch. "Do you need help? Maybe we should all stay with Aaris and leave the pixie from hell here."

"What the hell did you just call me? I'll have you know that I'm still alive, no thanks to you." I stepped forward until our toes were touching, putting me eye level with his impressive pectoral muscles.

Max ignored our standoff and retrieved Aaris from the couch and tossed her over his shoulder. "C'mon, let's get you home before the shit hits the fan."

She made a noise that sounded vaguely like consent.

"Do you know where you're going?" I paused to ask.

He turned back toward me. "I think I can manage. I hope you two enjoy the rest of your evening."

The door slammed shut and we resumed our staring contest.

"Do you feel better now?" I asked primly.

"Better?" Jake frowned.

Feeling emboldened, I moved closer, the toes of my ballet flats resting on top of his boots. "Yeah, better. Max said you were in the middle of an 'interrogation.' Did you 'interrogate' the orgasms right out of her?"

Jesus, I was going to have a rage aneurysm if I envisioned Kamdyn and Jake having sex one more time.

Instead of getting defensive, he smirked down at me. "I'm assuming 'interrogate' is innuendo for fucking?"

I shook my head. "Don't say it like that, but yes."

"I'm sorry I offended your delicate sensibilities, sweetheart. I meant to say that I assume you're using interrogate in place of 'having sex.' And in response to that, I would like to remind you that I was only gone for five hours." His hands moved down to his hips.

"And?" I matched his stance, trying to hide my complete confusion.

He pursed his lips, obviously pleased with what he was about to say. "And I find that it takes me most of the night and into the morning to get what I need to 'complete my investigation,' if you catch my drift. I follow every lead, relentlessly pursuing every hole I find. I don't stop until I've coaxed every last drop of information from them. You knew that already though, right?"

My breath faltered and I worked to remember how it went. *Was it exhale and then inhale? Or the other way around?* I wanted to clench my thighs together to alleviate the sudden ache but knew that he would notice and I refused to give him the satisfaction in knowing that he'd gotten under my skin.

"Yes, well, that all sounds disgusting," I finally managed.

"That's funny. You say you're disgusted, but your expression says you want me to demonstrate." He rocked back on his heels with a full smirk.

"Gross."

"Two words." Jake held up his index and middle fingers to emphasize. "Bedroom. Eyes."

I wrinkled my nose and turned to walk toward my bedroom. "Three words. Barf. Gag. Vomit."

"I'm glad to see you're finally putting that thesaurus to use. How many synonyms do you think there are for desire?"

I spun back around to face him. "Desire? Please. This expression is nothing but barely concealed rage. You just want me to have Munchausen Syndrome by Proxy, but I won't."

Jake scratched at his jaw with a frown. "Munchausen's?"

I sighed. "Don't tell me you don't know what it means. Aren't you supposed to know everything, Detective? You held me captive, hoping I'd develop feelings for you so that you could exploit me."

He pinched the bridge of his nose and closed his eyes. "Hayden, I think you're confusing Munchausen syndrome with Stockholm syndrome."

SHANNON MYERS

My face grew warm. Damn it. He was right. "Regardless," I tried to recover my composure. "I'm not interested. If I put my hands on you, believe me, it'll be because I'm strangling you."

He closed the gap between us and leaned down, his hands resting lightly against his thighs. "You can't even begin to fathom the things I'd do if I put my hands on you."

I backed up until my heels came into contact with my door. "Well, as much fun as this has been, I'm going to get some sleep."

"This conversation is far from over." He narrowed his eyes in victory as I shut and locked the door behind me before falling face down onto my mattress with a muffled groan.

Instead of feeling safer, I was keyed up and in need of a release. I forced myself up off the bed and into the bathroom to brush my teeth and wash my face.

I wasn't going to dwell on Jake's words. He'd just said it to get a rise out of me. I'd just focus on my nightly routine before sliding under the covers and into oblivion for a few hours.

I pulled the blankets up around me, working to ignore the way they clung to my damp skin. I was balanced.

I don't stop until I've coaxed every last drop...

I was centered.

It takes me most of the night...

I was... in need of an orgasm.

I kicked the covers off the end of the bed and worked to center myself. I heard Bootsy as she rearranged them into a nest for herself.

If I gave into my urges, then it was like he was winning. That strengthened my resolve until I realized that if I didn't get myself off, then I was still losing.

I was going to do it and I wasn't going to think of him or his dirty words the entire time.

With that resolved, I slid my left hand down the front of my pajama pants. My body thrummed in anticipation as I stroked lightly along the folds, working to think of a celebrity to help me 'get the job done.'

When that failed, I thought of Max.

I pushed myself to the edge as my fingers circled my clit before slowing it back down. My pajama pants migrated somewhere down around my shins, as my hand moved faster, feathering against raw nerve endings.

I imagined that it was Max's hand rapidly moving between our bodies and let a soft moan escape. My breath came in short bursts as I imagined the way the veins would stand out on his forearms as his hand moved across my skin.

I traced his forearms up to muscular biceps and a chest with a set of familiar tattoos.

No.

I was thinking of Max.

Max.

It was too late. My thighs clamped together, and I watched, horrified, as Jake pushed me over the edge with his smug smirk. My back arched up off the bed and I came, with a soft cry of surprise and some very confused feelings.

Someone sends me another death threat and I decide to masturbate in response.

That seemed like an appropriate solution... for a psychopath.

TWELVE

Jessa pulled the edges of her jacket closer to her body in a poor attempt to stay warm. When that failed, she began bouncing on the balls of her feet.

Her mystery guest was late, and she was slowly freezing to death on the fire escape. She wondered what it said about her intelligence that she'd shown up alone to meet a complete stranger for clues on a murder.

A quick check of her cell phone revealed more missed calls and messages from Chad, but still nothing from Jake. It should've worried her, but when he'd gone undercover to bust up a local sex trafficking ring, there'd been no contact for over a month.

She shoved the phone back into her pocket and retrieved the long lens camera from the backpack at her feet.

Yellow tape cordoned off the entire balcony and there had been people coming and going since she arrived. Her view was limited to the balcony, and she briefly considered abandoning the plan and moving higher.

Curiosity was the only thing that kept her from following through. She snapped some more photos and searched for her brother's face in a sea of cops.

A younger man in a suit split from the others and stood near the broken railing, seemingly staring off into space. He appeared to tower over everyone else and Jessa decided it was in the way he carried himself.

He scanned the early morning skyline, back-lit by the light from the inside of the condo, and she documented it with each click of the shutter.

Several strands of hair poked out in different directions. He'd either been woken up by a call to come to the crime scene or he'd been running his hands through it in frustration.

He was young. It surprised her. With the exception of Jake, most of the detectives she'd met were older. Men who'd become jaded at a young age. Out of sheer boredom, Jessa studied his mannerisms.

His muscular body indicated that he spent a lot of time in the gym and his hardened jawline just screamed that he didn't take shit from anybody.

Then he smiled, a slow sexy smile like something about the crime scene amused the hell out of him, and she realized that he was charming; and charming was more dangerous than a body built for brawling.

One was in direct opposition to the other.

He might've been the type to fetch coffee for his wife or girlfriend in the morning before running out to rescue puppies from the clutches of evil. It wouldn't have made a difference to her.

She'd had her fill of men just like him. A man who'd seduce the panties off a woman's body before informing her that he was married and he wasn't looking for anything serious.

Detective Desirable turned and said something to another cop on the balcony before gesturing toward an adjacent building.

With the sun coming up and her contact nowhere to be found, Jessa packed up her stuff and began the arduous descent back down. The pain in her calves and hamstrings, along with her irritation at being stood up yet again, increased with every step.

She finally made it to the bottom and the soles of her boots hit the pavement below with a loud thud. When she straightened, she met the intense stare of Detective Desirable.

"Going somewhere?" he asked with an easy smile.

The smile was meant to disarm her. Instead, she took a step back, putting some distance between them.

"So, you obviously saw me and now want to question my motives," she stated with as much strength as she could muster.

Her typical cases didn't involve cops; well, at least where she was concerned. Whatever measures were taken by the affected parties after she left was out of her control.

"It's not illegal to be on a fire escape, you know," Jessa added, pointing up toward the zigzagged appendage. In the early morning light, it looked less like a piece of architectural history and more like a steel death-trap.

Detective Desirable flashed her another easy smile, one she didn't return. "Actually, it's considered trespassing, which is highly illegal."

She shifted the backpack higher onto her shoulder and moved to step around him. "Don't you have a murder to solve?"

He latched onto her arm and led her up against the bricks with a husky, "Not so fast. You seem to think you know why I'm here, but I don't know why you are."

"I wanted pictures of the sunrise. Can I go now?" Jessa's heart beat just a little too fast for her liking. Getting arrested was not in her plans for the day.

The detective looked up at the building. "Funny, I don't seem to remember the sunrise coming from a certain balcony. You were caught photographing an active crime scene; I'm going to need to see some ID."

"And I'm going to need to see a badge," she retorted with a growl, before wrenching her arm free.

"You mean this?" He flipped it open. "Detective Adam Keller. Your turn."

Knowing she'd definitely end up in jail if she didn't comply, Jessa fished her driver's license from the front pocket of the backpack and reluctantly handed it over to him.

His eyes widened as he checked it over and his smug expression slipped.

Good, she thought. Maybe he recognized her name. Her little business wasn't much, but she stayed busy. It wasn't unreasonable to think that a cop might know who she was.

"Jessa... Hopkins. Any relation to Jake?" He was no longer smiling.

She sighed. "He's my brother. Why—what'd he tell you? That I can't handle myself? I'll have you know I'm here on official business—"

Detective Keller held up a hand. "Stop. I need you to just listen to me. When's the last time you spoke with your brother?"

Jessa paused to think about it. "Last Tuesday? I've been trying to reach him since last night, but he's not picking up. The last time—wait, why are you looking at me like that? You're freaking me out."

"Ms. Hopkins, I'm going to have to ask you to come with me."

JAKE SAT AT MY DESK, reading over the manuscript for Angel of Death, while I sat on the couch, eyed glued to him. I'd been on pins and needles since he sat down but resisted the urge to ask what he thought, knowing it would only earn me a sarcastic remark.

That wasn't what had pulled the air from my lungs and kept me captivated for the last thirty minutes though.

Jake was wearing glasses.

Thick black rims, favored by hipsters the world over, rested on his perfect, upturned nose. Incidentally, they were the same style worn by geeks like me.

If my damp panties were any indicator, then my sexual orientation had just become Jake in glasses.

He made an odd sound of interest and I snapped to attention.

"What? Find a grammatical error?" I teased before taking a sip of coffee.

Look at how normal and unaffected I was acting.

He turned to me and I sucked in a breath, so struck by him in glasses that I ended up inhaling the second sip. I began coughing and spluttering while he watched me amusedly.

"Wrong. Way," I croaked, pointing to my throat.

"Apparently." He looked at the screen and then back at me before clearing his throat. "I... I guess I have some questions with this."

I wiped my streaming eyes and nodded. "It's terrible, isn't it? I just thought I'd make Jessa more of a—"

"Will you let me ask the questions?"

I swallowed and nodded again. "Absolutely, Detective."

"You can't even begin to fathom the things I'd do if I put my hands on you."

I was reminded of the conversation we'd left unfinished. He hadn't mentioned it again, and I wasn't going to bring it up. I was confused enough as it was.

Sleep hadn't come easy; every time I closed my eyes, I saw Jake holding himself up over me, his smug smirk on full display. When it wasn't that, it was him on a date with Kamdyn, touching her hand, while watching my face for a reaction. Every bit of it made me twitchy.

I wanted him.

Desperately.

And I hated myself for it.

It wasn't like we had great chemistry. We weren't even capable of being in the same room without it turning into a fight. And I'd tried, but he just brought out the worst in me.

I pulled myself from thoughts of self-loathing and tried to focus on his issues with my manuscript and not on the way his button-up shirt hugged his frame.

"It's good, Hayden. You've nailed Jessa—"

"That doesn't sound like an issue," I pointed out. "Get to the bad stuff."

He leaned back in the chair and crossed his arms over his chest. "You don't want the compliment? Fine. I have a couple of issues with where this story is headed. If you're running with the idea that my sister is about to find out I was thrown off a building, the chances of me making a reappearance are slim. How are you going to bring me back?"

I curled my legs underneath me and gnawed absently at my lower lip. "I don't know yet. I'm working on it though. Since we're on the topic though, how are you going to keep me safe? I received a threatening email last night and Max—"

"Max told me all about it and I'm working on it." Jake rose to his feet and began pacing. It wasn't something I'd written, but I knew it was something he did when he was thinking.

"Well, when you can guarantee my safety, then I can guarantee your return to the story. How about that?" I sweetly asked, secretly enjoying the way his face began to take on a reddish tint.

Jake clenched his jaw and nodded. "Oh, I'm keeping you safe, sweetheart. You're still breathing, aren't you?"

Bootsy tried to creep out from under the couch without either of us noticing. Obviously, she wanted no part in our 'discussion.' I put my coffee mug on the table and scooped her up into my arms.

"I really should call and thank Max," I said, stroking the black and white fur along Bootsy's back and earning myself a head bunt. "If he hadn't been here—"

"If he hadn't been here?" Jake roared. "You got an email; not a singing telegram from a gunman. I'm only a detective, but I'm fairly certain that your life wasn't in danger at any point last night."

My hand moved up to Bootsy's neck, and she began softly purring against my shirt. "I like Max. He's very nice."

Jake smirked. "Well, he's an assassin, so I'm not surprised. You both kill people for a living—sounds like you're perfect for each other."

What kind of man carried treats in his pocket?

An assassin, apparently.

It actually made more sense than anything I'd come up with.

I stopped petting and Bootsy immediately began nudging at my hand, urging me to continue. "What? I thought you said he was ex-military."

"He is—former Army Ranger, turned assassin. The name Max Grant doesn't sound familiar to you?" Jake seemed to get as much pleasure from toying with me as I did with him.

Max Grant...

I turned the name over in my mind, trying to place it. There was something familiar about it, but I couldn't put my finger on what that something was.

"Let's try this," he added, fully committed to taking me down. *"The Killing Hour."*

"Wasn't that just in theaters? Is he an actor?" I had no idea.

"Josephine Rothschild."

I frowned. "She's an author, uh..." I wracked my brain frantically. "Oh, she writes crime thrillers!"

He crossed his arms over his chest again and grinned, his tongue peeking out from the corner of his mouth. "And?"

Realization struck and I paled. "And her main character is Max Grant. No! How? You brought another fictional character out with you? Oh my god, he's with Aaris!" I jumped up, sending Bootsy into the carpet. I ignored the pins and needles sensation in my legs and jogged toward the front door. "He's an assassin—I told her he was real! She's not safe."

Jake held out an arm and I ground to a halt before he could clothesline me. "Aaris is fine, I swear to you. And yes, I called in reinforcements once I knew your life was in danger."

I put my hands on my hips. "You brought more than him?" I hissed. "What is wrong with you?"

He shrugged. "I have a few guys. Listen, it's not really important. What is important is you telling me why, out of all the guys on the force, you chose Adam 'Dickhead' Keller for my sister?"

"What's wrong with Adam?"

Jake rubbed at the back of his neck with a heavy sigh. "What's wrong with Adam? Where should I start? Oh, for starters, the guy's a rule follower. Everything has to be by the book—"

"What's wrong with following the rules? Isn't that like imperative to your job as a cop?" I interjected.

He sank down onto the couch with a bitter laugh. Bootsy, completely oblivious to the tension in the room, jumped up into his lap for attention. His hand moved across her fur distractedly.

"Jake," I prodded. "What's wrong with him?"

"He's just such a goody-goody, you know? The guy's this smug, virtuous prick whose idea of romance is reciting the penal code. I can't stand him."

I cocked my head to the side, completely dumbfounded. "So, the nice guy thing isn't an act?"

Until a week ago, I assumed that every character I wrote was based on some version of me or the people I knew. It was perplexing to know that, in actuality, I was scripting someone's life.

There was no room for error.

I had one surly detective on my hands, I didn't need other characters getting the same idea.

Jake stood up suddenly, sending Bootsy sliding back down to the carpet. She scowled at both of us before marching toward the bedroom, tail whipping back and forth.

He sat back down at the desk and hunched over the keyboard. "Where is it?" He used the mouse to scroll up the screen. "Here. Going somewhere?" he asked with an easy smile. Okay, that is one-hundred percent Adam—always smiling. I bet he goes home and jacks off into a pair of handcuffs every night with a big grin on his face, because gosh dang, he just loves his job."

My lip curled up. "And how might one 'jack off' into a pair of handcuffs, Jake?"

"Really, Hayden?" He rolled his eyes. "You need the logistics of that? I'm just saying that knowing Jessa, she's going to eat him alive."

"Maybe they'll be perfect for each other—the rebel and the rules guy. It'd make a great movie, don't you think?"

Jake shook his head and leaned over the desk again, rereading.

My phone began playing the opening bars from Mariah Carey's 'All I Want for Christmas is You.'

He cocked his head to the side with a raised brow. "Isn't that a—"

"Great way to alert me to text messages? Yes, yes it is." I retrieved my phone from a couch cushion. Aaris. Right on cue.

Who was that guy? Call me ASAP!

My heart hammered in my chest as the phone rang. What if Max had hurt her? I'd let her leave with a man who murdered people for a living. *What kind of friend was I?*

"Hello?" she answered breathlessly.

"Are you okay?"

"Am I okay? You send me home with that guy and you want to know if I'm okay?" Her voice was laced with hysteria.

"Aaris, I can explain—"

"Sweetie, I want to marry that man and carry his babies. He takes me home and I was feeling, uh, amorous, if you will." I cringed.

Drunk Aaris would hump a light pole, something I had unfortunately witnessed on more than one occasion. "I used my best moves and do you know what he said?"

Knowing what she considered her 'best moves,' I could only imagine. "No?"

She giggled softly into the phone. "He said that I'd had a lot to drink and what seemed like a good idea now might not feel so good in the morning. And I thought he was blowing me off, but he had me drink this stuff that he swore would keep me from feeling hungover and put me to bed like a goddamn gentleman."

Jake gave me a look and I whispered, "Aaris," before resuming my conversation. "Well, that sounds nice, but it doesn't really explain why you've decided to marry him."

"He brings me home safely, refuses to sleep with me while I'm intoxicated, ensures that I get to bed safely and don't wake up with a hangover and you're confused?"

"Well, when you put it like that. Have you told him any of this?" I asked hesitantly. The quickest way to lose a man was to tell him about your feelings.

It was obvious by the way Jake was leaning over that he was no longer reading anything on my laptop and was instead listening in to my side of the conversation.

"That's the thing. I woke up this morning, feeling amazing, and he's nowhere to be found. He did leave me a phone number though."

I debated whether to tell her what Max did for a living, but it had been a long time since I'd seen Aaris head over heels for anyone, minus Jeremy Piven, but he didn't count.

"Did you call him?"

She sighed. "It wasn't his number that he left..."

"Okay... whose number was it?"

"It was the number to the local AA. Isn't that a sign?"

A sign that she needed to stop drinking? Yes.

"I mean, what kind of man leaves that information for someone he just met? A man who's found the love of his life and wants to make sure she's making good choices, I think." Her voice had taken on a dreamy quality and I winced, knowing that Max was probably long gone, leaving me to pick up the pieces of her soon-to-be shattered heart.

"Um, don't you have to work later?"

She groaned. "Yeah."

"Well, try to get some sleep. We'll talk later."

She agreed and I ended the call. Jake turned his head to the side. "She fell for Max?"

I nodded. "It seems that way, which should be fun seeing as to how he's not only fictional but a trained killer as well."

"I think Max has that effect on people. It's why he's good at what he does." Jake was still standing, with his forearms resting on the desk. It was almost comical the way he'd folded himself in half instead of just sitting down in the chair.

"You better watch it; if you keep hunching over like that, you'll shrink down to six-five or," I let out a mock gasp, "six-four before you know it."

He gave me the side eye. "And what do you suggest I do to prevent that?"

I grinned widely. "Yoga."

"Yoga," Jake repeated.

I nodded. "Yeah, it's great for posture."

He stood and stretched before leaning down to grab his ankles, limbering up for the track event we were apparently hosting in the living room. "Okay, let's do it."

"Okay," I replied with narrowed eyes. "Just like that. You're not going to pick a fight?"

"No. If you think I need yoga, then I'll do it." He lifted his arms above his head, and I was momentarily distracted by the distinct lines of abdominal muscles that ran down the center of his stomach, disappearing into the top of his jeans. That was an eight-pack. Easily.

I frowned and crossed my arms over my suddenly hard nipples. "Are you sick?"

"No, why?"

"You're acting weird. At least fight with me so that I know you're okay."

"Alright, let's get this hippie-dippy bullshit over with so that we can get back to solving cases. Better?"

"Much... but you can't wear that."

Jake looked down at the dark denim and frowned. "What's wrong with this?"

I demonstrated a lunge. "You need something that you can move and stretch in. You'll never get loose in those."

The corner of his lip turned up. It was like a little baby smirk. "Is that so? What would you recommend?"

"Yoga pants!" I exclaimed. "Or gym shorts... or sweatpants."

Jake nodded to himself. "I might have something down in my bag. Are you wearing that?"

I looked down at my *Cats Meowt Side... How Bow Dat?* tank top and yoga pants. "Absolutely. This is perfect for exercise."

"It has a cat shaking its fist on it," he muttered, before disappearing into the bathroom.

"It's not shaking its fist," I argued. "He's snapping his fingers. He's a sassy cat."

"Whatever you say," he called from behind the closed door.

I pushed the coffee table into the couch and laid out the yoga mats. Jake was probably going to fall in love with yoga, thanks to me. He'd have me work it into his next book as a way of showing readers that he took his health seriously.

I bet some of my readers would demand that I host an author/reader yoga retreat. We'd get heavily meditated and just become one with nature. We could sit around a campfire and talk about our crystals.

Maybe if things went well, I'd try introducing Jake to some crystals during corpse pose.

The bathroom door opened and he strolled back into the living room, wearing nothing but the hottie glasses and a pair of grey sweat-pants. I was wrong. It was a twelve-pack.

If I was a cartoon character, my eyes would've bugged out of my head, while my tongue rolled out like a red carpet.

Grey. Sweatpants.

My lust had to be written all over my face. I looked down at my yoga mat with flushed cheeks. I needed to say something, or it was only going to get more awkward. "So, we'll just start," I squeaked out.

"Is this not okay?" Jake questioned. "You said something loose and comfortable."

I dragged my toe along the rubber mat, refusing to look up at him. If I did, he'd read my mind and then I'd never hear the end of it.

"Most people wear a shirt, but you're Jake Hopkins, so why would you?" Without waiting for a response, I dove right in. "We're going to start with some light stretching to warm up before we begin."

He copied my every move and the few times I risked a glance from under my lashes, I was met with a speculative stare. I stretched down and hooked my fingers around my big toes.

"What's this called?" Jake exhaled softly as he replicated it.

"Well, there's a fancy name for it, but our teacher just calls it Big Toe Pose. It's good for your hamstrings." I exhaled and released my toes. Half a second later, he did the same.

"What's a good one for lower back pain?"

Where I expected facetiousness, his eyes remained serious. Soft. So far, my plan appeared to be working. He was open to yoga and all that it had to offer.

I laid down on my back and lifted my hips up into Bridge Pose. Jake had paused to take a drink from his water bottle as I switched positions and now stood frozen, with water running from the side of his mouth.

"Jake?" I asked, still maintaining the pose.

He nodded slowly, his Adam's apple bobbing up and down in a swallow. Realizing that he was dumping water onto his face and the mat beneath him, he lowered the bottle and replaced the cap.

I paused for thirty seconds, deepening the stretch by lifting my heels off the mat. "This," I exhaled, "is Bridge Pose and it is so good for your lower back. Try it."

I could've sworn I was imagining it, but his eyes no longer looked sleepy. Jake stared at me like a man who was completely and utterly famished.

He dropped down to his knees beside me. "Show me again."

I shook my head with a soft laugh. "Jake, it's not hard. You just..."

And there it was. The way he knelt over me brought back my masturbatory vision of him, biting down on his lip in concentration as he worked to find the best ways to get me off.

"You just what?"

A flush crept up my neck, heating my face. "Uh, you just lift your tailbone, like you're drawing it up toward your pubi—abdomen."

I was fumbling over words, making it completely apparent that I was having lustful thoughts toward the detective crouched next to me.

I decided to switch gears and poses.

"Another good one is the Feathered Peacock pose." I moved onto all fours and then pushed up onto the balls of my feet, walking them toward my head. Maybe if I continued twisting myself into poses, then I could avoid having to have an actual conversation.

Jake sat back and watched with wide eyes as I kicked one leg up in the air and then the other, resting all of my weight on my forearms.

He exhaled before asking, "Are there any stretches you can do with a partner?" There was still no trace of humor in his voice.

I slowly brought my legs back down and wracked my brain. "I know of a couple, but we mainly just work on our own in class."

"I think I'd like a partner." There was nothing erotic in his words, but his tone left me wanting something. Anything at this point. Maybe just a good ice-cold shower.

I kept waiting for the other shoe to drop and him to admit that he'd just been fucking with me, but he continued watching me with a ravenous expression.

I swallowed the saliva that had pooled in my mouth. "We could do a forward fold, but you're a lot bigger than me, so your head might end up in my lap." I laughed nervously. "Um, maybe we could try a twist instead?"

"Yeah, show me that."

"Okay." I chewed at my lower lip. "It starts with Lotus pose; that's the one we did at the beginning. We do that sitting back to back."

My throat felt like it was closing up as he sat down behind me and I almost laughed when I saw our reflections on the small TV screen in front of me. I was a tiny sapling compared to this redwood. My skin heated to the point of sizzling as he shifted around, getting into position.

"Like this?" His deep voice vibrated straight into my core.

"Um, I think so?" Even my voice sounded unsteady. I focused on the pose itself and tried to block out thoughts of becoming a bendy pretzel for him in a very sexual, completely non-yoga way.

"Inhale and raise both arms. When you exhale, twist to the left. You'll place your right hand on the outside of your left knee and your left hand on the inside of my right knee. I'll mirror it and then we'll hold before moving to the opposite side."

I inhaled and he followed my lead, sending goosebumps down my skin when his arms brushed against mine. We twisted in unison and my damp palm found his knee.

His hand rested on the inside of mine, taking up most of my thigh thanks to the height difference between us. I'd spent my life fighting the stigma of being little. Apparently, the majority of the world's population made it past five-one.

I wasn't taken seriously most of the time and had endured having my hair ruffled up like a small child's on the rare occasions I showed my anger, because I was just too adorable.

I'd scaled grocery store shelves like they were my Kilimanjaro in order to reach something on the top, because I refused to be the little girl asking for help.

As I sat behind this massive giant of a man though, with his hand covering my leg, I found that I liked my smallness.

"How are you doing back there?" he asked, the rumble reverberating into my back.

I exhaled the breath I'd been holding. "Good. Let's switch to the other side."

Jake agreed and we brought our arms up on an inhale before moving our bodies to the right. I stretched around him, placing my palm against something that didn't feel like the inside of his knee. I patted and moved my hand against it in an effort to discern how far off target I was.

He sucked air through his teeth. "Uh, Hayden." His voice sounded strangled. "Could you lower your hand?"

My cheeks flamed when realization struck.

"Lower... still lower. Okay." He guided my hand down to the safe zone while I sat in stunned silence.

Holy shit.

Jake was packing.

I'd unintentionally pulled the old switch and dick grab. I tried focusing on my inhales and exhales, but my heart was distracting me with its furious pounding.

"Um, Jake?" I needed to keep my mouth shut and think of becoming Zen and centering myself. "Are you not wearing underwear?"

Then again, when had I ever listened to reason?

He cleared his throat. "You said I needed something I could be loose and comfortable in, did you not?"

My fingers began trailing upward and were promptly put to a stop by Jake's hand. "Hayden," he warned.

"What? I was stretching my fingers." What I was doing was booting sanity right off the balcony in favor of copping another feel.

Just so I could describe it better later.

Research.

"I think that's enough yoga for today." Jake rolled away from me and onto his knees. I made a big show of unfolding my legs and doing some light stretches while continuing to sneak glances at his lap.

"You need a hand?" he asked roughly.

Do you? I thought.

It wasn't a rhetorical question and lines appeared on Jake's forehead as he awaited my response. I forced myself to look away from the impressive bulge in his sweatpants and nodded.

Still on his knees, he grabbed my hand in an attempt to pull me up. Instead, the momentum sent us both falling onto the carpet.

My breasts collided with his chest and I floundered uselessly against the floor, trying to right myself.

I expected to be bucked off at any moment. Instead, Jake's arms wrapped around my lower back pulling me closer. My hips rolled forward from the contact and I instinctively rocked back against his hands.

He surprised me further when his hands slipped lower and cupped my ass. *What the hell is happening?* I silently asked with wide eyes.

Just take it, he seemed to respond as his fingers dug into my soft flesh. When he bit down on his lip just like I'd imagined he would when he was concentrating, I let out a small gasp of shock.

He continued moving my hips in a soft rhythm while staring at my mouth. I was dry humping Jake's navel, but he seemed oblivious to it.

We were so lost in the moment that neither one of us heard the door open.

"What the hell is going on here?" Aaris shrieked.

I jumped to my feet and adjusted my tank while Jake dove for the couch and a throw pillow. When I frowned, he gestured with his head toward his crotch, as if the entire thing had been my fault. Judging by the pained expression on his face, he'd come down with a severe case of blue balls.

The fact that he even had an erection made me feel... empowered. I'd done that—all five-foot-one inches of me. Took that giant sequoia and made him my bitch.

"Anyone?" she demanded again.

I put a hand on my hip and grinned. "I think Jake's hard-pressed to explain this one. Make no bones about it; he is up for the discussion though." I said the last part with a wink, earning me a death glare from the boner king himself.

Aaris placed her index finger against her mouth and then held it up as she worked to articulate a response. "Okay," she finally said slowly. "First of all, sweetie, your high beams are on. Secondly, someone better start talking like right now."

A quick glance confirmed that my nipples were in fact in the process of cutting their way through the thin material of my shirt.

Jake smirked up at me and I snapped, "Nothing happened, okay? I fell. He caught me. End of story. Now, if you'll excuse me, I'm going to turn the heat up and change into something warmer. It's too cold in here."

THIRTEEN

AARIS POURED a bowl of cereal and waited patiently until Jake and his pillow left the room before leaning over the counter to hiss, "Did you see the dick print on that one? Holy hell, Hayden! I thought you two hated each other!" She was practically bouncing up and down in her seat.

The pipes in the wall gave a low groan as the shower kicked on. I picked distractedly at the sleeves of the sweatshirt I'd snagged after Aaris pointed out my excessive nippleage and took my time, pulling the sleeves over my hands and then pushing them back up to my wrists in an attempt to stall.

"Well, we do."

It didn't sound as convincing as it had before.

Before I accidentally groped him.

Before he had his hands on my ass.

Before I sexually assaulted his belly button.

"The whole thing's been one big dicktastrophe, Aaris."

She fought a smile and lost. "Did you say *dicktastrophe?*"

I groaned and covered my face with my hands. "C'mon, Aaris, enough. I said catastrophe, obviously."

"You did not. You said one big *dicktastrophe* and after seeing what I did when I walked in, I don't blame you. God, I almost ran home for some marshmallows."

At my utterly confused expression, she elaborated, "Sweetie, with that tent he pitched, I thought we were setting up camp. He's into you, no doubt about it."

I opened my mouth and then closed it. *What had happened?* One minute, we were doing yoga and the next I was riding him like a seesaw.

I'd been dickmatized. I got a handful and lost my ability to make rational decisions.

The bathroom door open and I shook my head at Aaris, silently warning her not to continue the conversation.

"So, I think it's great that you're going to come to VIP night at the bar. Really. You never get to attend these events." Her grin nearly reached her ears.

Damn.

She'd been begging me to go for weeks, but I'd been vague about my work schedule.

"What's VIP night?" Jake asked, running his hand through still damp hair. Beads of water clung to his cheeks and as my eyes drifted down, I was disappointed to see that the sweatpants had been replaced with jeans again. The fate of the bulge remained unknown.

Aaris quirked a brow at me before answering him. "It's something that Bryan, my boss, does every year as a way of getting our friends and family into the bar so that he can siphon away their money. I never have anyone show up. Having Hayden there will at least get him off my back a little, you know?"

I narrowed my eyes at her. She was going to play this until she got what she wanted. I pulled my notebook from my purse and began jotting down ideas for Jessa, ignoring the way Jake instantly reassured her that he'd be attending too.

I must've had the female equivalent of blue balls, because I was suddenly raring for a fight. I wanted to scream at both of them because of my own confusion. Fiction and reality had collided, creating absolute chaos.

I drowned out their voices with the one in my head. I needed to find out who killed Addison and Jake. The list of suspects in both cases was a mile long as neither one of them had been particularly well-liked when they were alive.

It would've been easy to pin it on an angry husband with him, but there weren't any that had been previously mentioned. To add one in now was lazy storytelling and definitely wouldn't pack an emotional punch.

Who would've gained the most from their deaths?

Jake had suspected the cartel in Addison's death, but that didn't fit with his. They had no reason to go after him even if he was investigating her murder. They would've paid off a judge to avoid charges had he gotten close enough to sniff out a suspect.

No. It was someone else.

I'd written myself into a corner with *One in the Chamber* by mentioning a mystery woman on the balcony.

Jake wasn't a small man, so what woman would've had the strength to knock him off-balance?

"Hayden?" Aaris waved a hand in front of my face. "Hello, earth to Hayden."

I blinked. "Sorry. I'm in my head right now trying to figure this story out."

"Have you got a lead?" Jake leaned in, apparently putting the 'yoga incident' behind him in favor of news.

I shook my head. "No. I've got nothing to go on, other than you and Jessa both saw a woman with blonde hair." I paused as the thoughts began flooding in. "Wait... wait... what if? Oh my god, what if Addison isn't dead?"

Jake sat back in his chair and rubbed his jaw. "You think she faked her death? Why? What would she have to gain by doing that? And, if she wasn't burned to death in her apartment, then who was?"

I rested my elbows on the table and massaged my temples. I had no ideas and nothing concrete to go on. It was like putting a puzzle together when half the pieces were missing. I needed more than just speculation.

"I don't know," I sighed.

Aaris's spoon hit the side of her cereal bowl with a clang and Jake and I both looked up at her.

"You know, you don't have to actually search for a killer, right? It's fiction—Hayden could say that a killer clown from the sewers killed you and Addison and that'd be it. End of story. Boom."

We both stared at Aaris like she'd suddenly sprouted three heads.

"You can't just throw a killer in all willy-nilly. You build up to it with a random mention or run-in. And I'm pretty sure that Stephen King would have something to say about me using Pennywise as the villain."

Jake nodded. "I agree. It'd be a slap in the face to the readers if she phoned it in on this."

"Oh, look. You two are finally on the same page about something." Aaris waved the spoon at us with a grin.

"Same page? Sweetheart, we aren't even in the same library."

I ignored the barb that seemed to land in the vicinity of my heart at his words and forced a smile onto my face.

"Still complete enemies. There's no need to worry about that."

Jake's eyes went dark, but he nodded again. "Absolutely. I'm just trying to get my life back."

"IS THERE anything on the menu that has some fucking meat in it? I'm a growing boy." Jake looked up from the menu he'd snagged as he followed me through the throngs of sweaty bodies in search of the bar.

I kept my word. We'd shown up for VIP night.

LED lights pulsed to the beat of the music. The bass reverberated through my skin and into my bones, leaving me with what I assumed would be permanent hearing loss.

I couldn't fathom how Aaris had managed to deal with the noise night after night without resorting to shouting like an elderly person in need of hearing aids.

The tip of Jake's boots brushed up against my heels and I rolled my shoulders to ward off the shiver that worked its way up my spine. It was the most contact we'd had since our nearly naked yoga session after his date with Kamdyn.

I'd gone to work the next day, expecting her to vomit up the details of the entire night onto my desk. Surprisingly, she'd stayed in her booth, avoiding me until I couldn't take it any longer.

When I demanded that she tell me everything that had happened, she'd given me a strange look before closing the door behind me.

"Jake couldn't be less interested in me—all we talked about was you."

I reassured her that he absolutely did not have feelings for me, but her words continued to ricochet around my head like a pinball.

Needless to say, it had been a weird week of dodging each other while living under the same roof. Not that it bothered me or anything. I had a book to write and a job to go to... plenty of things to keep me busy.

In another world, with a completely different person, I might've been up for more. But, this was Jake 'I'm A Real Boy' Hopkins and any interest he had in me was strictly case related.

I flagged the bartender down. "Um, hi. I was wondering if I could order an old fashioned? My friend told me all about them—"

"Is your friend eighty?"

I laughed and nodded; further proof that my backbone all but disappeared in social settings.

My friend was actually seventy-eight and came in every six weeks to the salon for a cut and color. She was lovely. The bartender, on the other hand, not so much.

Jake moved into my line of sight and yelled over the music, "Did you get me something?"

I shook my head. "Dude, I barely know how to order for myself, do you think I have any sort of clue how to order whiskey?"

I deepened my voice to sound like his and bellowed, "Hello, my good chap, I would like a whiskey with rocks in it. On the double."

Jake's nostrils flared and he ground down on his back teeth, accentuating his fantastic jawline. "Who says I wanted whiskey? Maybe I'm in the mood for beer."

I rolled my eyes. "Sure. Okay. You don't drink anything but premium whiskey. I'm not an idiot, Jake."

The bartender dropped off what I presumed to be an old fashioned and Jake ordered a beer.

"See. Unpredictable," he yelled over the music.

I was quickly reaching the point where I wanted to thump him right on his pouty lips every time he opened his mouth. Instead, I grabbed a miniature drink straw from the caddy on the bar and turned away to enjoy my old fashioned in peace.

It was surprisingly good—sweet and spicy rolled into one.

"It's weird, but I pegged you as a fruity cocktail drinker." Jake tipped the beer bottle back and, despite looking like he'd just sucked on a lemon, somehow managed to keep the liquid in his mouth.

"Really?"

He gave the room a once-over before returning his attention to me. "Well." He ran the pad of his thumb across his lower lip. "Maybe more like a Shirley Temple."

"Prick," I said under my breath before turning away. Keeping my back to Jake, I scanned the crowd for Aaris.

"She's just to the left of the wall of TVs," he noted.

I looked over to the wall and found her immediately. Reluctantly, I turned back to him with a frown. "How'd you find her so fast?"

"It's my job to know where people are," he matter-of-factly stated in that low voice of his. The same voice that made me act irrationally.

I discreetly clenched my thighs together in a warning and turned back to study the crowd.

Most of the women were wearing elaborate dresses or sleek jumpsuits while I was hanging out at the bar in my *I'm feline fine right meow* t-shirt and ripped jeans.

Well, the joke was on them because mine was the only ensemble that allowed me the freedom to pee without getting fully naked.

Music filled the entire building, yet only a few braved the dance floor. The majority of the 'VIPs' loitered around tables, continuously glancing up at the screens to see if their social media account was on display yet.

They weren't even talking to each other.

I pushed my glasses up onto my head and rubbed at my eyes before checking my watch. I'd promised Aaris no more than an hour. Given that only five minutes had passed since we arrived, it was going to be the longest hour of my life.

Without crystal clear vision, the club appeared to be a living, breathing thing. The walls swayed back and forth to the music, making the room appear much smaller. Even the television screens seemed to be reaching toward the hapless guests beneath them.

If the club was alive, then we were all trapped inside its stomach, just waiting to be digested. I settled my glasses firmly back on the bridge of my nose and watched as the room reverted back to normalcy.

Well, what constituted normalcy in a place like this.

Nope.

Knowing I'd never make it, I slipped a chocolate bar from the pocket of my purse and popped a small square of it into my mouth.

"What was that? What did you eat?"

"A piece of chocolate—I'm hungry."

Jake held out his hand. "I'll have one too."

I shook my head, ready to battle him if necessary. "They're special um, vegan chocolates. They ground up these... plants and extracted the plant's internal organs to mix with the chocolate. It's really an acquired taste. You'd hate them."

His eyes narrowed. "Weed, Hayden? Really?"

"Weed, Hayden?" I mimicked in his deep voice. "Fine. Yes, there is a chance that there might be some form of marijuana in these. It's for medical reasons. If I have to stay here for an entire hour, then I will do it comfortably."

"Drugs will kill you. You do realize that, don't you?"

"I'm not drunk enough to have this conversation with you." I downed the rest of my drink and signaled for the bartender. "Can I get a dirty martini with vodka?"

He nodded. "Leaving the old fashioned to the over-sixty crowd?"

To avoid yelling over the music, I stepped up onto the metal foot rail under the bar and rested my arms against the shiny metal surface. "It wasn't that bad. I just thought I'd stick with what I know I like."

"Do you like it extra dirty?"

Sensing my utter confusion, he held up the shaker. "Your martini, I mean."

Where Jake's attractiveness was instant and overwhelming, the bartender's was a gradual recognition. When he smiled, one corner of his mouth had a slight quirk to it. I pictured him spending his days off in a bookstore or coffee shop. The guy in the corner, too shy to approach anyone. Maybe I didn't despise him after all.

I gave him my cutest grin and wrapped the ends of my hair around my index finger. "I like it really dirty."

Jake began choking on his beer, but I kept my focus on my new friend. I searched along the bar, but there was nothing displaying his name.

Bars really needed signs above them that said something along the lines of, *'Your bartender tonight is Joe Blow and he is single.'*

Was it really that hard?

I held out my hand. "I'm Hayden."

He emptied the contents of the shaker into a martini glass before taking it. "Jack."

He added a wooden skewer of olives to the briny liquid before sliding it my way. "Let me know if that's dirty enough for you." He gave me a wink and moved down the bar to start his next order, but his eyes kept straying toward me.

"What the hell was that?" Jake growled.

"I don't know what you're talking about." I took a long drink and made sure Jack was watching as I licked my lips. He bit down on the corner of his and smiled.

It was just like riding a bike.

The behemoth chose that moment to invade my space and Jack's smile faded before he turned away.

"What are you doing?" I protested.

Jake shook his head and snapped, "What am I doing? What the fuck are you doing?"

I climbed up onto the stool, using the bar top for leverage. "I'm enjoying myself. That's what people in the real world do when they go out; they have fun."

Jake contorted himself into the chair next to mine in his dark wash jeans and black wool sweater. A very fitted wool sweater. The sleeves cut into his arms, forcing those bulging biceps into view.

I tossed my hair over my shoulder and discreetly checked out his backside. His jeans were showcasing his ass in a similar fashion.

"Hayden?"

"Hmmm?" I answered distractedly as I took another peek.

"My eyes are up here." He ran a hand down his thigh, smoothing invisible wrinkles.

I swallowed and tried for a distraction. "Why does it bother you that I was talking to the bartender? And why are you incapable of purchasing clothes that fit?"

He closed his eyes and pinched the bridge of his nose for far longer than was necessary. "I swear to god, Hayden. Did you not just witness the same thing I did?"

I began nibbling the olives off of the skewer and shrugged. "What? What did you 'witness' that offended you so much? Me, ordering a drink? Or was it the fact that a man might find me attractive?"

He crossed his arms over his chest. "That—the whole thing. It was... pathetic."

I closed my eyes and took another long drink of my martini, counting all the ways in which I'd like to see Jake die to calm myself.

Pathetic?

I frowned. It wasn't the weed that had me disoriented. It was him. This up and down, back and forth between us was wearing me down.

I'd played along for over a week, but tonight? Tonight, I just wanted to enjoy myself.

"Well, you would know, wouldn't you? I'm going to find Aaris. Enjoy your beer." I slid down from the barstool with my drink.

The cords in his neck went taut and he growled, "Damn it, I'm trying to keep you safe. You need to stay sober and alert, do you understand?"

I rolled my eyes. "Oh my god, Batman. Do you hear yourself?" I gestured around the club. "We're already in hell, what's the worst that could happen?"

"You're right. Go. Hook up in the bathroom with the bartender. Whatever." He took a swig from his beer bottle and his lips instantly puckered in disgust.

"Okay, Goliath." I patted his arm. "You can stop trying to prove a point. Order something you actually like."

"I like this just fine. In fact, I might just become a beer drinker." He took another drink to prove his point and winced. "Delicious."

"God, you're ridiculous." I left him and wove through the crowd toward Aaris.

"Hey," I called over the noise when I reached her.

She held an empty tray under her arm and sidestepped her way over to where I was standing. "You came! How long have you been here?"

I jerked my head back toward the bar. "Long enough for Colossus over there to piss me off."

She looked over my shoulder at him and nodded. "So, I'm guessing yoga didn't lead to passionate lovemaking on your balcony?"

I grimaced. "Ew, no."

She waved a hand over me and then gestured toward the bar. "That would explain the sexual tension that's literally radiating off both of you. Go! Drink! Screw his brains out in the bathroom. Whatever you need to do to get over this funk."

Why did everyone assume that I had a desire to copulate in a public bathroom?

Jake met my gaze and tipped his chin up in acknowledgment. My cheeks heated and I turned away. Obviously, he hadn't heard a word of what she'd said, but the switch had been flipped and now I couldn't help but imagine him up against the bathroom wall.

"What happened to not trusting him and watching my back?"

She gave me a knowing smile. "Well, I did walk in on you two 'doing yoga.' It's not crazy to think that it would've become more since then, right?"

I moved closer to her as a group of girls squeezed past. "That still doesn't explain why you've suddenly changed your opinion of him."

Aaris mashed her lips together and glanced toward the bar. "Let's just say that maybe he's growing on me."

"This is because of Max, isn't it? Jake 'grew' on you because of him? Jesus, Aaris, you had one night with him where you proceeded to get blackout drunk and then nothing happened! The guy left you a note for AA. How many more signs do you need that he's not into you?" I clapped a hand over my mouth, but it was too late.

Aaris reared back as if I'd slapped her and I belatedly realized that several VIPs had turned away from their beloved screens to witness the abuse.

"Aaris, I'm so—"

She held her hand up. "I have a lot of tables to take care of. Excuse me."

Knowing I needed to cool off before I said or did something else I'd regret, I stumbled through the crowd and toward the large frosted glass restroom sign.

I had to hand it to Bryan; for a guy who was a complete tool, he'd put a lot of thought into *Magenta*. Custom subway tiles created a border above dark stone walls and the lighting above the mirrors allowed just enough light to keep it sexy.

It was the perfect place to disappear into with a lover, escaping the chaos and noise from the bar. Given my track record for the night, I would've considered moving a table and some chairs in; you know, were it not a bathroom.

I shifted my purse higher onto my shoulder and massaged my temples. I'd spoken to my best friend like she was garbage and why? Because she'd suddenly developed an affinity for the womanizing detective?

A woman who'd been hunched over the sinks since I joined the small line turned her head and snorted a line of coke off the dark veined granite counter. She lifted her head and made eye contact with the small group of women, daring us to tell on her.

I kept my head down and slipped into a metallic stall on the other side of the bathroom and immediately got lost in thought again.

That was the only drawback to being high. My thoughts took over, which was great for writing, but now I was left with a video of my fight with Aaris on a loop in my brain.

I rested my forearms on my thighs with a sigh. Jake brought out the worst in me and now I was taking it out on the people closest to me.

Despite the spray and crystals, it turned out that I was the one with negative energy. I was operating out of a place of fear, just like my oil lady had warned me about.

I just needed to raise my frequency and operate from a place of love and light. Maybe when we got back to the apartment, I'd meditate for a bit and work on getting my body reset.

I realized that at some point, the bathroom had gone silent, leaving me with the paranoid suspicion that I'd been in here for hours and not just a couple of minutes.

"Be cool," I muttered to myself as I pulled up my jeans. "You are Zen as fuck, and you are just gonna march back out there and apologize to Aaris."

The lights went out in the middle of my deep breathing exercise, plunging the bathroom into darkness. Things went from self-contemplative to slasher film scary in half a second.

"Hello?" I tried, with a slight waver in my voice. "Someone's still in here."

A soft tapping sound came from somewhere near the door and my pulse picked up. Obviously, that was just the plumbing acting up. Pipes clicked when the power went out; I'd read that somewhere.

"Aaris?" I tried again.

Maybe this was her way of paying me back. I strained, but all I could hear was the blood pounding in my ears. The power had to be out in the entire building.

I calmed myself with thoughts of the VIPs losing their collective shit over not being able to view posts thanks to the blackout.

Not me though. I was calm, cool, and collected.

Later, when the news crews showed up, I'd somberly tell them how I kept a level head during a disaster even as everyone around me fell apart.

Well Janet, I knew that I had to stay calm to make it out alive. Why, I knew that my best friend needed me, so I did what had to be done to make it to her.

It needed polishing, but I felt like it captured the general idea.

Something scraped loudly against the wall, moving closer to where I was, and all thoughts of bravery vanished. My breath quickened and I pressed a hand to my mouth to stifle the sound.

• Confession: I was afraid of the dark... like, deathly afraid. I had this recurring nightmare where I entered a room and the lights either wouldn't come on or would flicker for a few seconds before plunging me into darkness. Inevitably, the door would always close behind me, trapping me in the dark. It never involved another person before, so this was an entirely new level of terror.

A soft whimper escaped my lips and the scraping sound stopped. I wasn't alone and suddenly Jake's warning to stay sober seemed like sound advice.

"Hayden?" Jake yelled from outside the bathroom door. "Open the door!"

How was I supposed to make it to the door in complete darkness without encountering a serial killer who sported a hook for a hand?

Because what other rational explanation was there for the sounds that were inching closer to where I was hiding. Suddenly fearful that the killer was going to come in from underneath the stall, I felt around for the toilet seat and quietly climbed up onto it.

I immediately realized that the killer could now just lean over the top of the stall to hack me to death. If anything, I'd just made myself more accessible.

Crouching on top of the toilet, I used the handrails on either side to balance myself. Both physically and mentally.

You are safe. You are balanced. You are calm. You are grounded. You are Zen.

You are not about to be gutted...

"Hayden!" What sounded like Jake's fist hitting the door and I jumped, nearly losing my balance and toppling into the floor.

The scraping turned to a crunching sound; like the *disemboweler of the dark* was grinding something into the tile with their shoes. I needed a plan.

I couldn't see my hand in front of my face, but it was only a matter of time before the killer found me. I wasn't even wearing my nice underwear. That alone was reason enough to stay alive.

The bathroom was unnervingly quiet, but fear kept me glued to my perch. Maybe it was a trick to lure me out. I took a deep breath and closed my eyes, listening for movement.

The lock on the door clicked, followed by a sliver of light and the heavy tread of boots.

"Hayden?" Jake's voice was laced with panic.

He hit the light switch and I blinked against the sudden brightness before weakly calling out, "Over here."

As an afterthought, I added, "Be careful, Jake. There's a murderer in here."

Janet, I knew that running would've just exposed the killer to more people. So, I stayed put in the stall and created a diversion so that others could escape safely. My only thought was of them.

Jake reached the stall. "Open the door."

I kept my death grip on the safety rails. "I... I can't."

He peered through the crack between the stall and the door. "You're not naked. I can see you, Hayden. Just unlock the damn door."

I shook my head and hissed, "I can't let go. He's still in here. I can hear him!"

Jake rested his forehead against the stall with a sigh. "That's Bryan, the owner. Now, let me in."

I reluctantly released the bar and slid the lock back before resuming my stance. Jake looked me over; no doubt preparing his lecture on drugs and their effects.

I knew that what I'd heard was no hallucination though.

"Are you okay? Are you—are you hurt?" he finally asked.

I shook my head and looked down to see that my knuckles were turning white from my grip. "Someone was in here with me," I squeaked. "They, they turned off the lights and scraping. There was a scraping sound!"

I began laughing as if the entire thing had just been some elaborate prank that I'd been unfortunate enough to get caught up in. I laughed until tears ran down my face and the giggles turned to sobs.

Now, who was the lunatic in the bathroom?

Jake's eyes widened and he reached for me. "Come here."

I brought one foot down and then the other before reaching for his hand. I continued hiccupping my way through another round of crying and, instead of running away like a normal person, Jake pulled me into his side.

He patted my back awkwardly as I whispered, "I'm telling the truth. Someone was in here. It wasn't the drugs."

"We're going to walk to that door right there." He pointed. "And then we're going to go downstairs and get you some water."

I wasn't sure what I was expecting when it came to Aaris' lecherous boss, but the man that stepped out from an open stall was not it.

I'd pictured Bryan as overweight with stringy hair that he greased back every morning; not the muscular Adonis that he clearly was.

Not that his good looks excused his behavior; if anything, it made it worse.

He exchanged a glance with Jake before shaking his head. "It's empty. I checked."

He looked me over and my spine stiffened in response. There it was. The sleazeball, unmasked. He was mentally undressing me.

"I'd guess she's under the influence of something, Detective Hopper. If you need to use my office—"

Jake gripped my shoulder to the point of pain before biting out, "It's Hopkins and I can take it from here."

I wasn't under the influence of anything. I knew that what I heard was real. I wrapped my arms around myself as Jake dragged me away from Bryan toward the door.

"But, but." I dug my heels into the tiles as he propelled me forward.

The bathroom looked much like it had when I entered. There was no trail of blood leading to a body or a masked man with a knife poised high above his head, ready to strike some unfortunate soul.

In other words, there was absolutely nothing to back up my claims.

Jake ignored my protests and flipped the lock on the bathroom door, opening it up to a long line of seriously pissed off women.

One was squatted over a large metal planter, apparently having made the decision to make lemonade out of lemons. *Literally.* She yelped in surprise as we appeared and began yanking her dress back down.

"Are you fucking kidding me?" another asked. "We've been waiting out here so you two—" Bryan must've been right on our heels, because she added a whispered, "Three," while looking both men up and down approvingly.

One woman began clapping as she swayed unsteadily on her feet. "You go, girl. Get it!"

They thought that I did... with Jake... and Bryan. At the same time. I made the mistake of looking up at both of them and my ears grew hot.

Thinking of Bryan turned my stomach, but Jake—I could clearly picture him holding me up against a wall and the way the sweat would bead on his brow as he...

A flush crept up my neck, quickly followed by a tingling sensation.

He blinded me with a panty-melting smirk, and I sucked a ragged breath, knowing what was about to happen. Jake wasn't going to let me off the hook that easily; no, he was going to go for my jugular.

His hand moved down to rest against my shoulder and, as if on cue, he drew his badge. "Ladies, I'm sorry to have kept you waiting. We've apprehended the suspect and should be out of your way shortly."

"What did she do?" one asked with wide eyes and I realized it was the girl who'd been doing blow off the counter. Like she had any right to judge me.

"Public lewdness. Isn't that right, Bryan?" Jake growled.

Holy hell.

Bryan reluctantly looked up from where he'd been ogling my ass. "Uh, yes. Lewd acts in the, uh, in the bathroom."

Instead of threatening to disembowel us, the women grew louder. Not with threats of violence, but with offers to be frisked and hand-cuffed, among other things.

"Ma'am, I'm going to need you to come with me." Jake pinned my bicep in his gargantuan hand.

I pasted a fake smile onto my face and dutifully let Jake lead me back downstairs, amid a crowd of very thirsty women. My claws were just itching to come out every time one of them approached him.

I found Aaris hovering near the bar and offered a hesitant wave. She frowned and turned away in response. A man chose that moment to approach the bar and palm Aaris's ass, much to the amusement of his buddies seated nearby.

Jake's jaw clenched and he gave me a pointed stare as we moved past the bar and out onto the patio.

"What?" I yelled. "What's that look for?"

He flashed his badge at a group of people and took over the newly vacated sectional next to a large fire pit. "I think you and I both know."

I looked around the nearly empty patio. "Where's Bryan? Wasn't he right behind us?"

The vein in his neck jumped. "If he knows what's good for him, he'll stay in his office. What's going on with you and Aaris?"

"Sounds like you like Bryan about as much as Aaris does."

He flagged down a cocktail waitress and ordered another dirty martini for me and a beer for himself. "I thought I was supposed to stay sober... keep my wits about me."

He frowned and tapped at his phone. "Yeah, well, now might be a good time for you to lose your wits." When he finished, he looked up at me. "What happened back there? You suddenly can't handle your drugs?"

The waitress walked back up and I snatched the martini from her tray before taking a loud slurp from the glass.

Jake sat back with his beer. "Nice, Hayden. Real nice."

"Sober as a judge, officer," I mumbled into the briny liquid. "Public lewdness, that's a new one. And here I thought murder was my only crime."

He propped his feet up on the table between us. "What would

you rather I have said? That you got high and locked yourself in the bathroom because 'someone was out to get you?'" His phone vibrated and he glanced down at it, his smirk fading slightly.

I cleared my throat and he looked up in a daze. "Where was I? Oh right, getting high and making bad decisions..."

I tuned out of his lecture and focused on his facial expressions. He was hiding something from me. His smile was forced, and his eyes went grim every time his phone lit up with a text.

I took another long drink of martini and nodded when it seemed appropriate, trying my best to channel the correct level of shame I was supposed to be feeling.

"So, do we have a—" Jake's phone buzzed, and he began scanning the patio. There were only a handful of people brave enough to withstand the cold air and none of them looked the least bit threatening.

It was funny. Jake's heart to heart almost made me forget that I hadn't imagined what happened in that bathroom. Almost.

"What's the matter," I teased. "Did you see one of your exes?"

He continued watching the people, both inside and outside the bar, not even cracking a smile at my joke.

"Jake?" I tried again.

"Not now, Hayden." He tapped something into his phone and placed it face down on his thigh.

I strained to see what he'd seen, but the inside of the bar was packed. "Did you see someone? Do you believe me now?"

He scratched absently at his temple before making eye contact with me and I swore that he'd grown another foot since we arrived. Maybe it was just the menacing look on his face that made him seem ten feet tall.

"Hayden," he chided. "Just sit back and enjoy your drink like I am." With that, he took a swig of beer and screwed up his face.

I sucked an olive into my mouth and chewed it happily. "I am enjoying myself but, as much as I'd love to sit and watch you choke down another beer that you absolutely hate, I kinda need to go talk to Aaris."

"Just, uh, stay where I can see you. I don't want to have to go searching for you when I'm ready to leave." He tipped the bottle back, looking completely at home on the sectional.

I couldn't help but notice the way his hand moved down to his waist. Guns weren't allowed inside the club, but the Jake I'd written had a holster hidden in the back of jeans. I suspected that the man in front of me did as well. He wasn't going into any situation unarmed.

I needed to find Aaris and apologize, but then, I was absolutely going to find out what Jake was keeping from me. I slipped around the horde of people stacked three deep at the bar, standing on tiptoe in my search for her familiar face.

My stomach gave an anxious lurch when I found her behind the bar with Jack and I suddenly needed the ladies room again.

"I tried the one upstairs. No, it's got little yellow placards outside the door and a sign that says out of order."

I froze at the conversation. Why would the bathroom be closed off? Hadn't Jake made it clear that he didn't buy the whole 'murderer in the bathroom' story?

I checked to see if Jake was watching and found him pacing the patio with his phone held to his ear. Knowing I wouldn't get another opportunity, I ran upstairs.

The girls hadn't been lying. Not only had the bathroom been cordoned off with caution signs, there was also a line of yellow tape blocking off most of the hallway too.

The music still pulsed beneath my feet, but it was quiet. Too quiet. I ducked underneath the tape and padded toward the door, resting my cheek against its cold wooden surface.

I jumped at the sound of a low groan. Someone was in the bathroom... *again*. A smart person would've booked it downstairs, but I'd never been accused of being one of those.

Besides, what if the person moaning was just the latest victim of ~~The Hooker~~ ~~The Hook Hand Killer~~ The Killer With a Hook for a Hand?

Well, it needed some work, but I had time to come up with some-thing clever later. Right now, someone needed my help.

"Yes, Janet, I did put myself in grave danger despite everything urging me not to. Even when the world disagreed, I knew that danger lurked in that bathroom and I wasn't going to rest until everyone was safe. I just asked myself, what would Jessa Hopkins—"

I pushed at the same time someone opened the door from the other side and I ended up falling right into a broad body.

FOURTEEN

"MAX?"

His hands went to my shoulders. "Hayden? Are you okay?"

"I thought..." I struggled to see around him. "I thought I heard something. What are you doing here?"

"Uh, taking care of a few things. Who's Janet?"

I frowned. "I don't know what you're talking about. I don't know a Janet." Even as I said it, my cheeks heated.

Max gave me a bemused smile. "You sure about that? You seemed to be having quite the conversation with her out in the hall."

"I have no idea what you're talking about." I laughed easily, but my relief at finding a familiar face was short-lived as another low grown sounded from somewhere near one of the back stalls.

"Uh, Max?" I questioned as I tried to move forward. His wall of a body prevented my efforts. "Max, what's going on?"

What if it had been him this entire time? He was there when I got the email and now he just appeared from nowhere after I was almost gutted. It didn't leave me feeling very Zen.

He casually drummed his fingers against his leg and smiled at me, like we were waiting in line to buy movie tickets, not hiding out in the women's bathroom. "So, how's Jake doing?"

I stepped back, colliding with the tile wall that I'd found so mesmerizing only a few hours ago. Now, it was nothing more than a barrier.

He placed an arm on either side of my head. "Why'd you come up here?"

"Please..." a voice whispered harshly. "Please, help me."

Max gave me a half shrug and a grin that seemed to convey he was just full of secrets. He had Nicolas Cage-level crazy eyes. How had I not seen that before?

I wondered if Jake would even notice that I was gone again. Would he come looking for me a second time or had this been his plan all along?

Maybe he and Max had been working together to take me down. I bet they'd formed some fictional character alliance, destroying the authors who'd given them a voice.

I glanced toward the door and then back up at him. There was a slight chance that I could slip under his arm and make it to safety before he murdered me to death, but was I willing to leave Groaning Greg behind?

I chewed at my lower lip as I debated the pros and cons. Surprisingly, Max seemed content to remain standing by the wall. That was probably what Jake had meant when he said that Max was good at what he did.

An efficient killer had to be patient above all else.

A quick, high-pitched burst of laughter escaped, and I clapped a hand to my mouth in horror. Now was not the time to crack up. "I think I need to go back downstairs," I mumbled against my fingers.

Max nodded. "That's a good idea. Go find Jake." He gestured for me to go ahead of him, but I'd seen enough thrillers to know how that was going to end. I wasn't getting capped by some fictional character I barely knew.

I waved my hand. "Oh no, after you. Please."

Once he turned his back, I bolted across the bathroom to where the sounds of moaning had emanated. When I rounded the corner, I stopped in my tracks.

The man lay in a heap on the tile. His wrist was cuffed to the doorjamb of the stall above his head, twisting his arm at a weird angle. His face was bruised, and both eyes were almost swollen shut, but surprisingly, there was very little blood. I took another step forward before stopping again.

I knew him.

"He's the guy who grabbed Aaris," I said dumbly while pointing.

Max hadn't run after me. No, he'd simply strolled over and was leaning against the wall with his thumbs in the front pockets of his jeans.

"Yeah," he stated in a flat voice.

Nothing seemed to phase this guy. He'd been in this bathroom for who knew how long, methodically torturing Groper Greg, yet he stood against the wall as casual as could be.

Someone could burst in and excitedly shout that the building was on fire and Max would probably just give a brief nod before moseying down to the exit when it suited him. There was just no reaction. The man was a stone-cold killer.

"I thought... I thought that you were in here because of what happened to me," I breathlessly stated. My stomach had gone fluttery on me and I was instantly regretting that second martini.

He shook his head. "No. Well, partly. I wasn't able to find the subject."

He walked over and opened up the door to a supply closet. "I'm thinking that the agent who sent you the threats was here tonight and they left right through this window. Maybe they knew we were babysitters. It could be that they're either a sleeper or operating naked—could even be a swallow."

"Of course. I hadn't considered that, um, possibility," I responded somberly. I had no idea what half of the words he'd just used meant, but he used them as if he thought I did.

It wasn't like he was going to suddenly demand, "What does operating naked mean? What's a sleeper, Hayden? Tell me, damn it!" I was a writer of thrillers. Obviously, I already knew those things.

And, if he did ask, I would just say that the villains in my stories operated clothed and didn't like swallowing. Easy peasy.

"Classic E&E. I kept up surveillance and found Chuckles here harassing the staff—"

"Harassing the staff or harassing Aaris?"

He gave a heavy sigh. "Does it make a difference?"

I nodded wisely. "It does, actually. Because if it's just some random staff member, then it's like a Good Samaritan act. If it's Aaris, then that changes things."

"How?"

I groaned loudly, startling Groping Greg out of his dazed stupor. "How? You took her home and, instead of leaving your number, you left her with the contact info for AA."

Max rubbed at his chin, obviously lost in thought. "I use burners, so my number's always different and she does drink too much. Plus, people spend way too much time attached to the damn things. I fail to see how any of that relates to this though."

I threw up my hands in frustration. "You made her think you liked her and this!" I pointed at Greg. "This is just confusing things!"

"Who said I didn't like her?"

"But you... you just left," I finished weakly.

"Does Jake know you're here?"

I shook my head. "No. Does he know you're here?"

He cocked his head to the side with a frown. "Who do you think called me? I was already on surveillance, so he reached out to me as soon as he got the door unlocked—"

I held up my hand. "Wait. You're trying to tell me that Jake called you down here?"

Max nodded nonchalantly. "Yeah, he wanted to stay with you, so he had me keep watch here...see what intel I could gather."

"But, then why the hell did he make me feel like I hallucinated the entire thing?" My mind raced like I'd missed some crucial point in the conversation.

Max shrugged as he knelt next to Greg. "I don't know. Maybe he thought you'd freak out if you knew that someone attempted to kill you. Some people react poorly to that, I guess."

I shook my head. Assassins were weird.

Had he really believed I was in danger? If so, then why try to convince me that it was all in my head?

"I'm, uh, I'm just gonna walk out the, um," I paused, trying to rein my thoughts into something resembling sentences.

Max stood up quickly and faced me. "Okay. Just keep your focus on the door." Having issued his strange warning, he turned his attention back to the unconscious man on the floor.

I bit my lip, debating whether or not to ask him to elaborate before deciding that it was better to just leave. I had to still be in shock. A normal person would've been rocking on the floor by now.

I sucked in a gasp as I passed the mirror. The middle section of glass had been shattered from one end to the other in a perfect line.

The crunching and scraping I'd heard had been this; I was certain of it. This was what Max hadn't wanted me to see. I'd missed it before; with Jake rushing to get me downstairs.

Jake.

I stumbled out of the bathroom and fell into the wall of the small alcove, struggling to hold myself up like a drunk. And maybe I was; because suddenly Jake 'I only care about myself' Hopkins was keeping secrets in an attempt to protect me.

My head spun with nonsensical images as I clung to the wall. Jake and yoga bendy pretzel shapes. "Don't let me down, wall. Keep me up just a little bit longer."

Using it for support, I managed to make it to the staircase. The man dominating my thoughts stood at the bottom with a panicked look on his face. Once he saw me, he visibly relaxed and without my trusty wall there to support me, my knees gave out.

"Jake couldn't be less interested in me—all we talked about was you."

He cared about me; maybe not in a, *'let's get married and have a house full of cats together,'* kind of way, but it was still a step up from, *'if you get dead, I can't get back in the story.'*

He knelt next to me, not even winded from his jog up the stairs. "Are you okay? Did something happen?" He brushed the hair back out of my face, and I wanted to weep at the contact.

Why couldn't he have been real?

"I—" I choked. "I think I want to go home now."

I'd find Aaris first thing tomorrow and apologize, but right now I needed my bed and a plan that got Jake his story without me losing my heart in the process.

"I'M READY."

Jake turned away from the *Angel of Death* manuscript. "Do you have anything that doesn't have a goddamn cat on it?"

"Why, what's wrong with my shirts?" I pulled the material away from my body and looked down at it.

Calm Your Kitties.

It was adorable and I didn't see the problem.

"Because in case you hadn't noticed, we're trying to solve a fucking investigation and your shirts are distracting."

"So, stop staring at them."

He'd been like this all day; snapping at me over the smallest slights.

"Is it typical for you to throw your used tissues on your desk?" He'd examined the pile with the same look of horror and revulsion that one might have if they found a cockroach on their dinner plate.

It wasn't my fault that my nose ran due to allergies. And really, I was being environmentally conscious by conserving my tissues for future use.

Of course our ceasefire after the club incident had only lasted for the night. By the next morning, it was back to business as usual. As if his hand hadn't rested against my knee for most of the drive home, squeezing every so often just to make sure I was still with him. As if he hadn't continuously asked me how I was doing or offered to stop and get some food.

Where I'd gone to bed completely convinced that he had feelings for me, I woke up in a completely different world. One where Jake was just a detective who wanted to get home and I was nothing more than a means to an end.

He clenched and unclenched his jaw. "You stick out like a flashing neon sign. I'm trying not to draw attention to us everywhere we go, okay? No cats. You with me now?"

He turned to the computer and I mouthed the words at his back before flipping him off.

"I saw that," he responded dryly. "Instead of wasting more of our time, you could be changing."

And we were back to being enemies. I briefly wondered if Max had told him that I'd gone back to the bathroom last night. Maybe that was the cause of all of this. He'd told me to stay put and I hadn't listened.

"And what's with Jessa?" He pointed at the screen. "It's like she's seconds away from slitting her damn wrists—"

"What do you mean? She's grieving the loss of her brother and trying to figure out what happened," I protested around the lump in my throat. I'd thought the story was starting to come together.

He pushed the laptop screen down to the keyboard with an ominous click before dragging his hand through his hair. "That's just it. You're so presumptuous—thinking you know everything there is to know about the Hopkins clan. Here's a newsflash: I haven't spoken to Jessa since I joined the department."

"But, you knew what she was doing and you said how she was as a person; it just seemed like you two were close."

He'd said that, hadn't he?

His hand dropped from his hair down to the back of his neck. "I keep in touch with my parents. They give updates, but it's not like I need to reach out to her, you know?"

I felt like a child; one who'd spent too much time playing make-believe. I'd made a major mistake by assuming I knew their family dynamic.

Once upon a time, I sat down and wrote what was in my head, researching the details as they came up. Now, I no longer knew the rules to a game that I'd mastered since I was a kid.

How was I supposed to write a novel when the major characters were keeping crucial details from me?

"I... I just thought—" I began.

He cut me off. "What, Hayden? You thought that after spending a week together that you'd somehow have the whole story? That we'd have a few drinks and I'd forget why I was here? Can you please just go change so we can leave?"

He growled the last part and the lump in my throat grew until it stretched against my skin painfully. Because he was right. I'd hoped that after some time together, he'd see that I wasn't out to destroy anyone's life. I'd stupidly thought that he'd eventually want to be my friend.

"Where are we going?" I managed softly.

He massaged his forehead with his thumb and middle finger. "Dinner. I need some air. I can't stay cooped up in this apartment. So, if it's alright with you, I'd really like for you to change clothes so that we can get the hell out of here. Bring your notebook, I'll give you some plot tips."

I dug my fingernails into my palms, leaving little crescent moon shapes of anger embedded in the skin. I was going to be convicted of murder before this book was done.

"Oh, I've got just the thing," I bit out.

I pulled the black blazer from the back of my closet and dusted the shoulders off, deciding to pair it with the dark skinny jeans and leopard print stilettos.

Now, there'd only be a fourteen-inch difference between us. Just to level the playing field.

I hadn't planned on wearing makeup or styling my hair, but knowing that he was anxiously waiting to leave in the other room suddenly left me with the desire to make him wait as long as possible.

I frowned at my reflection in the bathroom mirror and began the arduous task of digging through my makeup bag for the products that had all but guaranteed to take me from sleepless zombie to a red carpet ready A-lister.

My eyebrows looked like angry caterpillars who'd been woken up before they could transform into beautiful butterflies. I grabbed the tweezers with a sigh and tweaked out a few hairs until they resembled something seen on humans again.

I carefully applied eyeliner and mascara, taking my time to add loose curls to my long chestnut-colored hair. I slipped my glasses back on to observe my handiwork.

Maybe Jake saw me as pathetic for flirting with the bartender, but as I pushed my lips into a pout and coated them in blood-red lipstick, it hit me. He was so obsessed with proving that I didn't know anything about him when in reality, he knew nothing about me.

I was a goddamn catch.

Deciding that my look was complete, I fired off text number eleven to Aaris. None of them had been read and even though her car was in the parking lot, she hadn't answered the door when I'd gone over earlier today.

This was worse than the fight we had in high school when she'd insisted that the Mona Lisa had been painted by Leonardo DiCaprio; or the time we went to a concert and I spent all of our extra money buying each of us a shirt from the nice man hanging around outside the bathrooms.

Shirts that had half of the concert dates and locations cut off on the back.

I buttoned up the blazer and checked my phone again. I'd just go over there after dinner and bang on the door until she let me in.

"Hayden, sometime this century!" Jake growled in his Batman voice.

"Coming, Satan," I muttered under my breath.

FIFTEEN

THE DRIVE to the restaurant was silent, which suited me just fine. Jake flipped through radio stations while I tried to distract myself from the fact that Aaris still hadn't responded to my texts.

I checked emails, scrolled through all of my social media accounts, gagging when I saw my brother's smug face in yet another random city. It didn't help. I still had this sinking feeling in the pit of my stomach that I may have gone too far with what I said.

"This place seems casual," I noted dryly, as Jake parallel parked in front of a large glass building with stone columns flanking the front doors. Two stone lions glared straight ahead, daring us to try to enter their fine establishment.

"That's because it is. You eat too much fast food; I thought it'd be good to get something good into you."

I bit down on the corner of my lip and turned back to my window with a grin. I'd been trying to get something good into me since he'd shown up.

"What?" he demanded. "What did I say?"

"Nothing. Let's eat. I'm starving."

He helped me down from the truck and handed the keys over to the valet before leading me past the beasts of the apocalypse. I tried to ignore the heat from his hand as it pressed against the small of my back and the way it made me want to rub my head against him like Bootsy did when she was marking her territory.

The hostess gave me a polite smile before her eyes moved up to rest on the mountain of a man behind me. I had to admit that he was impossible to miss in the charcoal gray suit that had to be custom made to fit him the way it did.

And I was clearly underdressed.

Her eyes turned feral as they moved back down to me, clearly sizing me up for a fight. I crossed my arms and stared her down.

"Just two?" She looked up toward Jake, dismissing me.

"Just two," he replied with a smirk, as she led us past cloth-covered tables to a booth in the back.

I determined that, along with citrus and spice, there appeared to be a distinct undertone of *ménage à trois* layered into his cologne.

"Your server will be right with you," she said while giving him what was probably her best seductive pout.

I waited until she gave up and walked off before rolling my eyes and pantomiming jacking off into my hand. Jake pretended not to notice as he looked down at his phone, but I was certain I saw the corner of his lip turn up.

"Is it warm in here, Jake?"

He looked up with a frown. "No. Why?"

"I'm feeling a little warm." I stood up and unbuttoned the blazer and his eyes turned murderous.

"What. The. Fuck?" he bit out through a clenched jaw.

"Is something wrong? Are you hot too?" I grinned before slipping back into the booth.

I pointed at my *Detective Claws: Solving Mysteries with Purrfect Precision* shirt. "Oh, do you have a problem with this? I thought it was *purrfect* for solving investigations. Isn't that what you said we were doing?"

He pinched the bridge of his nose and picked his phone up again.

"I thought we agreed that you were going to pick something without a cat on it."

"That's the thing. The only things I have without cats on them are cut down to here." I ran the back of my hand down the center of my chest, stopping in between my tits. "And that just doesn't seem appropriate for a professional dinner, does it?"

He shifted in the booth and picked at the sleeves of his suit jacket, suddenly doing everything in his power to avoid making eye contact with me.

"Hello there. How are you doing this evening?" our waitress asked before placing a hard-backed menu in front of Jake. She didn't even spare me a glance as she dropped a paper menu and crayons in front of me.

I stared down at it in confusion. It was a kid's menu, which was puzzling on multiple levels. This didn't seem like a place that catered to the twelve and under crowd and I had passed the cut-off fifteen years ago.

"Uh." I held up my hand. "What is this?"

She looked down at me with her highly glossed lips turned up into a condescending grin. She'd probably applied it specifically for Jake's benefit. "Is there a problem? Would you like some different crayon colors, sweetie?"

I watched Jake, waiting for him to intervene. He was a decent human; surely he wasn't going to let her get away with talking to me like I was three.

Sensing my stare, Jake looked over his menu at mine and smirked. "You know, I think we might need a booster seat. She can barely reach her water glass."

I ground my molars together and growled, "Martini. Top shelf. And an adult menu if you think you can manage such a difficult task."

"Oh, sweetie, I'm sorry," she purred. "But I'm going to need to see some ID."

Jake chuckled and brought the menu back up over his face with a whispered, "Good luck," as I dug around in my purse for my driver's license.

"Here." I slapped it into her palm.

She frowned and brought it up to her face. "Five-one... wow. And what about you, big guy?"

He gave her a panty-melting smile. "I'll have the Pappy's, on the rocks. Thanks."

She handed me my ID and disappeared. Meanwhile, I continued staring daggers until he gave up any pretense of looking over the menu.

"What?" he grunted.

"Why—" Wet anger crept into my voice and I paused until it seemed to pass. He wasn't worth my tears. "Why did you do that? Why would you go along with her?"

He shrugged. "I thought we were just having fun."

"Oh, silly me. Fun. Of course." I looked down and began rifling through my purse. I needed a distraction before I launched my probably expensive water goblet across the table.

"Hayden, I wasn't try—"

"Oh, it's fine. I get it. We're not friends."

I waited in vain for him to apologize, but he didn't say another word. We sat in silence until our drinks arrived and I immediately ordered another before draining the glass in front of me. "Just keep them coming."

After everything I'd done for him, he was just going to let people talk down to me? So, maybe I'd thrown him off a building. That was in the past.

By the time the fourth martini arrived, I was picking olives out of the empty glasses with my fingernails and devouring them in the hopes that they'd sober me up, while Jake watched me with a horrified expression.

They were full of protein, weren't they?

Jake had suggested the lobster and crab cakes and prosciutto-wrapped mozzarella, but I hadn't wanted to fill up on appetizers.

Well, that, and I took sick pleasure in denying the Titan his pre-meal.

I tore into another olive, wondering what the hell kind of fancy restaurant didn't serve bread? How was I supposed to soak up all the alcohol?

"I'll be right back," I mumbled before sliding out of the booth. My hip caught the edge as I stood up, sending a cascade of water down the side of my glass and onto the pristine tablecloth.

Jake reached for my hand. "Hey, are you okay?"

I nodded. "Yep." *Other than this inexplicable desire to pelt you in the head with the cutlery.*

I stumbled into the bathroom and immediately checked for supply closets with secret windows before slipping into an empty stall.

What a damn prick.

This was the nicest restaurant I'd ever been in and I couldn't even enjoy myself. I swallowed hard and blinked until my vision cleared.

How had I let myself get tied up in knots over what a fictional character thought of me?

I was going to march back out there and enjoy my seared tuna and ginger rice. And once I'd sobered up a bit, I was going to give him a piece of my mind.

I worked on my speech while washing my hands. I'd tell him to put down his damn phone and have a conversation with me, for starters. Then, I'd demand to see a manager over the way the staff was treating me; judging by the prices on the menu, they were going to need to comp about ninety percent of the meal in order for me to afford it.

I nodded to my reflection and Detective Claws before grabbing a small terrycloth towel from the intricately woven basket on the counter.

It was a good plan.

"What a mess—do we need to get her a sippy cup?" Slutty Susan the Server giggled as she put our food down, leaning over just enough to ensure that Jake could see down her shirt.

I stepped behind a column, anxiously awaiting his response.

Please tell her to fuck off... please tell her to fuck off, I repeated in my head.

I wouldn't have let anyone speak about him like that. I'd gotten defensive when Aaris suggested that he was behind the death threats.

Jake looked down at his plate and then back up at her. "Could I get some steak sauce?"

Could I get some steak sauce?

It was one thing for him to read my bad reviews and tease me over them, but to let a perfect stranger tear me to shreds because of my height, while remaining silent? Was he fucking kidding?

Something I had absolutely no control over was tonight's main attraction. And the man who'd sworn to keep me safe just betrayed me in the worst way.

You are calm. You are centered. You are balanced. You are safe— you are going to kick some motherfucking ass.

I had been stressing about his story, doing my best to make it perfect. Well, no more Ms. Nice Writer. I stepped around Susan and slid into the booth with a low growl.

Jake looked at me with a content smile. "I'm glad you're back. I was about to gnaw my arm off waiting for you."

Was this before or after you gnawed off some of the buttons on Susan's shirt?

"I'll be back with that sauce," she said with a wink before disappearing.

"She is soooooooo nice, isn't she? Taking such good care of you."

His eyebrows drew together. "Are you okay?"

I laughed. "Why wouldn't I be? Everything is just so nice."

He pointed to my plate. "You're not even cutting your food... just your plate. Are you sure you're feeling alright?"

I dropped my knife onto the plate and retrieved my notebook from my purse. "I'm fine, silly. Eat up."

Jake cut into his tenderloin while keeping a wary eye on me. I flipped through the notebook until I came to a blank page.

"Oh good, you're going to get some writing done after all," he said around a mouthful of steak.

I smiled up at him sweetly. "Of course. I know how important it is to you."

If you pissed off a writer, you died in the next book. It was as simple as that. Unfortunately, I'd already thrown this one off a building. I was going to have to get a little creative.

Jake sat across from the mysterious brunette in one of the city's swankiest restaurants. It was supposed to have been a nice dinner between friends, yet Jake hadn't appeared to notice anything beyond the medically enhanced breasts on the female waitstaff. The brunette had been patient and accommodating for as long as possible.

He paused with the fork halfway to his mouth and frowned. "Hayden?"

I shuddered with barely concealed rage but continued writing. Within seconds, all traces of humor had vanished from Jake's face as he slid free from the booth and moved to the center of the room.

Holy shit.

It was working.

"Hayden, don't you do it," he warned, even as his hands moved up toward his face.

He was suddenly overcome with a need to express himself through dance. How else would the waitress know his true feelings?

Jake's arms and legs moved as if they were connected by a string. He was the perfect marionette, throwing his elbows back in sync with his legs.

Our waitress froze with the bottle of steak sauce in her hand. "Is he... doing the Running Man?"

I tried and failed to hold in my triumphant grin. "Why, yes. Yes, he is. And that one would be the Macarena."

From across the room, Jake noticed the dashing gentleman having a quiet dinner with his wife. His hair was combed over in a style quite popular with the men over seventy and although he was trying to be sly, Jake knew that this was a very special meal for him.

When I scratched out the next part, his nostrils flared in anger. *You wouldn't*, he mouthed.

I sank my teeth into my lower lip and nodded happily.

Oh, yes I would.

He sauntered over to the man's table. "Excuse me, sir," he nodded. "Ma'am. I understand that someone here is having a birthday."

The man frowned and shook his head, his heavy jowls swaying back and forth from the movement. "Young man, I believe you're mistaken."

I took a bite of my tuna and moaned in ecstasy. And then, because I was such a good friend, I snagged the lobster tail off of Jake's plate before it went cold.

Several of the tables were under the impression that his antics were some weird mid-dinner skit and had turned away from their tables to watch.

Jake brought his hands up to frame his eyes and gave a soft chuckle before leaning down. "Hap-py Bi-rth-day to you..." He crooned breathlessly. "Hap-py Birthday... to you... Hap-py Birthday, Mr. President. Happy Birthday to you."

The other diners clapped softly as Jake blew the man a kiss. I raised my glass in a toast. "To the birthday boy!"

The man looked like he was on the verge of having a massive coronary and his wife kept looking around the room in confusion.

I rested my forehead against my arm and shook with laughter as he stormed over to the table for act three.

Jake knew that he now had the female's attention and there was only one way to claim her as his for all eternity.

He sidled up next to Susan and jerkily extended his right leg. "You put your right leg in..."

I cracked open the lobster tail with my knife and fork. "You put your right leg out?"

His jaw clenched and he bit out, "Yep, that's it. You put your right leg in, and you shake it all about. You do the... hokey pokey... and you ... turn yourself around. That's what's it all about."

Slutty Susan began stumbling over her words. "Okay, big guy. I think maybe you've had too much. Why don't you have a seat right here with your, um, friend—"

She continued stammering out half-sentences while looking to me for help.

"But, what if that is what it's all about?" I asked around a piece of buttery lobster.

Even the hostess had abandoned her stand to witness the debacle, along with several members of the kitchen crew.

Jake sat back down in the booth with a thud and growled, "Are we done here?"

I continued chewing and nodded to poor Susan. "Sweetie, can you bring us the check and box these up? Jake, you barely touched your tenderloin. And the lobster tail—" I gave her a thumb's up. "Definitely top-notch."

The fork that was still in Jake's hand was bending under the strain of his fist. "Give me the goddamned pen," he demanded once she was gone.

I handed it over with a satisfied smirk and leaned back in the booth. He dropped it into his suit pocket and stared down at the empty table as anger rolled off of him in waves.

Susan came back with our doggie bags and the check, which she automatically slid toward Jake. I stopped her with my hand. "Oh, I've got it."

Jake kept both hands flat on the table, not bothering to look up at either one of us.

I opened it and nearly choked. It was double what I spent on groceries every two weeks. I dug around in my purse for my emergency credit card. "Here we are."

She took it but lingered for a few extra moments in the hopes that Jake would snap out of his stupor and beg her to date him. I'd sort of expected him to come to and offer to pay the damn bill, seeing as to how it was his idea to come here.

Obviously having given up, Susan sent the manager out with my card and a strong suggestion to never come back again. I slipped the credit card back into my wallet and signed the receipt, adding a $.10 tip before scrawling in the margin, *Children are just terrible with math.*

Jake suddenly stood up and yanked me from the booth amid appreciative applause from several nearby tables. I fought to get my arms into my blazer while giving them the royal wave.

I stopped to pet the stone lions before being dragged over to the valet stand. "Hey, I wasn't done with those pussies," I protested.

He handed the ticket over and turned to me with a growl. "I'm going to beat you."

I wrenched my arm from his grip. "Yeah, well, unless it's with your dick, don't bother," I snapped as I buttoned the blazer and adjusted my purse.

His eyes widened in shock. "What the hell did you just say?"

I looked up at him demurely, feeling the heat from his stare as it blazed against my skin. "Uh, I said don't bother."

I really thought I'd said that in my head.

"Why the fuck would you do that?"

"I thought we were having fun."

"Fun? You call that fun?" His voice went up in volume and I jumped. "I made a fucking fool of myself back there and for what—some revenge plot against the waitress?"

"You made fun of me," I murmured like a petulant child.

"Jesus, Hayden." He ran his hands through his hair. "I wanted to take you out to have a real meal. Yeah, I may have gone too far with the teasing, but once you told me you were uncomfortable, I stopped." He scowled at me from under the streetlight, his eyes positively murderous.

But, he hadn't stopped.

"Instead of sticking up for me, you asked for the steak sauce. You let her treat me like I was a small child!"

"Do you hear yourself?" he hissed. "What was I supposed to do; make a big scene and get us thrown out? I ignored her, thinking that she'd take the hint and go away. It's the same reason I stopped reading the negative reviews to you. Because I realized how much it was hurting you. I'm not perfect, but goddamn, I'm trying here."

Suddenly, the game no longer seemed fun. I'd humiliated Jake and probably convinced our waitress to look at a new profession all because of my own insecurities. I was a complete idiot.

He continued tersely. "From now on, it's strictly business."

"Until when?" I blurted out defiantly. "The next pair of tits distracts you and I end up trapped in a bathroom with a psychopath?"

Jake's truck arrived with a deep rumble, effectively ending any further conversation between us. The driver came around and helped me up into the passenger seat and I turned until I was facing the window.

The drive back went about as well as the drive to the restaurant had gone, only this time there was no music to break up the silence.

I trudged up the stairs and into the apartment where Bootsy greeted me with an impatient yowl before kneading at my legs. "Not now," I mumbled.

I wasn't sure whether I wanted to cry or vomit... or both. The door slammed shut behind Jake and I jumped. It was definitely going to be both.

"Jake, can we talk?"

He put the boxes of food in the refrigerator and turned to me. "Sure." He walked back out of the apartment, rattling the wall as the door banged closed behind him.

"Okay, I'm just gonna take that as a no."

Bootsy ran to the door, meowing for all she was worth.

"Yeah, good luck, sister. I don't think he's coming back." Then, I laid down on the couch and cried myself to sleep.

"HAYDEN."

I flinched but kept my eyes closed. "Shhh... I don't wanna lose my sleep."

"Hayden. Look at me."

I blinked up at Jake, lit by the moonlight streaming in from the door to the balcony. "You came back." My voice had gone scratchy like sandpaper thanks to my tears.

He tucked a strand of hair behind my ear and pulled me into a sitting position. "I came back. I've been thinking about what you said back at the restaurant. Do you blame me for what happened at the club?"

I stretched like a cat and yawned. "I don't. This whole thing is just really confusing, you know?"

The coffee table creaked as he settled his weight on it. "I do. It'd be a lot to take in under normal circumstances, but I'm not going to stop until I find this person—"

"Why did you let me think that I'd imagined what happened at *Magenta*? You knew someone was in there with me and that they broke the mirror."

Jake looked down and nodded. "I thought it'd be better if you didn't know. I thought that you'd become too scared to leave your apartment and I didn't want you living in fear like that. I knew, and that was all that mattered."

I swallowed past the lump in my throat. "Thank you for that and for coming back. I thought you were gone forever," I finished with a weak laugh.

"I'm sorry I left. I needed to drive around and clear my head." He stood up and walked to the balcony door and then back over to me. "Have you ever just needed something? To feel it—more than you need your next breath?"

The pulse jumped in my throat and I nodded. "Yes."

This was it. The moment of truth.

His hand cupped my cheek before sliding down to rest against my collarbone. "Because when I looked at you earlier, I needed my hands on your body," he paused to smirk as I moved closer. "After what happened between us at the restaurant, I wanted to wrap my hands around your tiny throat and just squeeze with everything I had."

I fell back against the cushions with a rough exhale. "Really?"

"What? Did you think I meant something else? Were you hoping for it? You can admit it."

I stood up and moved away from him. "Hoping for it? More like hoping it would never happen! Why won't you admit that you've wanted there to be something between us since you got here? One word, Jake. Yoga. You were turned on by me!"

He rolled his eyes and followed me. "Turned on? You grabbed my cock. It doesn't matter who you are; if he gets attention, he's coming out to play."

"You're disgusting. And I didn't intentionally grab your—junk, it was a mistake. If you weren't as big as a damn tree, it wouldn't have been an issue."

"Funny," he said with a smirk. "I've never had a woman refer to it as a tree before."

I dropped my shoulders. "Oh my god, you're such a guy!"

"Yeah? Well, you're a pint-sized pain in my ass!" Jake cut the distance between us in half and I instinctively stepped back, only to collide with the wall.

I forced myself up to my full height and stood toe to toe with him. "There you go again! Making fun of me because I'm smaller than you—"

"You called me a tree!"

"Because you are! You're a goddamn giant—" I froze and stared dumbly at my hands. Hands that I'd thrown up in frustration were now holding onto the lapels of his suit jacket.

Jake followed my line of vision and let out a rough exhale. "Fuck, Hayden."

You can't even begin to fathom the things I'd do if I put my hands on you.

"I'm still very mad at you," I whispered with shrinking resolve. "So. Mad."

"I know." His hands covered mine.

We both struggled to get our next breath while anxiously waiting to see what the other was going to do. He moved until I felt the warmth of every exhale across my skin.

We were rubber bands; each pulled to the limit and any moment now, we were going to snap. He'd make good on his promise of strangling me and that'd be it.

I stared up into his eyes and decided that there were worse ways to go. When he leaned down, I didn't even hesitate. I hooked my hands around his neck and brought his mouth down over mine.

I expected him to fight. I wasn't prepared to feel his full lips moving against mine. I'd been right. His lips were made for mine. He lifted me up into his arms with a growl and I wrapped my legs around his waist, holding on for dear life.

I was kissing Jake.

He was kissing me.

My back connected with the wall and he shifted us until his... tree... was against my... *oh my god.*

The blood thundered in my ears as his teeth caught my lower lip. His hands roamed over my ass, moving me up and down against him until all coherent thought ceased to exist.

We were going to hide out from the person who wanted me dead, right here. Just like this. We'd order our groceries online and make Aaris take Bootsy to the vet. It was going to be perfect.

His right hand moved up into my hair and he twisted it around his fist, angling my head as he saw fit. His tongue slipped into my mouth and I gripped him tightly with my legs as sparks rained down on us.

I'd used him as a puppet back at the restaurant. Now, it was my turn to dance on the strings. I deserved it, and given the outcome, I would take that punishment again and again.

I couldn't remember the last time I'd been kissed like this. Hell, I couldn't remember the last time I'd been kissed, period. What we were doing had moved beyond that and into something deeper.

More, I silently begged as Jake tilted my face up. He squeezed my jaw and brought his mouth down roughly against mine again in response.

His tongue tasted like the whiskey he'd had at dinner—caramel and honey with hints of spice. It reminded me of the clove cigarettes Aaris and I used to smoke in high school when we'd sneak out.

"You're the best thing I've ever written," I mumbled against his lips.

He pulled back abruptly and stared at me with narrowed eyes. "Where is it?" he panted.

I reluctantly removed my hands from the nape of his neck and pointed. "My bedroom? That way."

There were no traces of humor on his face as he lowered me down to the ground and stepped away. I gripped the side of my desk to keep myself from melting into the carpet. "Jake?"

He ran a hand down his face. "The notebook. Where's the notebook?"

I frowned. "In my purse?"

"Jesus," he laughed to himself. "I almost thought this was real."

I shakily held onto the desk and wall for support before gasping, "What the hell? It felt real!"

Instead of crossing the room to take me in his arms before proclaiming, *'our love was always real,'* Jake pushed his lips into a pout and moved even farther away. "Did it? Isn't that how you wrote it?"

I slid down the wall and onto the carpet as my legs gave up the fight. "I'm confused—"

"Are you? Because that makes two of us. Why won't you just confess," he snapped before shoving his hands into the pockets of his slacks.

My eyes followed his hands down to the evidence of our encounter. His friend had not only come out to play but brought along the entire playground for good measure.

Jake cleared his throat and I blinked slowly before looking back up. "I don't understand why you're mad. Did I do something wrong?"

My breath came in short gasps and I closed my eyes, trying to commit every detail to memory. I wanted to remember how he kissed me for the rest of my life. I needed something to hold on to when I was old and gray, wasting away in a nursing home.

When the nurses would ask me, *"Hayden, do you remember this little girl? She's your great-granddaughter,"* I would shake my head and say, *"Don't know her, but I can tell you how it felt to have Detective Jake Hopkins' tongue in my mouth."*

Jake chuckled and my face heated with the thought that he could suddenly read my mind.

"You're a real piece of work, aren't ya? Hand it over."

"Excuse me," I sputtered. "Hand over what?"

"The notebook. I know you've got it. How else would you explain — whatever the fuck that was?"

"You think I wrote this?" My voice cracked. "I didn't, I swear!"

The scene that was playing out in my head fought with the one in front of me, leaving my head swimming. I'd gotten pretty good at predicting where a story would go once I envisioned it, but he'd gone and made it impossible.

Jake stripped off his suit jacket and wadded it into a ball before tossing it onto the couch. "You think I'd suddenly forget what happened at dinner? Have you lost your damn mind?"

I jumped up. "You kissed me back!"

"Yes, because you wrote it," he explained slowly.

I furiously chewed at my swollen lips and ran my fingers over my mantra necklace, but I wasn't calm or grounded... or any of the other bullshit I was supposed to channel.

I slipped my heels back on and snagged my purse from the floor beside the couch.

"Where are you going?" Jake took a tentative step toward me and then stopped, as if I was going to produce my magical notebook and force him to kiss me again.

I sighed, "I'm leaving, Jake. What does it look like?"

"You can't just leave. There's someone out there who wants you dead."

I nodded. "Given the choice between you and the homicidal fan, I'll take my chances with the one out there."

He held out a hand. "Wait. Just let me think."

"There's nothing to think about. I didn't write it. Trust me, if I had, you would've known."

I ticked a point off on my finger. "For starters, I would've written something better than dead fish lips and a partner who didn't put an ounce of effort into it."

That was enough to break the invisible barrier he'd put up

between us and he stomped over to where I stood. "No effort? You enjoyed it, you did the thing with your legs—" He swallowed hard.

I shook my head. "No. No, I didn't."

I left him standing in my living room, looking like a child who'd just been told that Santa wasn't real. The wind whipped my already tangled hair into my face as I made my way downstairs; reminding me of Jake's massive hands twisting and pulling.

A whimper escaped and I pressed a hand to my throat to stop the ache. I wasn't going to cry again. I crossed the courtyard and climbed another four flights before reaching her door.

I didn't care if she was still mad. We were going to stay up and work this out and maybe, just maybe, I'd work out a way to finish Jake's story without ever having to see him again.

SIXTEEN

I KNOCKED on the door and wrapped my arms around myself. "C'mon, Aaris. Just let me in. It's freezing out here."

I frowned at the sound of heavy footsteps coming from inside the apartment and again when the door was pulled open.

"Hayden," he said respectfully before tucking the gun back into his waistband. I tried not to gawk at the fact that he was shirtless. The muscles on his body made that an impossible task; they were practically screaming, *look at us!*

In spite of my confusion, I managed a shaky laugh. "Max. Is Aaris here?"

He nodded. "She's in the shower." His hair was messy, and I tried to decide whether it was from sleep or something else.

I waited patiently for him to push the door open and invite me in. When that didn't happen, I tried again. "May I come in? I need to talk to her."

"Oh. Sure. Come in. Do you like coffee? I was just making a pot."

I stepped into the warmth of her living room and checked my watch. "It's two-thirty, Max. Isn't that a little early for coffee?" I smiled up at him and half a second later he repeated the gesture.

Assassins were odd creatures.

"I like coffee," he stated matter-of-factly before turning away. Any questions as to why his hair was wild were answered by the red scratches running the length of his back.

"Me too," I mumbled. "So, how long have you been here?"

Max checked his watch as the coffee maker fired up. "Twenty-four hours and sixteen minutes."

I raised my eyebrows. "Really? So, you took her home from the... bar?"

He sat down on the arm of the overstuffed chair near the fireplace, watching me curiously. "No. I followed her home."

Did she know that?

I nodded, keeping the question to myself. For now. "I see. I'm just going to get that coffee and leave you to it, then."

"You should reconsider your footwear."

I turned around. "What?"

"Under-pronation can lead to ankle sprains or breaks if you're not careful."

"What are you—an assassin and a foot fortune teller?" I snorted at my own joke. Max remained stone-faced.

"Well, it's apparent that you're a supinator by the way your shoes lean to the left. See how they're worn down more on the outside? The force of impact is concentrated along the edge there, putting more stress on your foot."

"What else can you tell about me just by looking?" I challenged him.

Max narrowed his eyes and looked me over. I sat perfectly still, afraid to move and break his concentration. "You were crying as recently as two hours ago. Your lips are swollen, and the surrounding skin is irritated, indicating recent intimacy... or a severe allergic reaction. The way the pulse just jumped in your throat tells me that it's the first one."

He steepled his hands under his chin. "The person you were intimate with is the reason you're here now. You had a fight, and it led you here. How am I doing so far?"

"Holy shit," I exclaimed reverently. "Max, that's amazing! You should be working with the FBI or writing horoscopes! How did you know?"

"Most of it I picked up on when you were at the door. Jake filled in the rest; said you two got into it and he thought you'd be coming here," he said with a grin.

So, he did have a sense of humor.

I groaned and sank back down on the couch. "Seriously? I thought you were like a psychic or something. What did he say?"

"Exactly what I just told you; you two got into—"

"Okay... I'm clean. You wanna dirty me up again?" Aaris sang from the bedroom.

Max's eyes widened. "That might be a problem. You've got company."

She appeared in the doorway, wrapped in the comforter. Her damp hair was pulled back into a French braid and her cheeks were flushed, making her look younger. "Hayden? What are you doing here?"

I gave a small wave. "Hey, I didn't mean to interrupt—" My words broke off in a sob. "I, I just—"

She took a couple of steps and then paused. "Sweetie, I want to hug you, I do, but I'm not quite decent. Can you hold that thought for like thirty seconds?"

Max patted me roughly on the back, like a choking victim in need of aid. "You came over because you feel badly about the things you said last night and you want to make things right. You also need advice. You have feelings for Jake and that... complicates things."

"Max, can you not with the weird *Long Island Medium* shit? I don't have feelings for Jake and, if Aaris bothered checking her phone, she would know that I've been trying to reach her all day."

"I don't get that reference," he deadpanned. When he didn't crack a smile, I realized that he wasn't joking.

I sighed, "Of course you don't. Just... stop trying to read my mind. Yes, I came to apologize. No, I don't have feelings for Jake."

"Okay, what'd I miss?" Aaris had swapped the comforter out for a pair of baggy sweats and I didn't miss the hungry look in Max's eyes as he watched her stalk toward us.

Someone in this room had caught feelings, but it absolutely was not me.

"Hayden fell for her target."

I glared at Max. "I just finished telling you that I didn't have feelings for him. It's like you're not even listening."

Aaris sank down beside me on the sofa. "Who, Jake? Sweetie, we already knew that. That's why you're here?"

I shook my head in frustration. "No! I mean, partly. God, will you two just give me a second to collect my thoughts?"

"No feelings, no regrets," Max stated flatly as he walked into the kitchen. "Coffee?"

Aaris waved him off. "What happened?"

I took off my glasses and rubbed my eyes. "I don't know. One minute we were ready to kill each other and then he was kissing me. Or maybe I kissed him. I can't even remember, but it's over and we're back to hating each other again. Hooray!"

Tears spilled over onto my cheeks and I swiped angrily at them. "But, that's not why I'm here. What's going on with you two?"

She smiled and glanced toward the kitchen before lowering her voice. "I'm surprised you don't know already. Didn't you help orchestrate the entire thing?"

I frowned. "What I said at the club was wrong and I shouldn't have opened my mouth. I'm sorry. I never meant to hurt you; I was just feeling frustrated by Jake and being at the club and—"

"Then you found me. Let me know what a dick I'd been." Max recited the words much like a newscaster reading from a teleprompter.

"I, um, I..." He gave me a look that convinced me to shut up and nod instead. "Yes. Yes, all that happened. Really gave him an earful about leaving and whatnot."

You know, in between him kicking a guy's ass for touching you.

Aaris cocked her head to the side. "None of that happened, did it?"

Max handed her a steaming mug of black coffee. "It did. She was inebriated. Drink up. It'll get cold."

I leaned down, unable to contain my laughter for a moment longer. The assassin had lied to Aaris. In spite of his social ineptness, he'd somehow managed to bridge mine and Aaris' relationship.

He turned to me. "Hayden, I'm going to get your coffee and then we'll discuss your problem."

"Oh, no, that's really not necessary. I can come back when you're not here or, you know, never."

Max continued into the kitchen and Aaris shrugged. "He's a little different but really nice."

"Aaris, David Bowie in *Labyrinth* was different. Max is... well, Max is something else entirely."

"I heard that," he called from the kitchen.

I cringed. "He's totally going to poison my coffee and then you'll have to finish Jake's book for me. Good luck with that."

Max handed me a mug. "If you hadn't let your emotions get in the way, you wouldn't be rewriting Jake's book. Oh, and if I was going to kill you, you wouldn't see it coming."

"Duly noted." I took a hesitant sip of coffee, recoiling at the bitterness. "Is there creamer or are we being forced to drink it like savages?"

"He's right," Aaris chimed in as she took our mugs back to the kitchen. "You wrote *One in the Chamber* to make a publisher happy. What could Jake's story have been if you'd written for yourself?"

Max raised his eyebrows. "Don't fall for your target. Rule number one: stay professional. In this case, it's already too late for you, so now it's time for a little UW." At my blank expression, he added, "Unconventional warfare."

"Right. Unconventional warfare. That's exactly what I was thinking. Conventional warfare just won't do in this, um, situation."

"Sweetie, just say you have no idea what he's talking about." She handed me my coffee.

"How far are you willing to go to get your story, Hayden? There's sabotage. Hit and run. Ambush. Pick your poison—poison is also a good strategy; a bit overdone with women though."

"Wait. You're suggesting I kill Jake?"

Max nodded. "Pencil through the ear or eye. You're a writer; it'd be believable. I would suggest something less messy, but let's keep it on the table."

I held up my hand to stop him. "Why am I killing Jake again?"

"Because he's forcing you to change the ending to your last book? We don't negotiate with terrorists."

And, apparently, that was the only explanation I was getting.

"Aren't you guys friends, Max?" Aaris asked with a yawn.

"Friends? He paid me for a job and I'm doing it. Whether he lives or dies is not my concern. I got my money."

We both stared at him in horror.

"You can't just kill someone who brought you here!" I exclaimed. "What about the bro code or whatever the hell you guys call it?"

"Bro code? Is this like the medium islands you were talking about earlier?"

Not only was he an assassin, he was a mercenary as well.

"So, you're saying if I offered you money to kill Jake..." I let my voice trail off, waiting for a response.

"Depending on the amount, I'd take it. What? What's wrong with that?"

"Okay, Mr. Roboto. I will keep your offer in mind, but in the meantime, I need to get back to my apartment. I've got to work in a few hours." I drained my coffee mug and carried it to the sink.

"I'm surprised you haven't asked the most pressing question," Max noted dryly.

I forced a laugh. "And what's that? How you'd kill him?"

His mouth turned up in an amused smile. "No. How Jake feels about you."

Aaris bounced up and down on the couch. "Oh, yes. How does Mr. Hopkins feel?"

Max moved over to the couch next to her. "Well..."

I held my breath as I waited for him to finish his sentence. Not that it mattered because Jake was fictional and I was clinically sane. No, I was just holding my breath out of curiosity.

"Well..." I snapped. "Sometime today, Max."

It didn't change a thing.

"Let's just say that he broke protocol pretty early on—"

Aaris interjected, "Max, no. None of your random bodyguard jargon. Tell us in normal terms. Please."

He nodded. "Okay. Jake developed some, unprofessional feelings for Hayden. Is that better?"

I crossed my arms over my chest and rolled my eyes. "Really? That was your big revelation? I already know that he wants to murder me. He even told me how he'd do it."

Max's eyes lit up. "He did? How? Was it strangulation?"

Aaris patted his arm. "That's not really something you should get excited over... or ask about... ever."

I straightened with a sigh. "I'm gonna head home now. Thanks for letting me interrupt your sexathon for a little bit."

I turned away before their eyes went heavy-lidded, like two people who were going to have each other's clothes off before the door had completely closed.

Max's voice stopped me at the door. "I'm not going to lie and say he loves you, mainly because I don't know that he's capable of it, but Jake cares a lot about you and that makes you dangerous."

"I'm dangerous?" My voice went up an octave, and he cringed. "He's the one who barged into my life and demanded a re-write; at gunpoint, I might add!"

"Oh, what's this? Dirt? I'm gonna go grab another shower." Aaris fled the room, leaving me alone with the assassin.

He watched her leave before pinching the bridge of his nose. "You call the shots. You're in charge of his entire life. As a man, that's pretty fucking emasculating, Hayden. He has to be able to trust you to keep you safe from whoever's out there. Just remember that."

I QUIETLY OPENED the apartment door and tiptoed in, doing my best not to disturb Jake. The couch was empty, so I tiptoed down the hallway to my bedroom.

Bootsy lay on the bed with the tablet, happily watching what appeared to be a nature documentary. I gave her a quick scratch behind the ears before checking the bathroom.

Empty.

"Did Jake leave?" I asked the empty room. Bootsy looked up and gave a soft meow before going back to her movie.

I walked back out into the living room. If he left, then I'd have to go and find him. The only problem was I didn't have a phone number or even the slightest idea as to where he may have gone.

The glowing ember of a lit cigarette caught my eye through the vertical blinds, and I stopped pacing.

I slid the door open and stepped out into the cold to face the firing squad. I knew he heard me, but he kept his focus on the court-yard down below. "What happened to all that talk about cigarettes killing you?"

Jake exhaled a stream of smoke. "It will, but maybe I needed to numb myself a little to stay alive, you know?"

I did.

"Which part are you numbing right now?"

He took a long drag, still not looking at me. "Fear."

I laughed, but he continued to stare straight ahead. "C'mon, Jake. You're a detective. What could you possibly be afraid of?"

"You," he exhaled. "You win. I'm tired of trying to prove that I'm not the guy you wrote. So, here we are. I'm smoking. Are you happy now?"

You're in charge of his entire fucking life.

Jake was afraid of me. Given what I'd done to him at the restaurant, I couldn't say that I blamed him.

The smoke rings drifted off the balcony and disappeared before I found my words. "I don't want to fight you anymore."

He stayed silent and for a moment, I thought that maybe he didn't hear me. Then he rolled his eyes and my heart twisted in my chest and I knew that we were never going to be friends.

In fact, we'd be lucky to make it through this alive.

"Since when? You've been fighting me since I showed up. Why the sudden change of heart?"

I sank down into the chair next to his. "Jake, please. What happened at the restaurant was me, I admit it. But, the kiss? I didn't write that, I swear to you."

He pushed his lips out into a pout. "You wrote it. You didn't. I don't even know the difference anymore, Hayden. You want me to believe that you're helping me, but then you pull the shit you did earlier. What am I supposed to think?"

He turned to finally look at me and I was hit with the memory of our kiss. I'd had his hands on my ass twice now. His teeth had been on my lips. His tongue had done things to my tongue that I didn't know were physically possible.

It made me want to weep. I was never going to be kissed like that again. If I was lucky, I'd just live out my days with Bootsy, churning out novels as if I were an authority on love and relationships.

If I proved my family right, then I'd be adding eight to ten cats to the mix, while living in a ratty bathrobe coated in *Cheetos* dust and cat hair.

I wouldn't even make it to the nursing home to regale the staff with my witty stories. I'd just be found a month or two after my death, half-eaten by my horde of cats.

"Hayden?" Jake waved a hand in front of my face.

"I don't want to be eaten by pussies!" I blurted out.

His mouth fell open. "What the fuck? What does that even mean?"

I cleared my throat and settled back against the wicker chair. "Obviously, what I'm trying to say is that the pussies are a, um, metaphor for my books. And, eaten is, well, to be devoured. So, I don't want to let this story devour my morals."

"Yeah, that makes absolutely no sense."

"Just give me a second," I snapped. "It made sense in my head."

"Look, I don't know what you're getting at, but I just want this" — he gestured around the balcony— "to be resolved. I can't hold up my end if you're fucking with the script."

"I wasn't fucking with the script," I hissed. "I wanted to kiss you, damn it! Is it really that hard to believe that I'd want to kiss you and maybe, just maybe, you'd want to kiss me back?" A bubble of a sob rose up, and I slapped my palm over my mouth to stifle it.

Now was not the time for hysterics.

"Don't cry." Jake rubbed the back of his neck roughly and frowned.

I forced a laugh. "I'm not. That was nothing. It's not like it really matters to you whether I'm happy or not anyway."

Silence filled the space again, my pulse the only sound in my ears. I looked away from his intense stare and picked at the warped pieces of wicker, poking out from the chair like spikes.

"It does matter to me, Hayden," he finally admitted. "I don't know why, but it does. Maybe it's because you make me laugh. Maybe it's because you're unapologetically you, with your crazy crystals and mantras. Or maybe, it's simply because you know everything about me and it feels like we should be friends. I don't want to see my friends hurting."

I nodded along, feeling the arrows of humiliation as they pierced my skin. I wasn't sure what I expected; maybe for him to admit that he'd wanted to kiss me? That it hadn't been something he was forced into?

But, friends?

I didn't want to be his friend.

I felt a jolt of shock. I didn't want to be just his friend. I wanted more. But, I couldn't have it.

Max had been right. I had the upper hand. A relationship could never work under those circumstances.

I couldn't say that, so I settled for, "I don't know everything about you! Surely there are a few secrets you have."

Jake stubbed out the butt of the cigarette and immediately lit up another one. There was a small pile of them on the table between us, giving me the impression that he'd been out here a while.

"I do smoke. I've been using the patch since I got here, but tonight I just needed a little more."

I nodded, encouraging him to continue. "And?"

"I don't know, Hayden. I think you know the rest."

I shook my head. "No, I don't know who your best friend is or your favorite food. Just because I wrote it doesn't mean that it has to be true. Like, like... I didn't write that you have glasses, but you do!" I knew I was grasping at straws and judging by the bemused expression on his face, he knew it too.

"Alright. Did you know that I was going to ask Addison to marry me?"

I pushed down the swell of indignant anger. How could he tell me that after we were so close just a couple of hours ago?

Oh, right. Because I literally just asked him to do that very thing.

Obviously, that had been a stupid, horrible decision.

"Is that so?" I folded my arms across my chest to stop them from shaking. It had everything to do with the cold and nothing at all to do with the hurt his words had caused.

He bit down on his lip and looked away. "Yeah. She was single and my mom was pressuring me to settle down and give her grandkids. Said she knew that Jessa wasn't ever going to let herself get tied down to some guy, so it was up to me."

"Did you love her?" I asked nonchalantly.

Please say no.

Jake frowned and pursed his lips. "I don't know. We came from the same line of work, so we didn't annoy each other by getting over-protective when one of us needed to work late. It just made sense, you know?"

I nodded and tried to inject as much disinterest as I could into my words. "Yeah, sounds like you two would've been happy. Is that why you came here? So, I'd write you back into the story, I mean? You could find out what really happened to her."

"I never thought about it like that. I guess I never imagined that there was a chance that she was still alive. I just wanted my life back, but if she's out there, it changes things."

"Does it?" I realized that I was breathing heavier than normal and focused on getting my inhales and exhales into a normal cadence again.

He looked back at me. "Yeah. Look, I'm sorry about accusing you earlier, with the kiss."

I laughed quickly and jerkily waved my hand in the air. "Oh, that? It was bound to happen. Two people stuck in the same small space for so long. We were either going out like that or in body bags, am I right?"

"You really think that's all it was? Just the result of us spending too much time together?"

"Yep," I squeaked through the tears that were being held back only by sheer willpower. "We just need to hold up our end of the agreement; no more stupid mistakes. Truce?"

I held out my hand and he looked at it strangely. I bit down on my lower lip when he finally reached out, completely engulfing my hand in his.

"Truce," he said roughly.

I snatched my hand back and stood up. "Well." My voice cracked. "I have to get some sleep now."

"Hey, are you sure you're okay?" Jake touched my shoulder. "I could come back in with you."

I shook my head. "No, stay. I'll be fine."

I slid the door closed and we watched each other through the glass; less than a foot apart, but separated by an impenetrable barrier.

I made it to my room before completely losing my shit. I curled up next to Bootsy and held a pillow over my face to muffle the sounds of my sobbing.

I'd messed it all up and there was no way to fix it other than to give Jake the story he wanted. He'd needed to start chain-smoking again to numb himself to me. If I wanted to do the same, I'd be buying out an entire dispensary.

Bootsy's meowing grew louder as she moved under the pillow with me, her rough sandpaper tongue lapping up my tears as they ran down my cheeks.

"I'm an asshole, Bootsy girl," I whispered. "I just want to fast forward to the part where I'm married to a great guy—who's real, obviously—and wearing his shirt while I make him pancakes in the morning. Is that too much to ask?"

I'd have to learn how to make pancakes, but maybe I'd start with frozen waffles and work my way up.

She carelessly flicked her tail and settled back down in front of her movie. I lay next to her, hoping the monotonous narration on bird migratory habits would lull me to sleep, but all it managed was to stir up feelings of guilt.

He hadn't given much away, but what little he did was earth-shattering. Addison. I never imagined. I'd always pictured her as this blonde supermodel type, so it made sense that he'd want to marry her.

I just knew that if I visited their home, the dishes in the cabinets would all match and everything would be white: the carpets, the towels

—even the walls. They would've had two gazelle-like children and worn matching sweaters for their holiday photos. Even their fancy dog would be sitting perfectly in a red plaid sweater, smiling for the camera.

Meanwhile, my last holiday card had been made using a *Snapchat* filter where Bootsy and I looked like reindeer. Obviously, I was not in the same realm.

My perfect guy would probably be someone with interests that were a little more... enlightened. He'd wear his hair in a man bun, and we'd do yoga together every morning. It wouldn't be sexual like it was with Jake either. We'd respectfully align our chakras and open our minds before heading out to visit Damien at the coffee shop.

He'd proudly tell everyone that visited his shop that I wrote books as he wove rugs on a loom.

I frowned.

Obviously, that last part was a mistake. He would do something more interesting than rug-making. Maybe he ran a wildlife sanctuary and instead of magazines in the waiting area, there'd be copies of my books.

Yes. Maybe that was it.

I'd probably visit him there on the weekends and do readings from my latest work and one day I would realize that my life was incredibly boring—*no, that wasn't right.*

I'd realize that my man, Dusk Marley, was a much better fit for me than Jake ever was. In fact, I probably wouldn't even remember Jake's name. He would just be some nameless character I wrote ages ago.

He sounds boring as fuck, a voice that sounded suspiciously like Jake's said in my head.

I was outraged on Dusk Marley's behalf. Obviously, he was just trying to provide the best life he could for me and our three cats: Bootsy, Gypsy, and Leaf.

Jake couldn't understand a love like mine and Dusk's. It was messy and imperfect; all the things he hated. I was a free spirit, and I needed to find someone who was the same instead of worrying about what some uptight cop thought about me.

I belatedly realized that he'd never once asked me about myself out on the balcony; proving that our encounter had been just that; a drunken incident that we'd both work to forget in the days and weeks to come.

I hoped.

SEVENTEEN

"ISN'T THIS PLACE GREAT?" Aaris sipped her sparkling water and looked around the table with a grin. "I can't believe it took us a month to get reservations, but when it's the new hip spot in the city, what can you do?"

"Have we had a chance to look over the menu? Do we want to start with the tempeh stuffed avocado or maybe some walnut chorizo nachos?" our waiter asked the table with more enthusiasm than any one person should have.

Max and Jake exchanged a glance over their menus; some unspoken code that civilians were not privy to.

"Uh, I have a question." Max waved him over. "Can you direct me to the meat section?"

Aaris giggled at the same time our waiter muttered, "Oh, dear."

"Sweetie, *Pure Love* is a vegan place. We talked about this, remember?" She nodded at him encouragingly. He nodded back stiffly before turning back to the waiter with a plethora of questions.

Jake shifted in his seat and his leg brushed up against mine. He hadn't been acting much like himself lately. There were dark circles under his eyes, and his jaw was covered in heavy stubble that he refused to shave. It was painfully obvious that he hadn't slept in days.

He looked down at our legs touching and treated me to a smirk. It made me want to push him onto the table and straddle him until I couldn't hold myself up any longer. The glassware would fall to the floor with a crash, but we'd be so lost in each other that we wouldn't even care.

It was safe to say that my silly little crush had morphed into quite the problem. Every touch, every look killed me with the realization that there would never be anything more between us.

"So, are we stopping for a burger on the way home?" His eyes glinted mischievously.

I shook my head discreetly. "No, why would you say that?"

• Confession: Aaris told me that she was a vegetarian when we were in high school. Afraid to admit that I enjoyed eating the animals she was so fond of, I told a little white lie and convinced my parents to play along when she would come over for dinner. I meant to tell her the truth, but then one year turned into ten and it just didn't seem to matter anymore. Until now.

"Jake, Hayden is a vegetarian like me. Didn't you know that?" Her head was cocked to the side, the way it did when she was trying to figure something, or someone, out.

His massive thigh connected with mine again under the table, but I refused to look up at him.

"Hayden." His voice was low, taunting. "You never told me that you were a vegetarian."

Aaris talked Max into a tofu burrito bowl before ordering the seitan chops for herself. "So, you've lived with Hayden for a month now and you didn't realize that she wasn't eating meat?"

I jabbed Jake with my elbow. "You know him. So involved with the case that he can't be bothered to notice anything else."

He grabbed the waiter's attention as he passed by. "Uh, could she get a dirty vodka martini, top shelf?

I took one look at Aaris' stern expression and added, "In the biggest glass you have, please? Okay, thanks."

I turned back to see him watching me in fascination. "I notice a lot of things, but somehow, I missed that."

I tugged at my earring. Maybe it hadn't been such a good idea to bring Jake here.

"You are aware of how inhumanely most animals in slaughterhouses are treated, right Jake?"

Oh, good. Aaris had found her soapbox. Just when I thought the evening couldn't get any worse.

He looked up at her. "Is that why you don't eat meat?" She nodded and he looked over at me. "And what about you?"

I cleared my throat. "Well, obviously for the ethical reasons and the... spiritual ones, um, as well."

His lip twitched. "Obviously."

When Max and Aaris appeared to be deep in conversation, he leaned down until his mouth was right next to my ear. "Don't worry, your secret's safe with me."

His warm breath tickled my neck and a shiver moved through my body. He moved closer and my panties began their migration to the floor. His lips moved into a pout like he knew the effect he had on me.

It wasn't fair.

Men could just turn off all emotion while I was struck with the memory of our kiss every time he looked at me. I'd often wondered in the weeks that followed, if he'd obsessed over it like I had. If he lay awake at night, thinking about how I tasted and felt in his arms.

Guys like him were probably kissed like that all the time though. There was nothing special about what happened. It was just another ordinary day for Jake Hopkins.

I told myself that I was just in the right place at the right time, but when his leg was mashed up against mine and his arm was draped casually over the back of my chair, I pretended that it had meant something more. To both of us.

Apparently, I was a moron.

I watched Aaris and Max, whispering to each other with their heads pressed together and I wondered how they got through dinners out in public without tearing each other's clothes off the first chance they got.

With my head down, I glanced over at Jake in a black crew neck sweater that was once again, a size too small. If I knew that I was going to be going home to *Gigantor*, I wouldn't even make it to the drink order. Hell, we'd never eat out because I'd keep him hand-cuffed to my bed.

That is, if I had actual feelings for him.

Which I didn't.

He was just a friend.

A friend I wanted to see naked.

I groaned and the hand on my chair moved up to rest against my neck. "What's wrong? Just realized you're going to have to eat this shit and pretend to like it?"

I blinked and turned toward him, hoping that my expression didn't give away my thoughts. "I was just thinking... about Jessa. I feel like we're close, but it's just not coming together as quickly as I'd hoped."

His greenish-brown eyes stared back at me with an intensity that was almost too much to take. "You in that big of a hurry to get rid of me?"

I couldn't decide if I was imagining the worried tone in his voice or not. If I was playing it cool, I would've made a joke about how he took too long in the bathroom or how he'd convinced my cat to change allegiance only hours after arriving. Something to convince him that I didn't care.

Instead, I whispered, "No, you big lug. How am I going to live without you?" I meant it to be funny, but my voice caught, and my vision swam with tears. I rolled my shoulders away from his grip and stared down into my lap. I was probably about to get my period and when it happened, I'd exclaim, *"So, that's why I've been a weepy disaster. It had nothing to do with Jake. It was just my ovaries the entire time!"*

I reluctantly looked up, expecting to see the familiar smirk and to hear a comment about how crazy he thought I was.

To my surprise, Jake wasn't smiling. The expression on his face was unreadable. He continued watching me, struggling to find the right words. His Adam's apple moved up and then down, but he stayed silent.

I couldn't say another word. I'd feel stupid.

Actually, I already felt stupid. And awkward. I turned away and dabbed at my eyes with the linen napkin before smiling brightly at the waiter as he placed the appetizers in the center of the table.

"This looks amazing. Thank you!" I'd just taken a sip from my martini when I noticed his name tag. I inhaled sharply and began coughing violently.

Dusk.

The waiter's name was Dusk. Jake pounded me on the back while I tried to figure out if this was something I'd conjured or just a random coincidence.

I hoped it was the latter because this Dusk was tall but lanky and he was lacking the man bun that I'd imagined. I wiped at my streaming eyes and waited until he was gone before looking up again.

Aaris and Max were still lost in their own little vegan love nest, oblivious to everyone around them. Meanwhile, Jake continued to stare off into space, his nostrils flaring out with each exhale.

He got like this when faced with a problem.

If he was feeling stuck on a case, he'd sit at his desk and just zone out, trying to find the solution somewhere inside his head. I wanted to ask him what he was thinking about, but I wasn't sure I'd like the answer.

He was going to leave eventually, and it was going to smash my heart into pieces. But, right now, he was here, and I wanted to enjoy every second that I still had him.

Damn the consequences.

I rested my hand on his thigh and the muscle immediately stiffened. "Did you try the avocado?"

Jake stared down at my hand and then slowly brought his eyes back up to meet mine. "No," he finally managed. "It's good?"

I nodded. "So good."

I didn't know if it was good or not. It was taking every ounce of focus to keep my hand exactly where it was. I was caught between wanting to yank it back as though I'd been burned and needing to sink my fingers into his flesh, stroking and petting. Up and down... up and down...

Jake stood up with a loud sigh. "I—I need the men's room. I'll just be—" He clicked his tongue against his teeth and all but ran away from me.

My chest tightened as I watched him disappear, taking my time to appreciate the way his jeans cupped his ass. I looked down at my hand in wonder and suppressed a soft giggle.

How had something so small just taken down Grande the Giant?

"YOU GO ON INSIDE. I need to visit with Max." Jake guided me into the living room and then shut the door behind me.

He'd been on edge for the remainder of dinner and nothing seemed to cheer him up; not even a pit stop on the way home at the burger joint he loved. I still wasn't sure how he'd choked down a burger and fries on top of the stuffed avocado, two plates of nachos, chickpea stroganoff, coconut cream pie, and chocolate cheesecake he'd had at the restaurant.

I didn't know what had gotten into me, but I'd gone out of my way to touch him as often as I could.

He wanted the salt? I'd brush my fingers against his as I passed it. Dropped his napkin? I deftly slipped mine onto his lap, patting it down for good measure.

Friends touched each other.

Usually, it didn't leave one friend with a strong need for an edible and a vibrator though. On autopilot, I checked Bootsy's food and water before making my way into the bedroom.

I needed to get a thousand words down to stay on pace, but I was antsy.

Restless.

I took the pile of clean clothes that had been wadded up into a ball from the ottoman and began hanging them up. Once that was done, I made the bed. My clothes suddenly felt scratchy against my skin, the friction making me crazy.

Well, crazier than normal.

Perhaps, all the touching had been a bad plan.

I needed to be writing. That would help take my mind off of... whatever this was. I grabbed my laptop and sank down on top of the down comforter.

I wrote a couple of paragraphs before groaning in frustration. The sexual tension between Jessa and Detective Keller was too much. I was trying to write a damn cozy mystery, but they were fighting me every step of the way.

I checked my watch. Jake was still with Max. Who knew how long that would take—maybe hours. If I closed the door and turned off the light, he'd just assume I was asleep, right?

I closed the bedroom door with a soft click. My heart raced in anticipation as I turned off the lights and stripped down to bare skin, while Bootsy scratched at the door, demanding to be let in.

I just needed a few minutes with *Tumblr* and my vibrator and then I'd deal with the little Khaleesi. I opened my underwear drawer and evaluated the arsenal of toys.

What to take?

I passed over the plethora of vibrating eggs and rabbits, going for the Feminizer. It was my go-to in a pinch.

"Guaranteed to get you off in sixty seconds or less," I sang as I climbed under the comforter and settled against the pillows with my phone.

The man in the first video looked like Jake, with his scruffy face and starched dress shirt and instead of scrolling down to the next one, I paused, fascinated by the way he unbuttoned his shirt. His hands traced his partner's face and his tongue circled hers. He closed his mouth around it and I exhaled shakily as he drew it into his mouth.

Jake had done that.

No, I wasn't thinking of that right now. I was thinking of this nice gentleman, Dmitri and his lover, Tatiana. His tongue moved down her body and her head fell back at the same time mine did. That Dmitri really seemed to know what he was doing.

I reached between my legs and, as I increased the speed, the persistent whir began to fill the room. I had to hurry. Jake was going to be back at any second and it sounded like I was piloting a drone in here.

Tatiana repaid Dmitri before climbing up his body and I increased the speed again. "C'mon," I murmured. "Sooo close."

Dmitri thrust his hips up and Tatiana's mouth fell open. I came with a deep exhale and a death grip on my phone. It wasn't thoughts of Dmitri or Tatiana that pushed me over the edge. It had been Jake.

It was the way he walked around with confidence that life wasn't going to throw anything his way that he couldn't handle and the smirk that seemed permanently etched onto his face. And there was a glint that only seemed to appear when his eyes landed on me. I wasn't sure what it meant, but it seemed important.

The handle on the bedroom door began to turn and I frantically held the power button down on the vibrator. It switched off just as the door swung open, sending a sliver of light across my face.

"Hayden? Are you asleep?" Jake stepped into the room holding a bowl in his hand.

"No," I mumbled as I pulled the comforter up to my chin, effectively hiding myself and any evidence of what I'd been doing before he arrived. "What do you have?"

He held up the bowl. "I thought you were up late working, so I brought you some writing fuel—*Lucky Charms*, no milk."

When he extended the bowl toward me, I shook my head. "Can you just put it on the, um, dresser? I'm not—I'm not wearing anything, right now."

A slow smile spread across his face. "You're not wearing clothes, but you weren't sleeping? What exactly have you been doing?"

Shit. Why hadn't I just said that I was sleeping?

"I was... I was researching a... sex scene for *Angel of Death*." My face heated. I hadn't meant to say that either.

• Confession: 'Research' was code for, "I'm going to look at *Tumblr* and get myself off a few dozen times in between word sprints." It was sort of a Friday afternoon stress-reliever.

Jake flipped the switch to the overhead, bathing us both in light. "Okay, as much as I want to get into the reasons that you would be researching a sex scene for your non-sexy cozy mystery, I did come in here for a reason."

To tell me that you can't stop thinking about our kiss from a month ago and when I touched you at dinner, it ignited all of your pent-up lust?

"We found another note. It was left on your car. I saw it when we pulled up but didn't want to alarm you. Max is looking into what it might mean—"

I interjected, "What it might mean? Is it not the straightforward, 'You will die in seven days?' Or did they rhyme it again? Because that really takes the threat out of it, you know?"

He sat down on the side of the bed and scratched at his jaw, crushing my toes beneath his glorious ass. "It said, *'The curse is come upon me,'* does that mean anything to you?"

I shook my head and he continued, "Exactly. I'm not entirely sure it's even related to the other things that have happened, but Max wants to check it out..."

Jake's voice trailed off and I realized with horror that his focus was on the nightstand next to me; specifically, the still open under-wear drawer that doubled as a toy factory.

His lips parted and he leaned in. "Fuck, Hayden."

I was suddenly hyperaware of my own heartbeat and the flush that was working its way up to my hairline. "That's... personal." With a pant, I stretched out to close it, but my arm fell short.

He stood up and walked over, staring down into the depths like it was a treasure chest. And it was. For me.

"Jake," I warned.

Please don't make fun of me.

He ran a hand over his face before pushing the drawer closed. "Just get dressed. I'll be out in the living room."

The door slammed shut behind him and I rubbed my damp hands on the comforter. Well, that had gone about as well as I expected.

Next time someone barged in on me masturbating and asked if I'd been sleeping, I was definitely going to save myself the trouble and say yes.

My phone lit up under the blankets and began vibrating. I reluctantly pulled it free to see that it was my mother calling me. At ten o'clock on a Saturday. The lust was replaced with a queasy feeling in the pit of my stomach as I let it go to voicemail.

I couldn't talk to her right now. I was too keyed up. I stared blankly at the phone until it chirped with a voicemail notification. Knowing it was best to rip the band-aid off, I hit play.

"Hayden, I'm sure you're out right now, but listen— your dad and I were talking to Reid and Emily and they found a great place up in the mountains. I hate to do this, but we're going to cancel our annual Thanksgiving get-together next month and do that instead. We'd love to have you join us, but you'll have to purchase your own ticket and pay part of the cabin fee. Let Reid know; he can give you a break-down on costs. Also, let me know if you're still coming on the twentieth. I'm trying to get a final head count for the caterers."

I balled my hands into fists and inhaled slowly. It was so typical of Reid to plan these big family trips that I couldn't afford. He knew it too.

I pulled a sports bra on and then stomped into the closet for some clothes. My brother was the worst. I grabbed a handful of dry cereal and angrily crunched on it as I walked into the living room.

Jake was pacing the living room in a similar fashion. "It took you long enough. Okay, we need to figure out what this latest note means."

He grabbed a pen and began sketching out some sort of diagram on a scrap of paper. The pen ripped through the paper and he let out a low growl of frustration.

"Your energy is terrible."

He clenched his jaw before biting out, "And why do you think that is, Hayden? Could it be because we're a month into this and still no closer to finding out who wants you dead? We've stuck with your routine and, short of announcing to the world where you're going—" He froze.

"What?" I protested over a mouthful of cereal. "What are you thinking?"

He dropped his pen. "God, it was right in front of me the whole time. Have you ever done a signing?"

I began shaking my head before he had a chance to finish his sentence. "No, no. No. I can't do a signing. I can't talk about the books."

Jake pulled his glasses off and pinched the bridge of his nose. "You wrote them. Of course you can talk about them."

"But, but," I spluttered. "What if they ask questions?"

He blinked slowly. "Come again?"

"You know... questions. Like, why did you write this book? Tell me the plot."

"Okay, there was only one question in there. If they ask you about your books, you just talk about them. You wrote the damn things; it's not like they're asking you to explain quantum physics."

"No," I whisper hissed. "I can't talk to people. You went to 'Detective class,' so it's easy for you. You write so that you can tell people a story without having to look them in the eye while doing it."

Jake smirked. "Detective class? Jesus, Hayden. You don't even know what I went through to get where I am? That's like inter-viewing Hawking and only noting that he had a cool wheelchair."

I shook my head again. "I can't do it, Jake. I can't. I'm not ready."

"What do you mean, you're not ready? You've written six books and you're in the middle of your seventh. I think that just screams ready. This is good. We'll get you in front of your fans and see if we can't trap ourselves a stalker."

I frowned and looked down at my t-shirt. "But, what do I wear? Do I have to go find people to talk to, or will they come to me? What if they ask me to be friends? Do I say yes? Or stay professional?"

"You don't get out much, do you?" Jake noted with a heavy sigh.

EIGHTEEN

"I THINK THIS LOOKS GREAT." Jake stood back and surveyed the table with an appreciative nod.

The bastard had done it. He had finagled an invitation to one of the biggest indie signings in the country. Last-minute. We'd gotten in an hour ago and gone straight up to the signing floor for set up.

The majority of the tables had been set up the night before and seemed to be geared toward the romance genre, but Jake had convinced me that even if they didn't come for the *Detective Hopkins* novels, the *Blood Letters* trilogy would draw them in.

I'd wanted to puke since we landed and even more so once I saw the way the other tables looked. Some had mini neon signs that flashed while others had elaborate table decorations and intricate book stands.

I took in the hotel-provided plain white tablecloth and the books resting on the cheapest bookstands I could find. I didn't even have a banner or bookmarks to hand out.

My table was like Cinderella, pre-fairy godmother. What if the readers came up and saw that my table didn't have those things?

What if they demanded that I produce one or be kicked out the event?

I pointed at the tables flanking mine, suddenly wanting to run for the exit. "I don't have a sign with my name on it. How are people going to know who I am?"

"So, we'll make one. There are enough cardboard boxes around here. We tape a few together and write your name across it —boom, done."

I looked around at the vinyl banners and frowned. "You really think that will look like these?"

He nodded. "Yeah, it'll be great. I'll see if they have some markers we can use."

I tugged at the ends of my hair nervously and tucked a few stray pieces behind my ears. I'd gotten up hours before we needed to leave so that I could painstakingly straighten each piece and put on makeup. I had discreet gold studs in my ears and a pair of black slacks; just like a real grown up.

I was going to be confident and professional. It was my big chance, and I wasn't letting anything screw that up.

The girl at the table next to mine waved me over. The banner behind her said she was Marilyn Fox. I would've guessed her to be in her mid-fifties, with electric red hair that matched almost everything on her table. Judging by her book covers, she enjoyed writing about group activities. "So, you got to bring a model, huh? How'd you manage that?"

"Who? Jake? No, he's not a model. He's just here as a friend."

Marilyn nodded knowingly. "That's smart. I might do that at the next one. Helps get people to the table, you know?"

I picked up one of her bookmarks and turned it over in my hands. "You don't think they'll come because they loved the books?"

She cackled, drawing the attention of several other authors. "Girl, this must be your first signing ever. You bring a model and you can guarantee that you've got a line all day. Otherwise, you work on throwing yourself at anyone who comes your way. Sometimes, it pays off. Sometimes, it doesn't."

"So, what are your books about?" I asked politely, hoping that I wasn't going to have to pimp myself to anyone. I wasn't built for it.

Sweat ran down my spine and I tugged at the collar of my blouse, but the material was unforgiving, nothing at all like the t-shirts I'd left behind.

"Can't you guess?" she teased.

Making a sandwich out of a woman?

Perfecting the art of walking around half-naked?

"Um, threesomes?"

Marilyn cracked up again, sounding like a witch who'd just managed to snatch some stray children. "Shifter ménage. I tend to stick with wolves.

"Some people do bears, but I just can't even wrap my mind around making that work, you know? I used to write vampires, but that's been done to death. You need wolves to play up the 'one true mate' aspect. I like the idea of two different pack alphas fighting over their human woman. Really gets my engine revving. What about you?"

"Excuse me?" I asked in confusion. I hadn't understood half of what she'd just said.

"C'mon, girl, don't be shy. Is it bears?"

"No. I—" I glanced down at one with a handsome shirtless man gazing menacingly from the cover. Behind him was the silhouette of a wolf. I mashed my lips together to keep from giggling and shook my head. "No, I like wolves too. They seem, um, neat."

"Neat," she echoed. "They're perfect killing machines. I wanted an animal that mated for life—tried penguins and that failed spectacularly. It's just too cold to make the love scenes work and then with the man having to sit on the eggs, it just killed my heat factor."

I squeezed my eyes shut and turned away, unable to contain the hysterical bubble of laughter that was fighting its way out. "I'm sorry," I managed with tears in my eyes. "I just need to finish setting up."

I walked until I found Jake hunched over an empty table, pressing tape down over several pieces of cardboard. "I think I've just about got it," he mumbled without looking up. "Are you nervous?"

I squeaked with laughter and he paused. "Hayden? Are you high right now?"

I shook my head and lifted my glasses to fan my streaming eyes. "I just met—" I dissolved into another fit of giggles. "Jake…"

His lips turned up into a smirk. "What happened?"

"The author at the table next to mine writes shifter ménage; but not about bears because that would be unbelievable. She tried penguins, but—" I gave up and knelt down, certain I was going to pee my pants.

His brow furrowed. "Penguins? Who the fuck wants to read about penguin shifters? This is good. People will take one look at that and come straight for your table. Go back and I'll meet you in a second. I'm just going to add a few more things and check in with my guy."

I'd almost forgotten that we weren't really here to promote my books, but to find the person who wanted me dead. Marilyn gave me a tight-lipped smile before whispering something to the author behind her. They both looked me up and down before turning away.

Well, I wasn't here to make friends.

Jake came back over with the sign and I covered my mouth in surprise. He'd sketched out my name in big, bold letters and added a drawing of a cat face underneath.

"It's perfect. Thank you!"

"I thought maybe people would see it and think you write domestic cat shifter porn. Might be a good icebreaker." He taped it up on the front of the table and we stepped back to admire it.

My sign resembled something a homeless person might hold up on a street corner, but it was handmade and that made it better than anyone else's here.

Seeing my name in Jake's handwriting did weird things to me. I waited until he walked off to grab some bottled water before snapping a picture of it.

I resisted the urge to hug him, mainly because I knew I wouldn't be able to let go. I'd turn it into some embarrassing display of unrequited lust that Jake would assume I'd scripted. We hadn't really fought in a month and I wasn't going to be the reason our ceasefire ended.

Once the doors opened, things got a little crazy. Women of all ages swarmed the ballroom, nearly all of them dragging wagon-sized carts behind them.

"You might have a line in front of your table," Marilyn noted with a sour face. "I have quite the fan base here, so I'll apologize in advance if we block your table. My readers are vicious."

She gave another witch laugh before shuffling back behind her table. Jake rolled his eyes and mimicked, "My readers just have to know if the alpha penguin shifter is sitting on twin or triplet eggs."

I swatted his arm playfully and grinned. I was at my first signing and instead of hanging out in the bathroom, applying damp paper towels under my arms, I was sitting next to a gorgeous man who made me forget to feel nervous.

I wasn't the only woman who appeared lost in the presence of Jake either. Nearly every woman that stepped onto our row froze when they saw him.

A few tentatively approached and took their time browsing the backs of my books; their eyes darting up at him every few seconds. Others simply observed him from Marilyn's table.

If Jake knew what they were doing, he played it cool. His arm rested on the back of my chair and every so often, his fingertips brushed against my shoulder.

Several women that approached had read the *Blood Letters* trilogy and loved it. One had even made a cloth bookmark featuring the cover of book one.

"Jake, look." I held it up and a small smile appeared.

"Do you read her stuff?" the older one asked him.

He nodded. "You could say that. I'm more into her Detective Hopkins novels."

I bit the inside of my lip to hide my grin and signed the inside of their books, feeling giddy. I was at a book signing and people had brought copies of my books for me to sign.

If only my idiot brother were here to witness this. *No, I was Zen.* I wished him love and light… and a front-row seat to me being the center of attention for once.

"Can we get a picture with the two of you?"

I nodded and the two women crowded around us behind the table, practically pushing me and Jake together. His hand rested between my shoulder blades, pulling me into his side. Unable to resist a once in a lifetime opportunity, I let my cheek rest against a wall of pectoral muscles.

A familiar frosted bob moved through the crowd and I froze. Jake waited until the women moved on before questioning me.

"What did you see?"

I stood up on my tiptoes, trying to find her in the crowd. "I swore I saw—"

"Hello, Hayden."

We both turned toward the voice and I awkwardly stuck my hand out. "Anne Marie, hello. What are you doing here?" I kept glancing warily around the room, certain that Rob was going to jump out from behind a table to grope me. I never imagined that a politician's wife would be caught dead in a place like this.

Following my gaze, she added with a pinched expression, "Rob's not with me and I'd prefer if you not mention that you saw me. It wouldn't look…appropriate to the voters."

I nodded and glanced down at the rolling cart filled to the brim with books. "You've got quite the haul here."

Anne Marie gave me another tight-lipped smile before pointing toward *Body of Proof*. "I just need one more to complete my list."

"You've read my books?"

"I did. The Detective Hopkins books were your best yet," I

grinned like a madwoman and she added, "Until *One in the Chamber*. The writing was weak and the plot almost non-existent. Was there supposed to be a follow-up book to that because I just can't imagine how you go on from there."

Jake took the cash from her with an ear-to-ear grin, while I hastily scrawled my signature on the inside cover and shoved the book into her hands. "Great! Well, I will definitely keep your feedback in mind. So good to see you!"

She disappeared back into the crowd and I turned to Jake. "Don't say it. Please."

He gave me a half smirk. "Say what? Did something happen?"

"You were right. I'm wrong. There. You happy now?"

He squeezed my shoulder lightly. "Completely happy. So, tell me. How do you know her?"

I frowned. "Jake, she and her husband come into the salon all the time. You saw him the last time you were there; slimy little greaseball who can't keep his hands to himself?"

The grin faded, and he pulled his phone from his pocket.

"You don't think she might have something to do with the notes, do you?" I hadn't considered the possibility that someone I knew in real life would be after me.

"I don't know, but I gave a description to my guy. He'll follow her and see where she leads us. You just focus on the signing, okay?"

I nodded but kept an eye on the door.

Just to be safe.

———

"THIS ISN'T GOING TO WORK," I said into the phone. "I was told that we'd have two double beds."

Computer keys clicked rapidly in the background. "I'm so sorry, Ms. Michaels, but we're completely booked tonight. I don't have any double bed rooms left."

"Thanks anyway." I hung up with a heavy sigh.

The event had gone so well. The only book I didn't sell out of was *One in the Chamber*. It didn't sell out because not one person bought it.

Otherwise, I was calling it a smashing success. I'd signed books until my hand cramped and smiled for every picture. And the high was unlike anything I'd ever experienced.

"Jake, they can't switch our room. What are we go—" I came to a halt when I reached the small sitting area. He was folded in half on the couch with his face resting against his knees.

"Do you feel okay?" he mumbled through his legs.

"I feel fine. Why? Are you sick?" I placed the back of my hand on his neck and he jerked away with a groan.

"I don't know. I feel...weird. Maybe it's food poisoning. Aren't your fairy bullshit potions supposed to protect us against this?" He stood up suddenly and swayed on his feet. "I'll be right back."

I wasn't sure how I'd gotten him to agree to being spritzed with my oil blend this morning, but he had to have known that the oils only worked on negative energy and not tainted food.

"We ate the same things though. If you have food poisoning, then I should have it too."

When there was no response from the bathroom, I went back and began unpacking my suitcase. We were going to be leaving tomorrow afternoon, but I needed something to do. I fired off a quick text to Aaris to let her know how it had gone and to check in on Bootsy.

Afterward, I kicked my heels off and sank down onto the mattress and watched the sun set through the wall of windows. When the room grew dark, I realized that Jake had been in the bathroom for a very long time.

"Jake?" I called hesitantly. "Do you need anything? I can grab you some ginger ale or—" The door suddenly opened, and I jumped back in fright. "Jesus, Jake."

He gripped the doorframe in his massive hands and watched me curiously. "What are you doing here?"

"What do you mean? I just told you that they couldn't get us separate rooms...are you sure you're okay?"

He looked like hell. His shirt was unbuttoned and untucked. My gaze drifted lower and I froze. *Oh my god,* his semi-erect dick was hanging out of his pants.

I held up a finger. "Um, if you'll just, um..."

Jake grinned and tapped his index finger against my nose. "I got you, Hayden. I. Got. You." With that, he closed the door in my face.

I knocked lightly. "Hello?"

He flung the door open and this time stalked toward me like a predator in search of prey. He'd shed his shirt but hadn't bothered to put his dick away, and it swayed in a very distracting manner with each step he took.

I continued backing up until I reached the windows. "Jake? What's wrong with you?"

"Come here." He held out his arms. I hesitantly took a step toward the bed, but he caught my arm and pulled me back toward the windows. "Baby, do you know what I've been doing?"

Baby?

I shook my head and offered, "Vomiting?"

"No, I've been thinking about today. You conquered your fears. Just like that. Hayden, listen." He held up a hand. "You write so beautifully. The inside of your mind must be a fucked up place."

What the actual hell had happened to him in the bathroom?

I remained silent, but he held his hand up again. "Stop. Don't argue with me. I've been trying to work it out since I got here. How is a girl like you single? I've been trying to figure it out and tonight, it just hit me. The drawer in your nightstand was the key, don't you see?"

He laughed at his rhyme and I shook my head. "Are you drunk? Why are you acting like this?"

Jake mashed his finger against my lips. "Shhhh...I've been thinking about all of those toys. It was a sign that you aren't going out on many dates—"

"Thank you, Sherlock. You've been most helpful," I mumbled around his finger.

"Stop. I wanted to kiss you that night, okay?" He stared down at me with a serious expression. "I wanted to kiss you before that night, and I want to kiss you right now."

I felt light-headed at his revelation. "I can't have this conversation with you right now." He was completely shit-faced and not likely to remember saying any of it.

His arms came up to rest on either side of my head, caging me in, before his mouth dropped to the spot where my neck and collarbone met.

"Jake," I pleaded breathlessly.

His lips moved up and he whispered, "When I walked in on you in the bedroom, I wanted to watch." His teeth grazed my neck. "I wanted you to dump out the entire drawer and give me a demonstration on how it all worked."

A soft moan escaped, and I bit down on my lip until I tasted blood.

"And then." He pulled my hair up in his fist as his teeth connected with my ear lobe, nipping and sucking until I was just as impaired as he was. "Then, I wanted to fuck you so well that you had no use for any of it anymore."

When my legs began shaking, Jake bent down and carried me over to the bed, shedding his pants in the process. His boxer briefs clung to his hips and his dick jutted proudly over the waistband.

Possessed by the same madness, I sat up and pulled the blouse over my head. He grabbed my ankles, pulling me down toward the end of the bed. His hands made quick work of the hooks on my slacks and they quickly joined my blouse on the floor.

We were now in our underwear. This was a brand new development and I couldn't move or take a proper breath as I waited to see how he'd respond.

Jake covered my body with his, spreading my hips wide to fit around his massive body. One hand moved up to grip my hair while the other yanked the cups of my bra down so he could pay tribute with his mouth.

I arched my back and rolled my hips forward until his erection was right where I needed it. He lightly bit down on my nipple and I shivered, pushing the thin material of my panties against him.

"Please," I begged for something I couldn't put into words.

This was a horrible idea and I needed to stop. He was obviously fucked up and I would hate myself once it was over, yet I kept meeting his short thrusts, not caring that this would only end in heartache.

Once he was satisfied that my nipples were ready to cut glass, he moved up and sucked my bottom lip into his, keeping me pinned in place by my hair. Our tongues fought for control with each of us sinking our teeth in where we could.

Jake kissed me like the world was ending and I was his lifeline. Instead of arguing, I panted and moaned for him to continue his assault.

His hand moved down between us, pulling my panties to the side before I felt the head of his cock against my entrance. One hip thrust and he'd be inside of me. Well, as much of him as he could fit.

"I want in," he growled against my lips. "I want to mark you in ways that stick long after I'm gone."

Long after I'm gone...

It was enough to snap me out of my stupor. I sucked in a ragged breath and shook my head. "No," I whispered. "I can't."

I knew what this was, even if in his impairment, he'd temporarily forgotten. I already cared about him more than I should. Sex would just complicate those feelings further.

"Fuck," he growled before moving away from me. "Fuck." He swallowed hard and then nodded before standing up unsteadily. "You're right."

I felt along the comforter for my glasses. They'd disappeared at some point during the excitement, leaving me blind. Jake leaned across the bed and gently placed them in my hands before straightening again.

I took one look at him and everything in me begged for reconsideration. He tried coaxing his giant hard-on back into his boxer briefs, but it was having none of it.

"Just give me a second," Jake managed in a strangled voice as he tried corralling it with his hand. I worked to keep my eyes averted while wrapping my head around what had just happened.

He was fine at the signing. There was nothing that indicated he wasn't feeling well until we got back here. Something had happened between the end of the event and now. Maybe it was some sort of virus pumped through the air vents that made me irresistible to men.

He watched as I pulled my bra back up, his Adam's apple moving up and down in another long swallow. "Fuck, Hayden. You're gorgeous."

I didn't know what to do with the compliment. It was obvious by the way he was still swaying on his feet that he was impaired. Yet, a part of me wanted to think that he meant what he was saying.

Instead of trying to dissect the hidden meaning in his words, I went for a safer topic. "When did you start feeling bad?"

He slipped a hand into the front of his briefs to adjust himself and I wanted to applaud his efforts in wrangling the beast back to its cave. However, it didn't seem like the most appropriate time.

He backed up, using the wall for support. "I started feeling off when I got back to the room. Like really relaxed, but in a way that makes you think you might not wake back up if you fall asleep. And the room won't stop spinning, but I haven't had a drop of alcohol. I feel like I should just puke and get it over with, but I can't."

So, it wasn't quite the reaction I wanted after a guy made out with me.

I got up and walked over to him. His eyes were heavy-lidded, but that wasn't abnormal for him. I ran the back of my hand down his cheek and he let out a deep sigh.

"If I didn't know better, I'd say you were high," I laughed and then froze. "Wait, were you eating the candy in my purse?"

He groaned and shook his head. "No. I don't want to tell you. It's bad...like real bad..."

Jake trailed off as I crossed my arms over my chest, inadvertently pushing my breasts up and together. I rolled my eyes. "Just tell me what you took so that we can fix this. Okay?"

"It's fine, Hayden. I'm feeling better now. It's like it didn't even happen. I'm just thirsty."

He was high, but how?

I checked my purse on the way to grab him a water, but everything was right where it was supposed to be. To be as messed up as he was, he would've had to have eaten enough for me to notice.

When I returned, he was staring down to the street below with his forehead pressed against the window

"I can't feel my face. I think all the blood is gone," he grumbled, his breath fogging up the glass.

I glanced down at his boxers. I had a few ideas as to where it had gone, but again, it wasn't really the time or place.

Me and my shitty luck.

"Let's get you into bed, big guy." I handed him the bottle of water and pulled him toward the mattress. He drained the water as I tucked the blankets around him, just like he was a child.

You know, if the child happened to be a foot and a half taller than me.

"Water is so good, Hayden. It turns into blood when you drink it and then it flows back into the veins in your face. Did you know that?"

I frowned. "I'm not quite sure that's how it works."

He closed his eyes and I waited until his breaths became even before going into the bathroom. I wet a washcloth and laid it across his forehead. At some point, he'd kicked a leg out from under the blankets, letting it dangle near the floor. Probably to stop the room from spinning.

I'd hoped we'd go out to dinner and explore the city some, but I'd have to settle for room service. That brought me back to what he would've eaten—I knew he didn't smoke it. He hadn't left my side for more than a few minutes at a time. The entire hotel was a 'smoke-free' zone, so he hadn't had time to run out for a quick blunt with his homies.

I giggled at the image and reached out to put my hand on his chest, feeling the soft rise and fall of each breath.

"I stole something from you," he murmured without opening his eyes.

"You did? What was it?"

My heart?

My sanity?

He brought his arm up to rest under his head and looked over at me. "There were these cupcakes they passed out when you went to the bathroom. I was going to save it for you; the event organizer was adamant that they were for authors only, but I was fucking starving—"

"So, you ate it. All the other authors had cupcakes too?" The wheels started to turn in my head. Unfortunately, it was taking Jake a lot longer to reach the same conclusion.

He nodded. "I'm pretty sure they did. I thought if you never knew about it, then you couldn't get mad."

I sat up and faced him. "You realize what this means, right?"

His eyes drifted down toward my breasts again. "I'm sorry, what was the question?"

"You're such a guy," I sighed. "I'll put on a shirt."

"Don't." His hand moved to cover mine. "I like seeing that cattoo. I wanna put my mouth on it. Wait, what does it mean that I ate your cupcake? Is it a euphemism?"

I stared dumbly at our hands joined together. This connection somehow felt more intimate than his mouth on mine had.

I blinked slowly and tried to focus. "The cupcake was laced with something—I'm going to guess weed based on your symptoms."

He closed his eyes again and nodded. "Makes sense. Is this what being high is like?"

I laughed. "You've never been high before?"

"Never. There's something you didn't know about me. Are you surprised?" His thumb traced along the inside of my wrist as he talked, lulling me into a dream-like state.

"Very. I guess I just assumed you had. Being high is like— well, it's like nothing can bring you down. Your mind is focused, and things just make sense. But, that's not what you are, my friend. You are beyond high because you were given too much; which brings me to my next point. You said that cupcake was meant for me."

Jake opened one eye and peered at me through the narrow slit. "And? You want me to feel guilty? Because I do. I shouldn't have eaten the damn thing and I'd be feeling fine right now and you—Jesus!"

He sat up with a jolt, flinging the washcloth across the comforter.

"I see that you finally put two and two together over there," I noted dryly.

"Hayden, it would've killed you!" He was breathing like a bull ready to charge. Every muscle in his body had gone rigid.

Not that one.

I checked.

I tried to pull my hand free as his grip had tightened considerably in the last few moments, but he wouldn't budge. "I doubt that I would've died. I have a pretty high tolerance. I probably would've just slept it off."

Jake's nostrils flared and he shook his head. "Son-of-a—" He ran his free hand over his face. "I'm supposed to be keeping you safe!"

I squeezed his hand. "Stop. You did keep me safe... by eating all the drugs yourself." My teeth sank into my bottom lip and I grinned up at him.

He didn't return the smile. In fact, his eyes had gone dark and intense, giving me the impression that he was about to murder someone.

He shook his head. "Don't make that face at me, Hayden."

"What face?"

"That one. You're still doing it," he groaned.

I looked over his shoulder at my reflection in the window. "I don't know what the problem is. I'm just making a normal face."

"No, it's not. That face makes me want to strip those sexy panties off of you and finish what we started. I've thought a lot about it, and I'm willing to bet that you make that same face when I'm deep inside of you."

His fingers traced up the side of my arm before coming to rest against my hair. He took the strands and wrapped them around his fist, lightly tethering me to him.

For a few seconds, I was frozen solid; imagining what it would be like to not worry about the consequences. Who cared if we couldn't stand each other in the morning?

Oh, wait.

I did.

Right now, Jake wanted me. A quick glance down had confirmed that. But, tomorrow morning, he'd be sober and back in professional mode. I wasn't going to be accused of drugging his food just to get laid.

I pushed my cheek up against the hand holding my hair and shook my head. "We can't and you know it. We made a deal and as much as I want to say yes— believe me, I do— I don't want to compli- cate things. I'm sorry."

I was sorry too.

It had been years since I'd been close to a man and when I had what had to be the sexiest one alive throwing himself at me, I'd turned him down. Not once, but twice.

"Fair enough. If you change your mind, I'll be right here, somehow getting more high. Does it come and go in waves? I don't think I want to go any higher." Jake laid back against the pillows again, pulling me along with him.

"Maybe you're metabolizing some of it?" We were still holding hands, each of us laying on our side facing the other. It was nice.

Jake closed his eyes for a second and nodded. "It's multicomplying in my body. I'm more fucked up than I was an hour ago."

I thought back to an hour before when he'd been waltzing around the room with his dick hanging out of his pants. "Oh, I don't know that you are."

He closed his eyes again. "Lay here with me for a second?"

I mock-sighed, "I guess I'll cancel that hot date I had planned and stay here to take care of you."

His eyes remained closed, but he smiled. "Good. That guy was all wrong for you anyway."

"And how would you know?" The playful banter between us was safe. Familiar even. Territory I could easily navigate.

It was when Jake started telling me that I was gorgeous or describing the ways in which he'd like to defile my body that I felt unsteady.

I didn't know what to do with him when he was nice to me.

"He's not me. Simple as that."

And we were back in no-mans-land. We slipped into silence and I was bordering on that fine line between consciousness and dreaming when he spoke again.

"You lied to Aaris." He opened his eyes when I didn't respond and elaborated. "You convinced her that you're a vegetarian, but you're not. Why?"

A strand of hair fell over my eyes and he reached up to tuck it behind my ear. The scent of him filled my lungs and muddled my thoughts.

"I don't know, Jake," I sighed. "It was a long time ago."

"Yeah, but you did the same thing with Damien from the coffee shop."

He said all of it as a casual observation, yet I couldn't help but feel defensive. "What are you saying—that I'm a liar? That I can't be trusted?"

His fingers lingered in my hair. "I'm saying you've wasted all this time writing for other people— trying to change your story to fit the narrative they set. Well, fuck them. It's time to write for you. What's your story, Hayden?"

I propped my head up on my fist and deflected. "What's yours?"

Jake let go of me and rolled onto his back. "Come here. The room's spinning again."

I curled up against his side and rested my head on his chest. His fingers moved back to the nape of my neck and I realized that I didn't need the mantra necklace to feel zen as fuck; just his hands in my hair.

"You said that I joined the police academy after I lost my parents, but my parents are still alive. Truth is, they sent me away when I was a teenager. I was an epic fuck up. I'd been arrested twice— once for burglary and the other for possession of alcohol by a minor."

His chest rumbled against my cheek as he dismantled everything I thought I knew about him.

He shifted against the mattress. "My old man wasn't having it. Said he was sending me to military school. We came to blows in the garage. Being a former Marine, he kicked my ass, and off I went. Now's the part of the story when I should say that my parents changed my life for the better with their decision or that it brought us closer, but it didn't happen.

"I was still just as angry when I graduated as I was when I went in. He thought he could ship me off and let someone else deal with all my problems. Like it was too much for him. Went and joined the academy and still, to this day, I've been waiting for him to tell me that I've made him proud."

What was I supposed to say after that? That we were kindred spirits? That I understood what it was like to be a disappointment to your parents? Rage coursed through my veins, but I choked on uncertainty.

How could his parents not be proud of him? He'd done amazing things as a police officer.

If I told him what it was like growing up in Reid's shadow, would he understand or just see it as me competing with his pain? His face remained impassive, so I reined my anger and sympathy in and just held on to him.

Jake continued to stare up at the ceiling. "Thing is, I could've gone back to what I'd been doing before. I'd picked up a few things that would've made me hard to catch. In the end, I decided that I was going to make something of myself, in spite of him. And if the day ever came that I was a father, my son would know how much he meant to me, no matter what shit he got into."

We lay there in silence and I thought about how my parents and Jake's weren't all that different. Reid had been their golden boy, unable to do anything wrong, while I'd always been a bit of a letdown.

"Did you always want to be a writer?" Jake asked as he continued to massage my scalp.

"No. I didn't really know what it was growing up. I guess I thought that everyone had stories in their head. It never really seemed like anything other than a hobby." I yawned and looked up at him. "I'm going to turn the light off and get some sleep. Will you be okay?"

He nodded, watching me with that unreadable expression again.

The events of the day had left me exhausted and confused and in need of a dip in the ice machine down the hall. I flipped the switch, plunging us into darkness before he could see the tears that had suddenly appeared in my eyes. Jake pulled my body back over to his, draping my arms and legs around him like a blanket.

I drifted off to the sounds of the traffic on the streets below, only to be woken by his lips pressed against the corner of mine. It was brief; there one minute and gone the next.

Just like every good thing between us.

NINETEEN

"BAKER CHECKED OUT," Jake said by way of greeting as he sat down in the vinyl chair next to mine.

I looked up from my laptop and checked the digital sign to ensure our flight was still on schedule before turning my attention to him. "No one else got sick?"

He took a swig from his bottled water. "Not one, which makes me think that the cupcake was switched out. I still can't figure out how they ensured that it got to your table though."

I went back to Jessa's story, my mind still mulling over what little information we did have. Instead of a late brunch and some last-minute sightseeing, we'd spent hours going over surveillance footage and interviewing potential witnesses before rushing to the airport.

Jake was still convinced that I would've ended up in the hospital had I eaten the cupcake, but that was what bothered me. This person had been savvy enough to sneak a weed-laced cupcake into the ballroom, but hadn't chosen something more potent?

Out of every poison out there—arsenic... cyanide—they'd chosen weed? It was less how to get away with murder and more a study in how to become a massive inconvenience.

"How are you feeling?" I asked while keeping my eyes on the keyboard.

Nonchalant.

Casual.

He continued draining the bottled water before offering a gruff, "Fine."

I'd woken up feeling like we'd turned a corner and moved through my morning asanas with a clear head and a smile on my face.

That is, until Jake appeared in the room, looking nothing like a man who'd been drugged out of his head the night before.

He'd come to a stop in front of me as I held Wide Leg Forward Fold before making a rough sound of disapproval and looking away.

"You wanna get some clothes on, Hayden? We've got a lot to get done this morning."

Last night, he'd wanted me in nothing but my underwear, but given the fact that he'd looked at me like I'd just run over his grandmother, that opinion had changed.

It'd been naïve to think that we'd be friends just because he let his guard down with me. We'd just gone straight from the stadium parking lot to second base, leaving me keyed up and hopeful that things would be different.

It had been merely a fluke.

A lapse in judgment.

After that, he'd disappeared from the room while I dressed and had been avoiding me ever since.

I patted the arm of his chair. "Do you want to talk about it?"

"Talk about what, Hayden?" He kept his eyes on the cell phone in his hands. Obviously, we were playing the same game—*don't let the other person know you care about the subject being discussed. Whatever you do, keep your eyes averted.*

I picked at a rip in my jeans. "Last night. I just thought that—"

He cut me off. "Yeah, let's not do the whole 'discuss our feelings bullshit.' I was stoned. Now, I'm better. End of story."

Ceasefire over.

I fell silent again, digging my finger into the hole and watching the material fray.

Jake's leg bounced up and down before he stood up. "Are you hungry? I'm hungry. I'm just gonna grab some food."

I looked back up at the sign. "They're about to start boarding."

He pursed his lips and nodded. "Yeah, I've got time."

I spent the next twenty minutes wiping microscopic pieces of dust from my keyboard while watching the arrivals and departures board for the slightest change. When that didn't work at distracting me, I checked my horoscope.

Most of the time it's good to have strong opinions and be independent and willful, Libra. There are other times when your attitude pushes people away. There's a stubborn yet sensitive attitude in your world of romance that may be difficult for you to deal with. Perhaps you're taking a more rational approach to things while your loved one is taking a more emotional one.

Stubborn, yet sensitive? If that wasn't a perfect description of Jake.

When they began boarding and Jake still hadn't reappeared, I began to worry. I gnawed at my lower lip and looked around before packing up my laptop. He knew when the flight was leaving and said he'd be back.

A middle-aged woman with platinum blonde hair caught my eye. "Are you and your man having a fight?"

I turned around and looked behind me. "Me?"

"Yes, you. Silly girl." She slipped her paperback into her oversized purse and came over to sit next to me. "So, tell me, how bad is it?"

I frowned while zipping my backpack shut. "How bad is what?"

She glanced around, presumably for Jake, before leaning in to whisper conspiratorially, "The fight between you and your husband."

The heavy scent of booze nearly knocked me back.

I paste a polite smile on my face. "Oh, he's not my husband—"

"Fine. Boyfriend. Fiancé. Whatever. Look," she barked out, running a hand down her tracksuit. "You might think I'm just another attractive woman, trying to butt into someone else's business, but you're wrong."

I hadn't thought that.

Not at all.

"Okay?" I answered weakly before sitting back down.

"I have quite the knack for helping couples in need. I couldn't help but overhear what sounded like a lover's spat and I'm here to offer my services."

I looked up at the screen and retrieved my boarding pass from my purse. "Oh, well, as much as I would love to do that, it's my turn to board. Nice to meet you..."

"Emma," she beamed. "And what a lucky coincidence, it's my turn to board too."

I gave one last look around the gate, suddenly desperate to find Jake. "I just need to find—"

She swatted the air between us. "No. You are an independent woman who does not need a man to board a plane. He knows where you are."

I quashed down the urge to laugh hysterically and joined the line to board. The flight attendant came over the loudspeaker to give details for the flight, but Emma managed to drown out most of what he was saying.

As we inched toward the jetway, I heard about couples who were much worse off than me and 'my chap.' Couples that had inexplicably given this woman money and their trust to fix their relationships.

"Now, Joe had just gotten caught up in making the money and then he was done. This left Valerie to raise the kids, run the household, the works. Now, can you imagine what happened when their kids graduated?"

I shook my head politely and handed the gate agent my ticket, willing Jake to come back and put me out of my misery.

She latched onto my arm like we were old friends. "Well, I'll tell you. Splitsville. Just like I'd predicted four years before. By then, it was too late to save either of them. That's why it's so lucky for you that I was sitting where I was."

"Mmm hmm..." I made eye contact with the flight attendant and raised my eyebrows.

Help me.

Obviously, he wasn't fluent in the subtle art of eye speak. Instead of, *"Ladies, we have assigned seats for this flight and you two cannot sit together,"* I got, "Welcome aboard, feel free to sit anywhere there's an open seat."

I ground my molars together. "Thank you."

I navigated the narrow row with Emma right on my heels, still rambling on about the miracles she'd worked.

It would've been helpful had my horoscope mentioned her showing up. I would've hidden in the bathroom until they made the last call announcement.

Emma herded me into a row with two empty seats. An older man looked up from his newspaper and nodded at the two of us.

I glanced over the seats and past the line of people, wishing that Jake would've given me a way to contact him. "I'm sorry," I apologized to Emma. "I'm just going to wait for my chap."

Oh god.

Now, I was talking like her.

"Please find a seat and stow your carry-on in the overhead bin. We've got a full flight today. Don't block the aisles," chirped a peppy flight attendant as she moved past us.

Sweat trickled down my spine and the ceiling was suddenly too low for my liking. People grumbled as they moved around me, but I stood like a deer in the headlights, governed by indecision.

"Sit down," Emma urged. "Let him wonder where you are for a change."

Someone's carryon caught me in the back of the head, forcing me back toward Newspaper Ned. Emma took the aisle seat, and I'd officially reached the threshold of hell.

I kept straining to see over the seats, waiting for the grumpy gargantuan to make an appearance.

And he did.

Finally.

He scanned each row before landing on mine. When he saw me, he relaxed his shoulders and gave a small wave before sitting down in a seat near the front.

No last minute white knight rescue for me.

The universe felt that Jake and I needed a time out. And, after last night, I was inclined to agree.

Maybe I was supposed to give Emma a chance. She counseled couples of all sorts, so she probably had loads of insight into what to do if one found oneself falling for a fictional character.

Instead of judging her, I needed to remember that we were all beings of light and goodness with an important role to play.

I inhaled deeply and centered myself. I was not going to think about Jake or last night. Instead, I was going to open myself up to everything the universe had to offer.

Including my new friend.

I took a swig from my bottled water and tried to focus in on what Emma was saying.

"...So, that brings me to you and your man. And it sounds like the same type of situation. Am I right?"

I nodded wisely. "Absolutely. You really have a talent for this."

Ned began chuckling from behind the newspaper. The woman in the row in front of us turned and peered at me through the crack between the seats.

Like a sideshow act.

So, I might've missed the first part of her spiel. I was just going to nod and agree until I sorted it all out. Then, I'd bare my soul and she'd recognize that we were kindred spirits.

We'd probably end up becoming the best of friends; friends who took expensive plane rides and talked about making a difference in the world.

Emma leaned in, exhaling the remnants of whiskey my way. "When did your fear begin?"

Perhaps agreeing with whatever she said had not been the right plan, but it was too late to admit that now. "Um, I guess back when I was a kid. The thought of it just weirded me out. Then, as I got older, it seemed like something I wanted, but I just couldn't fit it in."

The chuckles grew louder until Ned's paper was practically vibrating. He was probably reading the comics and feeling jealous that he hadn't chosen the middle seat.

"Well." She dropped her voice to a whisper, yet managed to sound louder than before. "It's normal to feel an aversion to it. Did you tell anyone of your fear?"

I took another drink of water. "Yeah. I told my parents and my dad said I better make room for it or else I was going to end up dying alone with my cat."

The woman from the seat in front of us was making no attempt to hide the fact that she was listening in and I frowned at her.

Emma choked on the gin and tonic she'd ordered right after takeoff and rasped, "You—your father really told you that?"

I shrugged. "Well, yeah. He said if I refused to let a man in then I was going to spend my life alone. So, you can see my dilemma here."

There we go.

Back on track.

Maybe now was the time to mention that Jake was fictional. Really get into the meat of the story.

"What it is about the act itself that scares you?"

I thought about the previous night and how close I'd come to letting my guard down. "I don't know exactly. I know it's going to hurt."

There were more snickers from behind the paper and I rolled my eyes at Emma as if to say, *'Can you believe this clown?'*

She urged me to continue.

I took a deep breath. "The hurt isn't what scares me; it's the destruction that's going to be left behind once it's over. Like how am I supposed to put the pieces back together?"

Ned rocked in his chair, wheezing with laughter like an old man.

I pulled the paper away from his face. "I'm sorry, but you are being incredibly rude right now. My friend and I are trying to have a serious conversation and your laughter is very distracting."

Tears ran from the corner of his eyes and he shook his head before wheezing again. "Just... just give me a—"

I folded my arms across my chest and watched as his face turned crimson. "Love is not a laughing matter."

"Love?" he forced out. "Who said anything about love?"

I turned to Emma. "Tell him what we're talking about, so he'll go back to his boring old paper."

Emma drained the gin and tonic and slurred, "Anal."

I froze in horror as the people in the rows around me began laughing. This was worse than the recurring nightmare I had of appearing on the *Today* show in my underwear.

I knew two things then. One, the universe had a sick sense of humor. And two, I was going to be completely drunk by the time this plane landed.

JAKE STOOD WAITING for me as I race-walked off the jetway. I looped my arm through his and began dragging him toward baggage claim.

"Whoa. Slow down. What's the rush?" he protested as I pulled him past fast food kiosks and overpriced gift shops.

"I really need to get back to the story, Jake," I snapped. "Or did you forget why we're all here?"

He pointed at my backpack. "Don't you have your laptop? Why weren't you writing during the flight?"

I glanced behind me to see if Emma was following, but there was no sign of her. There were, unfortunately, several faces that matched the ones I'd seen peering over seats at me though.

"We have to hurry and get back to the apartment. Bootsy needs me."

He let me keep my death grip on him, but slowed our pace. "Have you been drinking?"

"Yes," I forced through clenched teeth. "That is really the least of our problems right now. Where the hell did you go?"

"I went to grab food. Just like I said. The line was long. End of story."

We stepped onto the escalator down to baggage claim and I noticed several people down below had their cell phones trained on my face.

Jake frowned. "Are they taking your picture?"

A nervous burst of giggles escaped, and I grinned until my cheeks ached. "No. I mean, maybe. I mentioned that I write books back on the plane and you know how people are; everyone wants proof they met a celebrity. Hurry, our bags are waiting."

Our bags were not waiting. The little siren was blaring above the carousel, but it remained empty. I had to get us out of here before Emma showed up, demanding to meet my chap.

She'd somehow managed to get drunker on the long flight and let it slip that she wasn't really a therapist. At least not from a legal standpoint. Apparently showing up to class with a flask was frowned upon.

The fact that I was beyond humiliated escaped her notice as she rambled through the remainder of the flight about how she was a self-taught sex therapist with a completely unique approach.

I had to keep her away from Jake. I kept my death grip on him, trying to make myself invisible.

Proving that the universe didn't give you what you wanted, but what you needed, our bags were the first two off the conveyer belt and I lunged for them without hesitation.

"Okay, we got them. Let's go."

Jake trailed behind me toward the exit. "Are you sure you're okay? You're acting really strange."

"Hellooooo," a voice called from the escalator. "Wait up!"

I dropped my shoulders in dismay and turned to see Emma.

"Hayden? Do you know her?"

She began stepping around other travelers to get down to us faster and I didn't even think. I just took off for the sliding glass doors.

"Freedom!" I exclaimed as I reached the other side and continued jogging down the narrow sidewalk.

"Hayden!" Jake yelled from behind me. "Hayden, slow down!"

I wasn't stopping for anything. I was going to go home and forget that the flight had even happened. No one would ever know, and it wasn't as if I'd given Emma any of my information, so she had no way of contacting me.

Not only that, but I was going to forget what happened in the hotel room. When we got back to my apartment, I'd have Aaris set me up with someone who was both nice and real. I'd be back to my old self in no time.

The heel of my boot landed awkwardly against the pavement and I sucked in a lungful of cold air as the force propelled me off the side-walk and onto my right ankle. There was a pop, quickly followed by a burst of pain.

I scrambled onto my knees and stood up, but my right ankle gave out again almost immediately. So, I did the completely rational thing —I began hopping on my left foot while tugging my suitcase along behind me.

Jake dropped his duffel bag and ran over. "Damn it, Hayden! Why were you running in heels?"

My ankle protested every bounce and I sank down onto the side-walk again with a soft moan.

I rocked back and forth, holding my foot in my hand like an injured dove. "They're not heels. They're booties. The perfect fall accessory," I panted through the waves of pain.

He sighed and shook his head. "You're out of your goddamn mind, you know that?"

I looked over his shoulder at the exit, praying that Emma hadn't gotten her bag yet. "We gotta go. Like now."

New plan. I'd go home... sleep off the alcohol... and then vow to never remember this flight.

Jake pulled the bootie off and began digging into the tender skin. I yelped and the corners of his mouth turned down. "Yeah, we're going...to the hospital."

"No," I argued, still keeping an eye on the door. "I mean, yes, we have to go right now. But, we can't go to the hospital. I don't have insurance."

He took his bag and slipped the strap over his head like a cross-body purse before lifting me into his arms. "Alright. We'll get you home and get it elevated.

When I saw the top of Emma's head moving toward us, I began scrambling to gather all of my things. "We have to go right now... before it gets worse."

"That's not really how it works. It's going to get worse, whether we stay here or not." Jake adjusted the backpack straps on my shoulders. "Do you think you can climb onto my back? It'll be a hell of a lot easier to carry you to the truck."

I nodded and wrapped my arms around his neck, trying not to choke him as he lifted me off the cold ground.

I held the bootie in my hand solemnly. He managed the rest of our baggage and carried me piggyback toward the parking garage.

By the time we made it back to my apartment, my ankle had swollen to the point that my sock was beginning to cut off circulation. I reluctantly peeled it off while Jake carried our things up before coming back for me.

Purple and blue bruises spread up toward my shin. Had he not gotten my bootie off when he had, I was convinced it would've become permanently attached to my foot.

He used a fireman's carry to get me up the stairs and the full weight of my injury hit me. How was I going to get up and down the stairs with a busted foot?

This was all Emma's fault.

Jake placed me gently on the couch next to Bootsy and her beloved iPad before going into the kitchen. A few seconds later, Max and Aaris walked in.

She winced when she saw my foot. "Oh, sweetie. How did that happen?"

Max assessed the damage from across the room. "Supination."

"Yeah, yeah," I grumbled, while simultaneously trying to stretch my calf muscle. Everything from the knee down ached and I regretted the fact that I wasn't in a hospital bed being pumped full of intravenous drugs.

Jake came back in with an ice pack and a bottle of water. He retrieved a bottle of ibuprofen from his pocket and tapped three into my hand. "Go ahead and take these. Max is going to look at you."

I frowned. "Max? Why? So, he can tell me that this wouldn't have happened if I'd only been wearing the proper footwear?"

Max walked over and scratched Bootsy under the chin before addressing me. "No. I was a combat medic in the Army. I'm gonna get you fixed up."

"Now, we're just gonna dab the brush at the canvas like this and what the heck, we'll add a little tree right back in here..."

I realized that Bootsy hadn't moved an inch since I'd come in. "What is she watching?"

Aaris pointed at Max. "It was all his idea. I told him that you preferred bird documentaries, but he said she wanted to expand her horizons while you were away."

Jake wrapped the ice pack around my ankle, and I sucked in a breath as I leaned over to see the tablet. "Bob Ross, Max? You got her hooked on Bob Ross while I was gone?"

He shrugged and knelt next to my ankle. "She was knocking shit over in the middle of the night and I couldn't sleep, so I introduced her to Bob and she's much calmer now."

"She's a cat. That's what cats do. They hunt at night."

His fingers moved over my swollen skin much like Jake's had and I winced before reflexively pulling my foot back.

Jake caught it and gently lowered it back into Max's hand. "You've got to let him look at it. Hey." He sat down next to me, earning him a dirty look from Bootsy. "Hey, look at me."

I bit down on my lip to keep it from trembling. "Aaris, could you grab my purse?" I widened my eyes and tilted my head and she nodded in understanding.

"Here we are." She popped a gummy into my mouth like I was a small child. I put one hand on my abdomen and the other on my chest and inhaled deeply through my nose, letting my tummy push my hand out. I exhaled through pursed lips and then repeated until I felt in control of my emotions again.

Max waited until I nodded before turning my foot over in his hands. I waited for a comment from Jake, either about the weed or the belly breathing, but he just took the hand that was on my abdomen in his and squeezed. "Hayden. Look at me."

I turned my head against the cushion and faced him.

"Tell me about why you became a writer. Last night you said it was more of a hobby, was there something else you wanted to do?" His deep voice was hypnotic, as was his large hand covering my stomach.

Despite all of my bluster about forgetting last night in the hotel, I realized as he spoke that I was full of shit.

I wasn't getting over him.

Not in this lifetime anyway.

I swallowed past the sudden lump in my throat. "You mean like when I was little?"

He continued stroking the back of my hand with his thumb and nodded. "Yeah. What did you want to be?"

Our faces were inches apart, each breath shared between us.

Pain blurred my thoughts, making it hard to concentrate. Max pushed my toes toward my shin, and I let out a startled gasp of pain before biting down on my lip. He said something to Aaris and she left the room.

"Hey, eyes on me." I reluctantly looked up at him again and he continued. "You've got this. Just talk to me."

I nodded shakily. "Um, I didn't know I wanted to be a writer; not like what you mean anyway. I actually started with writing song lyrics. I watched a lot of *Star Search* and I had this idea in my head that I was going to be discovered when I least expected it, so I wrote out my songs."

He brought his hand up and brushed the hair off of my forehead. "Song lyrics, huh?"

"What does huh mean?"

Jake smirked. "Nothing. It just makes sense now."

I was going to ask what made sense, but Max shifted my foot and I ground my teeth together to keep from screaming at him. He looked up at me somberly. "It's sprained."

"You think?" I bit out through clenched teeth.

He nodded. "Yes. Completely sprained. You don't have the stuff I need, so Aaris and I are going to run down to the VA and—"

"Wait." I stopped him. "What am I going to need?"

He began ticking items off on his fingers. "Bandages to keep it immobile, a walking boot, and a good pair of crutches."

"But, how long will I need these?" I couldn't be on crutches for my parent's dinner next weekend. Reid would never let me hear the end of it.

Max shrugged. "Two...maybe three weeks?"

So much for making a grand entrance.

TWENTY

I PULLED the hem of the red dress down toward my knees, frowning at my reflection in the mirror before casting a longing look at the jeans and t-shirt wadded up on my bed.

The jeans would've been better for covering up the monstrosity on my right leg, but that wouldn't have fit my mother's dress code.

"You'll just go for dinner and then make your excuses to leave early," I told myself.

"Hayden?" Jake tapped his knuckles against the door.

"Come in." I continued glaring at the girl in the mirror. A girl who felt like a stranger. My face was suffocating under the layers of makeup and it took everything in me not to gnaw at the crimson stain on my lips.

"Hey, are you—" Jake froze in the doorway. "Fuck. What's all this for?"

I looked over my shoulder at him. "I have to go to my parent's house for dinner, remember?"

He nodded slowly. "And your parents... they live in the White House? Or is it Buckingham Palace?"

I ran my fingers through the soft curls, hoping they didn't frizz up on the way over. "Something like that," I answered distractedly. "I'll be home before ten."

"You can't go by yourself, Hayden. You can't even drive," he noted with a wry smile.

I hobbled over to the bed to grab my purse, ignoring the perfectly good pair of crutches leaned up against the wall. "I'll just call Uber or something."

Max had insisted I use them at all times for the next two weeks, but Bootsy had become fascinated with them and made a game of darting out in front of me. After tripping over her repeatedly, I decided I was better off taking my chances with just the boot.

"Is my gray suit formal enough for dinner?"

"Why?"

Jake rolled his eyes. "Because I'm writing a book on etiquette. C'mon, I'm going with you. Someone's got to make sure you don't break the other leg while you're there."

I thought about it. It would be nice to have someone to talk to, and then I remembered why we were having dinner in the first place.

"I—" I hedged. "I'm not sure that's a good idea. It's usually a pretty intimate affair with just family." Well, and Reid's girlfriend, Emily, but she'd been considered a part of the family since day one.

"Well, I think they can make an exception for your... who can we say I am? A boyfriend, maybe?" He said it all nonchalantly.

Meanwhile, the floor had dropped out from beneath my feet, sending me spiraling into a mess of emotions.

He'd said the B word.

"But, what happens when you leave?" I hadn't meant to say it.

I temporarily lost my train of thought, along with all the reasons he couldn't go to dinner, when he stripped off his shirt.

"I don't know," he said from inside the closet. "I guess you could say it didn't work out."

I could say that.

I could also join the Peace Corps and change lives all over the world.

Could and would were miles apart.

I sighed. "Fine. I have to leave in five minutes so that I have enough time to stop at the bakery on the way."

Jake walked back into the bedroom as he fastened the buttons on his dress shirt. "Ah, classic. You didn't make anything, so you're stopping at the bakery," he teased. "Are you going to put it on a fancy plate and pass it off as your own too?"

If he only knew...

I laughed and hobbled into the living room. "Not quite. No one in my family would expect me to cook. My mom asked me to pick up an order for her. I guess she ran out of time."

Bootsy watched us from the couch with her precious iPad resting on the cushion beneath her. Max had turned her into a damn monster. If I tried to put a nature documentary on, she meowed incessantly and batted the damn thing off the couch.

Only Bob Ross would do for the little Khaleesi.

I waved at her and she flicked her tail in response before dismissing us. The temperature outside was in the fifties, so I grabbed my coat on the way out.

"Hop on?" Jake gestured toward his back as we reached the stairs.

I pointed down at my dress. "I'm not sure this is appropriate attire for piggyback rides."

He nodded. "You're right. Plan B. Come here."

I limped the three steps over to him and he scooped me up into his arms. "Is this better?"

I nodded dumbly just as a door opened and Eddie stepped out, looking more impaired than usual. "Fuck, you look nice, Detective. I really like that red dress. Brings out the color of your eyes."

Jake frowned at him. "I'm going to assume you're talking to my girl and not me, in which case I'll let it slide. I'm taking her to dinner."

"The dumpster said you might be heading out soon. The dumpster says a lot of things though." Eddie swallowed nervously and scurried back into his apartment like a cockroach.

He really needed to find friends who were actual people, not inanimate objects. This was coming from someone who had developed feelings for a fictional character, but that still seemed like a step up from a waste receptacle.

"That was... strange," I noted dryly.

"Yeah, he needs to lay off the drugs. Maybe get out of his apartment more." We continued down the stairs, with Jake acting like nothing was amiss.

First, it was the *B* word.

Now, *my girl.*

Detective Hopkins was dangerously close to me swooning in his arms from all the sweet talk.

He offered me the use of a motorized cart when we stopped at the bakery. I refused, having made the split-second decision that hobbling was much less humiliating.

The rest of the drive was quiet, but not like an angry or uncomfortable silence. It was different this time.

Anticipated silence.

Like we were looking forward to something.

Jake let out a low whistle as we pulled into the long driveway. "This is not what I expected..."

I ran my damp hands over the hem of my dress, smoothing it against my thighs. "Yep. This is where they live."

His eyebrows drew together as he looked at me. "Are you shaking?"

"No," I laughed. "Low blood sugar. Let's go eat." I was going to vomit before we even made it inside.

There were luxury cars everywhere. Jake parked behind one, his truck sticking out like a hillbilly cousin at the country club. "I thought you said this was just a small family dinner."

I shrugged. Maybe they'd decided to make a big thing of it. "It usually is," I murmured as I counted the vehicles.

He took the bakery box from my hand and helped me down from the truck.

"There you are," my mother trilled from the front porch. "I was beginning to wonder if we needed to send a search party."

I forced a smile onto my face. "Sorry. The bakery was a little backed up."

She shook her head and wagged her finger, sending some of her martini sloshing over the side of the glass. "Hayden, lack of planning on your part is not the bakery's fault. Oh!" She noticed Jake and smiled like the former beauty queen she was. "And who is this?"

Surprisingly, the King of Smirks didn't return it. "Detective Jake Hopkins. And you are?"

She extended a hand. "Anna Michaels, Hayden's mother. She's never mentioned you before- a detective... how interesting."

My mother led us through the arched foyer and into the kitchen. "Just put that box down there and we'll go find Craig."

"Mom?" I touched her arm and lowered my voice. "Um, could you, I mean, would it be possible for me to get reimbursed for the cake? It was a little expensive."

A hundred and fifty dollars was a drop in the bucket to them, but to me, it meant that Bootsy and I would both be eating tinned cat food until my next royalty payment.

She laughed uncomfortably before her eyes darted up to Jake. It was her classic, *we don't discuss money in front of strangers* look. "Hayden, I think you still owe your father for that editing business he covered for you. Let's not make tonight unpleasant, okay?"

I nodded. "Sure. I just thought..."

"I'll have your father take it off your tab," she answered sweetly before shaking her head at Jake. "Kids and money—what can you do? Now, everyone's outside."

She tottered out to the patio, but Jake held back. "Are you okay?" His hand came down to rest on my arm.

"Oh, yeah. She's just had a few too many martinis. It's fine." I stepped around him and limped out to the patio before he had a chance to see my eyes fill.

Sadness was quickly replaced by anger when I saw Reid and his colleagues milling about the expansive backyard. A band played in the corner and there was a long table of catered food set up. It looked like a goddamn wedding was taking place.

"What is all this?" I asked my mother.

She hesitated for a brief second and I knew; I knew it was too much for me to have even one night.

"Well, Reid's company finalized their merger with *PharmTech* yesterday and we wanted to celebrate. Emily's going to be out of town next weekend, so it left us with this weekend. It'll be too cold after that."

I stood in open-mouthed shock as I watched Reid and my father tell some hilarious story to a group of suits around them. Everyone laughed and drank while I stood frozen on the patio.

"Come on, Hayden. Go congratulate your brother. This is a very big accomplishment for him," she chided.

I navigated the first step with my air cast, something she'd yet to acknowledge and Jake stepped in, leading me down the stairs to the yard.

"Hey." His voice was low. "Care to tell me what the hell's going on?"

"Um, apparently Reid's company merged with some other company and we're celebrating." I began giggling hysterically and his grip tightened on my arm.

My father saw us and excused himself from the group. "Little Hayden... about time you showed up. Did your mother tell you the big news?"

I nodded as he pulled me into a rough hug. "She did."

He ruffled my hair. "See what happens when you work hard for something? You should go talk to Reid and get some pointers." He turned to Jake. "And you are?"

"Detective Jake Hopkins."

"Craig Michaels." They shook hands, but Jake once again wasn't smiling. He looked like he was trying to solve a mystery.

"Detective, huh? What trouble has this one gotten into now?" My father bellowed with laughter.

Jake's eyebrows were almost touching. "I'm dating your daughter, not investigating her. You're saying you've never heard my name before?"

Oh no.

I knew where he was going with this.

My father shook his head. "No, but you know how most women play hard to get? Well, this little one plays hard to want." He boomed with laughter again at his clever joke.

He was the only one.

My face heated with embarrassment. "Good one, Dad. We're just going to go get some food."

"Wait. Anna!" he yelled across the lawn. "Anna, the gift!"

My mother waved at him and nodded before disappearing back into the house. She returned with an envelope. "Here we are. A little something for the birthday girl."

Jake sucked in a breath beside me, but I kept my eyes on my parents. I hadn't wanted him to come for this very reason.

I took the envelope and imagined a check with a lot of zeroes inside. Instead, there was a picture of a leather couch. I frowned at it.

"A... couch?" I had a couch. I didn't have room for another.

My father nodded. "A couch. Something that won't collect cat hair like the one you've got now. That thing is more cat hair than sofa, am I right?" He chuckled.

I looked down at the picture again, buying myself some time before I opened my mouth and said something I was just going to regret. Bootsy would have the leather shredded within a week.

"Now, here's the best part," my mother chimed in. "This couch can be yours in three more payments. See! It teaches you to manage money and solves the cat hair problem."

My nostrils flared and my jaw was beginning to ache from clenching my teeth. Jake's hand dug into the place between my neck and shoulder. "You got my gift on layaway?"

They smiled proudly and Jake began steering me toward the food table. "Excuse us for a second."

"Absolutely," my father replied. "See if you can't get her to eat a little something. She's far too short these days."

His laughter echoed in my ears as we moved toward the white linen-covered tables.

"It's your birthday?"

I nodded. "You're using your Batman voice again, you know?"

He rolled his eyes. "Why didn't you tell me? We could've—"

"We could've what?" I hissed back at him. "It's just another day. We'll eat and then have cake. That's all I need."

He pursed his lips and studied my face. "This is what you want?"

I added a spoonful of mozzarella salad to my plate. "Absolutely. This is fine."

We moved through the line in silence before finding a round table near the house.

"Your parents don't know who I am," he stated flatly before snagging a meatball from his plate.

"You expected that they'd know about my make-believe boyfriend?" I snorted. "I'm crazy, but not that crazy."

"That's not what I mean, and you know it. Your parents should've picked up on that name immediately. I'm only the main character in three of your books."

I pushed a piece of mini quiche across the plate with my fork. "Well, they're not really into reading the genre I write. They prefer something a little more high-brow."

Jake's chair creaked as he leaned forward. "High-brow? It's a book your kid wrote! My kid could write a book on the mating practices of sea turtles and I'd read the shit out of it—"

"Got a thing for sea turtles, do you?" I asked with a grin.

"Jesus, no. You're missing the point. If your son or daughter creates something, you acknowledge that." He gestured at the crowd of people. "I mean, what the fuck did your brother do to warrant hijacking your birthday party? Cure cancer?"

"Well," I hedged. "Not quite, but that's the endgame from what I understand."

Reid's girlfriend, Emily, waved at me from the porch and I stood up. "Hey, just eat the free food and enjoy the music. I'm going to go say hello to my brother's girlfriend."

In a rare show of emotion, Jake reached for my arm and pulled me toward him. "You deserve better than this and you know it." He pressed a light kiss against the back of my hand, and I was on my way to the ground in a dramatic faint before I realized he was doing it for show.

We had to look like a real couple for my parents.

I patted his back awkwardly. "Okay, Detective. You're gonna give yourself diabetes if you keep it up with the sweet bullshit."

His mouth turned down and he sighed. "You would say that. Go, try to have some fun."

I pointed down at my boot. "But, not too much."

Emily met me halfway and took my arm in hers, leading me into the kitchen. "What happened to you?"

I explained the entire ordeal as we sat across from each other at the marble island, including the cupcake incident at the hotel. I managed to keep what happened after to myself.

That was the thing about Emily. She made me feel entirely too comfortable, which led to oversharing. I just changed a few details and made Jake the detective working my stalking case.

She popped the cork on a bottle of white wine and frowned. "So, someone tried to poison you and got him instead? Have you told your parents about this?"

I laughed. "I haven't told anyone but Aaris about this. It's too 'out there,' you know? Well, I take that back. Max knows too, but Jake told him."

"Who's Max?" She handed me a glass.

"Oh, um, like a bodyguard that Jake knows. He's keeping an eye on things at the apartment— well, when he's not with Aaris."

Emily paused with the glass resting against her lips and grinned. "Aaris found a man? Is he ancient?"

I explained how Max was the exact opposite of every man she'd ever been with. "I think she's really into him."

"And what about you, Hayden? Are you and the detective hot and heavy too?" She winked and took a sip.

"No," I blurted out with a laugh. "Not at all. He's just here to do a job and then things will go back to normal."

The thought of him leaving left me with an ache in my chest, but it was the reality slap I needed. "I'm surprised you aren't out there celebrating the merger."

Emily looked over my shoulder through the patio doors. "I'm sorry about your birthday, babe. I did get you a little something. Let me grab it."

She slipped off the stool and I dumped the wine into the sink. I couldn't stand the taste of it, but I wasn't willing to offend the only friend I had here.

She returned with a square box. "Here you are. It's nothing extravagant, but I wanted you to feel special tonight. Everyone deserves to feel important on their birthday."

It was a coffee mug featuring a cat wearing a ninja suit. Underneath were the words *Pawsassin*. "Em, I love it!"

She grinned. "I found it while we were in Chicago. It reminded me of you. Now, instead of hiding out in here like social rejects, let's convince your mom to cut the cake. Cake makes everything better."

I agreed and she left to go find her. A few minutes later, the two of them returned and Emily excused herself to go to the bathroom.

"You want cake, Hayden?"

"Pretty much why I'm still here," I joked, earning myself a frown.

"I had to check with Reid first, but he said it was fine."

"Wait," I interjected. "You had to check with Reid to see if it was okay for me to have my birthday cake?"

She bit down on the corner of her lip. "Well, don't be mad, but we changed the cake. It's just that not a lot of people like strawberry."

I hopped over to the counter and lifted the lid on the bright pink box.

Congratulations, Reid!

I stared at the icing letters until they blurred from my tears. "Excuse me," I growled before hobbling out to the backyard.

"Reid!" Every head whipped my direction. Even the band stopped playing.

He looked up from his conversation and smirked. "Yes, Hayden? Is there something I can do for you?"

I gripped the railing and side-stepped my way down the steps toward him. "Yeah, you can explain to me how my birthday cake turned into a congratulatory cake for you."

I felt a wall of muscle at my back and knew that it was Jake without having to turn around.

"I don't believe we've met. Reid Michaels." He extended a hand to Jake.

"Detective Jake Hopkins. What exactly are we celebrating?"

Reid smiled, much like a teacher would to a small child. "Well, my company *Genetistry* finalized the merger with *PharmTech* yesterday. I'm sure you've seen our commercials."

Jake shook his head. "Nope. Never heard of either one of those."

Reid's smile faltered slightly, but he managed to recover before it was noticed by anyone other than me. "Well, we completely redesigned the field of genotyping. Until my company came along, people had to put in a lot of legwork to discover their ancestry. I developed a saliva DNA kit that simplified the process. My product is accurate to .01% and more importantly, the only company backed by the FDA."

Jake nodded along and smiled at the appropriate times, but I didn't miss the discreet eye roll. "And how does *PharmTech* factor in?"

The grin took over his entire face. He'd probably made a boatload of money in the merger just like Scrooge McDuck. He'd probably install a safe room filled with gold coins that he could swim around in too.

"Well, *PharmTech* will use the information we've stored to better understand genetic mutations and diseases, which will lead to scientific discoveries and, if I'm being candid, hopefully a cure for cancer. Just think, never having to watch a loved one suffer through the agony of illness." He spread his hands wide, looking so much like a magician that I almost expected him to pull a rabbit from a hat.

"So, you're taking information from your current clients without their consent?"

Reid shook his head. "Not at all. The participants are receiving the opportunity to participate in groundbreaking research. This is a good thing. Have you considered having your DNA tested? I could make you a deal."

Jake slung his arm around my shoulders. "You know, I'm good. Hayden's handled my family tree stuff up until this point and I'm pretty satisfied."

I tried to keep a straight face.

Reid's jovial used car salesman persona slipped again. "Hayden? Let me guess, she's using *Ancient Tree*. I'm telling you right now, it won't be as reliable as my saliva test."

I frowned at his words. "I'm a wonderful researcher of genealogy and ancestor-like things."

Reid shook his head condescendingly. "Hayden, you spend more time lost in your head than you do in the real world. It's like you're content to remain a receptionist the rest of your life. *Hello, thank you for calling Salon Wicked, this is Hayden, your hairfessional. How may I assist?*"

He'd called the salon one time, yet made a point of mocking my mandated greeting every time I was around him.

"She's a writer too, you know," Jake added and I sighed.

Here we go...

"Oh, that's right. A 'writer.' Anyone can call themselves a writer when there's no research involved."

Jake's hand slipped off of my shoulder and he took a step toward Reid. "Have you read them? Because there's a lot of research that goes into them. Your sister stays up late putting hours of work into them."

Reid apparently missed the unmistakable threat in Jake's tone and slapped his shoulder. "Yeah, bud. Sure. *'His hard member throbbed against her creamy thigh...'*" He mimed jacking off. "She writes romance... I wouldn't even consider that a real genre."

I gasped. I mean, I knew they hadn't read anything I'd written, but to completely dismiss my entire career as fake. I wasn't sure whether I wanted to cry or stab him to death with my salad fork while casually noting that his DNA was going all over the lawn.

Jake reached out and gripped the front of his shirt before growling, "They're cozy mysteries, you fuck." He released him and Reid stumbled back. "Let's go, Hayden."

I reluctantly trailed after him, feeling like I'd committed a crime. Nobody dared to raise their voice in the Michael's household. We let our success speak for us.

Feelings were something best kept to yourself, or as my father had so tactfully put it, *"Don't tell me about the labor pains, just show me the baby."*

It was why they hadn't read my books. Unless I'd hit number one on the New York Times bestseller list, I wasn't worth reading.

"I have cake," my mother called from the patio as we approached.

He took one look at the cake and roared, "Are you fucking kidding me?"

The band stopped playing again and my father speed-walked across the yard over to us. There was no running. Running might give our guests the impression that things were less than perfect.

"Young man, you would do well to remember where you are," he pointed at Jake as he climbed the stairs. "And you, young lady, are ruining your brother's big night by bringing this man and his foul language here."

"Ruining his big night? Do you hear yourself? It's her goddamn birthday and not one of you assholes has done a thing to celebrate her!" Jake's face was turning a dark shade of red and I worried that he was going to stroke out on me.

"We did celebrate her," my mother argued. "We gave her a very expensive gift."

He ran a hand raggedly down his face before biting out, "You gave her a couch on layaway. A couch she didn't ask for, but is now expected to foot the bill on because you have this warped idea that you're teaching her money management skills."

"You don't like the gift? Fine. We'll give it to Reid. At least he knows how to appreciate things," my father snapped.

I glared at Jake. *Thanks a lot.*

This would go down as the worst birthday in history, and that was counting the time that Reid faked being sick to get out of going to my party. Instead of finding someone to stay with him, they'd simply canceled the party completely.

Jake turned to leave but stopped at my father's words. "Reid would appreciate it more? Did Reid appreciate the money you gave him to start his company? Money he was never expected to pay back?"

My father's face was mottled with anger. "You are out of line—"

Jake stood toe to toe with my father, towering over him by at least half a foot. "And you are missing out on an amazing woman. She is intelligent and so damn talented, but you would know that already if you ever bothered to pick up one of her books."

My father interjected, trying to reestablish his authority as the patriarch of the family, but Jake wasn't having it.

"Did she tell you she had a book signing? No, of course not," he answered his own question. "Why tell the people who belittle your career. Well, I'm going to tell you that she sold out of almost every book she brought. There was a line of people waiting to see her; not pretty boy Reid over there. Her."

He looked at Jake and then at the sea of interested faces. "Young man, I—"

"Don't deserve her. Sit and piss all over her work and who she is as a person. One day, she'll be on the top of every book list and you'll be trying to peddle some bullshit to the media to remain relevant. By then it'll be too late, because some of us knew she was worth something from day one." His voice remained low and even. He could've been discussing the weather or some other monotonous subject; not me or my life.

Snapping out of his trance, Jake looked out over the lawn. "I'm sorry to have ruined your evening." He turned back to my parents. "I'm excluding the both of you and fuckboy over there. You three deserve to have your evening blown to shit. C'mon, Hayden. We're leaving."

Jake took my hand and pulled me through the glass patio doors, past the expensive furniture and top of the line everything, and out to his truck.

His breaths were coming in short bursts and his face was still an alarming shade of red. He helped me into the truck. "You can tell me off now. I fucked up. I know it wasn't my place to say anything, but damn it, Hayden, I couldn't just sit back and let them rip you to shreds."

I burst out laughing and it took me a full minute to get it under control enough so that I could speak. "Oh my god, Jake. Did you see their faces? You called my brother a fuckboy!"

I wiped my streaming eyes with the back of my hand. I wanted to kiss him for what he'd done but settled for squeezing his hand. Soon, he'd be gone and all I'd have left would be the memories of him telling my parents where to go and the feel of his hand in mine.

He grimaced. "I did. God, I'm not getting invited to the family Christmas party, am I?"

I shook my head. "I don't think either of us will. How did you know that my dad gave Reid money?"

He walked around to the driver's side and climbed in before answering me. "I didn't. It was a hunch that proved to be correct. I can't believe they're on your ass about paying it back, while letting him off the hook."

I hadn't known about the money, but it made sense. To have heard Reid tell it though, it was implied that he'd built his empire from the ground up all by himself.

I let out a frustrated sigh. "Can we go home now?"

He hit the accelerator, letting the pipes loudly announce our exit. "I've got one stop to make first, if it's alright."

We drove back to the bakery and Jake left the truck running while he ran in. He came back out a few minutes later with a small pink box.

"It's the best I could do last minute."

Happy Birthday, Beautiful!

I was struck dumb by frosting for a second time. Some of the letters were slightly smudged, indicating they'd been done in a hurry, but it was perfect for me.

I was caught between wanting to play it cool and needing to snap photos to post on every one of my social media accounts.

"Hey." He reached for me. "As clumsy as you are, you don't wear your scars on the outside. They're on the inside. Every time you were told that chasing your dream was stupid, it cut you."

I blinked away the tears.

"Now, let's get you home. We've still got a few hours left to celebrate."

TWENTY-ONE

"SO, SHE'S CLOSE THEN?" Jake asked around a mouthful of cake.

Strawberry cake, thank you very much.

I licked the pink icing off my fork and nodded. "I feel like we're close, but I still can't picture the villain. Jessa and Laura are quite the team though, don't you think?"

He scrolled through the manuscript before looking up at me. "They're something, alright. I thought you were out of your mind when you paired them up, but it works. You're a fucking genius, you know that?"

I rolled my eyes with a laugh. "Sure. Okay."

He reached out and gripped my chin in his hand. "I'm serious, Hayden. Because of people like your parents, you can't face the truth that you're great as you are. You don't need the damn sprays and spells or whatever the fuck else you keep around here. If people don't like who you are; then fuck 'em."

I cleared my throat and shifted on the couch. "We better get some coffee going. It's going to be a long night of writing."

Jake kept his hand on my face. "Let's take a break for tonight."

I grinned at him. "C'mon, Jake. You're not getting soft on me, are ya?"

He closed his eyes and took a deep breath, psyching himself up. "Baby, there's not one part of me that's soft. I'm fucking rock hard. And in watching the way the pulse is jumping in your throat, you know exactly what I mean."

Baby... swoon.

"Holy shit." I exhaled faintly. A quick glance down at his dress pants confirmed that he was indeed rock hard.

"It appears that I've rendered the writer speechless," he teased with a smirk.

I placed a hand tentatively against the back of his neck and his eyes widened. When I leaned up and pressed my lips against his, he let out a rough exhale of his own, one that made me think he hadn't expected my reaction. His hand moved down to the strap of my dress and his fingers roved under and over the material.

Our mouths moved together with an urgency as we explored the other's body. I trailed a hand down his dress shirt, coming to rest against his pocket. I tucked it inside, feeling the beat of his heart against my knuckles. I wanted to be carried around in Jake's pocket, safe from the world.

The stubble on his face scraped against my skin and I shivered with pleasure. Jake's hands tangled in my hair and our knees bumped together, but our mouths remained connected. I shifted on the couch until I was sitting on his lap with my dress bunched up around my hips.

His tongue traced my lips and I smiled before opening up to let him in. He kept one hand fisted in my hair while the other found the zipper of my dress and began coaxing it down.

"I think that maybe you want this as badly as I do," he whispered, moving his hand down to stroke against the front of my panties.

"I do," I panted and thrust my breasts up against his chest as the straps of my dress slipped down my arms.

Damn the fact that he was leaving. I could feign writer's block and drag the story out for another year or two. I could force him to stay and feed me strawberry cake every night. I could demand that his mouth kiss every square inch of skin.

I loosened his tie while lifting and lowering my hips against the front of his slacks, forcing a moan out of both of us. "Until you leave, I'm yours," I murmured against his lips.

The words were scary, and I pulled away after saying them. It was too much. I was basically prostituting myself out for as long as he was here.

I'd just laid all my crazy cards out on the table, not even bothering to keep them close to my chest for a while longer.

"Hey." He managed to pull me right back in. "You're my girl. I'm not going to hurt you, okay?"

"I'm your girl?" I blurted out.

He smiled. "The only girl I care about." With that, he wrapped an arm around my lower back and pulled me up against his chest before bringing my mouth back down over his.

No one had ever defended me like he had...or gone out of their way to make my birthday special, even when the majority of the night had been shit.

His tongue stroked my bottom lip and I opened my mouth to let him inside again while keeping my emotions on lockdown.

Jake suddenly pulled back. "I think we need to do some yoga. Your energy is all wrong."

"Yoga? Really?" I disagreed. My energy was in need of sex. Lots and lots of sex.

He stood up and carried me toward the bedroom.

"Wait, where's Bootsy?" I shuddered as his lips found my ear lobe.

"I gave her the tablet and started a Bob Ross marathon. She's good." He lowered me to the carpet with a smirk and kicked the door closed behind him. "Hands on the wall, Ms. Michaels."

I did as he asked and moaned softly as his hands patted down my body, lingering in between my legs.

"You wouldn't be carrying any pencils or pens on your person would you, sweetheart?" he whispered against my ear.

"No, Detective," I whispered back.

"Good girl. Because you're going to let this happen. Your job isn't to write it—none of your fade to black bullshit, okay?"

I nodded and held onto the wall for support. He wrapped my hair around his hands. "Now, what was the move you were doing in the hotel room?"

I thought back to last week. "A wide..." His teeth moved down to my neck. "Um, a wide leg forward fold."

He released me and began unbuttoning his shirt. "Do it."

I let my dress fall to the floor and clasped my hands behind my back before stretching down toward the floor, doing my best to ignore the decidedly unsexy walking boot.

Jake cursed and kicked off his shoes and pants before bending down next to me. "The first time we did yoga, all I could think about was the ways I would bend and stretch your body around mine."

My muscles lost their tension and I fought to hold the position as he placed his tie around my wrists, knotting it lightly. He rested one hand against my rib cage, letting his thumb stroke against the lace of my bra.

"You know what else I've been dying to do?" He yanked the lace panties over my thighs, and I moaned loudly as his teeth sank into the soft flesh of my ass. His thumb continued teasing my nipples and I arched my back, trying to relieve the ache.

"No, no. You're not in charge here," he whispered before pulling me upright. The sudden change in direction left me unsteady and he kept his arm around my waist until the waves of dizziness passed. Despite my arms being bound behind my back, he managed to unclasp my bra and his hands roamed freely over my breasts, caressing the sensitive skin.

I hadn't even touched him yet, but I was getting high off of his rough exhales as he trailed his lips down my neck.

"Do you think," he paused to catch his breath. "Do you think you could do that back bend thing if I held your foot?"

I grinned. "I think you might need to untie me too, don't you?"

He nodded. "Yeah, that. Can you do it?"

I let my bra fall to the floor and stretched my arms over my head as soon as they were free. My foot protested the stretch and after several tries, I realized there was no way it was going to work. "I—can't," I sighed.

"I've got another idea," Jake growled before scooping me up and carrying me to the bed. My head hung off the side, putting me at eye level with the dick straining to break free from his boxer briefs.

I lifted my head up and watched as he forced my panties down to my knees and spread my thighs. His tongue lapped at my stomach before coming to rest on my tattoo and my skin raised with a shiver. He let his mouth trace a circle around it before gasping, "Goddamn, I love your cattoo."

When his mouth moved between my thighs and his finger dipped inside my body, my head fell back, and I groaned incoherently.

He let out a soft curse and added another. "You're so wet, baby."

I nodded shakily and opened my eyes to see that my entire body was covered in Jake and I suddenly had a wicked thought. I reached up and snagged the waistband of his boxers, dragging them down toward his thighs. His cock sprang free and I didn't hesitate before guiding it into my mouth with my hand.

He made a small sound of praise and rolled his hips forward, urging me to continue. I moved my grip up and down, letting him in a little bit at a time. He was so thick and hard that I wondered how on earth he was going to fit inside me.

Why hadn't I noticed this back at the hotel?

My mouth became greedy and I relaxed my throat to accommodate all of him, lightly digging my nails into his ass cheeks to anchor him.

Not one to be outdone, Jake began using his mouth and hand

simultaneously and I whimpered against his cock before coming with a full body shudder.

He thrust forward and held himself deep in my mouth, causing my vision to blur around the edges. Tears leaked from the corners of my eyes and I sucked in a ragged breath when he pulled back.

"Baby," he growled. "Can I fuck you now, please?"

I nodded, completely intoxicated, and he kicked out of his boxer briefs with a smug grin before sliding a condom over the hard ridge of his cock. I followed his lead and threw my panties onto the floor.

He dragged me to the edge of the bed and lined the head of his cock up against my pussy. "Say it. Say you want this," he demanded. His full lips were coated in a light sheen that I knew was all me.

I'd marked him.

"Hayden."

I nodded. "I want it. I want you."

"Once this happens, there's no going back."

His words were ominous, and I should've heeded the warning and tapped out. Instead, I stared at his magnificent body and realized that he'd been right; there wasn't one part of him that was soft.

I made my decision. I was going to forget the fact that someone wanted me dead. I was going to forget that he was going to be leaving me soon. I was going to forget everything but this moment right here, with Jake trying to hold himself back with everything he had.

I used my hand to hold his cock steady before guiding it slowly into my body with a hiss of pleasure. Jake growled my name in a warning before thrusting his hips forward and spots danced before my eyes as my body stretched. I wrapped my uninjured foot around his lower back and pulled him closer, wincing at the twinge of pain as he moved deeper.

He stopped moving and breathed out, "Baby?"

"Don't... don't stop."

He wrapped fistfuls of my hair up in his hands and tightened his grip before bringing his mouth roughly down over mine. I couldn't move; I was completely filled up and pinned down with him.

I'd never written it, but I'd often wondered about how Jake was as a lover. I imagined him as forceful or even degrading, but never like this. He was the culmination of every fantasy I'd had. He moved and shifted against my body, knowing exactly what I wanted.

What I needed.

He lapped at my breasts and sucked a nipple in between his teeth, holding me in place. I began meeting his thrusts with my own, forcing his mouth down harder on my sensitive flesh.

"You can't be real," I gasped.

I'd been so wrong.

That was what he meant by there was no coming back from this. This was a once in a lifetime thing and I was never going to experience anything like it, or him, again.

My hands scrambled against the sheets and I groaned his name as I came. Not satisfied, he placed his palm right above my pelvic bone, forcing my body to grip him tighter and my orgasm to stretch into the next.

"That feels pretty fucking real, doesn't it?" When I didn't respond, he lifted his hand.

I moaned something incoherent before pulling his hand back to my body. "Jake," I panted.

"Yeah, baby?" His teeth grazed the shell of my ear. "Tell me what you want."

"I want." My breath came in short, desperate little bursts as his thrusts increased. "I want you to shut the fuck up and do that again!"

He chuckled softly and obliged and I lost count of where one orgasm began and the other ended.

"I- I don't understand how you're this good. I made you."

His hips surged forward brutally. "You didn't make me, baby. I made me." With that, he pushed in as deep as he could go and growled my name as he came.

I'd assumed that he was the type of man who left once he got what he wanted, not the type of man to collapse in bed beside me. Not the type to pull me up against his sweaty body and press soft kisses against my forehead. And absolutely not the type to whisper, "I knew you'd fit me perfectly."

I was so wrong.

The realization almost forced the air from my lungs. I was catastrophically in love with him.

TWENTY-TWO

I OPENED my eyes and let them adjust to the early morning light. The mountain next to me inhaled deeply before rolling over. Even in his sleep, his hands reached out for me.

"I find that it takes me most of the night and into the morning to get what I need to 'complete my investigation.'"

I'd lost count, but judging by the ache between my legs, that assessment had been accurate.

I slipped out from underneath his arm and stood watching him sleep. It was perfect like this. We could almost pretend that we were a normal couple.

I mashed my fist against my mouth and hobbled toward the bathroom. The apartment suddenly felt too small for the both of us and I hastily threw on a pair of sweats, fighting to get the material around my cast.

Jake sat up in bed, bleary-eyed. "Babe, what are you doing? Come back to bed."

I nodded. "I will. I just need a minute, okay?"

His eyes drifted closed as he nodded back at me, already on his way back to sleep. I blinked away the tears and softly closed the door behind me.

Bootsy was curled up under the dining room table, still watching Bob Ross. I didn't want to know how she'd gotten past the *Are you still watching?* check-ins.

I pulled my down jacket off the back of one of the chairs and stuffed my cell phone into the pocket. The air outside was so cold it almost took my breath away.

Gone was the balmy fifty degrees from my birthday. Now, the sky was dark and heavy with snow. I forced myself to walk faster down the stairs in spite of the air biting through my jacket and settling into my bones, never mind the ache in my foot.

Just like the sleet that was blowing through the breezeway, my mind was a vortex of thoughts.

I slept with Jake.

I knew his M.O. and I was just another in a long line of women. It didn't mean anything, no matter how desperately I wanted to believe the opposite. He'd called me his girl, but that was something he probably said to every one of them. I bet it made them feel as special as it had me.

I loved him.

I doubled over in agony on the stairs at the reminder, wanting to scream at the unfairness of it all. His entire reason for being here was to get back to his story. He wasn't going to stay, hadn't I told myself that? Tears froze to my lashes as I remained bent in half, grieving something I never had.

How had I even considered that I could sleep with him and keep my feelings in check? *I'm yours for as long as you're here?* What the fuck was that?

Eddie's door opened with a crack and he peeked through. "Hayden?"

I rubbed the back of my hand roughly across my eyes. "Hey, Eddie, I'm just going on a little walk."

His eyes widened as he took in the precipitation. "The dumpster. We have to tell the dumpster."

I patted him lightly on the arm and shook my head. "Okay. Have a good morning."

I continued my descent. I couldn't second guess myself now. I'd made my bed and now I had to lie in it.

"I know," I mumbled under my breath. "I'll just... I'll just get him back into the story and then we can pretend that this whole thing never happened."

I'd lost my damn mind, but Jessa was close. I knew it. The second woman on the balcony that night. She was the key in all of this. From the way she stuck out with her formal dress—as if trying to emphasize the fact that she was a woman.

Go where the money leads...

Aaris had said that before, but it hadn't made sense. No one would profit off of Jake's death, except for one person.

Someone who had taken Addison out in an attempt to get to Jake. Someone who could come and go from crime scenes without being noticed.

I froze at the base of the stairs.

That was it.

I knew who the killer was. It had been staring me in the face the entire time. I knew who pushed Jake. All that was left was to determine who wanted me dead.

Well, not dead, but inconvenienced.

I limped briskly through the small park connecting the buildings as the sleet gave way to fat flakes of snow.

First, there was the door. The glass had been broken by a brick, not bullets, which indicated that it had been a warning and not intended for anyone. The *Detective Hopkins* novel seemed to support that theory.

Then, there was the email, demanding that I return what was stolen before the next full moon. It hadn't made a damn bit of sense because I hadn't stolen anything.

At the club, the mirror had been shattered from one side to the other. *The curse is come upon me* note was found later. Max had determined that the note was a line from the *Lady of Shalott* by Alfred, Lord Tennyson for all the good it did.

That brought me to the poisoned cupcake.

I frowned. It was right there—*something I'd stolen that needed to be returned... the curse is come upon me.*

Whoever was behind this wasn't actively trying to kill me or they would've succeeded by now.

There was a connection between all of them. I sank down on a park bench, letting the ice soak through my sweatpants. Ignoring the cold, I pulled my phone out, tapping in *the curse is come upon me,* only to see results we'd already researched. I tried again but added *cracked mirror* to my query. Similar results popped up, with the exception of one.

Agatha Christie had written a novel, *The Mirror Crack'd from Side to Side.* It was a detective novel based upon the poem, featuring the unforgettable Miss Marple investigating the murder of a woman who drank a poisoned cocktail meant for someone else.

While it wasn't a poisoned cocktail, Jake had eaten a poison cupcake intended for me just like the main character in *The Mirror Crack'd from Side to Side.*

Once I knew what I was looking for, the next piece of the puzzle fell into place. *Return to where it came from before the next full moon* was a line from *The Adventure of the Western Star.* It was the infamous detective, Hercule Poirot, investigating a case of stolen jewels.

They were using plot devices by the late Agatha Christie as a way of intimidating me into... doing what exactly? I was supposed to return something before the next full moon... a jewel, if the text was any indicator.

What did I have that was precious?

I gasped when it hit me.

Jake.

I was supposed to return Jake to his story before the next full moon. The use of Agatha Christie novels, the half-assed attempts made on my life; I wasn't dealing with an upset reader.

Only a few people knew that I was trying to rewrite him into the story. I was up against someone who knew that he was here. Someone whose idea of intimidation relied heavily on the books that they'd read.

Someone who had no idea how the real world worked.

I wiped the flakes of snow from my face and struggled to tie up the last loose end. Whoever considered Jake a jewel had obviously never seen the man eat.

"Maybe it's—" I exclaimed just as the back of my head exploded in a blinding flash of pain. The last thing I saw was the snow-covered ground as it came up to meet my face.

I GROANED and rolled to my side. Instead of Jake's pouty smirk, I was met with my brother's terrified face.

"Reid?" I croaked. "Where are we?"

He shook his head from side to side and whimpered in response.

I rolled my eyes and hissed, "Jesus Christ, Reid. Words! Use your words!" My head ached something awful, but I pushed myself into a sitting position to see that we were in a bedroom.

A bedroom I'd never seen before in my life. My sweatpants were still damp from the snow, so I hadn't been here long.

I glared at him. "Did you do this? Is this your idea of payback for last night? If so, Jake was right. You really are a fuckboy."

He continued shaking his head and I watched in sick fascination as a tear rolled down his cheek. I'd never seen Reid cry before. Usually he was the one causing tears, which meant one thing. He wasn't here voluntarily.

"What happened?" I dropped my voice to a whisper, just in case our captors were listening in on us.

He hiccupped. "...Took me. I can't—"

"They took you? Why? You're worthless."

Obviously, this was about me and my books; there was no reason on earth for involving Reid.

And if they thought for one second that they could use him as leverage, they were sorely mistaken. They could use him for kindling as much as I cared.

"Emily." He moaned from the fetal position.

"What?" I barked. "Did they hurt Emily? Damn it, Reid, why didn't you sacrifice yourself for her?"

My head ached with every movement and I didn't trust that I could stand without tipping over. I moved onto all fours and began crawling toward a grimy window in the corner. From what I could gather, we were in an abandoned cabin. Either that or the home-owner was in desperate need of a good contractor.

Maybe an intervention by HGTV.

I wiped a small section of glass with the sleeve of my jacket and peered out. The trees were so thick that I couldn't make out any definitive landmarks.

Okay. So definitely in an abandoned cabin in the woods.

"Reid," I sighed. "Do you know where we are? It's important if we're going to get out of here and save Emily—"

The door swung open and I began clapping. "Emily! Thank god Reid didn't screw up and get you killed. Now, it's going to be up to the two of us to get out of here because he's gone bye-bye." I twirled my index finger around my throbbing temple.

She held up a gun and it took my brain a good fifteen seconds before I realized that she wasn't here to help.

"How was your nap?" she asked, her eyes damn near twinkling with excitement.

Reid whimpered again and scooted back against the wall. He kept looking to me, silently pleading for me to rescue him.

I rocked back on my knees. "Is this because of last night? You're upset because we made a scene at Reid's big merger party?"

Emily threw her head back and laughed. "Oh, Hayden. You

never did catch on, even when the answer was sitting right in front of you. I thought the glass of wine would do the job and I could just smuggle you out of your parent's house, but you didn't drink it, did you?"

"Um, no?"

"Do you know how much *Genetistry* crap I had to listen to just to get close to you? Two years of my life wasted, Hayden. Do you know what that feels like?"

I shook my head, eyeing every potential exit in the room. "No, but I have a feeling you're going to tell me."

I was still wearing the damn walking boot and had the worst headache of my life. Oh, and I'd lost my glasses at some point.

So, blind and lame with a probable concussion.

Even if I managed to stall her, my odds of escape weren't great. And if I was responsible for rescuing Reid too—well, we'd both be leaving in body bags.

Emily walked closer and grinned widely. "Damn right I am. Two years of steering you in the right direction only for you to blow it by throwing Jake off a building. Please tell me in which of our many conversations I suggested that? I mean, Jesus, I practically wrote the book for you and you botched it!"

"So you sent me threats from Agatha Christie's novels?"

She nodded like it made all the sense in the world. "In *Body of Proof,* you compared Jake to Hercule Poirot, Agatha Christie's beloved detective. I was once again trying to helpfully guide you back to where he needed and wanted to be."

I played off a hunch and asked, "So, which one are you? Addison's sister? A cousin perhaps?"

Her lip curled up in disgust. "Please. You think I would've suggested offing my sister? No one was more shocked than me when I casually mentioned an apartment fire and you followed through. My reminders were what kept you focused and driven!"

So, she'd been the one to kill Addison, but not Jake. That little plot twist was going to cost me twenty thousand words.

"Agatha Christie? More like *Nagatha Christie*, am I right?" I chuckled at my joke while both Reid and Emily stared blankly at me.

"Are you done?" she asked.

"If you're not related to Addison, then who are you?" I bit out. "Someone who was jealous of their relationship and decided to get even?"

"Relationship?" She slapped her knee and cackled, "What relationship? Neither one of them could stand the other, yet you kept forcing them together. I did Jake a favor by getting rid of Addison and you—I told you that you needed a strong female love interest... which was the exact conclusion that Rachel at *The Janice Morrison Agency* came to as well."

I was so caught up in trying to figure out why Jake would've lied to me about Addison that I almost missed the part about Rachel. It was enough to send me crawling full speed across the carpet toward her. "You? You're the reason I lost my chance at getting traditionally published? Why? Because I wouldn't write you into the story?"

Hadn't Jake admitted his guilt?

"I was in the story!" she screeched. "Nameless blonde that Jake meets at the bar in *Body of Proof*? That was me! We had one amazing night together and he was supposed to call, but you sent him off on another investigation and I disappeared off the pages! I gave you until the next full moon to return me to my rightful place in the story, but you didn't listen."

I tried to remain calm, even as the steady thrum of my pulse fought to drown Emily out. I gave her a half-hearted shrug and picked at some fuzz on the carpet. "Jake sleeps with a lot of women," I began, and my chest tightened with pain.

Now wasn't the time for my broken heart. I would deal with that can of worms as soon as I wasn't looking down the barrel of a gun.

"He's a player and to think that you were somehow different, well; I'm sure you're not the first. Unfortunately, he has that effect on women. I can't imagine how that must've felt." This was good. I was remaining calm, while silently siding with her.

I'd get her to bond with me; part of the sisterhood of traveling crazies or whatever. She'd realize that I had no more control over Jake than she did and she'd let me go. We'd give Reid hell over being such a pansy and then off we'd go back to the city.

Emily nodded in agreement with me and I lowered my shoulders. "You're right," she said grimly.

Good, she saw that this entire thing was asylum-level crazy. I smiled and pretended to pay attention while working on the speech I'd give the reporters later.

Well, Janet, I just thought like a detective would. My poor defense-less brother was relying on me. You see, writers put a lot of work into creating their characters. I just happened to pick up a few tricks from mine.

I briefly registered the click of the safety being switched off before the barrel of the gun dug into my forehead painfully. I thought we'd made a connection. There was a chance I'd missed a few key points in her monologue.

"You see, I can't just walk away from this. I tried to helpfully guide you to the right story, but now, you've got no other choice. Fix the story or die," she giggled.

I stared blankly at her. "So, you want me to write you and Jake into the story as a couple or you'll kill me?"

She sighed. "It's like you're not even listening."

I remembered something Jake had said after we first met and hid a smile. "You can't kill me... well, you could, but you won't. Without me, there's no way for you to get back. I wrote you into the first book, therefore, I am the only one who can bring you back."

She shrugged. "Maybe, but I can kill him." She turned the gun on Reid.

"And? How is that going to get me to do what you want? The man's made my life a living hell every chance he's gotten. You kill him and you're doing me a favor."

Reid's eyes widened and his entire body shuddered in fear. "N-n-no," he pleaded.

Emily's jaw clenched and she cursed under her breath before turning the gun back on me. "Maybe you're right. Maybe you're not. Maybe I'll just keep you locked in this room until I get what I want."

Her expression softened. "For what it's worth, I do think you're a wonderful writer. I wouldn't be going to this much trouble for anyone, you know."

I sat up straighter. "Really?"

She nodded. "Yeah, *The Janice Morrison Agency* wanted to represent you—"

"She's just trying to flatter you to get what she wants," Reid muttered, having decided to come back to reality just as things were getting interesting.

We both turned to him and said at the same time, "Shut up, Reid!"

Emily bowed her head. "Anyway, I just want you to know that our friendship was never fake. No matter how badly your family behaved, I really did enjoy spending time with you. I'm going to give you some time to think about your options, okay?"

"Okay." I smiled up at her. This was exactly what I'd been aiming for with my earlier comments. Emily and I were both cogs in the great wheel of life; all it took was finding that common ground. It was just like my yoga instructor was always saying; cherish the connections that the universe sends—

"I'll give you thirty minutes and then I'll blow his head off and we'll see where we stand, okay?" She cackled, before slamming the door shut behind her.

I didn't feel like cherishing my connection.

I felt like whipping my walking boot at her big dumb head while screeching at the top of my lungs all the ways in which I wanted to watch her die. She'd ruined my career and then gone out of her way, trying to sabotage every other aspect of my life.

I belatedly remembered my cell phone and began patting the pockets of my coat. Of course it was gone. I was stuck in the middle of nowhere with Reid *"I probably pissed my pants"* Michaels as my only ally.

"What are we going to do?" he whispered harshly.

I drew in a breath and exhaled before looking over at him. "Oh, are you done crying over there?"

He ran a hand over his face and nodded. "You try being in a relationship with someone for two years and then finding out they were just using you to get to your sister. Like I needed another reminder of how much better you are."

I snorted, "Did you just say better? Don't you mean worse?"

Reid shook his head. "No, I said what I meant. Do you know how frustrating it is to be the brother of the girl who writes—"

"Oh, poor you!" I seethed. "How embarrassing to be related to such a lowly individual. I bet you've had to field so many questions during the press conferences that were called over it."

He pointed a finger at me. "Can I finish? Mom and Dad pushed for me to run my own company and make a name for myself since elementary school. But you, you had this freedom to do what you wanted, and you wrote books—damn good books too."

Reid suddenly looked sheepish as if he'd just admitted that he enjoyed putting on a nice pair of *Louboutin* heels every evening before taking a stroll around his penthouse apartment.

"Emily was right about that," he admitted. "And I thought, how hard can it be? I'll write a book too... except, I couldn't. I didn't have the patience or the creativeness to come up with a solid plot. Meanwhile, you continued to publish these books like it was nothing."

I pursed my lips. "So, you've read my books? But, that doesn't make sense. You always teased me about them."

"Yeah, what was I supposed to do? Admit that you were better at something. Not a chance in hell of that happening," he said with a soft laugh.

"So, at the party last night, did you—"

"Wonder how the detective from your novel ended up here?" he asked with a smirk. "Yeah, I had a few questions about that. Obviously, I couldn't ask you or you would've known I read your stuff. Next thing I knew, I had a few drinks and woke up here."

"Where is here exactly?"

He clenched his jaw. "Not a damn clue. She took me home last night, said I'd had too much and made me drink her homemade 'hangover cure.' So, I'm fairly certain she roofied me and now, I can't tell you shit about where we are."

Well, this posed quite the problem.

Reid pointed at my foot. "I meant to ask you last night, but what happened?"

I rolled my eyes. "Fell off the curb at the airport."

He didn't need to know all the horribly embarrassing details behind it. He was under the impression that I was better than him and I wanted to keep that going for as long as possible. Plus, we were on a little bit of a deadline to keep his head attached to his body.

His eyes narrowed. "When was this?"

"I don't know, a week ago?"

"Oh my god," he exclaimed. "You're the planal girl!"

I tried to lift the window, but it wouldn't budge. "The...what?" I panted.

Reid joined me and we tried again with no success. When he didn't answer, I looked up only to see that he was trying to hold it together with little success.

"What? Say it."

His body shook with laughter. "There was a *Twitter* thread about a woman who sat next to some sex therapist on a plane and their conversation was documented in its entirety for the world to enjoy. She ran out of the airport to get away from the therapist and ended up tripping and falling off the sidewalk. The hashtag *planal* began trending not long after. It was you!"

My cheeks heated and I shook my head. "No, it wasn't." I cleared my throat. "Anyway, we're supposed to be finding a way out of here, not discussing stupid things we saw on the internet."

Reid continued chuckling. "It was definitely you. You're blushing, which is a dead giveaway—"

"I should've let her shoot you," I grumbled. "Look, do you want to get out of here or not? We need a plan. Do you have a phone?"

He shook his head. "I don't even have my wallet. She took everything."

"Okay. We need to find a way out of here..."

Reid sat down and put his head between his knees. "I can't believe I was dating someone who's completely mental. I even slept with her! I mean, to think that you're a fictional character...that's Stephen King level crazy."

I stared through the layer of dust on the window and toward the trees. "So, you think she's just cuckoo? What about Jake? Who do you think he is?"

He rested his chin again his knees. "I don't know; some guy who happens to share the same name? The man you based the character on? It's not like fictional characters are actually showing up in real life though, Hayden. You do know that, right? You can't write a few words and send her back into the book."

I stood up, trying to keep most of my weight on my good leg. "That's it! Reid, you're a genius! Do you have a pen and paper?"

"Yeah, she didn't let me have my cell phone or wallet, but she supplied me with a notebook and a pen to journal my feelings while being held hostage."

I inhaled sharply through my nose, reminded again why he and I never hung out. "A simple no would've sufficed."

I hobbled around the small room, but there was nothing. I was just debating how to make myself bleed so that I could write on the walls when it hit me.

I limped back over to the window and used the dust to send a message.

Jake sat up in bed with a start, knowing deep in his bones that Hayden was in trouble.

"Is this that witchcraft shit you're into? Are you summoning a demon to come to our aid? Because I want no part in that," Reid complained from his spot on the carpet.

"Shut the fuck up, Reid," I snapped.

She was trapped in an abandoned cabin somewhere in the middle of nowhere, but like every great detective, Jake knew exactly where to find her.

I debated whether or not to add more, my finger hovering over the grime. I didn't know if it would even work. If I didn't know where I was, how was he supposed to?

Reid scanned the words and looked at me in confusion. "What is that supposed to do? Are you finishing your novel on the window?"

I tried again.

The nameless blonde that Jake spent one night with decided that her plan to win him back was futile and handed her gun over to Hayden.

Nothing.

I frowned. Maybe it only counted on paper. If so, then I'd just wasted valuable escape time. Reid appeared to be fussing over his manicured fingernails, which clearly indicated that I was in charge.

"Don't you know some magical science trick that would get us out of here?"

"What? Like run DNA tests to distract Emily with her lineage while we make a break for it?" He laughed softly and continued picking at his nails.

We jumped as a window broke in another room. There was the sound of a brief struggle and then silence again.

"Maybe she committed suicide by jumping through the window? Did you write that down?" He looked over my head at the window.

"No." That would've been a better idea though.

The door flew open and slammed into the drywall behind it with a bang.

"Jake!" I cried. "You found me!"

The corner of his lip turned up in a smirk and he relaxed his shoulders. "Jesus, Hayden. You don't believe in sleeping in?" He crossed the room and began checking me over. "Are you okay?"

When I nodded, he abruptly turned to Reid and punched him in the jaw, sending him sprawling back onto the carpet with a yelp.

Jake growled, "Kidnapping your own sister? You son-of-a-bitch, I am going to fucking tear you apart!"

I was in love... with an idiot.

I jumped in between them, earning myself a nice little warning from my ankle. "Wait! Wait! It wasn't him! It was Emily! Didn't you see her?"

His brows creased in confusion. "Who?"

"Me." She grinned from the doorway with the gun very much in her hand. "Who the hell are you?"

Reid and I exchanged blank looks.

She'd slept with him and was desperate to get back to her story. *How could she not recognize him?*

His right hand moved down to his waistband. "Detective Jake Hopkins and you are?"

She shook her head. "Nice try."

"But," I protested. "But, you said you were Nameless Blonde in *Body of Proof*!"

Jake chuckled and discreetly moved his fingers toward his holster. "Her? Please. That was Kendra."

"No, Emily is Reid's girlfriend and the woman from *Body of Proof*."

He shook his head. "So when I asked if there was anyone who knew about your habits and you said no, that was a lie. I don't know, Hayden, but if someone thinks they came from one of your books, it might be a good idea to mention it to the investigating detective."

"Are you really getting on to me right now because I forgot to mention her? How was I supposed to know that she was a psychopath? Honestly, I always felt a little sorry for her having to date Reid for two years. Who has that kind of dedication?"

Jake shrugged. "Mentioning her at least once would've been a smart move. We could've avoided this entire fiasco."

"Fiasco?" My voice rose. "Had you disarmed the suspect upon entering, we could've avoided all of 'this.'"

"Can you two stop fighting?" Emily snapped.

Jake looked back at me. "I'm just saying, I've never seen this broad before in my life."

She rubbed at the back of her neck with her free hand, her eyes tearing up. "I'm Nameless Blonde! He's lying!"

Jake looked her up and down. "Nah, I never forget a face or a pair of—"

"That's quite enough, Jake," I forced out through clenched teeth.

"What?" He shrugged. "She's not fictional."

"I knew it!" Reid exclaimed triumphantly.

There was a flash of movement from the hallway and then Max was directly behind Emily. Gone was the goofy guy who made me coffee. He moved silently and I shivered when I saw the look in his eyes. It was blank; completely devoid of emotion.

He raised his hands and took Emily to the carpet before I could blink. She managed to get her hand free and pointed the gun at me. I knew I needed to run, but one foot was incapable, and the other had become glued to the floor.

In the nanoseconds it took for me to register that I was in grave danger, Jake dove forward and knocked me to the ground with a pop. I fought to get air back into my lungs as he shielded me with his body. *We were okay.*

We were going to get out of here. Jake would go back, and my life would return to the way it was before. Just me and Bootsy. Day in and day out. Nothing to look forward to but dying alone.

"Hayden."

There was something in Jake's voice that snapped me out of my depressing daydream. His head jerked back, and his eyes went wide with shock. He exhaled a soft laugh before rolling off of me and onto his back. Blood pumped steadily from a hole in his side.

I scrambled over to him. "No! No, no, no."

He'd been shot.

Jake had taken a bullet meant for me.

I looked to Reid, suddenly incapable of being in charge. "Do we put pressure on it? What do we do?" I was hysterical.

Reid quickly stripped out of his t-shirt and held it against Jake's ribs. "He's losing a lot of blood. We need to get him to a hospital now."

Jake's eyes fluttered closed and I shook his arm frantically. "You stay awake—do you hear me? Don't you dare close your eyes, Jake! Not now!" Tears coursed down my cheeks and fell onto his blood-soaked shirt.

He opened his mouth, frantically trying to speak, but nothing came out. He was dying all because he'd chosen to jump in front of me.

Jake groaned and gestured for me to come closer with shaking hands. I knelt down and cupped his cheek in my hand, using my fingers to wipe at the tears on his face. "I'm here, babe. I'm here. This is all my fault—"

His hand bumped against my arm, but I continued vomiting up

words, "I'm going to fix this. The doctors will get you all fixed up. You'll see."

He made another small sound of protest and began fumbling with the front pocket of his jeans. I laid a hand on his arm to still his movements.

"Stop struggling. Just stay calm. We're going to get you help, okay?" I continued blubbering, unsure of how we were going to keep him alive until we found a hospital.

With a clenched jaw, he thrust a pen into my hand before growling, "Change...it."

Change?

Oh my god.

Confusion gave way to clarity and I snatched the pen before searching the room for a blank surface. The closest object happened to be Reid's back and I didn't hesitate.

"What are you doing, Hayden? We need to get him out of here!" he snapped while keeping pressure on the wound.

It made me seriously consider placing the bullet somewhere else.

Emily fired a shot as she was taken to the ground. The bullet shattered the window, but surprisingly, everyone escaped unscathed.

Please work, I silently begged.

The window exploded behind us as I knelt over Jake again and cupped his cheek again. "Jake, open your eyes. Stay with me."

He forced out through clenched teeth, "Sweetheart, she didn't hit me, but your knee is embedded in my balls."

I moved off of him with a shaky laugh and swiped the back of my hand across my damp face. "You prick. You almost gave me a heart attack. I thought that was it."

Reid pointed at Jake's shirt dumbly and I looked down, noting that any evidence he'd been shot had suddenly evaporated.

"How? Why? How?" he stuttered. "But, you—"

Jake rolled to his side and sat up with a groan. "Sorry about your jaw, man. No hard feelings?"

Reid took his extended hand while still frowning at the floor. "Was that... was that magic?"

I forced the sob in my throat back and sighed, "We have to turn Emily over to the cops. She needs to get help."

I almost lost him.

I was still going to lose him.

"That's gonna be a problem," Max noted in a flat voice. "I kinda broke her neck."

Jake pinched the bridge of his nose. "You what? Why? We didn't even question her yet."

Max looked down at Emily's body and shrugged. "I turned her head and her body didn't follow. That's more on her. Am I taking care of pretty boy in the corner too?"

Reid's shoulders curled forward, and his hands trembled as he shook his head. Any second now he was going to piss his pants and cry.

"He's fine, Max." One look at Jake and I completely fell apart. "Can you take me home?"

TWENTY-THREE

"YOU SOLVED THE ENTIRE CASE, Hayden. It was right in front of my face the entire time, but I missed it." Jake poured a second glass of whiskey from the bottle in front of him.

It had been in front of us the entire time. Eddie had been conversing with Emily inside the dumpster, giving her information under the misguided notion that he was Moses and she was the voice of God. In his drug-addled mind, God had taken the form of a trash bin, instead of a burning bush.

Jake looked wretched and had been quiet since we left the cabin. Max assured us that he'd remove any evidence that we'd been there and, against my better judgment, I left Reid to help him.

I had to bite down on my lip to keep from asking Jake about what we'd done last night. I needed to know that it meant something, but the investigation was over.

There was nothing keeping him here now.

So, I turned my rose quartz ring in a slow circle around my finger and stayed silent. I'd gotten the ending I always wanted—the woman solved the mystery on her own. But what good was it when she was going to lose it all in the end?

Everything until him had been two-dimensional.

Fiction.

He was the realest thing I'd ever experienced, but it was temporary. Shakespeare himself couldn't have written a greater tragedy.

The list of things we weren't talking about had grown until there was nothing left between us but silence. It wasn't even five o'clock, yet Jake was sitting across from me, drinking like it was his last night on earth.

Maybe it was.

"I know you've got something on your mind. Just say it, Hayden."

I bit my lip. So much of what Emily had claimed was based on the delusions in her head, but I had to know for sure. "The email from Rachel, the one where they turned me down, you didn't have anything to do with that, did you?"

"I didn't," he admitted. "I saw the email pulled up on your laptop when you locked yourself in the bedroom and I used it to my advantage. What else?"

His tone was rough, and I hesitated.

"C'mon, tell me," he said, softer this time.

"Emily said that you and Addison couldn't stand each other, but I kept forcing you together and I know she wasn't fictional or whatever, but—"

"You wanna know if what I told you that night was true."

I nodded and slid my hands underneath my thighs to keep them from shaking. "It's stupid. You don't have to answer."

Jake pinched the bridge of his nose and stared down into his glass of whiskey. "What do you want me to do, Hayden? You want the truth, here's the truth. Addison was a colleague. Did we hate each other? No."

I swallowed around the lump in my throat. "But, you weren't going to marry her?"

His head shot up and he glared at me. "No."

I should've left it at that, but I couldn't stop myself from asking, "Why did you lie to me?"

He stood up and walked over to the balcony door. "I wanted to hurt you like you'd hurt me. Are you happy now? I'm a dick."

"Jake." I limped over to him and took his hands in mine. "Stop. We both said and did a lot of things."

He squeezed my fingers. "You know what happened to me that night on the balcony. You know and you've been keeping it from me. You know how it all ends, don't you?"

I bit down on my lip until the copper tang of blood coated my tongue and nodded fiercely. Yeah, I knew. I knew when his lips were mashed up against my jaw. I knew when he rocked into me and my inhales were timed perfectly to his and it was like we were one person.

I knew exactly how this was going to end and I dove headfirst off the cliff anyway. His eyes rested on the bottle again, debating the pros and cons of getting drunk.

I wanted a drink... an edible... anything to take the edge off, but my stomach was in knots. Anything I ingested was liable to come right back out, so I stayed sober and oh so painfully aware of it all.

I took a deep breath. "I was going to surprise you. I'll be finished tonight and then you'll be free of me." My voice cracked, but I forced myself to smile.

He nodded and walked back over to the table to drain the remainder of his glass before calmly pouring another. "What if you didn't finish tonight? What if you put it off until tomorrow morning?"

You are calm. You are centered. You are balanced...

You are hopelessly in love with him.

I grabbed his glass and took a swig, letting the whiskey burn away the emotions trying to bubble up to the surface. "Why? Did you get attached to the couch?"

Joking was safer than the truth, which was that I wanted him to stay because he'd fallen for me as hard as I'd fallen for him.

He stared down at his hands. "Maybe I want one more night with you. What would you say to that?"

My world, which had been close to spinning off its axis, slowed at his words. One night. An alternate ending.

"Okay," I whispered. I knew the rocks were sharp and likely to cut me to ribbons, but I was prepared to swan dive off of the ledge one more time.

Jake pushed away from the table, rattling the whiskey bottle from the force. His eyes had gone feral and he stared at me like he had that night in the hotel, like I was something he wanted to possess.

He easily plucked me out of the chair and carried me down the hall. One arm gently cradled my head while the other was tucked under my knees. I turned my face into his chest so that he wouldn't see the tears.

He laid me back against the comforter and paused to look me over. Last night, the dark had hidden so much, but the snow-filled sky this afternoon wasn't as kind. I tried to look away, but his hand moved down to my chin, holding me in place.

"Hey," he whispered. "Don't cry."

I wished that I hadn't spent so much time fighting him. We could've been doing this the entire time. Then maybe I would've been ready for him to leave by the time the book was finished.

"I'm fine," I insisted with a watery smile.

He grasped the hem of my *In the event of an emergency, place cat here* t-shirt and pulled it over my head. Another tear slipped free and he bent his head to kiss it as it made a trail down my face. His finger brushed down my chest and settled between the swell of my breasts.

"You're fine?" he asked before roughly yanking my sweatpants down.

I pressed the heel of my hand against my chest to alleviate the ache and nodded. "Yep. Fine."

He pressed another kiss to my cheek and then my jaw before thrusting up against my panties. I wrapped my legs around his waist and pulled him closer, earning myself a low growl in response.

His eyes were a dark shade of amber as he stripped off his sweater, never once looking away. It was too much, but every time I tried to turn my head, his finger hooked under my chin, drawing my gaze back to his.

My thoughts blurred into one as his tongue dipped into my mouth and his hands found the clasp of my bra. Jake dropped onto his forearms to take my breasts into his mouth, one at a time, until my moans turned into incoherent sobs.

He moved his hand up and tightened it against my throat, pushing me down into the mattress. He wasn't cutting off my air supply. He could break me if he wanted to though, and somehow, knowing that he would never hurt me made me even wetter.

I moaned against his lips when his fingers slipped under the elastic band of my panties and dug my fingernails into the sheets. I was wild with lust and I arched my hips up into the palm of his hand in frustration.

Touch me.

Fuck me.

Mark me like you swore you would.

His hand left my throat and joined the other between my legs. The thin material ripped under his grip and he grinned triumphantly before tearing the lace off of me completely.

"You're soaked, babe." Jake said something else after, but I was fairly certain it wasn't English, which was weird because he didn't know any other languages.

He stroked and kissed along my body until I was thrumming with desire. This wasn't farewell sex. If anything, it just reinforced my belief that I was going to die alone as a crazy cat lady because no one would ever measure up to him.

He lowered his mouth down between my thighs and I wanted to clench them together; to hold him hostage until he agreed to stay.

Instead, I braced my forearms on the mattress and watched as Jake worshiped my body. His fingers moved in and out of me steadily and when he caught me staring, he lowered his mouth again. With his eyes on mine, he sucked my clit into his mouth and my vision swam.

"Jake," I moaned.

I wasn't on the bed anymore. I was floating somewhere up in the atmosphere; maybe on a cloud.

I saw us as a couple; arguing over counter space while we got ready in the morning. He'd brush his teeth with a towel slung low around his waist and I'd start wearing makeup every day just so that I'd have an excuse to be in there with him. I'd tease him in just my bra and panties and our argument would end with us making love up against the wall.

Jake was waiting with his cock in his hand when I finally came back down to earth. "I thought you were fading on me," he smirked.

Marry me.

Choose me.

I can make you so much happier than a book.

His mouth moved back over mine impatiently before he ripped a foil packet from the nightstand and rolled it on. His lips tasted like me and I wondered how long it would be before they tasted like someone else.

Would he be able to go back to the guy he was before?

Jake ground his teeth together as he sank into me. I clenched around him and he let out a low groan. "You don't play fair, Ms. Michaels."

I let my body bear down on him again before breathlessly exclaiming, "I don't know what you mean, Detective."

He exhaled something that sounded suspiciously like a laugh before rolling his hips forward to pin me in place. "Brat."

We moved together like we'd been doing it for years. His hand wrapped around my hair, tethering me and just when I thought that there was no way to top the last orgasm, he'd shift my legs and get deeper.

"You fit me perfectly, baby," he murmured against the top of my head. I tightened around him and he growled, "You like that? How about this? The thought of anyone else having you like this makes me feel fucking insane—"

"Jake," I warned as my body climbed higher again.

He dragged a finger through the wetness and pressed it lightly against the one hole he hadn't investigated. I should've tensed up, but the pressure against raw nerve endings had me bearing down on him for all I was worth. I needed it. I needed it all.

"Come, baby. Come all over my cock—I wanna feel you."

I came with a whimpered groan, but he didn't slow down and just like a roller coaster, I moved up the track again. As the next orgasm hit, his finger pushed in fully, past the tight ring of muscle and I shook as waves of pleasure washed over me.

His finger and cock worked out a rhythm that managed to wring orgasm after orgasm from my body until I wasn't sure where he ended and I began.

"I'm sorry, Hayden," he panted. "I'm so fucking sorry."

I didn't have to ask what he was sorry for. I already knew. He was going to leave tomorrow morning. It wasn't a question for him.

I ignored his apologies and pushed against his chest. "I want to be on top."

If it was all going to come crashing down tomorrow, I needed to be in control one last time. His finger slipped out and he rolled onto his back, pulling me across his massive body as if I was weightless.

I exhaled slowly as my body sank down, adjusting to the new angle. Jake thrust his hips up with a grin. "We didn't try this yoga pose last night. I damn near came just watching you do it though. Will you ever know how it's fucked with my head seeing how flexible you are?"

Inexplicably, another tear broke free and I looked away from him toward the ceiling. I couldn't take much more of this. There'd be nothing left of me by the time we were done.

"Use me," I panted. "Use me to make yourself—" My skin prickled as another orgasm ripped through my body and I dug my nails into his chest to brace myself.

Jake caught my meaning and reluctantly moved his hands from my breasts to my hips, forcing my body to move at his speed. My head fell back as his cock moved deeper and faster inside of me before he tightened his hold and groaned his own release.

I lowered myself and placed my head against his chest, our heartbeats still fighting against each other. I'd solved two cases but was still no closer to wrapping up my feelings for Jake.

My panting turned to silent sobs and I soaked his chest in tears. He tightened his arms around me, his fingers stroking down my spine. Until now, I never knew that a heart could break without making a sound.

I decided that if I stayed awake, then maybe I could convince him to stay. Unfortunately, the events of the day had left me exhausted and despite my best efforts in fighting it, I drifted off to sleep in his arms.

I LOOKED at the blinking cursor on the screen and then back up at him. "It's, uh, ready. Jessa's in her apartment, waiting on the results of the autopsy. When the phone rings, that's your cue to knock on the door, okay?"

My voice was scratchy, and my eyes were puffy from crying in secret. I'd sobbed against the tiles of the shower until it felt like my chest would crack open from the pain and then again while putting on clothes in my closet. Pretty much anytime he wasn't in the room, I was weeping.

Instead of his normal tree-like posture, Jake had been slouched over all morning. "So, just like that? It's fixed?"

I swallowed past the lump in my throat and smiled. I only hoped he hadn't noticed my watery eyes or quivering chin. "Yep," I squeaked. "Just like that. You got your life back."

His jaw clenched and he straightened. "Look, Hayden, I just need to say one—"

"Don't. It's better if we don't say anything. You belong in your world and I belong here..." My voice broke with a sob. "I belong here, with Bootsy."

Jake sniffed and looked away. "Right. Can I at least have a hug before I go?"

I nodded and let myself be held by him. A torrent of tears ran down my face as I reminded him, "Now, don't forget to do your daily yoga or you'll be all stooped over again. I packed you some crystal spray—it's just a little travel-sized bottle, so it doesn't take up much room. Oh, and I added a piece of black tourmaline for protection."

His arms tightened around me and his chest vibrated with a soft laugh. "I think you've got my spiritual needs covered. Anything else?"

I could feel his shirt growing wet beneath my cheek, but I couldn't stop the tears. My body was purging my grief the only way it knew how. "Um, wear your glasses more. They make you look sexy as fuck. And maybe a hat—I bet you'd look really nice with a hat."

Really distinguished.

I was never going to see it. I mashed my lips together and brought my fist up to stifle the sobbing.

"Hayden." Jake brushed the hair out of my face. "Look at me."

"I can't," I said with a sharp gasp. I was going to start hyperventilating any minute now. My nose was a snotty mess and my throat ached like I was choking on something.

And maybe I was.

"Alright. Just give me five minutes, okay?" Jake abruptly let me go, grabbed his duffel bag, and walked out.

That was it?

No kiss goodbye?

I stood shell-shocked. Even Bootsy let out a yowl of anguish and batted frantically at the doorknob.

"He's, he's gone." I sank down to my knees and released the floodgates again.

I couldn't fall apart.

Not now.

I promised him the ending he deserved. I forced myself up and over to my desk, gulping for air like a drowning person.

I opened a new document. I had to get the words out before they suffocated me and Bootsy was forced to eat my corpse to survive.

They say you get one great love in your life. Well, Jake was mine.

It was a start, but I had a feeling that I could write volumes on my love for Jake and it wouldn't even begin to scratch the surface. My feelings for him would be pouring out of me for years to come.

I'd just reopened the Detective Hopkins novel when the door burst open. Bootsy hissed in surprise and bolted for the bedroom.

Jake stood, wild-eyed and covered in snow. "I've been trying to figure out why you left me the morning after we had sex and I came to the conclusion that it was because you didn't feel the same way. And I was going to leave it, but I can't. I can't leave until you know how I feel."

I opened my mouth, but he stopped me. "Please. I need you to just listen to me before you say anything."

He took a deep breath. "Your eyes scrunch up when you smile like they're competing with your mouth and it's so fucking adorable that I find myself looking for ways to make it happen again. You'll lie to people to protect their feelings, even if it means sacrificing your own. You have a big heart, Hayden. You give yourself to people, even assholes like me who don't deserve it. You and your damn cat are bat shit crazy, but I want to take care of you both." He held his hand up as I opened my mouth again. "I know you can take care of yourself, but I want to do it just the same.

"Your coffee is really just cream with a splash of coffee and you love a good bowl of kid's cereal, dry, to snack on while you write. You hum, you hum rap songs—mostly Nicki Minaj, but I've definitely heard some Lil Kim in there. I don't even know if you realize you're doing it; you're usually lost in thought."

He paused before exclaiming, "Oh, when you eat olives off a toothpick, you do this shoulder shimmy thing, like nothing in the world could ever make you happier. See, you knew everything about me from the beginning. It put me at a disadvantage, so I decided I was going to learn everything I could about you. I just never planned on it working out like this." Jake stood by the door, out of breath and with all of his cards on the table.

My mouth went dry and the tears stopped as he described a me that even I didn't recognize. "What are you saying?"

Jake walked over and knelt down in front of me, dwarfing my hands with his. "I'm saying that I love you, Hayden. And, let's be honest, I never would've survived that fall."

He loved me.

And I loved him.

We were going to move out of the city together and start our own cat sanctuary. They would interview us on the *Today* show and we'd tell the story of how we fell in love—well, maybe not the entire story. Parts of it were pretty unbelievable. Maybe I'd rewrite our love story for the people who asked. We fell in love while doing volunteer work at the animal shelter and decided to start our own no-kill shelter where we rehabilitated cats and adopted them out.

Now, what would we call it?

The Purrfect Pet?

Meow is the time?

Feline fine?

"Hayden?" Jake waved a hand in front of my face. "Can I get a response?"

I nodded and grinned. "I think we should go with the *Purrfect Pet*. We can add rescue at the end if you think it sounds too much like a pet store."

His brows drew together. "What the fuck are you talking about? I pour my heart out and tell you that I love you and you're talking about a pet rescue?"

I might've jumped ahead a little too far.

"Oh, obviously I love you too!" I threw my arms around his neck. "So, this means you're staying?"

Jake placed a hand on either side of my face. "Seriously, were you not listening to a damn thing I said?"

I frowned. "Don't get all grumpy. You just said all those nice things about me."

He rolled his eyes. "I'm thinking of taking a few of them back. You were already imagining us starting our own pet rescue, weren't you? Did Kathie Lee interview you in your daydream too?"

"Well, you interrupted before I got to that part," I grumbled.

"It's a damn good thing I love you, you little psycho," he laughed and pressed a kiss to my forehead.

EPILOGUE

JAKE

"They're going to be here any second, are you almost ready?" Hayden asked, with a sly smirk.

Detective Jake Hopkins couldn't believe that this was his life. In his wildest fantasies, he never imagined that one year later, he'd be living with the woman of his dreams, running their cat sanctuary, *Purrfect Pet Rescue Co.*

He fastened the jingling bell collar around his neck and took a long look in the mirror. He had to admit, it looked pretty damn good on him. The silver bells really completed the ensemble.

Who would've ever known that falling thirty stories would be the best thing to ever happen to him?

Jake never planned on dressing up like a cat, but when your pint-sized princess of a girlfriend was a *USA Today*, *New York Times*, and *Wall Street Journal* bestseller, you did what she asked. Plus, they needed a Christmas card that really captured who they were as a couple.

After pictures, they were going to meet Aaris and Max

for an early dinner before getting back out to the sanctuary to tend to their nineteen beloved cats: Bootsy, Gypsy, Leaf, Mr. Winkles, Giblet, Naughty, Donna Lynn, Jemimer, Tigger, Jake Jr., Ginger, LaLa, Poppy, Alfie, Dusk Meowrley, Cathulhu, Purrgie, Kitty Prrryde, and Tabbytha King.

The cats would gather around for their nightly bedtime story and asanas before being tucked into the soft blankets that he'd woven for them on his loom.

Afterward, Jake had plans of laying Hayden down on the handwoven silk rug in front of the fireplace before making sweet, sweet love to her.

After all, they were celebrating.

Hayden Michaels, the Indie author who had turned down multiple offers from a variety of agents, had sold her latest Detective Hopkins novel to Stephen Spielberg. It only made sense after he'd made her last three books mega-blockbuster hits.

Her parents had choked with envy at her massive success and begged to be a part of her life, even offering to take over litter box duty at the sanctuary to make up for all the years they didn't believe in her.

Reid left his job as CEO of *Genetistry* to become her personal assistant after realizing that he owed his very life to Hayden and her quick-thinking actions with the Emily situation.

All in all, Jake thought that their lives had worked out perfectly.

HOLY SHIT.

No.

None of that was real.

Jesus Christ, the things I ran across while using Hayden's laptop. This one had been titled, *Plot Ideas*. Usually, she stuck to inane things, like Bootsy finding the love of her nine lives on a nearby balcony.

And 'pint-sized princess of a girlfriend?'

Try pixie from Hell.

I realized early on, that the longer I was here, the weaker her control over me became. A year in and I'd become immune to anything she tried—*and thank Christ for that with these kinds of ideas floating around in her head.*

Life for us had remained relatively unchanged for the past year, despite the fictional world that Hayden seemed to reside in, which was a nice change of pace for me.

While *Angel of Death* hadn't become a global phenomenon, it had sold more copies its first week than *One in the Chamber* did in its entire run.

So maybe *The Janice Morrison Agency* had decided to stand by their decision to pass up Hayden's work; her readers had gone crazy over the direction the books had gone. Jessa had eclipsed me in popularity, but given what I had now, I wasn't all that upset about being upstaged.

The front door opened, letting in a frigid blast of air. "Hey," Hayden greeted me breathlessly and dusted the snow from her coat. "It's really coming down out there."

"Yeah?" I tapped the mouse, exiting out the document as she walked over and climbed into my lap. She wrapped her arms around my neck, sending bits of ice down the back of my sweater.

"What are you doing?" Her eyes narrowed at the blank screen.

"Nothing. Just waiting on you." I tilted her face toward mine and struggled to bring her lips down to meet mine. Unfortunately, she was on to me and jutted her chin up defiantly at the last second.

"You're acting weird—"

Did I say pixie from Hell? I meant hellhound. The woman could sniff my bullshit from a mile away.

I went for casual in an attempt to throw her off. "Hey, baby. How was your day? Mine was great, thanks for asking."

The furrow between her eyebrows disappeared, and she relaxed against my chest. "Hey lover, my day was wonderful. I sold so much shampoo. How was yours?"

This was it.

I wiped a damp palm against my thigh and shifted her to the side so I could reach the desk. "I—well, I wrote a book and I'd like to read it to you; just to see if it's any good, you know?"

Her mouth stretched into a grin and her teeth sank into her lower lip. "You wrote a book? Like a whole book? When did you get off work?"

I shrugged. "I had a couple of hours to kill. You writers make it seem like the process takes months."

Hayden rolled her eyes. "Oh, I can't wait to hear this."

I took a deep breath. "Okay, but you have to sit on the chair. I don't want you getting bored and trying to skip ahead by reading over my shoulder."

I smacked her ass as she stood up and her lip twitched as she fought a smile. She drew her knees up under her chin and adjusted her glasses with a skeptical grin. "The floor's all yours, Detective."

Maybe Pixie from Hell had been an overstatement.

I turned the laptop screen toward me. "Okay. So, a writer once told me that the best way to capture a character was by making a list of all the things the world would never know about him or her."

"Wait," Hayden interjected. "What's the title of this story?"

"It doesn't have one. It's not important. Can I continue?"

She nodded and I took another deep breath in an attempt to calm my racing heart. "Said writer was completely insane, but she had a good point when it came to character development. But, some characters have their secrets locked up so tightly that even the best writers can't crack the code. Here were the things that Hayden Michaels would never know about Jake Hopkins."

I glanced up to meet her raised eyebrows and forced myself to continue before I chickened out completely. "Despite what I may have told her in the past, I actually look forward to seeing what the cat shirt of the day is going to be—"

"I knew it!" She grinned triumphantly and raised her fist in the air.

I shook my head. "I've seen the #Planal video and read the *Twitter* thread more times than I can count. I find if my day's going to shit, nothing cheers me up more than knowing my girlfriend spent an entire flight discussing her fear of anal with a complete stranger. A fear that, quite frankly, surprises the hell out me with as eager as she is to—"

"Skip that part," Hayden choked out through the hands covering her face. "Oh my god, I can't believe you know about that!"

I chuckled and continued reading. "I speak fluent Spanish, French, German, and Italian. I find I use them most, not when I'm on the job, but when she's lying naked beneath me. I'm convinced that she thinks it's gibberish as I describe all the things I want to do to her in four separate languages."

The hands covering her face moved down to reveal her wide eyes as she whispered, "Jake..."

"I found a fail-proof way for her to bring me back into the story by the end of our first week together, but kept it to myself in a half-cocked scheme to get closer to her."

Her mouth fell open in shock and I fought back the smug grin that was threatening to take over. There were still things she hadn't known about me. It felt damn good. "I'd already interviewed and accepted a job offer with the city's police department before she was halfway finished with *Angel of Death*."

"You did? Why didn't you tell me? You kept acting like you were so ready to get back to your story!"

I sighed. "I didn't think you felt the same way and I'd already fucked up your life by showing up and demanding you fix the story that it didn't seem fair to say I'd changed my mind. But god did I hope that you would."

She pressed a fist to her mouth and nodded.

"I fell in love with her gradually and I can't even pinpoint the moment it happened. I just knew one morning when I woke up on her couch that she was it for me. Anytime she asked though, I told her it was the first time I saw her naked. You know, just so I could watch her face turn red with embarrassment." My arms went numb and I stood up unsteadily. "Bootsy." My voice cracked, and I coughed to hide it.

Hayden frowned. "Babe, what are you doing?"

"Bootsy, here girl," I tried again. I'd practiced this for over a month with her. She knew her cue and everything.

"Sweetie," she tried again. "Cats don't come when they're called or really do anything that you want them to."

I gave up and went into the bedroom to find her curled up on the foot of the bed, her tail flicking back and forth lazily.

Goddammit.

Would there ever be a day when the females in this apartment listened to me?

I scooped her up and carried her back out into the living room while she purred happily up against my chest. "Okay, slight delay. We're back and everything's fine."

"You're acting weird again," she noted dryly.

I nodded, the blood roaring in my ears. "Yeah, but I have a point and I am going to get to it right now. Um." I cleared my throat. "For the last two weeks, next to the black tourmaline and jet in my pocket, I've been carrying around a ring, trying to work up the courage to ask my girl a pretty important question."

Both hands came up to her mouth and she began shaking her head back and forth. "What? No. You're lying to me."

I grinned and dropped to one knee before presenting Bootsy to her. "Check her collar, babe." My voice had gone all husky on me like I was the one about to cry, which was... *fairly accurate, actually.*

Her small fingers fumbled against the collar and she sucked in a startled gasp when she found the ring, nestled in next to Bootsy's ID tags.

I undid the collar and slipped the ring onto her finger. Bootsy watched us with a bored expression.

"Hayden, will you—" I began.

"Oh, hell yes." She gently set Bootsy down on the carpet before launching herself into my arms, sending us both sprawling back onto the carpet. This time there was no resistance as I guided her mouth down over mine.

A thirty-story fall and a writer who was a little too obsessed with cats. It didn't sound like the makings of some great love story, yet I'd found my happily ever after right here in her arms.

Fuck, that was awful.

I had to lose everything to find the love of my life...

Nope.

Who could've predicted that my life would be this good after getting thrown off of a thirty-story building?

Now I sounded like her.

Looked like I was going to have to stick with my original ending.

I came here, certain of what I wanted. Absolute in what would make me happy. And then I met her and found that I'd never been more wrong. My ma always joked that the right woman would be the one to keep me on my toes.

Well, I'd been walking a fucking tightrope since the day I met her.

She wasn't the ending I'd planned, but she was without a doubt, the one I needed.

The end.

ALSO BY SHANNON MYERS

From This Day Forward Duet

(David & Elizabeth's Story)

From This Day Forward

Forsaking All Others

Standalone Novels

(Katya & Travis's Story)

You Save Me

Operation Series

(Dakota & Zane's Story)

Operation Fit-ish

(Kate & Nate's Story)

Operation Annulment

Renegade Series

(Mike & Lauren's Story)

Renegade (Book One)

Traitor (Book Two)

Fairest Series

(Charm & Neve's Story)

Through The Woods

Fictioned Series

Protagonized

ABOUT THE AUTHOR

Shannon is a born and raised Texan. She grew up inventing clever stories, usually to get herself out of trouble. Her mother was not amused. In junior high, she began writing fractured fairy tales from the villain's point of view and that was the moment she knew that she was going to use her powers for evil instead of good.

In 2003, she moved to Denver and met the love of her life. After some relentless stalking and a few well-timed sarcastic remarks, the man eventually gave in to her charms and wifed her so hard. They welcomed a son in 2007 that they named after their favorite Marvel superhero, Spiderman.

Sick of seeing beautiful mountains through their window every day, the three escaped back to the desolate landscape of the west Texas desert in 2009. She welcomed her second son not long after and soon realized that being surrounded by three men was nothing at all like she'd imagined in her fantasies.

After an unplanned surgery in 2014 and a long pity party, she decided to pen a novel about the worst thing that could happen to a person in order to cheer herself up. She's twisted like that. Thus, From This Day Forward was born and the rest, as they say, is history.

Not only does Shannon enjoy stalking people, she also has a fondness for being stalked.

Find her on online at: http://shannonshaemyers.com
Or on Facebook in The Forsaken:
https://www.facebook.com/groups/630229377127363/

www.ingramcontent.com/pod-product-compliance
Lightning Source LLC
Chambersburg PA
CBHW060941030726
47503CB00003B/679